Praise for (

'A light book with heavy themes
are important and urgent.'

Books + Publishing

'An alarming—albeit funny—glimpse into life beyond those white coats . . . a light, pacy read.'

Who Magazine

'Anyone with first-hand knowledge of [Henry's] subject will find this story true to life . . . There's plenty to shock, but also black humour, camaraderie, sex, drugs and moments of poignancy wrested from a dehumanising culture.'

Sydney Morning Herald/The Age

'When focused on hospital life, Henry's experience and expertise shine through, illuminating the difficulties her characters—and her real-life colleagues—face.'

West Australian

'A really good read . . . Steps are being taken to remedy the culture in teaching hospitals but, judging from this story, there is still a long way to go.'

Blue Wolf Reviews

'A book that has a vital role to play, *Going Under* is a conversation starter, an astute and penetrating tale that strikes at the very heart of our country's health care system.'

Mrs B's Book Reviews

'An important, timely book. The story gets smarter and darker as it moves on, but that only adds to the enjoyment. Here is someone who gets it [being a junior doctor], and has written about the experience clearly.'

Sam Still Reading

Sonia Henry is a doctor and a writer. Prior to her career in medicine she qualified and worked as a physiotherapist. She has been published on a variety of platforms, including the physician blog KevinMD, the *Sydney Morning Herald*, the *Australian Medical Students Association* magazine, and the *ANZ Journal of Surgery*. She enjoys wine, skiing, her friends and black humour (not necessarily in that order). She lives in Sydney. This is Sonia's first novel.

going under

sonia henry

ALLEN&UNWIN
SYDNEY • MELBOURNE • AUCKLAND • LONDON

This is a work of fiction. Like most works of fiction it is inspired from observations of real life experiences and events. However every character in this book has been created by the author and any resemblance to a living person is simply coincidental and readers must not assume that any part of this story has any real or factual basis.

This edition published in 2020
First published in 2019

Kind permission received from Faber and Faber Ltd to quote from 'Four Quartets' by T.S. Eliot on pages vii, 283 and 289.

Allen & Unwin
83 Alexander Street
Crows Nest NSW 2065
Australia
Phone: (61 2) 8425 0100
Email: info@allenandunwin.com
Web: www.allenandunwin.com

NATIONAL LIBRARY OF AUSTRALIA

A catalogue record for this book is available from the National Library of Australia

ISBN 978 1 76087 864 1

Typeset in Garamond Premier Pro by Bookhouse, Sydney
Printed in Australia by McPherson's Printing Group

10 9 8 7 6 5 4 3 2 1

FSC® MIX Paper from responsible sources FSC® C001695 www.fsc.org

The paper in this book is FSC® certified. FSC® promotes environmentally responsible, socially beneficial and economically viable management of the world's forests.

This book is for all the doctors who have ever felt lost or alone inside a system that should care for you better

Footfalls echo in the memory
Down the passage which we did not take
Towards the door we never opened
Into the rose-garden. My words echo
Thus, in your mind.

T.S. ELIOT, 'FOUR QUARTETS'

prologue

THIRTY-THREE YEARS AGO, TOBY HENDERSON WAS working in the emergency department of a hospital on the outskirts of the city. With a grand total of thirteen months' experience, he was the most senior doctor on the floor.

When the patient came through the doors, he didn't look that sick. He was holding his left arm above his head and it was wrapped in a towel, but he was walking and talking, which is always a reassuring sign. But as he came closer, Toby noticed that his skin had the pale, sweaty sheen of someone about to collapse.

He did collapse, and let go of the towel. Toby struggled to repress the urge to vomit as he saw half a stump where the patient's hand should have been, the rest of the fingers dangling by a few bits of muscle and skin, and blood spurting out from what Toby dimly knew to be one of the main arteries supplying the bottom half of the man's limb. Or former limb.

'I wanted to kill myself,' the man gasped, 'so I tried to chop off my hand. But then I realised that I'd made a huge mistake.'

That was a bit of an understatement, Toby thought as he grabbed the towel and rewrapped it around the stump, trying desperately to reposition the remaining piece of hand to stem the flow of blood.

'What are you going to do, Doctor?' a nurse whispered as together they heaved the man off the floor and towards one of the resuscitation trollies.

Toby had the unusual sensation of being inside a large fishtank. Everything was happening so slowly, as if they were moving through water. He watched as the man's face went from pale white to ivory to grey. Tombstone grey, Toby thought. Death grey.

'Doctor!' The nurse was yelling now, startling Toby from his dreamlike state, plunging him back into an awareness of his own helplessness.

'Get me an anatomy textbook!' he shouted, grabbing a needle to start an IV line before the peripheral circulation disappeared.

He stared at the gaping hole between the man's hand and his wrist. 'Saline—more saline!' he instructed.

Someone thrust a book into his hand and he peered at the page, trying to identify what was being revealed by the saline wash. The ulnar artery. No, the radial artery. No . . .

This is easy, he chided himself. You topped anatomy at uni. You know which artery runs down which side of the hand. This is first-year medical student stuff.

For some reason, his brain was scrambled. It was the blood; it was confusing him, making him disorientated. Was the man's thumb missing? His ring finger?

'You've got the book the wrong way around!'

By this time, the patient had lost consciousness. Toby felt a small sense of relief.

The nurse flipped the book the other way.

'Radial,' he muttered.

He swallowed. He knew that before he woke the plastic surgeon on call he'd have to know exactly which vessels had been severed, otherwise the surgeon would start yelling at him or, worse, refuse to come to his assistance.

'I reckon it's the ulnar,' the nurse said unhelpfully, looking first at the book then at the bleeding half-hand, half-stump that lay between them.

'Get plastics on the phone,' Toby said, 'and get a cross match now. He needs blood.'

'You ring the surgeon,' the nurse snapped. 'I'll get the blood.'

Toby called the plastic surgeon.

'Are you sure he's severed his radial artery?' The surgeon sounded irritated at being woken up and also doubtful. 'What can you see?'

'His thumb is hacked off,' Toby said, 'so it must be his radial.'

The nurses had taken over now. Hanging blood, applying pressure, preparing the defibrillator paddles.

'We'll handle this!' a nurse bellowed at Toby as he ended the call. 'There's a guy who's arresting in cubicle four. You need to get over there—now!'

'Was he dying too?' asked one of the two medical students listening to the story with wide eyes.

Thirty-three years later, Dr Toby Henderson leaned back in his chair in the emergency department where he was now regaling the doctors of the future with his cautionary tales. 'Of course,' he replied. 'Everyone dies at two am when you're the most senior doctor on. It's Murphy's law.'

'What happened afterwards?'

Toby smiled. 'The head of medical administration hauled me into her office and tore me to shreds for failing to respond quickly enough.' He frowned at the memory. 'God, she was a bitch,' he added.

Kitty Holliday, a final-year medical student soon to be known as Dr Katarina Holliday, shuddered. 'I don't know how I would have coped with that,' she said honestly.

She expected him to reassure her; he'd coped, after all.

'Well, you just don't,' Toby said. He glanced at his watch, signalling the end of his shift and the conversation.

'Excuse me?' said Estelle, Kitty's fellow medical student and friend. Surely he'd meant to say, 'Well, you just do.' Doctors always did seem to cope.

As Toby stood to leave he looked each girl in the eye and repeated: 'You just don't.'

'What a load of crap,' Estelle said some hours later. They were having their standard end-of-day debrief at the pub down the road from the hospital.

'I know,' Kitty agreed. 'I mean, of course he coped. He's still working in emergency, isn't he?'

The conversation gradually meandered towards other topics. Exams, men, what they'd do when they finally finished university and had some money. The thirty-three-year-old story of the near-severed hand and the idea that doctors might not cope was quickly forgotten.

PART I

birth

'But I don't want to go among mad people,' Alice remarked.

'Oh, you can't help that,' said the Cat: 'we're all mad here. I'm mad. You're mad.'

'How do you know I'm mad?' said Alice.

'You must be,' said the Cat, 'or you wouldn't have come here.'

Lewis Carroll, *Alice's Adventures in Wonderland*

one

'YOU'VE DONE THIS BEFORE, HAVEN'T YOU? LIKE, I'M NOT your first?'

There's a moment in which I consider being completely honest with the agitated half-naked man lying on the bed in front of me.

Yes, darling, I will say. *You're my first.*

'You're going to put that into me? But it's huge!' His eyes dart across to the long metal device I'm holding, then he winces involuntarily and shifts away from where I'm perched on the edge of his bed. I see a white flash of his exposed buttocks. They look even more frightened than he does. Or I am.

We both glance down at the 18-gauge cannula gripped in my sweaty right hand. My mental picture of a virgin high-class escort and her nervous virgin client dissolves into reality. For a moment, I almost wish I *was* an escort. Better that than, on my first day as a doctor, inserting an enormous metal needle into a patient's skinny-looking vein—a feat I've never yet managed to accomplish, though as a medical student I had plenty of opportunity to master it. 'We'll learn on the actual job,' Estelle and I used to tell each other with the confidence of people who could put off any unpleasant tasks into a distant future. Well, this is the job, and that distant future is suddenly the present.

'Yes, I've done this before,' I lie, trying to smile but knowing it's coming out more like a demented grimace. If I told him the truth we'd probably both pass out with fear, further delaying the inevitable.

He doesn't respond, but he grants me implied consent by extending his arm in front of me. I have a mental image of Jesus on the cross, arms outstretched, the stigmata of crucifixion mirroring the icon on the wall above the bed. I'm meant to be his angel saving him from his fate, but instead all that happens is I stare at his juicy, bulging vein, slightly purple underneath the translucent skin, and swallow.

Lord, grant me the serenity to accept the things I cannot change . . .

I pull the tourniquet on his upper arm tight. I see him tense slightly, but to his credit my virgin cannula client says nothing. He surrenders to his unexpected angel, and waits.

Courage to change the things I can . . .

I unsheath the cannula, stare at the end of the sharp needle, and take a breath. With my free hand, I tap along the vein, hoping desperately it will get bigger and more obvious. *Tap tap tap. Tap tap tap tap tap.* I'm merely delaying the inevitable, though. At some point I will have to attempt to pierce his skin and insert the needle.

'Just do it, please,' he says through gritted teeth.

I stare at the vein, now so enlarged by the tourniquet I feel certain I won't miss. Just push it through the skin, I tell myself. One quick movement.

'Sharp scratch!' I bellow enthusiastically and, trying not to think too much, I plunge the needle directly into the vein (I hope).

And wisdom to know the difference . . .

'ARGHHHHHH!' screams the patient, jerking his elbow and knocking my now-shaking hand. The cannula pierces the vein all right, but thanks to the unexpected movement it travels straight through it—coming very close to his brachial artery, I realise in horror.

I try to unclip the tourniquet but by now the patient is completely hysterical. I must have nicked his artery because there's blood squirting from his arm in a pulsating red stream.

At this point I am definitely a better potential escort than angel, I realise mournfully. Or doctor.

'Is everything okay in here?' Lawrence, the medical student assigned to me, appears out of nowhere. 'Did you get the cannula in?'

I refrain from pointing out the obvious, letting the blood-soaked patient, sheet and doctor speak for themselves.

'You have to keep your arm still,' I scold the patient. 'Otherwise this happens.'

'You didn't say anything about that!' he snaps back at me. He looks past me to Lawrence. 'Is he the doctor? Why isn't a doctor doing it?'

'She is the doctor,' Lawrence says at the same time as I say, 'I am the doctor.'

The patient, clearly not convinced that someone of my gender is capable of earning a medical degree, pleads with Lawrence—the final-year medical student doing his surgical term under my supervision—to put the cannula in.

Lawrence, being one of those medical students who stays back after hours and stalks the ward on weekends to learn handy skills like cannulation, agrees.

The patient, calmed by the fact that a tall strapping man is taking the reins, relaxes.

'It'll be a great learning opportunity for you, Lawrence,' I say supportively, backing away from the bed. 'Let me know if there are, ah, any problems. I'll just be sorting out some . . . other jobs.'

I leave the ward as quickly as possible and text Estelle, who texts back to say that she is in the hospital cafeteria with my housemate Max. Like me, they are interns—though I prefer the term 'junior doctor', which at least confers some sense of what the job actually entails—struggling through their first day on the wards at a major teaching hospital in Sydney.

I arrive to find them slumped over a table at the back of the cafeteria.

'I fucking hate this,' Estelle says as I join them. 'I want to go home.' She runs a hand through her long blonde hair and sighs. I watch in awe, amazed that someone can be so beautiful even when wearing an expression of extreme disgruntlement.

Two nurses walk past and give us a glance that hovers between disgust and pity. 'The baby interns,' I hear one say to the other, not bothering to lower her voice. 'That time of year when the hospital death statistics, like, triple.'

I can't help but feel their lack of confidence is justified. My first night shift is approaching and it fills me with fear. The public hospital where I work—a big old rabbit warren with kilometres of corridors and staircases—is huge. And on night shift those hundreds of patients, along with a skeleton staff, will all be under my inexperienced care.

The hospital is called Holy Innocents Hospital, which is as macabre as it sounds. Despite the fact it's almost directly on the ocean (these religious institutions always did know how to buy up good real estate), the glorious view of the waves crashing from the windows of the surgical ward is rather mitigated by the icons that loom down on us as we walk through the corridors. My favourite is an enormous painting which depicts the Massacre of the Innocents, which the hospital is named after. I said a better name would have been St Trinian's (a bit of a personal joke that I had to explain to Max). Nothing inspires a sense of confidence in your medical team more than gigantic paintings of young children being massacred on the order of King Herod.

It's like another planet compared with the scenes outside. Holy Innocents Hospital is in a relaxed beachside suburb in northern Sydney, and most patients who attend the place are either wealthy retirees or surf bums. It makes a good mix. One day you'll see a stoner surfie, the next a retired barrister. It's also not that far from the city so you also get a good mix of general bad behaviour, like people with weird things inserted in their rectums.

There is an affiliated private hospital, but that's a good ten-minute walk up the road. The consultants like that because it means they can keep to themselves in the glorious land of private practice and stay in their ivory towers while their juniors sweat it out in the trenches. I can't complain too much. Being so close to the water means that, hypothetically, after work I can rip off my doctor's badge and clothes and, in a small section of the beach not seen by the general public, swim in my undies. Even on day one of doctoring the idea of that kind of freedom is truly fantastic.

'You've got blood on your shirt, mate,' Max says, removing me from my fantasy of the ocean by slurping on his milkshake. 'Good first day then?'

'I tried to put in a cannula,' I admit. 'It was a bloodbath. I left my medical student to sort it out.'

'Yeah, that happened to me too,' Estelle says gloomily, staring into her coffee. 'In emergency I think I'll have to put in heaps of cannulas. It's awful.'

Max is shaking his head. 'I'm so glad I haven't started on a surgical or emergency term like you guys. Respiratory is so great.'

Max has had the incredibly good fortune of being rotated to a respiratory term in summer. Pneumonia being traditionally a winter illness, he only has two or three patients to look after. Sadly, neurosurgical patients don't seem to have a climatic preference.

Interns operate on a system of terms. You have some choice in this, but there are standard experiences every junior doctor needs to have under their belt before the medical board deems us fit to progress. At a bare minimum, you need to do a surgical term, a medical term and an emergency term. I've requested nearly all surgical terms. It's inevitable, really, that I will be a surgeon. My fate was sealed years ago in a delivery suite at the

Royal Hospital for Women, with an innocuous comment by an unsuspecting midwife. I was nine minutes old.

'Look how long her fingers are,' the nurse said to my mother, touching my hands as she cradled me. 'Maybe she'll be a concert pianist . . .'

Mum, despite having just gone through labour, snapped to attention. 'Maybe she'll be a surgeon,' she said firmly, examining my hands.

Thanks, Mum—no pressure or anything. I'm certainly doing my best to live up to my mother's expectations. My first term is neurosurgery, before we're shipped off to the middle of nowhere in the great Aussie outback for our rural medical secondment. Then, aside from a single mandatory term in the emergency department, I'll spend the rest of the year inside the operating theatre. Or attempting to get in there, at least, as a lot of the time surgical interns are stuck trying to manage the catastrophes sitting on the surgical ward.

'Why are you so keen to be a surgeon, Kitty?' Estelle asks me now, as if reading my thoughts. 'I hate the operating theatre.'

I consider this. Even as a student the surgical terms were always my favourite. The whole romance of the operating theatre appeals to me. It's the closest you can get to treading the precarious line between controlled life and equally uncontrolled deterioration and death. And it isn't called a theatre for no reason. It's a stage of sorts. The surgeons are movie stars with egos to match. The patients play their role to perfection, being helpless and unconscious. Bodies are cut open, lives are saved and lost—and everyone acts as if it is just another day, which for them it is, I suppose. I've heard other doctors say they enjoy surgery because it's straightforward; they can just 'go and get things done'. It's a world away from the complexities of human interactions with difficult patients on that other planet—the ward. But that's not at all how I see surgery. I like the grace and precision it requires, while all the time being aware that at any moment things can go wrong, that the careful choreography of the theatre can descend into chaos. The fact that so often it doesn't is, for me, miraculous. The operating theatre is a place where magic happens.

Estelle is staring at me. 'Earth to Kitty . . .'

I snap myself back to the present. 'You know,' I say, in answer to her question, 'blood and knives and power and pain and mercy and magic. It's all in there.'

Estelle smiles. 'There's the Kitty Holliday I know and love: half surgeon, half writer.'

'How's the book going, mate?' Max asks, upending his milkshake to drain the dregs.

I sigh. Despite the subliminal pressure to become a doctor—a surgeon, no less—I also grew up in a house full of literature with an English teacher for a mother. She instilled in me a love for language; words are my oldest and greatest friends. Mum's texts asking if I was studying for my medical exams were always peppered with quotes from obscure poets. No wonder I have an identity crisis. It's because I'm on the Pisces–Aries cusp, I reckon. The creative dreamer is always doing battle with the pragmatic, determined future surgeon. I write to escape, and for the last few years—ever since I started medical school—I've been working on a novel. But progress has been slow; there was always another anatomy lecture to attend, or exam to study for. And now that I'm finally a real doctor, my dreams of a literary life seem further away than ever.

'Badly,' I admit. 'But as my mum always says: novelists starve, doctors don't.'

'I can't believe this is our first day as real doctors,' Max says dreamily, no doubt envisaging his almost-empty ward and blank to-do list. 'I reckon I'll finish early. I told Winnie we could have a drink to celebrate. Want to walk home with me?'

Our housemate Winnie is the only person in our group of friends who isn't a doctor. She's a lawyer, which she generally hates. She texts me between billable hours to ask if I've met any hot surgeons yet like on TV. Her favourite little joke is that if I do finally ever write my novel I should call it *Fifty Shades of Grey's Anatomy.*

'I'll be here for hours,' I tell Max. 'My registrar's at a course today so I haven't even met her yet; I've sort of just been going it alone.'

The hierarchy of medicine is confusing, even for people inside the system. Interns are at the absolute bottom of the food chain. Above us are the consultants in training, or registrars. And above them are the godlike fully blown consultants, junior and senior. Most departments have a few of each. Junior consultants have a bit more to do with us interns than their senior colleagues, who are so far removed from their years as junior doctors it's like they never happened. They spend most of their time (when they're not on the fairway or in Aspen) making money in the private hospital. The hospital, in all its wisdom, has scheduled registrar orientation for the same time as our first day as interns, and the junior consultant who might have been able to offer me some direction has been in theatre the last five hours. I have thus spent my morning with no supervision and perpetually confused.

'I should have stayed a stripper, I reckon,' Estelle says suddenly. 'I was such a good stripper.'

I'd met Estelle at the start of my medical degree when we ended up at the pub together after sneaking out of the last lecture early. Half a beer in, Estelle told me that she'd worked on and off as a stripper for the last few years, as well as engaging in some hard-core partying, but had decided it was time to go straight, so to speak. After blitzing a year of a science degree, she'd transferred across to medicine. I can still picture Estelle standing next to me in the coffee line on our first day of medical school, in her white summery dress with her Longines watch, lying through her teeth to the guy next to us that she wanted to become a doctor to save the masses. Even at the time I thought she looked like she'd be more comfortable in day spas rather than medical tents inside third-world war zones.

'Do you think I'd be a good stripper?' Max asks hopefully. 'We could leave all this behind and start a doctors' strip show. What do you reckon, Kitty? Stripping would have to be more fun than surgery. Think about it—no more cannulas.'

'It'd definitely be a niche market, the stripper who nearly gives you a heart attack with their amazing sex appeal but then turns around and is able to save your life with effective CPR,' I agree, 'and kind of hot.' But even though I know he's only joking, it makes me think. What is it that I really want? Why have I spent the last billion years of my life struggling through medical school? It's for a purpose, something far more than just a job. That's why I'm here, now: because being a doctor is the most noble and worthy profession I can think of. I picture myself in a surgical mask under the bright lights of an operating theatre, knowing I have the absolute confidence to pick up a scalpel and press it down onto skin, watching the blood spring up as I complete the first incision. Only doctors have that kind of power, born from years of training to hone their skills, all to make another human being's life better, or even, hopefully, save it. That's the whole point of being a doctor . . . isn't it?

two

EIGHT HOURS LATER, I'M FINALLY ABOUT TO LEAVE THE hospital and head home. I have just walked out the front doors, the words HOLY INNOCENTS HOSPITAL glowing blue above me, when my phone starts to ring. The sound immediately sets my pulse racing.

I pull the phone from my pocket and stare at the screen. Maybe it's Max, I think hopefully, wondering why I'm not home yet.

'Is this Katarina?' a man's voice demands before I can say 'hello'. He has a slight accent which I can't quite identify.

'Ah . . .'

'Katarina Halliday?'

'Holliday.' I knee-jerk correct my mystery caller.

'What?'

'It's Katarina Holliday,' I explain, wondering for a second why I'm bothering. 'Like vacation. Holliday, as in going on a holiday.'

'Whatever. Where are you? I'm on the ward.' The voice sounds irritated.

Sounds like you need a holiday, I want to remark. Instead I say, 'I was just . . . leaving.'

There's a silence, during which I wonder who's on the other end of the phone. It must be someone senior. This is a rather bad start, I can't help thinking.

'I'm at bed seven thirty-two,' the voice informs me bluntly. 'I need the chart.'

I sigh and retrace my steps to the surgical ward. It's 9 pm, and I've been at work since 7 am. Aside from my coffee with Estelle and Max, I haven't eaten or drunk anything all day. I am going to be thin enough to be faxed in a few weeks, I think, using one of Max's favourite lines. Thin enough to be faxed. Holy enough to be canonised. Dedicated enough to be surgeonised. Scared enough to be miserable. Tired enough to be dead. The thoughts come from nowhere, but Dr Halliday, definitely not having a holiday, suppresses them quickly. She wants to be an angel of healing, and this is just what must be done. If it was easy, everyone would be doing it, I remind myself, quoting one of my lecturers from medical school. Doctors aren't everyone. We just can't be.

I arrive at bed 732 with the chart to see a man standing there prodding at the stitches in Mr Jacobsen's head. Mr Jacobsen looks terrible—he has just had a massive brain tumour cut out. I smile at him, then feel bad for smiling, so look at my shoes instead. They're really scuffed and dirty, I notice. I need a new pair. I also need a pay cheque, to buy the shoes.

'Don't ever leave the hospital again without telling me first,' my mystery superior snaps as I follow him into the doctors' room.

'Sorry,' I say. 'It's just that it's past nine o'clock, so I figured it would be okay.'

'When I was an intern I never left until I'd done a night round with my registrar.'

He starts scrolling through the CT scans on the computer, then stops and looks over at me. 'Can you scroll?' He sits back and rests his foot on the desk, his hands behind his head. The implication is clear: I'm WAITING.

For a second I am filled with disbelief. Like, can't he use a mouse? But no, I realise: he actually means it. He is going to sit there, with perfect motor function and the ability to use a mouse, and make me do it instead.

What I really want to do is tell this guy to Fuck. Right. Off. Instead, I reach for the mouse.

'I'm your boss, Dr David Hyde,' he says, finally identifying himself. 'You have three bosses: me, Dr Prince and Dr Bird.'

I nod, not taking my hand from the mouse nor my eyes from the two-dimensional black-and-white brain in front of me.

'Dr Prince and Dr Bird are too senior to spend much time with you. I've been in this job a year and I'm only staying because I think I'll get a senior consultant job here next year.'

I don't know what to say to any of this. I feel my phone vibrating in my pocket and this time I'm sure it's Max. I picture him and Winnie drunk and happy on cheap white wine, and feel an overwhelming urge to cry.

'Keep scrolling.'

I keep scrolling.

'Normally Rachel, the registrar, would be dealing with you on the ward, but since she's away I've had to cover for her.'

Scroll, scroll.

'Stop scrolling.'

I stop scrolling.

He peers at the image. 'What do you see?'

I look. Subdural, I think to myself. Subdural haemorrhage, but not totally white, so maybe a bit old. Subacute subdural, then?

'I don't know,' I say finally, scared to get it wrong.

'It's a subacute subdural,' he says. 'You should have known that.'

I hate myself.

'I thought that—'

'You didn't think anything,' he says flatly. 'Don't pretend.'

Our eyes meet for a moment. He has brown eyes, and is tall with blondish hair. If I'd met him at a bar, I would have thought he was good-looking—sexy even. He would tell me he was a doctor—a brain surgeon, no less—and I would be impressed. I'd hope that he would buy me a drink. Maybe more than one. I would tell my mother about him and hope that he wanted to be my boyfriend. A real-life brain surgeon. Wow.

'Interns always pretend,' he says, 'but we always know when you're lying.'

I stretch my lips in a smile, as if he has made a joke. I read an article once that said even if you're feeling really unhappy, when you smile it triggers off the happy response in your brain. So even in the worst of situations, the article advised, force yourself to smile and you'll feel better. Simple brain connections and chemistry. Happiness is just dopamine, a few neural pathways, and a big, fake smile. I should know. I am a happy young doctor, after all.

He smiles back at me. We sit there, stretching our lips at each other. His teeth gleam, reflecting the light of the computer screen. I have an image of the Joker, with his painted-on red grin, teeth bared.

I am saved when his phone starts to ring. It's recovery. The last patient on the list, the cervical spine fusion, has a neck swelling that is getting bigger. His presence is required.

'Don't forget the morning trauma meeting is tomorrow,' he says as he stands up. 'It's held every Tuesday. We go through all the emergency trauma cases that have come in. You need practice, and you need to look at more scans. I can't believe you didn't pick up that subdural. Dr Bird will be there. He's the head of department so make sure you're on time.'

'I'll be on time,' I say to his retreating back.

I take a deep breath, and let out a very long sigh. I feel my pocket vibrating again. I answer the phone. As I expected, it's Max.

'Where. The Fuck. Are you?!' he shouts into my ear.

'She's not *still* at work, is she?' I hear Winnie say in the background.

'I'm on my way,' I say, suddenly sure that if I don't leave this place immediately I will suffer some kind of catastrophic cardiac event.

Even though we're not meant to use this exit, I take the fire escape steps four at a time and burst through the door leading onto North Avenue, my street.

I walk up the road quickly. When I reach the little white cottage with the overgrown front yard I almost cry in relief. It might be only two hundred metres from the hospital, but 19 North Avenue feels like it is on the other side of the planet.

Outwardly, our house doesn't have a lot going for it. It's extremely old and rundown, and it floods at the first hint of rain. We have to use an umbrella to go to the bathroom in bad weather because it used to be an outdoor toilet. The previous tenants we suspect used this indoor-outdoor bathroom area as some sort of greenhouse to grow illegal hydroponic vegetation. We haven't ruled out continuing their legacy but I've a feeling our neighbours have above-average scent detection, if their formidable hearing is anything to go by. Max always says there'd be better money in flogging Endone on the deep web but, as I remind him, this is unethical and could lead to deregistration, so Operation Oxycodone remains his pipe dream.

We pay way too much rent, our neighbours hate us, and we are definitely the worst house in a good street. But none of that matters to me. With its steep staircase and high ceilings and fireplaces, number 19 North Avenue is my own little slice of paradise.

'Let's have a house party,' I can hear Max saying as I walk down the hall towards the living room. His voice is slow, meaning only one thing.

'Have you been taking valiums out of the shoebox again?' I demand as I enter the room, stepping over a squashed grape which has been sitting on the floorboards for at least six days. I ignore it.

'We've earned it,' Winnie says, leaning back on the couch and gesturing at the cardboard shoebox which houses our more questionable pharmaceuticals. 'Did I tell you about the date I went on last night?'

Winnie has a dating track record even worse than mine. Her experiences are so random and bizarre, it's like she has set herself a personal challenge.

I met Winnie when I was nine years old and we have been inseparable ever since, other than a period when her family relocated to the UK for a few years during our teens. We don't talk about that time too much, because Winnie's mother died over there after a sudden diagnosis of pancreatic cancer. I know she thinks about it, though—sometimes a dark cloud will come over her face, and Max and I sense to leave her alone.

'The fitness instructor?' I say.

Winnie rolls her eyes. 'I should have known. A fitness freak who doesn't drink. Stupid.'

'Non-drinking is a huge red flag,' Max offers helpfully. 'Madness.'

'Anyway, forget about the fitness instructor—we want to have a house party,' Winnie tells me. 'This house would be great for a party.'

I can feel number 19 smiling.

By the time we finish another bottle of wine it's settled. We were born to party, and number 19 is a house born to be partied in.

'How was the rest of your day, mate?' Max asks. 'Do you reckon you'll have to stay that late every day?'

I shrug, feeling demoralised. 'I hope not.'

'Did you meet any sexy doctors?' Winnie asks.

'Just one guy, the junior consultant,' I say, suddenly realising I'll have to see the Joker again in the morning and feeling even more dejected.

'And?' Winnie looks hopeful.

'And I've nicknamed him the Joker because he's so horrible.'

Max looks pained. 'One of those then.'

'Yeah.'

Winnie leans over with the wine. 'Shit, mate, that sucks.' She tops up my glass, then launches into a hilarious account of her date.

I lean back into the old couch, and feel myself relax into laughter. By the time I go to bed an hour later, I've almost forgotten I have work in the morning. I am reminded by the view of the hospital through my bedroom window. I sigh and close the shutters.

I set the alarm then get into bed and try to will myself into sleep. It's only day two of doctoring tomorrow, I remind myself. It's a marathon, not a sprint. Just take it one day at a time.

I hug my pillow for comfort and, just for a minute, forget myself and wish that Fabien was lying next to me. He always knew how to lift my spirits. But you don't think about Fabien anymore, I remind myself. I banish the thought, immediately.

My phone pings on my bedside table. I pick it up and see a message from Max.

BREAKING NEWS, it reads. *Surgical intern contaminates sterile field with tears!*

I LOL for real.

three

'EVERY STEP OF THE WAY IN THIS PROFESSION, SOMEONE will try to derail your career. No one tells you that, of course, but it's true. Every. Step. Of. The. Way.' So says Dr Bird, the head of the neurosurgical department.

I am underwhelmed with inspiration.

'Don't be fooled!' he booms, making everyone in the room jump slightly. 'They don't teach you this in medical school but, rest assured, your main problems aren't going to be the operations or the patients or the fear or the loneliness.'

'Gosh, he's really selling it,' Lawrence mutters next to me.

'It's the fact that at some point in your future, some other doctor—or an administrator, or a nurse, or some other colleague, maybe several of them—will actively try to destroy your career.'

Dr Bird looks around the room, his beady little eyes lighting on each of us in turn, letting the words sink in. He might have a birth certificate that says Bird, but he reminds me of a shark eyeing his prey. *Last words, little fish, before I devour you whole. Chomp, chomp, chomp.* I immediately christen him the Shark in my mind and forget his real name for the rest of my life.

'Anyway, that's just some food for thought,' he concludes, as the rest of the department starts to file into the room, obviously wanting to scare the pants off the new junior doctors before the meeting even formally begins, and succeeding. 'You can't say you weren't warned.'

Someone turns on the overhead projector and the image of a mashed-up brain beams onto the screen in front of us. A man stands up, and I cringe as I recognise him. The Joker returns. After our less than positive meeting last night, I'd been hoping he might fall sick or something and stay home, but no such luck. Not that that would ever happen; doctors aren't allowed to get sick. So here he is, once again pointing at a brain scan.

'Twenty-six-year-old female, assaulted with a king hit to the face two nights ago, brought in unconscious by ambulance through emergency.'

As his voice drones on I replay the Shark's words.

Every step of the way in this profession, someone will try to derail your career.

It's hard to remember at this moment why I'd ever wanted to become a doctor. I'd been so sure when I embarked on my medical degree: so committed, so driven, so convinced I would be able to make a difference.

'For the prestige and the scripts,' Estelle always says when people ask her the question. 'Why else would you do it?'

'Katarina!'

I snap to attention to see the Joker glaring at me. The mild ache that's been sitting behind my eyes immediately declares itself as a full-blown throb.

'Ah . . . yes?'

'Describe the scan,' he snaps.

NOT THIS AGAIN!

I stare at the image, and try to think clearly. Blood is white, and ischaemia is darker. There's some white, and some inflammation. The midline looks off; maybe there's a shift. Bleed likely from the middle cerebral artery with midline shift and oedema, I think to myself.

As I open my mouth to speak I see the Joker smirk. I freeze.

'Well, Katarina?'

'Ah, maybe a bleed, from, ah, the . . .' I feel sweat beading on my brow. The room is totally silent. All eyes are on me. 'Ah, the middle . . . cerebral . . .' I squeak out.

He looks disgusted. 'And?'

I clear my throat and try to continue, but my voice fails me.

'Bleed from the middle cerebral artery with midline shift!' my boss roars. 'That is a simple scan!'

'I . . . I thought that was . . .' I stop. Just speak next time, I admonish myself. Trust your instincts.

My instincts are urging me to flee—all the way to the south of France. One way.

Stop being so ridiculous, I tell my instincts. Surgeons don't run away. They stay inside the operating theatre and just cop it sweet. Toughen up, princess!

'You need to spend some time looking at more scans, Katarina,' the Joker says. 'I'm going to quiz you this afternoon, so you'll need to actually be prepared rather than relying on me to tell you the answers.'

I sink back into my chair, relief washing over me as he starts to interrogate a registrar on the other side of the room.

No surgical terms are easy, but brain surgery is as bad as it sounds. As we go through more scans, it's clear that most of the patients on the ward are at risk of crashing. And by crashing I don't mean a bit of a temperature spike; I mean like a train crashing. As in death. And no doubt, I think to myself sadly, it will happen when the rest of the team is in the operating theatre and I'm alone on the ward.

I can't handle this, I think, suddenly. *I actually cannot handle this.*

I mentally kick myself, hard, and force myself to concentrate.

'You must have seen some decent trauma in the States,' the Shark is saying to the Joker as the last scan mercifully vanishes from the screen. 'Good experience.'

The Joker, I soon discover, spent a year in a big-deal hospital in America after completing his PhD at Harvard; that explains the accent—he must be trying to remind us that he's no longer Australian but an honorary member of the Boston elite. Impressive as this is, it's clear that he feels he's taken a step backwards in returning to Australia, and he's trying to boost himself up by lording it over the more junior members of the team. I'm easily the softest target both because I'm at the bottom rung of the team ladder and because I'm female.

How can I make him like me? Not even like me, but just be marginally less horrible? I wonder as I hear my pager start to beep.

Dr Holliday draws a blank. Ask Kitty Holliday the writer, I imagine Estelle suggesting.

She'd probably flirt her way out of it with clever words. Weapons of verbal mass seduction, rather than scalpels of destruction, or something along those lines. Hmm, perhaps not. If I tried to flirt with him I might accidentally vomit, which would only make matters worse.

As we file out of the room, the Shark, to his credit, pulls me aside.

'I know you don't have a registrar for a few more days, so just call on me or Dr Prince if you need to,' he says, quite kindly. 'Things can get a bit messy up there on the ward.'

I must have looked a little confused at the mention of Dr Prince. As far as I knew, he wasn't at the meeting.

'Dr Prince doesn't attend many meetings,' the Shark says, sounding peeved. 'I've told him he has to, but he doesn't often listen to me.'

I nod.

'Anyway, Karen,' the Shark says heartily, looking over my shoulder as if the conversation has already gone on too long, 'I'll see you for a round later.'

'It's, ah, Katarina,' I correct him.

He nods vaguely and hurries away.

No problems, I tell his retreating back. Call me whatever you want, just don't be too mean.

Thank goodness the registrar will be here in a few days, I think as my pager starts up again, signalling that it's time for the nurses to start harassing me. I am relieved to learn that the registrar is a woman. I can't wait to have an ally, a fellow female warrior to stand between me and the Joker.

I only need to get through another few days, I remind myself as I walk into the ward, then the new registrar will start and I'll be out of the line of fire.

Just a few more days.

four

I TRUDGE INTO THE DOCTORS' ROOM, FIGHTING AN OVERwhelming urge to throw my beeping pager out the window. How can something so small have so much power? Outside, the sun is shining, and as I look out the window I wonder if I should have made different choices. It's only day two and I'm already starting to question if I'm really cut out for the world of medicine. If it was a TV show it's feeling, awkwardly, less *Grey's Anatomy* and more *Prison Break*. That is to say, rather than steamy encounters with my incredibly attractive colleagues, I can see myself spending more time plotting methods of escape. I suddenly wish I didn't want to be a surgeon and that I was sunbaking on a Spanish beach drinking sangria instead of sitting here, about to do battle with the ward printer, which doesn't work.

The beeping of my pager is drowned out by the sound of my phone.

It's the Joker. 'Prince wants to do a round,' he snaps. 'I'm needed in theatre. Go to the ward. Now.'

He hangs up before I can ask if he means the north or south side of the surgical ward, which is huge. On top of that, I have no idea what Dr Prince even looks like.

'No one knows that much about Prince,' Max told me last night when we were discussing our new bosses. 'Like, he's a bit of a mystery. Apparently, he's loaded. Maybe that's why he doesn't speak to anyone. He's so rich he doesn't need workmates.'

I don't care about Dr Prince's financial situation one way or the other, nor about who he chooses as his friends; I just hope he isn't a total jerk.

I walk quickly to the north end of the ward and hail a nurse.

'Have you seen Dr Prince?' I ask.

She shakes her head.

I walk back to the south end and sit down at the nurses' station. My phone beeps with a message from the Joker.

I need a coffee. Bring it to theatres.

I imagine buying the Joker a coffee and lacing it with arsenic.

Lawrence walks into the nurses' station. 'Hey, Kitty, I've been look—'

'God, he's such a fuckhead,' I say with feeling, waving my phone at him. 'Read this! Like, what does he think I am? His fucking receptionist? You know, I'd love to turn his knife on him,' I say, savouring the thought. 'Next time he quizzes me about some arterial supply—*bam*! It's a scalpel straight to the carotid.'

Lawrence is looking uncomfortable, I notice.

'Not enough to kill him,' I explain hurriedly. 'I'd just incapacitate him for a while. Like maybe . . . eleven weeks,' I specify, since that's how long I have left of my term. 'I mean, he can go back to operating when he's properly recovered.'

I hear someone clearing their throat behind Lawrence.

There's a short silence.

'Ah, I was looking for you because Dr Prince wants to do a round,' Lawrence says awkwardly. 'But now we've found you, so . . .'

'Thanks, Lawrence,' the man behind him says, stepping into my line of vision. 'I'm sure Dr Holliday and I can take it from here.'

I wait for the floor to open up and swallow me, but unfortunately nothing happens. I can feel my entire body flaming red. I wonder if Dr Prince has a fire extinguisher handy.

We stand there, looking at each other.

Dr Prince is taller than me, but not by much. He's wearing navy surgical scrubs and the hair poking out from beneath the cap is dark brown. His blue eyes crinkle at the corners when he smiles at me; he's at least forty-five, I realise. Maybe even fifty.

'You must be my intern,' he says mildly, holding out his hand. 'I'm Jack Prince.'

I wonder whether I should apologise for my homicidal rant against the Joker, his surgical colleague, but since he hasn't brought it up I decide it would be wiser not to mention it.

'Katarina,' I say, shaking his hand. 'My friends call me Kitty, though.'

I'm not sure why I feel the need to share this. The Shark barely knows I have a name, after all.

Dr Prince nods.

'I mean, I don't need to know *your* nickname,' I say quickly. 'Katarina is a bit of a mouthful, that's all. Obviously, I'll just call you Dr Prince.'

I don't know what's happening. My frontal lobe has hyperactivated to a point where complete drivel is spewing out of my mouth. I can't believe I tease Winnie about being a hypochondriac. Clearly she's right: a brain tumour can strike at any moment. I need an MRI urgently.

Dr Prince is looking at me with an expression that for the life of me I can't interpret.

'I don't really have a nickname,' he says thoughtfully. 'People usually just call me Jack.'

'Not short for Jackson, I guess,' I say, unnecessarily.

His eyebrows knit together. 'No, just Jack.'

'Oh,' I say.

'So, I suppose we should start the round.' He gestures towards the patient rooms.

I jump to attention. 'I'll get the charts,' I say, quickly walking to the alcove where the patient files are kept.

I return with charts in hand, relieved that I've managed to do something successfully, and hand them to him.

'So how are you finding neurosurgery?' he asks.

'It's all right,' I say half-heartedly. 'I mean, good. No, it's good.'

He raises his eyebrows.

'I like it,' I add unconvincingly as we walk towards the first patient.

'Have you been into theatre yet?'

I shake my head. 'Not yet . . . I went all the time as a medical student, though,' I say, 'and I found it so fascinating.'

He looks at me, interested. 'What did you find fascinating about it?'

I consider this. I'm about to make a joke, to keep things light, but for some reason he makes me want to be honest. 'It's hard to articulate,' I say slowly. 'The whole idea of taking away someone's consciousness, of cutting through their skin, to have that kind of power and control, is just, well . . .' I stop, feeling a bit foolish. 'Blood and knives and power and pain and mercy and magic,' I say, repeating the words I'd used to Estelle yesterday in the cafeteria. 'It's all there, under those bright lights.'

His eyes crinkle. 'You're a poet,' he says. 'My intern is a poet.'

I laugh. 'I wanted to be a writer,' I admit, forgetting myself.

'Why do you say it in the past tense? Once a writer, always a writer.'

I want to hug him, then feel depressed. I'm not really a writer, I remind myself. I'm just a wannabe writer who'll probably never make it.

'Well, you know,' I say defensively, 'I want to be a surgeon, and it's a bit hard to focus on both.'

'The two can coexist,' he says very simply, encapsulating all my desires and exposing my insecurities in one sentence. 'Why can't they?'

Suddenly I feel a bit light-headed. Here I am, revealing my secret dreams to my consultant neurosurgeon, and rather than laughing at or scorning me, he is responding with kindness.

'I don't know,' I say as we walk from the nurses' station to outside the patient curtain. 'I have the impression that surgery and creativity don't go that well together. I've had kind of a rough start. Although, it's only day two, I guess.'

He looks at me directly. His eyes aren't really blue at all, I realise. Not quite blue, not quite green and not quite grey. I don't know how to describe them.

They say the eyes are a window to a person's soul but I know from doing neurosurgery that this isn't true. Eyes are just an extension of the brain. Eyes aren't kind or cruel or anything else. They're just eyes.

'You should come and assist me in theatre sometime,' Dr Prince says, and then he opens the curtain, thus closing the conversation, and asks Mrs Boyd how her head's feeling after her operation.

I open the chart, and her CT scan falls out. The sight of another CT scan I'll probably be quizzed on makes me die a bit on the inside, but Dr Prince just picks it off the floor and holds it up to the light, considering.

'What do you see, Kitty?' he asks.

It is obvious to me, so I tell him. 'She's had a meningioma excised,' I explain. 'They do the post-op scan to check there's no bleeding or complications, and this looks pretty good. I saw her original scan yesterday.'

'We'll make a neurosurgeon of you yet,' he says, and he smiles.

Suddenly, I love being an intern. I love being a doctor. I love everything, and I feel as if I have just won the lottery.

'It really makes a difference when people are a bit pleasant,' I blurt out.

'Sounds like some people aren't being so pleasant,' he observes mildly.

I clear my throat and focus on putting the scan back into the chart. 'It's fine,' I say quickly.

We're interrupted by Mrs Boyd.

'You doctors are so young these days,' she croaks. 'And ladies! A lady doctor!'

Dr Prince and I both smile.

After we've seen all the patients we stand at the end of the ward. The round is over, but I find myself reluctant to leave.

'Well, thanks for the round,' says Dr Prince. 'You're doing very well.'

'Thank you,' I reply, feeling ridiculously pleased.

He looks like he's about to say something else, but instead he raises his hand, and half nods at me. 'Okay . . . Bye then,' he says.

'Bye,' I say, finding I'm doing my own weird half nod.

As he walks away I stand there, wondering why I feel so odd.

I walk to the nurses' desk near the front of the ward, and take a few deep breaths. Is it nausea? A headache? It's a sensation I can't quite put my finger on.

It isn't until the end of the day, when I meet Max in the cafeteria and describe my round with Dr Prince, that I realise I'm not suffering from a brain tumour or viral gastroenteritis or any other kind of illness.

'You must be getting used to neurosurgery,' Max says, looking at me closely. 'You actually seem a bit happy.'

five

MY PHONE IS RINGING, AND I'M DEBATING WHETHER OR not to answer it.

'Is it the Joh-kerrrr?' Max asks with an exaggerated Bostonian drawl.

'Just hang up on him,' Estelle suggests.

We're in the hospital cafeteria at our favourite table, which is tucked into a sort of alcove, concealing us from people we're trying to avoid. It's Thursday, which is tantalisingly close to Friday and then the weekend. It's almost the end of our first week and we are all still alive, as are most of our patients. The only death was Max's, a ninety-eight-year-old man with pneumonia, leaving him, to Estelle's and my envy, with only one patient on his list.

'It's a private number,' I say worriedly as my phone keeps ringing.

'He's just trying to trick you,' Max says. 'He must realise you've started to screen his calls so he's doing the old "call you through switch" move.'

'The new registrar is starting today,' I remind him. 'Maybe it's her. I should answer it.'

Max shrugs. 'It's your funeral.'

Angry that I am so weak, I press answer. 'Hello?'

There's a short silence.

'Katarina speaking,' I say. Maybe it's about my overdue electricity bill, not anything work-related at all, I think hopefully.

'Hello,' a male voice says, sounding slightly hesitant.

'Hello?'

'It's, ah, Jack Prince.'

I almost knock over the coffee cup in my haste to stand up, moving away from Max and Estelle's chatter so that he won't be able to tell that I'm at the cafeteria.

'Oh, hi, Dr Prince!' I say. 'Do you want to do a round? I'm just heading to the ward now.'

'No, that's all right. I was actually ringing to see if you'd like to help me out in theatre tomorrow. For my Friday list.'

'Sure,' I say. 'Of course.' I'm torn between dread and excitement at the prospect.

'I thought perhaps I could try to improve your experience of neurosurgery,' he offers.

I laugh nervously. 'That's really decent of you.'

'Well, the only way to know if surgery really is for you is to come into theatre,' he points out, sounding like my boss all of a sudden.

'Of course, yes, absolutely,' I agree.

'Theatre six,' he informs me. 'Tomorrow just after midday.'

I'm about to thank him again when the phone goes dead.

'Well, that obviously wasn't the Joker,' Estelle remarks, as she and Max stare at me. 'Why is your face going red?'

'I reckon Prince likes you, mate,' Max says. 'You obviously like him.'

'Of course I like him!' I snap defensively. 'He's the only person who isn't a total arsehole!'

Max smirks. 'Why'd you straighten your hair this morning, Doctor?'

Estelle raises her eyebrows. 'You never even brush your hair.'

'I am a normal human being!' I protest. 'I am capable of basic hygiene!'

'Wouldn't know it by your bedroom,' Max says.

I try to glare at them, but I start to laugh instead. 'Guys, he's like fifty,' I point out.

'Since when has that stopped you?' Estelle says reasonably. It's true that my less-than-stellar romantic history is littered with inappropriate liaisons with inappropriately aged men. 'Remember David the lawyer?'

'Though there was that guy Kitty met in Switzerland,' Max says in my defence. 'He was only thirty. I seem to remember her calling him her soulmate.'

'Yeah, what happened with him anyway?' Estelle asks.

'He's skiing in Switzerland and having the time of his life while I'm sitting here in this stinking cafeteria with you two,' I reply, irritated.

My appropriately aged soulmate, Fabien Pho, is a tall good-looking man I met on a ski holiday the previous winter. He's so different from me that it never would have worked, I remind myself whenever I'm overcome by longing or regret. I skype with him every now and then, and tell myself the joy I feel on seeing his brown eyes and white smile is only a comparative reactive emotion, contrasting ski holiday happiness with my current stress levels, and the entire thing is just a silly fantasy.

Still, even just hearing his name in conversation makes my heart squeeze a little uncomfortably, and I'm oddly relieved when my phone rings yet again.

Everyone's eyes go to the screen.

'This time it probably really is the Joker,' Max warns.

Thankfully, it isn't. It's my new registrar, wanting me to meet her on the ward to go through the patient list.

'Enjoy,' Max says, leaning back in his chair and putting his hands behind his head, the relaxed posture of a man not doing a surgical term. He looks over at Estelle. 'Hey, on a different note, have medical admin emailed to tell you when you have to go out bush?'

Estelle nods. As interns we all have to spend ten weeks out in rural Australia, to work at Holy Innocents' sister hospital that isn't staffed by enough local doctors. 'Next term, mate. Me and Kitty are going together. God, I can't believe that they're shipping us out to the middle of fucking nowhere,' she continues, bemoaning the fate of junior doctors forced to go on remote secondments. 'Do you think I could get out of it somehow?'

'At least we're going together,' I point out, grabbing my bag. 'Imagine if we were going it alone.'

I'm not really looking forward to living in the bush for ten weeks either, but that's a while off yet and, in the meantime, things here seem to be improving, what with Dr Prince becoming an unexpected ally and a new woman on the team.

I take a wrong turn on my way up to the ward, and find myself lost near the operating theatres. Theatres are on level five, and I feel irritated with myself. The surgical ward is level seven, so I have no idea how I've somehow exited the stairwell two floors below it. The long corridors and fluorescent lights, connected by lifts and staircases, make the hospital almost impossible for me to navigate. I'm bad at map-reading at the best of times; I need a GPS just to find certain parts of my workplace.

I've decided to use the stairwell as much as possible; at least the stairs act as some kind of familiar starting point. I feel like I spend half my day trying to find things, or places. Conveniently, there are phones everywhere. This is good and bad. It means as soon as my pager beeps the nurses know there's no excuse to not respond immediately. Every corner has an internal hospital phone sitting on it. Even then it doesn't really matter, because they'll just call my mobile number anyway. All of the interns' phone numbers are splashed all over the wards. So much for respecting my privacy. I run from the surgical ward on seven, down to theatres on five (so far the only reason I've gone to theatres is to give the Joker his coffee), back to seven, and the cycle goes on. My favourite level is three, because that's where the cafeteria is.

'Shouldn't they pay for us to have a work phone, don't you think?' Max asked me earlier as my phone rang continuously, with the dreaded extension of the hospital switchboard. 'You are on your phone constantly.'

'They don't even pay us overtime,' Estelle rightly said. 'Can't really see the combo company–car phone deal, you know, mate?'

Amusing myself with the memory of this conversation, I finally arrive on level seven, covered in sweat.

I see the new registrar as soon as I enter the ward. She's standing at the nurses' station squinting up at the patient board.

'Hi,' I say. 'I'm Kat—'

'Yes, I know who you are,' she snaps, tucking a strand of hair behind her ear. Not that I could have picked there was a hair out of place; her immaculately styled blonde hair makes me all too aware of my own customary dishevelment. 'Where have you been? I've been going through the blood results and there are about fifteen different things that you've obviously ignored.'

I gape at her.

'And where's my list? You never meet a registrar without a list for them. Go and print one. Now.'

Then, as if she's just made a benign comment about the weather, she smiles. 'I'm Rachel, by the way.'

And just like that, my newfound happiness evaporates.

six

WHEN I WAS FIFTEEN ONE OF MY RELATIVES ASKED ME at a family lunch what I wanted to be when I grew up. I didn't even hesitate.

'I want to be a Bond girl,' I replied.

I was trying to sound clever, but I also actually meant it. Fifteen-year-old me wanted a life filled with European beaches, attractive and dangerous men, fast cars and dry martinis. *So, tell me, James—do you still sleep with a gun under your pillow?*

Being a junior doctor has the potential for some Bond-esque moments—after all, nearly every Bond movie features an attractive female medic in some form or other—but so far I haven't had any. Unlike me, Bond movie medics aren't constrained by the walls or protocols of a teaching hospital. Their expertise seems to lie in the realms of the art of seduction, rather than the supposed art of medicine. The doctor in *The World Is Not Enough* clears Bond prematurely for fieldwork because they'd had extremely hot sex, and all I really remember is her expensive black underwear and white doctor's coat. She doesn't seem to have any qualms about sleeping with her patients. Where's the medical board intervention in her case? How could she have cleared him medically anyway? She didn't even check his X-rays properly!

If only I'd pursued acting, I say to myself mournfully as I approach the hospital entrance. It's been the same story every morning for the last five days. I allow myself the luxury of a small existential crisis in the short walk between home and the hospital, just to make myself feel better. Maybe it's not too late? If I lost a few kilograms and had a nose job I could still be in the running. I have dark hair and green eyes, and men often compliment me on my bum—maybe it's time to capitalise.

At least it's Friday, I tell myself as I open the door to the stairwell. The stairs, I remind myself, are good for me. The incidental exercise won't go astray if I'm to secure an acting agent and an audition for the next Daniel Craig feature. I'm charging up the steps two at a time to increase my heart rate when the door to the fifth floor flies open, forcing me to halt in my tracks.

I stand there gasping, demonstrating how horrendously unfit I am.

A man in scrubs is staring at me.

'Hello,' says Dr Prince.

I'm so out of breath I have to bend over. No doubt my face is the colour of a beetroot.

'Oh, fuck, hi,' I wheeze, dragging in a breath and wiping sweat off my face.

'Are you all right?' He looks concerned.

'Sorry for swearing,' I choke out, leaning on the handrail. 'I'm just puffed after running up the stairs.'

'Will you be right to come to theatre, do you think?' he asks, peering at me closely. I'm relieved to see that he's smiling.

'Yes, yes,' I reassure him, attempting to look calm and collected.

'Well,' he says, 'I'll see you later then.'

'Bye!' I bellow cheerfully, waving gaily as I resume my passage up the stairs.

After our round together I had hoped I could impress Dr Prince with some more neurosurgical insights, but alas my nerves get the better of me. I have no idea why I can't just have a normal encounter with the man, one in which I look together and attractive. Even better, one in which I make a sage remark on arterial supply of the brain, or something equally surgically impressive. Instead, usually when he sees me I'm either swearing my head off or covered in sweat.

Embarrassment and poor cardiovascular fitness aside, today, I remind myself, is going to be a good day. Once I get through the morning round I can look forward to going to the operating theatre to help Dr Prince.

The round. I grimace. Each morning it's been the same. Me and the Joker charging around the ward, dissecting and analysing every single error that's been committed the day before and reaching exactly the same conclusion in every case—it's all my fault. And I have a sneaking suspicion from yesterday's brief encounter with my new registrar that things are only going to get worse.

I'm not wrong. Dealing with one of them is bad enough, but the double act is excruciating. I watch a lot of crime drama and recognise immediately I'm now witness to my very own *folie à deux*. Three patients into the morning round, I'm already exhausted by the realisation that this new game of 'who can be meaner to the intern' is one I'll be forced to play every morning. I walk behind my superiors, dragging the charts, and wonder if they'll object to me lying in front of them before the round as a little bonding ritual so they can kick me a few times and then at least we'd get it out of the way.

'What's wrong with you?' the Joker sneers when I ask the new registrar to repeat which antibiotic the patient is on. 'You look half asleep.'

Ah, sleep. If only. What I wouldn't give to return to the sanctuary of my bedroom and be granted a reprieve from these horrendous people.

'You really need to focus more,' the new registrar informs me. 'When I was an intern I knew all the blood results off by heart and I'd arrive at work at six every morning to make sure I'd familiarised myself with all the patients. You should really be doing a pre-round, you know.'

I should be doing a pre-round at 6 am? This is news to me. The round itself is horrific enough!

Although we'd got off on the wrong foot yesterday, I'd still held out some hope that she and I would bond, both being women currently in surgery. The new thing in medicine is to support each other, after all, and be generally a bit, well, pleasant towards your colleagues. At least, that's what the email from medical admin this morning said.

After our first round together, I quickly dispel the hopeful illusion that we'll ever be friends. Everything I do or say is a personal affront to her own enormous intelligence.

'So, let's try and be better tomorrow, okay?' she says to me at the end of the round, as the Joker smirks.

There's something very wrong with this woman, I text Max immediately as she walks away. I get that she's a grade-A bitch, but do her putdowns have to be delivered with a big saccharine smile? She's like a smiling assassin, delivering her poisoned barbs with an expression of serene happiness. To make things even weirder, she looks like a cross between a friendly librarian and the pretty girl next door. Today, her outfit consists of a short bright red dress, set off by sparkling layers of expensively highlighted hair. The perfect symmetry of the layers amazes me. It took me years to accept that I can only wear my out-of-control hair in a permanently messy bun.

The Joker, also blond and shiny and fake Bostonian, loves it. Now he has his perfectly layered comrade—the Smiling Assassin. I run my hand over my bun, almost subconsciously. Maybe I should try that keratin treatment Estelle swears by. When in doubt, sort your hair out, is one of her life mottos.

Bad hair day aside, they've left me with a mountain of tasks which I have only a few hours to complete. I know if I don't get everything done there's no way I'll make it into theatre with Dr Prince. He seems genuine in his desire to show me the surgical ropes, and I desperately don't want to disappoint him.

I rush through my tasks, and by quarter to twelve I've changed into my scrubs to be ready for the operating theatre. I'm about to leave the ward when Sally, one of the young nurses, approaches me.

She looks worried.

I immediately begin to feel worried too. If I need help, it's far, far away. The Joker and the Smiling Assassin are both by now down in theatres, doing separate operations. The operating theatres are only two floors down but may as well be Siberia. A patient can deteriorate in five seconds; two floors away is as far as two light years.

'Kitty, it's Mr Waters . . . I think he's sick.'

Not Mr Waters—anyone but Mr Waters!

Mr Waters, who has just undergone a major brain operation, is our number one, most important, must-be-kept-alive-at-all-costs, VIP patient. Both his daughters are physicians who work at the private hospital and they're mates with the Shark. Lucy and Christine Waters come to the ward every day to 'visit' their father, which really means to supervise his medical care. I don't blame them. If I was the doctor caring for my family I'd put myself under supervision too. I like Dr Waters and Dr Waters. I also like Mr Waters. I also want to impress the Shark, who as head of the neurosurgical department is essentially God on Earth. It's only taken a week for me to start developing full-blown Stockholm Syndrome, which must all be part of the conditioning of a big teaching hospital.

'What's the problem?' I ask Sally, trying to sound confident and together, and like, you know, a doctor. (The truth is that whenever someone approaches me in the hospital and opens with, 'Excuse me, Doctor', it's enough to make my heart sink so fast I'm surprised blood doesn't start seeping out of my shoes. I feel my testicles retracting and I don't even have any. There aren't really any words to describe the all-encompassing dread that grips my entire body.)

'He's shaking. I think he's got a fever.' Sally looks as scared as I feel. What she doesn't look is confident in my abilities, which I find strangely comforting. It's as if we're soldiers together, in a situation neither of us can handle, but at least we have each other. We're Batman and Robin. Sherlock and Watson. Dr Who and companion. We are—

Except that, as a nurse, Sally doesn't really have any responsibility beyond informing a doctor what is going on—and that doctor is me.

There's no Batman and Robin; there's just Batman. Sherlock has no Watson. Dr Who has no . . . whoever Dr Who usually has.

I walk quickly to Mr Waters's bedside. The sight that greets me makes me want to curl up into the foetal position and start crying. Sally's right. He's sick. He isn't even just a bit sick. He's fucked. I stare at Mr Waters, the Shark's number one VIP patient, in abject terror.

Mr Waters is shaking so hard that his IV pole bangs against the metal bedframe with every convulsion. He has beads of sweat running down his face, and his teeth are chattering.

'Get . . . Dr . . .' he gasps as his eyes plead with me for help. I have a feeling that Mr Waters knows I'm totally useless and is giving me the right advice. I need a doctor. A real doctor. STAT!

I ring the Joker, who declines to answer. So I try the Smiling Assassin. The call goes straight to voicemail. With little time to spare I bite the bullet and call the Shark. I stammer something incoherent into the phone but manage to convey the important details. The Shark, who I've never seen or heard looking anything other than iceberg cool, sounds extremely angry. He yells something about a CT scan and hangs up. Time starts moving very quickly. I run to the computer to try to order a CT scan on the internal hospital system, but I can't find the right code name of the scan. I'm so flustered I can barely function. Sally runs back over to report that Mr Waters is simultaneously vomiting and shitting blood! His blood pressure is dropping! His heart rate is through the roof!

'Should I do a PACE call?' she asks me, looking frantic.

This is the best idea I've heard in years. 'YES!' I shout. 'PACE CALL NOW!'

The hospital's PACE team is called whenever a patient starts deteriorating. In this instance, they arrive promptly, to my overwhelming relief. Not surprisingly, the medical registrar comes over to ask where the treating team is.

'Ah, that'd be me,' I admit, feeling a bit queasy. I'm hiding behind the desk, still trying to work out how to order the CT scan.

At this point the Joker has been informed of the situation by the Shark, but instead of coming to my rescue he has been texting me instructions.

The medical registrar is disgusted. 'Tell your team to get here now,' he snaps. Then, seeing my look of uncertainty, he rolls his eyes. 'Oh, for God's sake, give me the phone and I'll ring them.'

'Good luck.'

As I could have predicted, the Joker tells him to bugger off.

By now Mr Waters has stopped breathing anyway so it's escalated to a code blue. As he is taken away by the intensive care doctors, Sally and I stand next to each other.

'Thanks,' she whispers, still sounding terrified. I've no idea why she's thanking me. If anything, I feel like I should be thanking her.

All I can think is that I want to go home but my work here isn't done. I sprint all over the hospital, trying desperately to organise an operating theatre to save Mr Waters. The Shark ends up performing emergency surgery.

Mr Waters finally makes it to theatre, but I'm thoroughly shaken up. I return to the ward and stand there for a moment, trying to process what just happened.

My phone buzzes with a message. It's from the Smiling Assassin.

Could you get me a coffee? You didn't bother showing so I'm in theatre 6 assisting Prince.

The realisation that the Smiling Assassin has taken my spot next to Dr Prince in the operating theatre while I was caught up in the Waters drama hits me like a sharp knee to the gut.

I pull off my scrub cap and blink hard. Pull yourself together, I tell myself fiercely. It's just one theatre list. You're on a surgical term. There are heaps of theatre lists.

A lone tear betrays me and tracks down my face. I use the cap to wipe it away, then walk quickly to the patient toilet on the ward. I shut the door, turn on the tap and splash my face with water. Then I go to the cafeteria to buy the Smiling Assassin a coffee, feeling ridiculously sad.

Chin up, I tell myself. It isn't the end of the world, missing one operation. I try not to imagine what the Smiling Assassin has told Dr Prince about my non-appearance. I'm sure you can explain it to him later, my brain reminds me rationally. No need to act like someone's died. Mr Waters isn't dead, which is the most important thing, isn't it?

I hand my last $3.50 over to buy a soy latte for the Smiling Assassin, a woman I am starting to truly despise. I dutifully walk to the operating theatre front desk and leave her the coffee, then return to the ward.

I work until the end of the day, check with one of the nurses that Mr Waters is still alive (he is), then walk home and drink an entire bottle of wine.

By the time Winnie and Max roll into number 19 from their dinner out (something fun normal people or doctors on respiratory terms in summer do) and ask me how my day was, I can't even respond. I stumble to bed, dreading the morning.

Somewhere else, somebody else is stepping onto a film set dressed in a white doctor's coat over skimpy lingerie, playing the role of the sexy doctor as she unethically clears Bond for his dangerous fieldwork. Damn that woman to hell—she has stolen my life.

seven

I AGE TEN YEARS IN A FEW WEEKS. IT DOESN'T HELP THAT I'm staying back at work till 9 pm every night to make sure Mr Waters, the Shark's VIP patient, remains alive. I don't trust the Joker or the Smiling Assassin enough to ensure that he does.

Mr Waters has now developed a pleural effusion, and looks uncomfortable every time he breathes. The Shark, in consultation with Dr Waters and Dr Waters, decides to have the fluid from his lungs drained using a special radiological method. This involves me contacting the radiology consultant, which means making a bit of an effort.

The Smiling Assassin and the Joker laugh in my face when I tell them that this is what the Shark wants. 'That's ridiculous! It's not big enough to drain,' the Joker says bluntly. 'Bird is being an idiot. He's just trying to impress his VIP patient's daughter. I don't know why, she's a hag.'

I bite my lip, fighting the urge to jump on him and commence manual strangulation.

'It's not going to happen, Katarina,' the Smiling Assassin says, smiling sweetly. 'Sometimes you need to recognise when the boss wants something that's not possible and you need to be smart enough to say no.'

'I think I should at least try,' I say awkwardly. 'Like . . . I can just go into radiology and ask.'

We're in the doctors' room at the end of the ward. I'm standing by the door.

'Why ask?' the Joker says. He's reclining in the only comfortable chair in the room. 'Just tell Bird no.'

'Katarina,' the Smiling Assassin says slowly, as if I'm a child, 'I know it's hard for you as an intern to understand this, but I've noticed that your clinical judgement needs a lot of work.'

Behind her, the Joker nods.

'Sometimes the things you're doing just simply aren't appropriate.'

By now other doctors have come into the room and are listening curiously to the conversation.

'I don't think this is inappropriate,' I argue, my neck and cheeks getting hot.

'But you clearly don't know the difference between what is appropriate and what isn't,' the Smiling Assassin replies.

Tears have started to well in my eyes, but I will not back down. The Shark and Dr Waters and Dr Waters and Mr Waters, whose life I goddamn helped to save, stand silently behind me in my mind's eye.

'Listen, I've got one boss in this situation,' I say. 'And I'm going to do what he says. If he wants me to sort out the lung tap, that's fine. To be perfectly frank, my main concern is to do the right thing by the patient, something neither of you seem particularly interested in.'

My insubordination is met with deafening silence. The Smiling Assassin's smile falters. The Joker looks bored.

I leave the room in what I hope is a dignified manner then run down the stairs to the radiology department, blinking furiously.

Thankfully, I've developed quite a good relationship with Martin, the radiology registrar. He offers me a cup of tea and we sit in the darkroom together as he stares at an X-ray.

'Look, being an intern is fucking shit,' he says, kindly ignoring my bloodshot eyes and dripping nose. 'There're a lot of dickheads in this place, just don't worry about it. I've gotten used to it. Some of the surgeons who come in here hassling me for scans, one minute they're nice, next minute they've flicked the prick on. Only takes them half a fucking second.'

For every arsehole in the hospital, there's also someone who's actually okay. Martin calls his boss, who agrees to perform the tap. The Shark finds out I've successfully organised the unorganisable and texts me directly, telling me I have it in me to be a surgeon. *I like the way you just get things done*, he writes.

Dr Waters and Dr Waters buy me a bottle of fancy champagne when Mr Waters is discharged home the following week. They write on the card: *Thank you, Kitty, you've been brilliant.*

Estelle, Winnie, Max and I drink the champagne on a Tuesday night in the backyard of 19 North Avenue.

'Here's to Mr Waters,' I say, raising my glass.

We toast: to Mr Waters, to me, to life, and to friends. The things that make it all worthwhile.

'I feel like we should be saving this champagne for a special night,' Winnie says. 'I mean, we're all in our work clothes and it's a Tuesday.'

'We've got the party on Saturday,' Max points out. 'Heaps of people have RSVPed on Facebook.'

The house party. I'd almost forgotten about it, what with all the drama at work. Every single intern we know is desperate to cut loose after the shock to the system of our new lives as junior doctors.

'It'll be morale-raising,' Max says happily.

'Or sorrow-drowning,' I say. 'I can make my famous punch. It turns an okay night into the best party ever.'

'Well, I can't fucking wait,' Estelle says emphatically. 'I'm so sick of that fucking hospital, I am going to get as drunk as a human can get.'

Winnie looks concerned. 'What if I have to take you to emergency?'

Estelle laughs. 'Don't be ridiculous, Winnie. I'd rather drown in my own vomit than go to that place as a patient. Just help write my eulogy, that's all I ask.'

'I've heard doctor parties get pretty loose,' Winnie says doubtfully. 'One of the girls at work dated a doctor and she said all he ever did was go to work and get high—not simultaneously,' she adds quickly.

'It'll just be some punch and a few laughs,' I tell her. 'Everyone is so tired from working such horrible hours it probably won't even go that late.'

'Famous last words,' Estelle says, grinning. 'Just you wait.'

eight

'DO YOU WANT SOME COKE?'

I stare at the anaesthetics registrar who's sitting on my bed. In my drunken haze, Tom looks pretty hot. Or does he? I tilt my head. His nose is kind of big, which proves awkward when we're kissing, but he's still pretty sexy. Plus, the fact he's one of those naughty doctors who does drugs and smokes is also quite appealing. I prefer the subversive ones.

'I'm having some,' he says casually, pulling a small bag of white powder out of his pocket. 'Do you have a credit card?'

Did I ever. One thing I'm proving particularly successful at is accumulating multiple lines of credit; banks fall over themselves to offer you loans and credit cards when you become a doctor—they don't realise how paltry our salaries actually are. Not to worry—with the magic of plastic I can play now and pay later. I wonder why Tom wants it, though. Maybe he carries around a portable EFTPOS machine for when he offers cocaine to people, I speculate. I suppose that's fair enough; cocaine's pretty expensive.

My confusion must be obvious. 'I need it to cut up the lines,' Tom explains.

'Oh, right,' I reply, thinking: Is this life in the fast lane? A hot anaesthetist, a house party, illicit drugs and my credit card?

I watch, fascinated, as Tom arranges the cocaine into neat lines. He pulls a fifty-dollar note from his pocket, rolls it up, then leans down and effortlessly snorts two lines in a row. He sits up and breathes in.

'God, that's good stuff,' he says, looking pleased. 'You want some?'

Through my cheap wine-induced haze, I stare at him. I see Tom, the cocaine, my bedroom. I catch a glimpse of myself in my full-length mirror and I wonder who the hell that woman is. Have I finally entered the medical twilight zone?

Before I became a doctor, I looked down on people who snorted cocaine. Only bad people did drugs, I reasoned, and I was never going to be like them. Doctors were good people with pure intentions.

'This blow is straight out of Colombia,' Tom says. 'Sure you don't want some? It's as pure as snow.'

What about me? I wonder. Am I still pure? Tom's cocaine is, evidently, pure as the driven blow, flown all the way from the cartels in Bogotá.

'I don't think so,' I say, feeling terrified by how tempted I am.

I'm saved by the arrival of three of the surgical registrars, who have no such qualms and leap onto the cocaine as if they've been in a desert without water for a week.

Tom looks over at me. 'Give yourself another year,' he says wisely. 'Then you won't be saying no.'

Maybe he's right. Could he be right? I walk carefully down my extremely steep stairs, so as not to sustain a head injury and be carted off, drunk as all hell, to the hospital emergency department.

'Fuck, mate, I knew it! Doctors are loose!' Winnie lurches towards me drunkenly as I reach the bottom of the stairs. 'Like, they're fucking out of control!'

'Where's Max?' I ask.

'Getting a blow job in the bathroom,' Winnie says. 'Well, I think he is. Someone is, anyway.'

'What?!'

Winnie and I look at each other and grin.

'Come on,' she says, giggling. 'We won't bust in, but if we bang on the door he'll get a real fright.'

We fight our way to the bathroom through masses of drunk, swaying bodies and people spilling drinks. I see Estelle berating one of her registrars about what a tool he is and wince, knowing she'll regret it in the morning but also feeling slightly pleased.

I'm just raising my fist to pound on the bathroom door when it's flung open. Winnie stumbles into me and I lose my footing, and we both collapse onto the floor, shrieking with laughter.

We look up, and I see one of the other interns emerge, vomiting.

'She was really drunk,' Max says by way of explanation. 'I just helped her into the bathroom so she could be sick.' He grins. 'What did you guys think I was doing?'

'Apparently you were engaging in a sexual act,' I inform him, bending over to check if the intern is all right.

'Wrong gender, mate,' Max says.

'So only sexual acts with a human possessing your genitals of your choice, then?'

'I was about to,' he admits, looking sheepish, 'but then this girl burst in and started vomiting everywhere and it sort of killed the mood, you know.'

Winnie looks down at our vomiting colleague, and nods. 'I can see that.'

Dr Vomit puts her head up, and purges all over my shoes. 'Sorry,' she groans. 'I'm so sorry.'

'It's okay,' I say. 'I actually hate these shoes.'

'I'll get you some water,' Winnie says. 'Kitty, maybe you should go wash your shoes under the hose.'

'Do you like being an intern, Kitty?' Dr Vomit suddenly asks, surprising me by knowing my name, as she grabs onto my arm and looks up at me with half-closed eyes. 'Like, do you really?'

'I don't know,' I reply, semi-honestly.

'I hate it,' she says, putting her head back onto the tiles. 'I really hate it. The thought of doing this for another year makes me seriously want to top myself.'

'Don't say that,' I say, alarmed.

She shrugs into the tiles. 'Nah, I don't mean it. I've just smoked so much pot tonight.' She stops talking and lifts her head off the ground to vomit again. It pours out, like lava from a volcano.

'You'll feel better after a bit of a purge,' I tell her.

'Shouldn't mix weed and booze,' Max says, with the air of doctorly and regular pot-smoking authority. 'You'll be vomming for hours.'

I prise her hand off my arm and leave Winnie to deal with the situation. Walking into the backyard to find the hose, I realise I am very drunk, and close my eyes. I lean against the fence and let my back slide down until I am sitting on the ground.

Do you like being an intern?

I hate it. I really hate it.

The thought of doing this for another year makes me seriously want to top myself.

I rest my head against the wooden fence and take a breath.

It's just a party, I tell myself, a stupid fucking party. People say stupid things when they're drunk at parties. We're doctors. We're fucking sensible and kind and caring doctors. We're allowed to get drunk and lose control now and then, aren't we? How else do you cope?

People say stupid things when they're drunk at parties.

I stumble to my feet, find the hose and turn it on full blast. I wash away the vomit and feel the cool water on my skin. This is a loose party. It's an out-of-control party. It feels like a loose, out-of-control, medical student party.

Except that when I was a medical student the world was clear, the focus sharp. This is who you are, this is what you'll be, this is where you draw your lines, and this is the slot you fit into. Here is your pre-determined path, so set forth, child, and walk confidently through your present and towards your glorious future. Here is north and south, and east and west. Here are your coordinates so you will never be lost.

I look up at the sky. It's overcast, so I can't see the stars, and the moon isn't bright. All that is there is the shadow of the hospital, looming over the house. The sound from the party is fading, and I stand there, a tiny speck inside a cloak of black.

In the darkness, I could be anywhere.

nine

'SO YOU'RE HERE TO SEE DR PRINCE?' I CLARIFY, SIMULtaneously fighting rising frustration and a day-old hangover.

The man in front of me gives me a look that suggests he isn't impressed. 'Who are you?' he demands.

He's at least sixty and judging by his clothes he's stepped straight off a farm.

'We've driven six hours to be here,' the woman with him—his wife, I assume—explains, looking anxious. 'We thought we'd be seeing Professor Prince.'

'Where is he?' the farmer snaps. 'Why are we talking to a nurse when I have an appointment to see the doctor?'

The mild ache behind my left eye is threatening to turn into a full-on migraine. Even though it's Monday and our house party was on Saturday night, I still feel wretched. For a second I picture the state the house is still in, knowing I'll be walking home to it this afternoon, and resist the urge to groan loudly. Winnie, Max, Estelle and I spent most of Sunday discussing whether Laura (Estelle knew her name), our intern comrade, needed (in the interests of collegiality) some fellow junior doctor support. I called Laura that night, but she said she was just drunk and didn't remember saying anything. Estelle followed up with another call, which only made Laura angry and upset; she told Estelle in no uncertain terms that she was perfectly fine, that being a doctor was great, she was just drunk, and suggested we should all just fuck right off as she had her career as a future cardiologist to focus on, and a PhD to finish. Case closed.

'I am a doctor,' I say, mentally returning to the patient in front of me. 'I'm Dr Prince's intern. I'm going to see you first and then he'll come by this afternoon.'

'What?' The man looks affronted. 'I can't stay until this afternoon, so he'll have to come right now.'

I raise my eyebrows. 'He's operating all day.'

I realise I need to actually figure out what this guy is doing here before the argument continues.

'Where's your paperwork?' I ask. 'If I could have a look at your referral that might make things a bit easier.'

His wife rummages through an old leather handbag and produces a folder with *John—Medical* written on the top.

I open the folder to see the letters *GBM* beaming up at me.

John's wife must have seen my facial expression, because she leans in. 'We tried to get him treated at the hospital near our farm,' she confides, 'but they said it wasn't worth operating on. The tumour is too close to something or other.'

GBM is the acronym for glioblastoma multiforme—unfortunately for John, as it is the most common and most deadly primary brain tumour. For a second, absurdly, I remember the Shark on a ward round telling me that in the latest WHO classification they've dropped the 'multiforme' and technically we should just refer to it now as 'glioblastoma'. 'Neurosurgeons are inherently lazy,' he said to me, looking irritated. 'They keep saying GBM instead of the correct term: glioblastoma.'

I look at John, who's staring steadfastly out the window, and doubt very much that he gives two hoots what we call the tumour non-consensually invading his mind. I could refer to it as 'Fred the Bastard' and it wouldn't make a difference.

'So, we got a bit desperate,' Mrs Wilde finishes.

Fair enough.

'Our daughter started googling surgeons who might want to operate, and we found Dr Prince on the internet.'

'So where is he?' John suddenly turns around. 'He's not even here. I knew these big smoke surgeons weren't going to be any good.' He folds his arms and glares at me.

'John!' his wife exclaims, looking at me anxiously.

I feel sorry for him.

'It's all right,' I say, 'Dr Prince will definitely see you. But you're going to have to stay on the ward at least overnight.' Then, seeing his frown, I add, 'I'll organise accommodation for your wife. The hospital will cover it.'

John's silent. I look down at his worn leather boots, slightly caked with mud, and I don't know whether to laugh or cry.

I turn back to the file. Mr John Wilde is a sixty-year-old farmer from somewhere west of the middle of nowhere, and now he's dying. No one wants to operate because no one thinks they can save him. His cardiac function is crap, his lungs are damaged by years of smoking, and now he has a huge malignant brain tumour. The hospital closest to his farm tried radiotherapy, chemotherapy and more radiotherapy to no effect, and now he's staring the end of the road square in the face. Or, as Mr Wilde says to me later, the horse has well and truly bolted.

John Wilde wants to be saved. I don't blame him, the poor bastard. Until you're dead in the ground the human instinct is to cling on. His brain tumour is a pit of crocodiles and he's found one surgeon who might offer him a rope.

Mrs Wilde had called Dr Prince's room's directly and, after battling with his less-than-pleasant receptionist, managed to get an urgent appointment. Dr Prince is clearly something of a humanitarian. Any other surgeon would take one look at Mr Wilde's scans and say, 'No fucking way.'

In a fairy tale, the patient would be grateful and happy. How fortunate for him that this big-time brain surgeon has agreed to see him. Mr Wilde acts like he doesn't care—and, who knows, maybe he's beyond caring. But it's clear that he's mortally afraid. His fear hovers around him like a thick grey fog. His eyes are tired, and his body's battered. The cancer has rendered him unable to swallow, so food is delivered via a tube that's been inserted into his stomach, like a grotesque abstract painting.

By the end of the day Dr Prince still hasn't shown up to the ward. It's getting dark and I'm about to go home.

'Where is he?' Mrs Wilde asks when I pop by to check on Mr Wilde. 'He is going to come, isn't he?'

I feel so sorry for her that I muster up the courage to call Dr Prince on his mobile.

He doesn't answer, and I leave a rambling voicemail message, like a complete idiot.

It turns out I needn't have bothered, because five minutes later he appears, looking at his phone, then at me.

'Hello, Katarina. Did you call me?'

'Yeah . . . just, ah, ignore the message.'

'Is everything all right?' Absent-mindedly he brushes his cap off. He's just come from theatre and is still in his scrubs.

His eyes are blue today. The scrubs make them blue.

'Everything's fine,' I say quickly. 'I just wanted to check when you were going to see Mr Wilde.'

Mr Wilde is looking at Dr Prince with a suspicious expression. 'Took you long enough,' he says grumpily.

Most other surgeons would have been annoyed, or snapped back, or even turned on their heel and left. Dr Prince apologises. 'I'm sorry,' he says, and he looks like he means it. 'I had a really difficult case. I got stuck in theatre. But I can see that Kitty has been looking after you.'

I raise my eyebrows at the use of my nickname, and he looks over at me and smiles. I find myself smiling back.

'She's a very good doctor,' Mrs Wilde says loyally.

'I know she is,' Dr Prince says. 'She's going to help me with your operation.'

I nearly fall over.

'So, you are going to operate?' Mrs Wilde asks hopefully.

'I think so,' Dr Prince says. 'I looked at your scans this morning, and I think we can probably manage it. It's in a very unusual place for this kind of tumour, the third ventricle of the brain. Extremely rare. I'm worried about the risk of hydrocephalus, as well as other things. I'll have to run it by some other doctors first—we always consult with the rest of the multidisciplinary team before undertaking a major operation.'

Mrs Wilde starts to cry. Mr Wilde thanks Dr Prince gruffly; he sounds as if he's on the verge of crying too. I realise even I have tears in my eyes.

Dr Prince and I leave the Wildes and walk through the darkened ward together. We stop at the doors. There's an awkward pause.

'Sorry I missed the operation the other day,' I say. 'I got a bit caught up.'

He looks at me. It's weird; he doesn't say that much, but when he does it always seems to mean something. Even though our encounters are brief and I always seem to be doing something embarrassing, when he looks at me it's always directly in the eye.

'I heard,' he says, something else in his voice. 'Did your senior doctors come and help you? How long did it take them to get there?'

I want to tell him the truth, that I'd been left alone on the ward while Mr Waters nearly bled to death, but I just mutter that it all worked out in the end.

He leaves it, but I know that he knows.

'Thanks for understanding, anyway,' I say, and without thinking I reach out and touch him on the arm.

He looks down at my hand on his arm. I quickly snatch my hand back.

He doesn't say goodbye. He just pushes through the doors and walks quickly away, leaving me standing there staring at his retreating figure.

I go to the doctors' room and grab my bag, then walk home.

For some reason I can't put into words, I'm feeling down. When Winnie asks me why I seem so morose, all I can say is, 'It's been a long day.' I slump onto the couch, completely exhausted.

'You could probably do with a break from the hospital,' Winnie remarks. 'Maybe the rural secondment isn't such a bad thing. I'll miss you and Estelle, though. And Max was saying he's going to try to swap so he can go at the same time as you guys.'

'I don't want to go,' I say. It's been hard enough getting used to Holy Innocents, which is a major Sydney hospital; the thought of an understaffed rural hospital gives me the willies.

'You never know,' Winnie says optimistically. 'It could be a relaxing escape from the city.'

'Unlikely,' I say. Although, I think to myself as I give in and walk into the kitchen to pour a glass of wine, Dr Holliday could sure use a bloody holiday.

ten

THE NEXT AFTERNOON, I SIT IN THE MULTIDISCIPLINARY oncology meeting and listen to consultants who've never met Mr Wilde discuss whether he should be allowed to survive.

'The tumour is near too much eloquent brain,' one of the surgeons argues, looking at the MRI on the screen in front of us.

I'm startled by the word 'eloquent'. It's almost poetic to describe important bits of brain tissue as eloquent. Maybe neurosurgeons do have souls, after all.

'We can't leave it,' Dr Prince says, 'otherwise he'll end up dying from obstructive hydrocephalus anyway.'

'If you do an open craniotomy you could easily damage his fornix, which would be a disaster. He'll end up a goldfish jack with no short-term memory whatsoever.'

'I'll go in with the ventriculoscope and have a look. I might be able to get some out that way,' Dr Prince counters.

I feel like I'm watching a verbal chess match. I don't really understand anything but realise that the tumour is in a bad and unusual place, putting a lot of pressure on important bits of brain, and operating is high risk, but leaving it means he's toast too. Caught between a rock and a hard place, as Dad would say, except the rock is horrific disability, and the hard place is death. Fantastic.

Everyone starts to argue with each other, loudly. The Shark is gesturing angrily at the MRI, the oncologist is shaking his head in obvious disgust, and the game continues. Check. Check. Check. Stalemate.

I nibble on my mini quiche, which is really rather good, and wonder if anyone would notice if I took another.

'I think it's pointless,' an oncologist sitting behind me says, sounding annoyed. 'It's too advanced.'

'It's clearly isolated,' Dr Prince responds calmly.

Go, Dr P! I cheer mentally.

'It's not worth the risk,' Mr Angry Pants oncologist snaps, gesturing at the MRI.

This is the problem with medicine. Too many decisions are made in big meetings by doctors who have never met the patient. They look at pictures and read blood results, but they have no idea who the patient is or even what they look like. I wonder how Mrs Wilde would feel if she and her husband had to drive all the way back to the west of the middle of nowhere after being told that no one is prepared to operate.

'The tumour IS very close to eloquent brain,' the Shark says, glancing at Dr Prince, then back at the MRI. 'What if he wakes up and you've destroyed his short-term memory?'

This is a loaded question. Everyone knows that there was a big complication earlier in the year and the mud is still being slung. Everything is suddenly very quiet. I try not to breathe too loudly. I look over at Dr Prince.

'Well?' The Shark smiles, and the tension in the room increases. I'm reminded of hyenas circling a wounded tiger.

Dr Prince looks at the MRI, considering. He clears his throat.

The Shark's lip curls slightly in anticipation.

'I'd definitely have to make sure I had a coffee before the operation,' Dr Prince says seriously.

I snort into my quiche and try to turn it into a cough as the Shark glares.

'I don't think the executive would take kindly to another big complication,' he says darkly. 'If you operate and make him ECOG 2 he won't even be able to tolerate chemorads. Then where will we be left? Tread carefully, Jack.'

I don't understand the neurosurgical jargon, but I'm in no doubt as to the barely veiled threat left hanging in the air. I sneak a look at Dr Prince, whose face is completely expressionless.

'I think it's worth going in with the ventriculoscope,' he says evenly.

The Shark's only response to this is to nod tersely.

After the meeting, I'm walking along the corridor back to the ward when I notice someone has fallen into step beside me.

'What do you think, Katarina?' Dr Prince asks. 'What would you do?'

I feel momentarily disappointed that we're back to Katarina, not Kitty, then remember I'm an idiot and answer the question. 'Well, seeing as I'm an expert . . .' I say with a grin, then, anger rising, 'I think it's shit that they can make all these decisions and write him off so quickly when they've never even met him!

I mean, I know it's in a weird place for a GBM, but the tumour's isolated—why can't we just have a look? If there's nothing to be done we can close up, but at least we've tried!'

I don't know why I keep saying 'we'. It isn't as if I'll be performing these amazing, death-defying surgical feats. I'll be snipping a stitch or two, if I'm lucky.

'If I mess this up,' he says, 'they'll tell me I can never perform this kind of operation again.'

'What?!'

'Welcome to the hospital.'

For a moment when I look at him the windows open. Light shines into my eyes and I see the struggles, the victories, the weight of being a surgeon performing the most difficult operations in the world. I touch his feelings and, strangely, they feel just like mine. In the hierarchy of medicine, I'm nothing and he's everything, and yet here we are.

I swallow and look away. You're nothing, I remind myself. You are a lowly intern who has only just mastered the art of cannulation. You can't make a difference, and your opinion doesn't matter.

'Actually . . .' I start speaking then stop, feeling a bit embarrassed.

He looks over at me. 'Yes?'

'What's a ventriculoscope?' I ask, annoyingly feeling myself start to blush.

He smiles. 'Usually we use it trying to resect a colloid cyst,' he explains. 'They live in the anterior part of the third ventricle, block off the foramen of Monro and cause hydrocephalus.'

I nod, pretending to understand.

'Well, this tumour, unusually, is in almost the same place as that. It's better to go in and have a look with the scope and try to remove it that way. If we can't, we can convert to an open craniotomy later.'

'Gee, sounds . . . hard,' I say, having nothing more meaningful to add.

He laughs. 'It is. The major risk with either approach is, like we said at the meeting, damaging the fornix. That could render the patient with terrible short-term memory impairment.'

'That's why the other surgeon said he'd be a goldfish.'

Dr Prince half smiles, half grimaces. 'We need to think of better comparisons. But, yes, the risk of the goldfish outcome is higher with an open approach, so it's better to have a look first with the ventriculoscope.'

'I sort of get it,' I say.

'Come into theatre this afternoon and you can see it all first hand,' he says lightly. 'It'd be good to have you there.'

'It's not like I can make a difference,' I protest, rolling my eyes. 'No one cares if I care. I'm just a shitty intern.'

'I was an intern once too,' he points out. 'Come along.'

Even though I'd meant it when I said that no one cared if I cared, as I stand in the operating theatre later that day watching the surgeons use the scope to look into Mr Wilde's brain, I can't help but feel as if caring does matter. I see the red mass of the tumour and even to me its ugliness is confronting.

When Dr Prince has finished, I ask the question that has been echoing so loudly in the room though no one has voiced it.

'Can you save him?'

I realise as soon as I open my mouth that it definitely isn't my place to ask sensitive questions about sensitive cases. I feel myself blushing as Dr Prince looks up and over the surgical mask, his eyes catching mine. For a brief, startling moment I find myself wondering what he'd be like in the bedroom, rather than the operating theatre. I frown and try to get my brain back on track. Tumour. Operation. Work. Doctors. Life. Death. Important. Stay focused, I tell myself. How can you be thinking about sex at a time like this? But another part of me is thinking that, when you're a doctor, life and death and sex are intertwined. We are constantly leaping from one extreme peak to the next, with little regard for the abyss below.

My mind rages at me to stay focused, but the battle is already lost. I stand there in my scrubs under the warm lights, next to the unconscious body of Mr Wilde as everyone else contemplates life-saving surgery, and realise I'm experiencing an overwhelming desire to have incredibly long, wild, alcohol-fuelled sex with my fifty-year-old surgical boss. I stand very still, in the most sterile environment in the world, looking into a man's brain tissue, with a vagina that has betrayed me by suddenly catching on fire. Brain tumour, operation, surgeons, vagina on fire. I leap from death, across to sex, and am brought down to earth with a mighty thud by the Joker replying to my question, even though he's not the one I asked.

'He won't survive an open craniotomy,' he says, sneering slightly.

'I can't get enough out with the ventriculoscope,' Dr Prince says. 'The only option is to open him up. Book him on the list for Friday.'

The Joker sinks into sullen silence.

I pull myself and my vagina together immediately, and manage to refrain from jumping in the air and yelling 'Wahooo!' as I leave the operating theatre. Dr Prince is like a knight in shining armour, a champion of truth and justice. He is kind of old and could lose a few kilos, I think as I smile at him, but at that moment he is the motherfucking sexiest man I've ever seen.

He can be a bit awkward at times, I feel myself fretting as Lawrence and I leave theatres to head back to the ward. I wonder briefly what he'd look like naked. I picture what underwear he'd most like to see me in. Black lace. No, white. G-string? French? Definitely French. God. Maybe it wouldn't be awkward. Maybe the sex would be really hot. Maybe not even just hot, maybe—

'Are you all right, Kitty?' Lawrence interrupts my tawdry thoughts and jolts me back to the present, and the decidedly unsexy scene of the stairwell to ward seven. 'You look a bit . . . flushed.'

'I'm just pleased they're going to operate on Mr Wilde,' I answer, mostly truthfully.

I open the door to the ward and vow to leave my unsavoury thoughts where they belong, locked in the operating theatre with all the other bodily fluids so they can be removed by the cleaners after hours.

eleven

EVERY WEEK ON A THURSDAY AFTERNOON WE HAVE A junior doctor meeting, run by medical admin. Most of the time my pager interrupts me so I don't get to stay, but I try to drop in for at least five minutes to scoff down some of the free lunch.

'I can't believe you've been an intern for nearly two months!' says Lawrence in awe as we walk into the conference room. 'I think you're doing super well,' he adds loyally.

Lawrence knows better than anyone how painful neurosurgery can be, especially with my good friends the Joker and the Smiling Assassin constantly breathing down my neck, so I appreciate the support.

On theme, the subject of today's meeting is Resilience. This is a deliberate move by medical admin. The results of a survey examining the experience of junior doctors in hospitals around the state has just been leaked to the media and most have scored extremely badly, including Holy Innocents.

'Resilience' is a word that has been shoved down our throats since medical school. I've lost track of the number of graphs

I've seen demonstrating that medical students and doctors have higher levels of resilience in harder times than the general population. Hospital administrators seem to think that if they keep telling us how resilient we are, and draw up pie charts to show us this, that it'll somehow make us even more resilient. We all must be walking around in a perpetual state of resilience overload. I'm borderline going to require resilience chelation therapy, if the pie charts are to be believed. The resilience must be just dripping off every wall of the place, in between the crucifixes. Overcoming suffering—a theme which adorns every spare inch of the hospital corridors.

Maybe I should start going to mass, I suddenly think. Lord knows my soul could use some soothing.

Lost in these existential thoughts I tail behind Lawrence into the meeting room. Max and Estelle have already arrived and are bearing plates loaded sky high with free nibblies. At least it's a break from the ward.

What is RESILIENCE? screams the PowerPoint slide on the screen, while members of the HR department hand out pamphlets to us detailing which hotline to call if our apparently boundless reserves of resilience should inexplicably dry up.

'We're here for you,' Nicole, the head of junior doctor admin, assures us. She clicks to the next slide. 'We don't want you to feel as if you can't speak out.'

I entertain myself by texting Max. *How's your resilience, mate?*

Shit, he replies immediately. *I need to do more mindfulness.*

MINDFULNESS IS MEDICALLY PROVEN TO BE GOOD FOR YOU, I read on the screen.

I stifle a laugh. The hospital's solution to everything is for us to attend the mindfulness classes which no one is allowed to go to because it would mean being away from the ward for too long. But not to worry, Nicole explains. If we can't make the classes, there's an app we can download on our phones! Forget patient deaths and bullying and job application pressures; as long as I can count to four and centre myself with my mindfulness app, I'll be good to go.

I mentally appraise Nicole as she instructs us all to put away our phones and pagers for one minute and take a big breath in and count to four.

Nicole is younger than me, maybe twenty-five, if that. Her youth is obviously an asset, as opposed to mine signifying only lack of experience, and she has already begun her stratospheric ascent up the ladder of medical administration. She has long shiny chestnut hair tapering into perfectly blunt ends. What is it, I wonder, thinking enviously of the Smiling Assassin, with every female in this hospital and their goddamn perfect hair? Her luscious locks tumble down over ample breasts and, even though she is a bit on the chubby side, she isn't trying to hide it. Her dress leaves little to the imagination. The whole image—the hair and the pink heels and pink-painted lips—oozes sexuality. From the appreciative glances of the male doctors, I can tell I'm not the only one admiring her outfit.

Are we going to drinks tonight? Max, also not breathing in or counting to four, is texting me again.

As if on cue, four seconds and a few more big breaths later, Nicole announces that a drinks night has been organised at the pub near the hospital for all the new interns, the admin staff, and anyone else who wants to drink away their sorrows. She doesn't put it quite like that, but phrases like 'morale raising' and 'team bonding' are well-known HR euphemisms.

Yeah, mate, I write back. *I'll be counting to four, all right—four wines.*

I hear a snort from three rows in front and see Max's shoulder shaking suspiciously, and grin. We have always loved making each other laugh.

After work, we meet Estelle outside the hospital. She has a maniacal expression on her face.

'If I could I'd inject alcohol intravenously . . .' she says, a dangerous glint in her eye. 'I have had the day from hell.'

'Fear not,' Max says, as we each sling an arm around her shoulders. 'We're only a few hundred metres away from bad wine and a good whine.'

For all the stresses and catastrophes that being a junior doctor brings, there's a sense of camaraderie among those in the trenches. My mates are everything. Just when I think I've lost north completely, Estelle, Max and Winnie appear, standing in the lighthouse that shows me the way, brandishing a bottle of cheap pinot grigio.

On our way to the pub we run into Nicole at the traffic lights.

'Love your dress,' Estelle says approvingly.

'Thanks.' Nicole looks pleased. 'I was worried it was a bit too tight.'

'No way—you look great.'

Nicole, warmed by the conversation, hovers near us as we take our usual seats in the darkest corner of the establishment.

Con the Greek, the publican, nods in our direction. 'Bottle of the house white?'

The pub on the corner is our home away from home. It's dark and seedy and full of shady-looking characters, but the last place you feel like being after a day in the hospital trenches is a brightly lit bar filled with happy people. Con the Greek is as jaded as we are, and our complaints about hospital life are matched by his relentless tirades about various government regulations.

We're just starting to argue over who's paying when Nicole breaks in to say, 'It's on us—there's a tab until nine. Don't pay if you don't have to.'

Normally I would be suspicious of anyone from medical admin trying to socialise with us, but Nicole is offering us a free bottle of wine and in any case she seems pretty all right. It isn't her fault she works in HR. She probably needs money too. We all have to do things we don't want to at work, present company included.

Two bottles of wine in, I am really starting to warm to her.

'What term are you on, Kitty?' she asks me.

'Neurosurgery,' I reply, feeling mournful. It's ticking towards 9 pm, which means soon it will be 10 pm, which means even sooner it will be 6 am and time to get up and do a ward round with the Joker and the Smiling Assassin.

She nods, opens her mouth as if she's about to say something, then catches herself.

'What?' Estelle asks, looking interested. 'What were you going to say?'

'Come on,' Max says, topping up her wineglass. 'Give us the goss!'

Her defences weakened by Max's relentless refills, Nicole starts to spill. 'Is one of your bosses Dr Prince?'

I choke on my drink. 'Yeah,' I say, trying to look casual as I wipe wine from my shirt. 'Why?' I add, suddenly fearing that she has carnal knowledge of my slightly overweight fifty-year-old surgical boss who, for some weird reason, I spend a lot of time thinking about.

'What do you think of him?' Nicole asks.

'I guess he's okay,' I say.

'Have you fucked him?' Estelle asks Nicole straight out.

It's Nicole's turn to choke on her drink. 'God, no,' she exclaims, laughing. 'No!'

'He's not that bad,' I say defensively.

Max gives me a look, which I ignore.

'I had a thing with one of his friends,' she informs us. 'This German surgeon who worked here last year.'

I feel such intense waves of relief washing over me I almost have to lie down.

'I had to organise all the paperwork to approve him to come to the hospital,' she explains, 'so by the time I finally met him we'd been emailing each other so much I felt like I actually knew the guy.'

'And then one thing led to another . . .' Max offers helpfully.

As it transpires, Nicole and the mysterious Dr Wolfgang Dietrich engaged in a torrid affair. Apparently, Wild Wolfgang is

Dr Prince's best friend and they operated together nearly every day when he lived in Sydney.

'Jack had us over for dinner,' she says, using Dr Prince's first name casually. 'It was just me and Wolfgang and Jack and his wife. Like, I thought things were pretty serious between us.'

I feel my stomach lurch at the mention of Mrs Prince, who I have tried to pretend may not exist. 'But?' I can't help asking.

'It turned out Wolfgang had a girlfriend back in Sweden. He'd been working on a research paper over there, I think. He left Germany to take some prestigious academic job and also got himself a hot Swedish theatre nurse, as I discovered.' Nicole rolls her eyes. 'Anyway, she came to Sydney to visit for a month and I suddenly stopped hearing from him.'

'Do you reckon Dr Prince knew?' I ask her.

'I don't know,' she says, frowning. 'Wolfgang might have just pretended we were over and that he'd got back together with his ex-girlfriend. Who knows?'

'Men,' Max says, rolling his eyes.

'Then, when his girlfriend left, he started calling me all the time,' Nicole continues. 'He was saying he loved me and all the rest of it, but then he went back to Sweden and I never heard from him again, so he's probably back with her.'

We all nod in sympathy.

'So it's weird seeing Jack now . . . but I think he still likes me. In fact,' she says, looking conspiratorial, 'I think he's a bit attracted to me, actually.'

It dawns on me that I need to start wearing tighter dresses. And brushing my hair more than twice a week.

'You know he owns an art gallery,' she says. 'He has this huge collection of Greek antiquities. They're so rare they get exhibited at museums all over the world.'

I feel my mouth start to drop open, and push my fist underneath it quickly.

'He's, like, massive in the world of high-end antiquities.'

Of course he is. That's probably why he doesn't talk much at the hospital. Who could blame him? If I was massive in the world of high-end antiquities I'd probably save my energy for hobnobbing with rare-antiquity-collecting billionaires, rather than wasting my breath on hopeless junior doctors or arguments with senior colleagues who are out to derail my career anyway.

'And he races yachts.'

'Does he?' I'm surprised by this. He doesn't look like he'd be out tugging ropes on the high seas, but I guess racing yachts is an expensive hobby for expensive people, and I'm starting to see the whole picture of Dr Jack Prince more clearly. He's starting to look very, well, expensive.

'He must think he's absolutely fantastic,' Estelle says with a yawn. 'I remember guys like him from the club. They were always so impressed with themselves.'

I think about Mr Wilde, lying on the ward waiting for his operation, and the only surgeon who's bothered to give him the time of day. I remember Mr Wilde snapping at Dr Prince for taking so long to see him and Dr Prince apologising for being late. I remember the other surgeons at the meeting who were ready to write off Mr Wilde after looking at a single brain scan and Dr Prince standing his ground, risking his reputation for some grumpy old farmer from west of the middle of nowhere.

It isn't until we pay the bill and walk home that I start to understand. The reason why I like Dr Prince isn't because he's a talented surgeon or is a big deal in high-end antiquities or races expensive yachts. Sure, those things make him different and exciting and they sound glamorous, but money and glamour don't mean anything to someone like Mr Wilde. In the incredibly complex world of neurosurgery, Dr Prince has done something incredibly simple. He's been kind.

I walk slowly down North Avenue, thinking. The one thing I know for sure as a junior doctor is that I don't know much. I'm reminded of this every morning when I walk into the hospital. Forever will come and go, and I still won't know enough. In two years I'll be a junior registrar, then a senior registrar, then a fellow, then a junior consultant, then a senior consultant. Knowledge will elude me for a lifetime, but I think I am learning my most significant lesson on that short walk home from the pub, in my first few months of training, at a time when I know the very least.

I think that the most important quality for a doctor to possess is kindness. Without kindness, I think, we're all lost in this maze of impossible perfection and constant self-punishment. Without kindness, we're doctors devoid of humanity. And without our humanity, we don't really have anything.

Even if Dr Prince fails to teach me the arterial supply of the spinal cord, he should be comforted by the fact he has taught me that. The art of kindness is shown to me in the painting he makes with his scalpel inside Mr Wilde's brain. Maybe that is the secret to the elusive art of medicine, who knows. Something as simple as just letting ourselves be kind, and letting people be kind to us in return.

It can't be, of course. That would just be too easy.

twelve

ESTELLE AND I ARE MUSING OVER THE STRANGE MICROcosm that is the hospital the next morning as we walk to the cafeteria for a coffee. In some ways, Estelle tells me, it's not so different to the strip club, which was its own little planet, with its own rules.

'I miss it sometimes, you know,' she says wistfully as we sit at our usual table, hiding. 'Anything has to be better than this shit.'

I have a quick image of another Estelle, sans stethoscope and frown, and imagine her completely naked and grinding around a pole as she makes eyes with the men who watch her. I can be your fantasy, I can be whatever you want me to be, baby.

'Got paid a lot more too,' she delivers the coup de grace on why being a stripper is better than being a doctor, with feeling. 'Like, a lot more.'

'I can imagine. I can't say our current salary is really helping to make the job more bearable,' I add, and on cue my phone beeps with an incoming text from the Smiling Assassin.

Why didn't you tell me Mrs Young's potassium was low?

I show Estelle.

'Wow, she's really into her social niceties, isn't she?' Estelle says. 'But it kind of proves my point. We're all on edge, all the time. Being a doctor is kind of like balancing on this very thin wire.'

'Fall off the wire and you land in the fiery pits of hell; make it to the end and you've still only got a night shift to look forward to,' I quip.

But Estelle is serious. 'Look, mate,' she says, 'this is a high-stress job. High stakes, you know. Like there's some sick fucking patients in this place, and it can get pretty overwhelming.'

I nod. Agreed.

'Lucky we have good mates,' I say.

'Yeah, that's just it, isn't it?' Estelle leans forward and looks at me intensely. 'A lot of other doctors don't have mates like ours. They just exist in their own heads, no one to booze with or laugh with or, you know . . .'

'Cry with,' I supply.

'Yeah. So what I'm saying is that we can never let each other down, okay? We have to drag each other over the line, kicking and screaming, to the bitter end. Like when we were in medical school, remember?'

'I remember.'

'And if one of us is ever trapped, or going mad, or about to lose the plot, we just have to reach out to the other person and we'll be there for each other, no questions asked. It doesn't matter what we're doing, where we are, whatever fucking important thing is happening in theatre or whatever—we will drop everything and go to each other's rescue.'

Our eyes meet. I recognise the fear and confusion in her look because I feel it too. We're both teetering on the thin wire we are standing on as junior doctors, gripping each other's hands as we try to stay upright in gale-force winds with no safety harness.

'I'll never let you down, mate,' I say to her, feeling an almost ridiculous urge to burst into tears. 'We will never let each other down.'

My phone rings. Without thinking, I answer it.

'Her potassium has been low for two days and you've ignored it,' the Smiling Assassin snaps.

'I told you about it on the round,' I say, attempting to defend myself, just for something different.

'I don't think so.'

'I can assure you I did.'

Estelle gives me a double thumbs-up and mouths, 'Fight back!'

'I can assure you that you didn't.'

I feel my frustration levels rising. 'Remember? It's only four point zero so you said to start her on oral potassium and recheck tomorrow. That's why I charted the slow K.'

I internally thank the Lord that it's Friday. Even though I'm on call over the weekend, it means a reprieve from the Smiling Assassin.

She doesn't answer, and instead ends the call.

'No time for goodbyes then,' I say to the phone.

Estelle looks amused. 'What a bitch.'

My phone beeps. Ah, back to the text.

Ward, it says.

I show Estelle. She looks confused.

'Ward what? Maybe it's a typo.'

I explain that when the Smiling Assassin wants to meet me on the ward she doesn't call or send a text like *Would you meet me on the ward?* or even *Meet me on the ward*, she just sends a one-word message.

'She's really minimalist,' I explain. 'Very word economical.'

'It's like you're a dog!' Estelle says, torn between laughter and horror. 'Like: "Fetch!" "Sit!" "Stay!"'

I laugh despite myself. 'I'd better go,' I say sadly. 'Dr Fido Holliday has to go and see her master.'

I arrive on the ward to see the Smiling Assassin waiting for me. She purses her lips but, incredibly, still manages to smile at the same time. Mercifully, she's stopped from speaking by my pager going off.

I'm being summoned to operating theatre six, which is hardly a reprieve as that just means the Joker, but I'm sick of feeling like her pet dog and feel a sense of dark pleasure that just as I've arrived I have to leave again.

'I'm needed in theatre,' I explain, backing away. 'I'll recheck the potassium tomorrow morning.'

Before she can argue I hurry off to the stairs. As soon as I'm out of sight I slow my pace.

All through the years of medical school, and even before then, I was desperate to get inside an operating theatre. And despite the stresses and strains of life as an intern, I still want to be a surgeon. I think I do, anyway. So I should be excited to go into that magical other world where incredible things happen and humanity in some weird way is suspended. The outside world simply no longer exists when you're standing over an open brain covered in green drapes. The operating theatre, I remind myself, is the place where the magic happens.

But the Joker is doing his best to ruin this for me. I dread going into theatre when I know he'll be there because I know what will happen. He'll fire hard questions at me and then belittle me when I fail to answer them. My self-esteem is already fragile after years of medical school and I could do without the stealth attacks from my emotionally delayed superiors.

But I discover as I walk into the change rooms and my phone beeps with a text from Lawrence that I've been gifted an out-of-season Christmas miracle.

The J's theatre list has been bumped for an emergency hemicolectomy so he's gone home. Prince wants you to help us in theatre 9.

I immediately look up at the list on the wall of the change room and confirm that the theatre nine patient today is John Wilde and the surgeon is Dr Jack Prince. Today really is the big day. The day Dr Prince is going to save Mr Wilde! I know Dr Prince joked that I could help with the surgery, but I was sure he didn't actually mean it. I try not to let my imagination run away with me as I pull a pair of scrubs from a cupboard and quickly change into them. I meet Dr Prince by the sinks in the scrub bay just outside the operating theatre.

'Hello, Kitty,' he says.

Stay focused, my brain screams at me. You are going into an operating theatre. *Keep it serious.*

I try not to smile too enthusiastically.

'Hi, Dr Prince.' To my horror I feel my cheeks start to burn. Honestly. I'm getting really sick of this. I'm a grown woman;

I'm too old for a crush. I'm also a doctor, and Dr Prince is an old, slightly overweight man who's just another doctor.

Doctor . . . Brain surgeon . . . Yachtsman . . . Purveyor of rare antiquities . . .

I drop the nailbrush in the sink, which makes a loud clang, but he doesn't say anything, just hands me another one, then another. We both know I'm hopeless, but he pretends not to notice.

'Is it true you lend ancient art to museums?' I can't help asking.

He looks over at me, using his elbows to turn on the tap, like the pro he is. 'Yes, it is true,' he says. 'It's a special interest of mine.'

'Cool,' I say, accidentally splashing water all over myself.

'Do you like history and art?' he asks me, as he starts to clean his nails.

'Yeah . . . I mean . . .' I pause, feeling stupid. 'I studied history at school, but I don't know much about art,' I admit. 'I like the idea of it.'

He doesn't say anything, and I regret my response immediately. I should have pretended, made some impressive statement about impressionism or something. Been impressive about impressionism. I almost laugh. I know as much about impressionism as I do about brain surgery—that is, nothing.

'I don't know that much either,' he says surprisingly, stepping away from the sink and turning to walk into the operating theatre, 'but I like the idea of it too.'

'Well, I guess art is just an expression of ideas,' I point out, following him through the door, reminding myself to hold my hands in front of me and not to touch anything.

He smiles. 'Exactly.'

I laugh. 'You're just saying that. You must know heaps.'

He laughs with me. In the operating theatre it's like seeing him in his living room, in a strange way. He's more relaxed, he laughs more easily, and he wants to chat.

'You know what they say . . .' I continue as we approach the steel trolley where Mr Wilde lies, drifting in and out of consciousness as the anaesthetist draws up more Propofol. 'Art is one of the only things in this world that exists solely for pleasure.'

I realise instantly that I've pushed it too far.

Behind his mask, his eyes find mine. I can't see his mouth, but I sense he's still smiling.

'That's true,' he replies. 'You'd know if you studied history that the ancient Greeks certainly realised that.'

The innuendo hangs in the air, languidly floating between our sterile masks and the beeps of the cardiovascular monitors. I want to ask him what else he does for pleasure and to tell him that, despite my baggy scrubs and awkward intern appearance and general daily misery, I'm capable of plenty of pleasure. I want to show him that, like the ancient Greeks, I know exactly where that pleasure is, and how to achieve it.

And how.

I don't, of course, and instead avert my eyes and busy myself with looking focused.

Mr Wilde stirs.

Dr Prince puts his hand on his shoulder, and he settles.

'It's all right, John. You'll be going to sleep now.'

Mr Wilde tries to speak, but I can't make anything out. Dr Prince leans in slightly.

'Try not to leave a bad scar,' Mr Wilde whispers hoarsely, attempting a smile. 'My wife won't forgive you. She thinks I'm ugly enough as it is.'

'I'll do my best,' Dr Prince assures him, but Mr Wilde is now under a sea of Propofol and has no idea if his last request will be granted.

'Stop making false promises, Jack,' the anaesthetist, who is sitting behind us, pipes up. 'You know you always leave ugly scars.'

Dr Prince is grinning so widely I realise they must be friends. 'Thanks for that, James.'

I turn and smile vaguely at the tall man in the little blue scrub cap.

'Kitty, have you met James Bond yet?' Dr Prince is still grinning as he picks up the betadine.

'It's actually Lloyd Bond,' the anaesthetist corrects him. 'But Jack does enjoy his super-original joke.'

I've never seen Dr Prince interact so easily with a colleague, and I'm pleased to see that he does at least seem to have one mate in the hospital.

'How's Margie?' Dr Bond asks as Dr Prince starts wiping betadine prep on Mr Wilde's head. 'I love that painting she gave me. I've got it hanging above my fireplace.'

I recognise the reference to Dr Prince's wife and try to suppress the churn in my gut.

'She's having an exhibition in Hong Kong,' Dr Prince replies, frowning down at the skin beneath him. 'While we're all here working she's schmoozing big-time art collectors.'

'Is your wife an artist?' I can't help asking.

He smiles. 'She is. And she knows a lot more about it than I do.'

'Jack's wife is famous,' Dr Bond chimes in behind me.

I force myself to smile, and try to drag my emotions into check. What exactly are these feelings? I ask myself as Dr Prince hands me the liquid to finish prepping. Envy? To be fair, who wouldn't be envious of a famous artist who dashes off to Hong Kong to star in fabulous art exhibitions.

Maybe it is envy. Not quite envy of another woman though, I realise as I watch him drape the blue material around Mr Wilde's head. I have never met Mrs Prince and don't even know what she looks like, but I can recognise the snake that writhes inside me at the time she must have spent with him, the things she must know about him. I imagine them sitting over a wine, talking about art, and I swallow.

God, I think. You really have got it bad for this bloke.

'Kitty, can you help me with the last drape?'

I snap out of my musings and tug the blue material down, and try to smile. I banish all thoughts of Mrs Prince, vow to never have these feelings again, and focus on the patient.

Dr Prince looks down. 'I've grown quite fond of John,' he says. 'I'd better make a decent effort with my sutures.'

'Pity these sutures are so ugly,' I say. 'Mrs Wilde won't be impressed.'

He laughs. 'How do you think we could improve them? Sutures of gold?'

'Why not?'

His eyes crinkle thoughtfully. 'Have you been to Japan?' he asks unexpectedly.

I shake my head.

'I have a friend who collects Japanese ceramics,' he says as a nurse ties the back of his scrub gown. 'They have this wonderful tradition: when pottery cracks, instead of discarding it, they fill the defect with gold. They call them precious scars. Some of the pieces are really quite something.'

Even though we are standing inside an operating theatre I am transported somewhere else. I'm walking down an avenue of cherry blossoms, past ancient potters, all fixing their broken pottery with rivers of gold inside a Japanese garden.

Dr Prince has a terrible and wonderful effect on me. Later, as we lean over Mr Wilde's open brain, I'm overly aware of his presence, and how close we're standing to each other.

We stay like that for hours. He leans in, his miniscule tools carving a delicate path through the mess of vessels and lobes and tumour in front of us. He occasionally sets me a task and nods his approval when I complete it successfully.

'You never know,' he murmurs, his eyes fixed on my hands as I carefully cauterise a piece of fat, 'we might make a surgeon out of you yet.'

'I don't know,' I reply, trying to figure out exactly how much finger pressure I need to put on the device so as not to burn away an important part of Mr Wilde's brain tissue. 'It seems like an awful lot of work.'

I'm not looking at him because I'm focusing so hard on the open brain in front of me, but I hear him laugh and feel inordinately pleased.

'A friend of mine and I need some help on a research paper,' he says, gently guiding my hand away from dangerous territory as I move to the next section of tumour. 'You should think about it.'

He takes the diathermy from me, to my intense relief.

'Sure,' I say, flattered. 'I'd love to.'

'If you do a decent job, you might be able to help present it at a conference in Sweden later in the year.'

I think back to Nicole from admin's tale about her European lover, and feel my eyebrows raise slightly.

'My friend Wolfgang is German, but he's been on sabbatical doing research at a university hospital in Sweden, where there's a centre of neurosurgical research. Wolfgang has published a lot on novel immunotherapy techniques for recurrent GBM. Him and another friend of mine, a Swede—Tomas—have been working on this paper for months. I won't be able to make it to the conference in Sweden where they are now unfortunately, but there's another one in Fiji towards the end of the year so we'll be able to catch up there.' He sounds uncharacteristically animated. 'You should come,' he suggests.

I laugh. 'Sure.' I'm not exactly a big-time brain surgeon in hot demand for fun-sounding conferences on Pacific islands.

Still, my mind immediately leaves operating theatre nine and runs down a palm-fringed beach. I'm four kilograms lighter and wearing a white bikini that looks excellent against my dark tan. I imagine Dr Prince and I enjoying a chuckle about how much we both hate the Joker as we sip a crisp Australian white . . . or five.

'Anyway,' I say, moving away from him slightly, 'the research paper sounds good. Should I email you about it?'

He tilts his head and looks over at me. I feel warmth flood my entire body; it's either premature menopause or what Sicilians call the lightning bolt. I'm embarrassingly attracted to him. It's becoming a bit hard to bear, if I'm completely honest with myself.

'You should,' he says encouragingly. 'Actually, why don't I email you the list today? If you get started on it now, there's a very good chance you'll be able to head over to Sweden and present it for the conference. If you really are keen on neurosurgery, now's a good time to start thinking about this sort of thing—building the CV, you know.'

'Yeah, I guess so,' I say. 'Thanks.'

'Not a problem,' he says. 'It'll be a good opportunity for you.'

Another hour passes, and by the time the last piece of tumour is cut away and I've sprayed the last bit of saline into Mr Wilde's brain, my back's cramping and I'm starving. I don't know how Dr Prince does it. He tells me that I can scrub out now, and I step away from Mr Wilde, relief washing over me as I'm able to move again. I pull off my scrub gown and gloves with relish; I'm free.

'I need to go to the ward,' Dr Prince says as his friend the anaesthetist starts to make Mr Wilde's settings ready for his move to intensive care. 'Kitty, can you round with me?'

As we walk out of the operating theatre together I remind myself, yet again, that I have an overactive imagination. I'm an intern. He's my boss. This isn't a big deal. It's work, not a date. We're going to look at extremely sick patients on a hospital ward, not liaise in a five-star hotel at lunchtime. Still, I feel strangely excited, as if something naughty is about to happen, even though it isn't. Being a junior doctor is an almost painfully grounding experience, but being near Dr Prince makes me feel as if I'm in the unusual position of having my head in the clouds while my feet remain firmly planted in the mud.

I sense something in him; something that's buried deep inside but that shimmers close to the surface when we're together. The need to escape, the desire to be somewhere different, far from the hospital and its politics and problems. I'm the most junior doctor in the operating theatre and he's the most senior, but sometimes I feel as if we're looking through the same window, separated only by a door that could easily be opened if one of us just leaned against it slightly.

Through the looking-glass, I can see the two of us, in our blue scrubs, getting into the lift and heading towards the surgical ward. We look like important doctors in a busy hospital, too busy and too important to fall into the rabbit hole.

We're the only people in the lift. I press the button, and we stand on opposite sides of the small compartment, sizing one another up.

'How's the writing going?' he asks suddenly.

I shrug. It's not going, actually. 'Writer's block,' I say. This is true. Being a junior doctor has rather sapped my creative drive.

'You know, I'm publishing a book,' he says, as the lift pings for level seven and we step out.

'Really?' I'm impressed, then envious.

'It's a book about the history of art,' he says. 'I've decided to start a publishing company.'

'Oh!' I say, laughing. 'I thought you meant you'd written a book.'

'The book launch is in Melbourne,' he says.

I nod.

'It's next month,' he continues. 'On a weekend.'

I have the sudden feeling he's trying to tell me something, but I'm terrified of misinterpreting him. Awkwardness overwhelms me. 'So which patient should we see first?' I call over my shoulder as I hurry towards the nurses' station to grab the charts.

And just like that we are in professional mode once more. I follow him around the ward, writing notes in the chart and trying not to dwell on the moment in the lift.

'I'll email you the details of the research this afternoon,' he says as we see the last patient. 'And I'll talk to Wolfgang and tell him I've found an intelligent and motivated junior doctor to help him.'

I feel a glow of pleasure at his words.

Before I can respond, his phone rings. It's intensive care. Mr Wilde has come out of recovery. He is awake, and doing well.

'He'll be on the ward in a few days, until I'm sure everything is okay,' Dr Prince tells me. He looks pleased. 'But I think it will all turn out quite well. He should make close to a full recovery.'

'To think those horrible people at that meeting didn't want to let you operate,' I say with feeling. 'And now look: he survived the operation and will get better and his wife won't have to drive in the city by herself ever again.'

He is surprised into laughter. 'What?'

'Mrs Wilde was really nervous about driving in the city because, you know, they live out on a farm,' I explain. 'And I felt so bad for her. Now they can just live out their days on their farm and never have to come back to battle Sydney traffic.'

My face is burning with embarrassment. 'It's the small human things,' I add, feeling a bit stupid.

Dr Prince looks over at me and frowns slightly. I have no idea what he is thinking.

'You're a very interesting young woman, Dr Holliday,' he says.

I'm so startled that by the time I open my mouth to respond he's already walking away. I think I see the other Kitty Holliday, the one standing on the other side of the looking-glass, smiling. I peer at her, hoping to get a better look, but she slips out of my sight, always hovering just in the periphery.

thirteen

'SO THEN HE JUST SAID YOU'RE A VERY INTERESTING woman?'

I'm standing in the kitchen the morning after Mr Wilde's operation. Winnie's looking at me sceptically.

'He said, "You're a very interesting young woman, Dr Holliday,"' I correct her.

'Like, he just came out with it? What was the context? Were you saying anything interesting?'

'Not really,' I admit. 'I told him Mrs Wilde hated driving in the city. Maybe he thought that was interesting.'

Winnie doesn't look convinced. 'Maybe,' she says. 'Do you reckon he was trying it on? Like, did he ask you for a drink after? Or try to get you alone in the change room?'

I shake my head. 'No, he just left,' I say.

'He wants to sleep with you,' Winnie says knowingly, sipping her coffee. 'When he says, "Interesting", he means, "I want to put my penis into your vagina."'

We start to laugh.

'It's really not like that,' I say, still laughing. 'I've got a massive crush on him and he feels sorry for me. Although he's also really nice. He's asked me to help him with this research paper. He reckons if I do an all right job I can go to Sweden in a few months and present it.'

Winnie looks surprised. 'Wow! That'd be cool!'

I agree. It does sound cool.

'You can combine your annual leave with a conference and make it tax deductible,' she says, suddenly reminding me she is a tax lawyer. 'Heaps of doctors do that.'

'Good idea.'

'Anyway, I have to get ready for work,' she says, jumping up. 'I like this guy who works on the floor below me and I want to make myself look so attractive he'll be forced to ask me out for a drink after work.'

'That sounds—' I stop '—almost normal. For you, I mean.'

Winnie grins. 'Apparently he's into weird fetish parties,' she says casually. 'Like where people get whipped and shit.'

'Oh, of course. He couldn't actually just be normal.'

'He told me he's only into ice cubes and stuff, though,' she says, her grin widening. 'He's not full fet, apparently.'

'So no dungeons, just the freezer?'

We both collapse into hysterical laughter.

'Sometimes I think we choose our romantic conquests based on how funny the story will be to tell each other,' I point out, gasping for air. 'Between my old surgeon and your "it's just ice cubes" fet guy from work.'

'You're an idiot,' she says, draining her coffee down to the dregs. 'He could be my soulmate.'

'Better get a bigger freezer then!'

Her laughter floats down the hallway behind her as she leaves for work. I let the lightness swirl around me and recognise it as an unusual sort of feeling these days, when everything is generally stressful. I wish, for a moment, the hospital was less intense and that Dr Prince was young and single and that we could go for a beer together and make a few slightly off-colour jokes, rather than hover over exposed brain tissue.

I'm pulled from this fantasy by Max emerging from his bedroom.

'We need to sign our timesheets, Kitty. We forgot last week and that's why our pay was late! Let's go do it now while we remember.'

Max grabs his stethoscope and bag, then my coffee.

'Mate!' I protest, as he downs what was left of my instant cappuccino. 'I was drinking that!'

'You snooze you lose, Doctor,' he says as I follow him out of the house. 'That's why you never have a boyfriend.'

We walk up the hill to the hospital together, bickering.

'What happened to the guy you met in Switzerland, anyway?' Max asks as we pass the homeless man who I see every morning asleep at the bus stop.

I sigh. 'You know we don't talk about Fabien, Max.'

Max looks sympathetic. 'You like him, though.'

It's true, I think to myself sadly. I do like Fabien. Or I did.

'Well, he's on a ski field having fun and I'm standing here with you not having fun,' I point out rather snappily.

'Just skype him,' Max says. 'It's not like you've got anything else going on.'

He's right: I don't. The last I heard Fabien was planning to head from Switzerland to South America to work as a scuba dive instructor. He'll be exploring physical shipwrecks while I'm turning into an emotional wreck.

Fabien Pho inspires feelings in me that I don't understand so I pretend they don't exist, which is a lot easier. We're so different that we might as well speak different languages. While I struggled through years of university, he was working as a roadie for famous bands and travelling the world. He decided to move to Zermatt, the coolest ski resort in Switzerland, just because he thought it would be fun, and the thought of skiing down Toblerone Mountain (the Matterhorn, which features on the Toblerone chocolate box) appealed to him. (Doing something . . . just for fun?! I could hardly imagine the idea.) Winnie and I had met him at a pub during après-ski drinks on a holiday to Zermatt we couldn't really afford. We had got merrily drunk—our inhibitions thrown to the wind—and I woke up the following morning next to the cutest man I'd ever seen in my life, even though I couldn't remember his name. Winnie woke up next to an eighteen-year-old, a moment that still holds a special place in her heart.

'Will you be my Toblerone Mountain boyfriend?' I asked the cute man in my bed.

'Okay,' he said.

'What about when I go home?' I demanded, despite the fact I'd just met him and couldn't remember his name.

'We can Facebook every day,' he said, smiling. 'And we can get a house overlooking Bronte Beach and get married and have two kids.'

'Wait a minute,' I said, sitting up in bed. 'How are we going to afford a house in Bronte?'

'You're going to be a doctor,' he said.

'Are you joking?' I asked indignantly. 'So I'll be slaving my arse off in emergency at some stinking hospital and you're going to be, what, a surf instructor?'

We both started laughing. Fabien, who has a Vietnamese mother and a German father, was born and raised in Sydney and was from, of all places, Avalon, a beachside suburb on the way to the hospital where I now work. That'd be right, I thought, admiring his lean torso. I'd come all the way to the Swiss Alps only to meet a ski bum from Avalon.

Fabien did end up becoming my Toblerone Mountain boyfriend. It was the most successful relationship I've ever had. He took me skiing all over the mountain, and even when we went off-piste, and I would start freaking out thinking that my father's warnings would come true and I would ski into a tree and die, he would just laugh at my worried expression, slap me on the arse and say, 'Come on, sexy bum! Let's see where we end up.' Every day with Fabien was like a fresh adventure, which came with a lot of joy. I didn't even know I'd lost the ability to feel that kind of joy until I finally let go and went with the flow.

Fabien's favourite thing to do after a hard day's skiing was to lie in bed and watch a clip from the movie *Meet Joe Black* on YouTube. Before Joe becomes Death, he meets the love of his life, a doctor, in a coffee shop next to the hospital. Joe says to the doctor that meeting her was like 'lightning striking'.

'That's like us, sexy bum. You're going to be a doctor, just like the girl in the movie,' he would say, grinning at me. 'This is when lightning strikes.'

I always had a good laugh whenever he told people how we found each other. Somehow, a drunken one-night stand at the seediest pub in Zermatt was translated into: 'We met at a coffee shop.'

'Kitty!' Max startles me out of my daydreams, and I recalibrate to see that I'm not perched on a snow-covered peak with a gorgeous ski bum but instead standing at the entrance to an old corridor with a stethoscope around my neck, and the only man in sight is my gay best mate.

'Snap out of it!' he orders. 'We're on a mission.'

We make our way down the dingy corridor towards the admin office where our timesheets are kept. This building used to be the old hospital, which is now decaying; the hospital's management haven't decided what to do with it, so they've made it a temporary home to administration.

'Fuck, it's creepy down here,' Max says, shuddering as we walk past an empty ward filled with old patient beds and random medical equipment from the 1950s. 'I don't know why they don't just knock it down.'

'It'd be asbestos or something,' I say, trying not to breathe too deeply. Medical admin has taken enough from us; I don't want their only gift to me to be mesothelioma.

Medical administration is in a tiny little office deep in the bowels of the old hospital, attached to the new hospital by a long, dimly lit corridor, so nondescript that you could easily forget it exists, except when there's a mistake with your pay—then you realise that this shitty little office in the basement of the old hospital is actually the controlling force behind everything: who gets hired, who gets fired, and who gets paid. The hospital capitalises on the fact that doctors have way too much other shit to worry about to pay too much attention to discrepancies on our timesheets. Doctors are too busy trying to survive, and ensure their patients survive too, to sit down and properly analyse the world's most convoluted payslip. This is perfect for medical admin; it means that most people won't bother trying to fight for the overtime owed.

Most of the stories that go around about administration aren't good. The brave junior doctors who speak out and demand they're paid for the overtime hours they work are treated like political dissidents. There are hair-raising tales of junior doctors who've dared to raise an issue about a disparity in hours or pay being taken in for private one-on-ones with the head of training, where it's suggested they have mental health issues and are 'harassing' admin by daring to question them. If you're marked out as a dissident, it's only a matter of time before you're shipped off to the proverbial hospital gulag, never to see the light of day of a specialist training program or a decent reference.

'Hi, Nicole,' Max says as we walk into the office. 'I love your shoes.'

Nicole's wearing extremely high leopard-print heels that make my ankles scream just from proximity. Her skirt is too short and her top too revealing, her hair too shiny and her lips too plump. Her dress hugs her curves so perfectly I almost have to avert my eyes. She is a Botticelli, a Victoria's Secret angel. I am in awe. She looks amazing.

Even Max, who is revolted by vaginas, can't stop staring. Nicole smiles, and her hair moves, a shimmering chestnut rug of Pantene and regular keratin treatments.

I suddenly feel self-conscious. My scrubs are so baggy the crotch hangs almost to my knees, making me look like a cross between a gangster from an early nineties MTV music video and an obese man.

'Hi, guys! I had a really fun time at drinks the other night.'

'So did we,' I say, making a mental note to find some smaller, more flattering scrubs and to book myself an appointment with my hairdresser (who am I kidding? find a hairdresser) as she hands over our timesheets.

'We must do it again,' Max agrees.

'I ran into Jack this morning,' Nicole tells me, leaning in conspiratorially.

'Really,' I say.

'I'm sure he wants to sleep with me,' she says. 'You know when you can just *tell*?'

Max looks at me but doesn't say anything.

'He's asked me to do some research with your German guy,' I say casually. 'The one on sabbatical in Sweden.'

Her eyes widen.

Instinctively, I regret telling her this, but I don't exactly know why. It's not as if I spend much time with Nicole. I also don't know her European surgeon lover from a bar of soap.

'I don't think I'll bother with it, though,' I say hurriedly.

'Oh my God, Kitty!' she exclaims. 'You have to tell me if you speak to him! Tell him you went for a drink with me!'

'Um, sure, definitely.' I look at Max, silently urging him to put an end to the conversation.

Max, being the good doctor that he is, picks up on my non-verbal cues. 'Anyway, Nicole, thanks,' he says cheerfully. 'Maybe we can go for a drink next week or something.'

We walk up the dim corridor towards the light of the main hospital, breathing shallowly to avoid inhaling too many asbestos particles.

'There's something a bit off about Nicole,' Max muses. 'Like, she's sexy and has great clothes, but don't you reckon she really thinks she's something special?'

'She's pretty hot,' I say. 'She's got that presence about her. There are plenty of women who are thinner and prettier than her who don't have that. I don't know. If I was a man I'd probably be into it . . . It sounds like Prince is,' I add dolefully.

'That's just what she's telling you,' Max points out as we reach the main foyer near the cafeteria. 'Who knows? He probably said hi to her once and now she's deluding herself he wants to get in her pants.'

'Yeah.' I'm not convinced.

'You should do the research with the Europeans,' Max encourages me, eyeing the coffee line. 'You never know where it might lead.'

Max is right. Just because the mysterious Dr Dietrich had sex with Nicole from admin doesn't make him a bad surgeon. Plus, whatever happened between them is none of my business.

'I have to go to the M&M meeting,' I tell Max, looking at my watch and realising I'm running late. 'See you later.'

'God, I hate those meetings,' he says with feeling. 'Enjoy.'

fourteen

NORMAL PEOPLE THINK M&MS ARE AN APPEALING chocolate treat, designed to make your day more enjoyable. For doctors, M&M means 'morbidity and mortality'. So the Wednesday M&M meetings are a benign way of describing a horrible process—it's when some poor sucker of a junior doctor has to stand up in front of the senior surgeons and present all the patient cases where somebody has fucked something up and the patient got sick and died. It's always a bloodbath. The only bright spot is that Dr Prince will be there.

I rush into the room, ignoring the Joker's glare and obvious glance at his watch, and see the only seat left is next to the Smiling Assassin. I accidentally grimace too obviously, which she notices.

'You're late again,' she whispers forcefully in retaliation, as I sit down. 'You and I are going to have a talk after this.'

'I was signing my timesheet!' I try to explain, but she purses her lips. 'Shhh.'

I can't help but smile when, five minutes on, someone arrives even later than me. There are no seats left, so Dr Prince stands up the back in a dark corner. The Shark's eyes follow him closely. The temperature in the room immediately goes up by about a hundred degrees.

'Glad you could make it, Jack,' the Shark says, looking anything but. 'Here's a question to start the meeting off. Do you think it is acceptable when senior staff don't answer their mobile phones when they're on call?'

Dr Prince doesn't respond, even though the question is clearly directed at him. I'd heard the Joker telling the Smiling Assassin on the round on Monday that Dr Prince hadn't answered his phone quickly enough on Friday night and the Shark had been forced to go into the hospital instead. I suspect Dr Prince failed to answer his phone because he spends his Friday nights having fun on his yacht or attending glamorous art functions with billionaire buyers of Greek antiquities, probably looking at exhibits painted by his wife.

'I seem to remember, Richard, a patient of yours who died a few months ago,' Dr Prince replies from the back corner, 'and you never really took any responsibility for it but blamed your registrar.'

'Is that an accusation?' The Shark's face has gone so red his head looks like it's about to blow off.

'Just pointing out we shouldn't throw stones from glass houses,' Dr Prince says in his usual mild tone.

'You're standing in a glass house, Jack,' is the retort, as murmurs from the other surgeons begin to grow louder. 'But you know that already.'

As Dr Prince starts to raise his voice, Dr Johnson, one of the neurologists, calls for order. 'I don't think this is the time or place to be having this conversation,' she says, looking deeply unimpressed. 'There are junior staff present, let me remind you.'

Dr Johnson takes over and starts asking the registrars questions about the first case. The Shark says nothing, but his face looks like a thunderstorm. I want to sneak a glance at Dr Prince, but he's behind me and I don't want him to catch me staring. I feel bad for him.

'Ask our intern a question,' the Smiling Assassin is saying to Dr Johnson. 'She needs to get better at her anatomy.'

I realise all eyes are now on me to start naming the damaged blood vessels in the mangled brain on the projector. I forget about Dr Prince and start taking deep breaths to combat my rising anxiety. I stutter something about the basilar artery which sounds semi-right, but Dr Johnson's look of disgust suggests otherwise.

The meeting passes in a blur of humiliation, and as soon as the last slide has been shown I nearly knock my chair over in my attempt to be the first to leave. Dr Prince, amazingly, beats me out the door, and I watch his back disappearing towards the safety of the private hospital.

The Shark is surrounded by his surgeon mates congratulating him on his show of dominance, including the Joker, and I use this opportunity to leave the area before they remember how badly I performed at question time.

'Kitty!' I walk out of the conference room and hear someone calling my name. I look up to see Estelle, charging down the corridor towards me. 'I came to find you. Let's get a coffee!'

Estelle has tracked me down to plan our trip to the country, which, unbelievably, is only a week away. I'm still not reconciled to the idea, but at least I'm now distracted by my research paper for Dr Prince and his German surgeon friend, the wonderfully named Dr Wolfgang Dietrich. With a name like that he must be a bit of fun, surely, I think to myself. Between Mozart and Marlene he's got all his creative bases covered. Dr Prince emailed me last night with the opening words, *Shouldn't take too long*, followed by millions of links to articles that looked like they'd take years to wade through. The quiet life of the country might be a good place to focus on my more academic, rather than alcoholic, pursuits.

Wingabby is around nine hundred kilometres from Sydney with a population of seven thousand and nearly as many birds, or so Estelle tells me, adding that the region is also famous for its orange trees. Every big city teaching hospital has a rural sister hospital, all in the spirit of helping out our smaller hospital siblings. In keeping with that spirit, the consultants refuse to go anywhere near the place, so junior doctors are sent to represent the hospital instead. The hospital newsletter always has photos of smiling city doctors standing with local Wingabby council members, proudly proclaiming what a great addition we make to the rural community. Max, on seeing one such photo, told me that he slept with one of the doctors in the picture and knew for a fact that the city doctors were only smiling because they were all high when it was taken.

'It can't be that bad,' Estelle says with an optimism that is clearly forced. 'I think it'll be fun to work somewhere different for a change. Everyone here is so obsessed with status. It'll be nice in the country. Surely they're a bit more relaxed out there.'

Our conversation is interrupted by the Joker calling to inform me that my show of ignorance at the meeting has reflected poorly on him, and that I need to go to the ward to discuss with him how I can improve myself. I sigh.

'See you on Saturday, mate,' I say to Estelle, reluctantly standing to go back to hell.

Maybe Estelle's right, I muse as I take the lift to the ward, where the Joker and the Smiling Assassin are waiting to administer my daily flogging. Wingabby could be a bit of a relaxing tree change, a chance to recharge the batteries.

The Joker pushes past me as I enter the ward. He looks annoyed. 'There's been a problem in theatres—get out of my way,' he snaps. 'We'll have to do teaching later. Go and round with the registrar.'

My momentary reprieve is short-lived as I realise the Smiling Assassin is waiting for me.

'God, I wish I was anywhere but here,' I mutter to Lawrence as we wrestle with the printer to sort out the patient list. 'I can't believe my next stop is the middle of nowhere for three months.'

'Where would you go instead?' he asks.

I let my mind transport me to all the places I dream about. 'I really like the south of France,' I say, considering. 'I've been there once, and I loved it.'

'The list is missing the new patients who came in overnight.'

Lawrence and I snap to attention to see the Smiling Assassin bearing down on us.

'Sorry,' Lawrence says, kindly taking the bullet. 'I was distracting Dr Holliday by asking her which part of the world she'd most like to visit.'

'Oh, yes?' She looks up. 'Where?'

Lawrence and I exchange a glance. This is some kind of trap, no question.

'The south of France,' I say finally.

A funny expression passes over her face. 'Do you speak French?'

I laugh. 'I wish. I did it for a few years at school but I'm pretty hopeless.' I make the little sign between my thumb and forefinger. '*Je parle un peu français.*'

For a second her face reminds me of my own when I'm transporting myself mentally to a preferred destination.

'I love the south of France,' she says suddenly.

There's an awkward silence.

'You know what they say: *speak in French when you can't think of the English for a thing*,' she says, looking up at us almost shyly.

I can't believe what I'm hearing.

She sees my expression.

'*Turn your toes out when you walk. And remember who you are!*' we recite together.

Lawrence's mouth is on the ward floor.

'Lewis Carroll, *Through the Looking-Glass*,' I say in amazement. 'How did you—?'

'Never mind,' she says abruptly. 'It's not important.' Her lips tighten, and she stares down at the patient list intently, as if it will provide the answers to the meaning of existence.

'Okay . . . well, we can fix the list for you,' Lawrence says, looking uncomfortable; it's bizarre to have an exchange with the Smiling Assassin that doesn't involve her yelling at anyone.

'Hurry up about it,' she snaps. 'I have to go to theatre.' She backs away, already pulling on her scrub cap. 'Call me if there are any problems.'

We watch as she rushes out of the ward, blue scrub jacket flying behind her.

Call her if there are any problems? What?

'Was she just being, like, nice?' Lawrence sounds confused. 'How did she know that quote? Do you reckon her mum's an English teacher like yours?'

I shake my head. 'God, who knows? Maybe she's getting the flu or something.'

I look at the list, and sigh. My pager starts to beep. I look down at it.

Mr Smith in bed 4 bowels not open five days pls review.

I make the executive decision to take the battery out of my pager and leave it on the desk.

'Come on, Lawrence,' I say to his shocked expression. 'Let's go get a coffee and look at how much flights to Paris cost.'

Mr Smith's bowels can wait. They've been waiting nearly a week with no movement; another hour won't be the end of the world, or his colon. Plus, I'm about to be deprived of city comforts for a while. Wingabby might be spoiled for choice when it comes to bird species, but I doubt you can say the same when it comes to coffee.

fifteen

I WAKE UP GRADUALLY, CLAMBERING OUT OF SLEEP, AND roll over slightly. What time is it? Have I slept through the alarm? I fumble for my phone, feeling the weird panic that assails you in the space between asleep and awake. It's only 3 am. Phew. Then, out of the corner of my eye, I see a shape lying in the bed beside me.

I gasp, knowing immediately that something is very wrong. Dread hits me like a blow.

Something's here.

I swallow.

Something is next to me. *Something is next to me. Something has come for me.* I know I have to look but I'm terrified. The fear is so intense it is visceral. *Please, just make it leave.*

Just breathe, I tell myself. Breathe.

I reach out tentatively to touch it but it doesn't move. I'm not surprised. I know what it is. There's a corpse lying next to me in my bed.

Just stay calm, I tell myself. It's only a dead body. You've seen lots of dead bodies. They can't hurt you. And you can't hurt them.

In my dreamlike state I vaguely wonder why there is a corpse in my bed. Is it haunting me?

Katarina, says the voice of reason buried deep in the layers of my subconscious brain. *Listen to me.*

How can I make the dead body go away? I wonder frantically.

Kitty, says the voice, *get up. Get up and turn on the light.*

I squeeze my eyes shut, and feel tears starting to form. The panic floods through my brain. It's roaring in my ears, hammering my chest. I feel bile rising in my throat. *Oh my God, I'm going to be sick.*

Get up! the voice commands. *Get up and turn on the light!*

I throw back the covers and in two giant steps have reached the switch on the wall. White brightness floods my vision.

In an instant I'm completely awake. I look down and see I am still wearing my scrub top from yesterday. I must have fallen asleep before I could get changed. I glance over at my bed.

There's nothing to see but crumpled sheets.

I shut my eyes. A nightmare. It was just a nightmare.

Just a nightmare.

I sit down on the edge of my corpse-free bed and run my fingers through my hair. My hands are trembling.

'Kitty?'

I look up to see Winnie and Max standing in the doorway.

'Kitty, are you all right?' Winnie asks.

I can only gape at them.

'Have you been called in to work?' Max asks, looking at

the scrubs I am still wearing. 'Is that why you were screaming? I thought you were going to the airport this morning.'

'I was screaming?' I say.

Winnie's forehead is creased with worry. 'We thought you were being fucking murdered! The whole street must have heard you.'

'I had a nightmare,' I say lamely. 'Sorry I woke you.'

'I think you're just a bit stressed,' Winnie says, coming over to sit next to me. 'You've had such a stressful time on surgery. And now going to the country.'

'I . . .' I clear my throat, but my voice is shaking. 'I . . .'

Winnie looks appalled. 'Oh, Kit. Look at you. My poor little Kitty.' She envelops me in a big, warm hug.

The tears fall like rain. I don't even know why I am crying, but I can't seem to stop. I keep trying to apologise but the sobs erupt from me, a tidal wave I cannot hold back. It's as if finishing my first surgical term and knowing I am leaving Sydney has allowed this small crack inside my subconscious to open, and now it won't close.

The images swirl around me. The Joker sneering as I answer another of his questions wrong. Mr Waters's face as he shakes on the bed, his heart rate dangerously high as he haemorrhages blood. Laura the intern vomiting on my shoes at our house party. Toby Henderson's voice. How do you cope? *You just don't.*

Was this me not coping? Was I acopic?

Acopic. You're acopic. Doctors and nurses love to use the word.

What the fuck does it even mean? We're ordinary people in extraordinary situations; who wouldn't be fucking acopic?

'I don't know what's wrong with me,' I say, fighting the weird rising anger, taking breath after breath, trying to will myself to calm down. I need to get control of myself and my emotions. Get a fucking hold on yourself, Holliday. Winnie keeps her arm firmly around me. She is an anchor in a wild ocean of I don't even know what. Max is looking worried.

I glance at my phone. It's 3.10 am. In four hours, I have to get up and go to the airport to fly to another hospital. All I do is go from one fucking hospital to the next.

I close my eyes. I'm standing in a ski field in Switzerland, staring at that fantastic mountain. I'm smiling. There's sunshine and powder and a beautiful man with brown eyes smiling back at me. My breathing gets easier. For a second, I forget about the hospital. Then I remember I'll be back to work tomorrow. I almost roll my eyes. No one will realise when I walk through the doors of the ward, but the truth is that I never actually left.

PART II

life

'Out beyond the ideas of wrongdoing and rightdoing there is a field. I'll meet you there. When the soul lies down in that grass the world is too full to talk about.'

—Rumi

sixteen

LOOKING DOWN FROM THE TINY PLANE ALL I CAN SEE IS light yellow, the grass starved by drought, and winding through it like a snake the deep brown of the Murrumbidgee River.

'It looks fucking hot out there, man,' Estelle says, craning to see past me.

'Apparently you can swim in the river,' I say without much enthusiasm.

She shakes her head. 'I can't believe they're allowed to just send us out to the middle of nowhere like this,' she says. 'But, you know, that's medicine, isn't it?'

'Indeed,' I agree. 'They did this to us as students and now again as real doctors. It's unbelievable.'

'Being a doctor is just one big game of rural bingo,' Estelle says mournfully, leaning back in her seat and massaging her temples. 'I can hardly wait to check out our new drinking hole—the RSL club.'

Not for the first time, I consider filing a lawsuit against the producers of *Grey's Anatomy* for false advertising.

Several hours later and the reality that we're stuck in Wingabby for a little over two months is starting to sink in.

We're sitting on the couch in a fibro house that is decorated exclusively in shades of brown. Estelle is staring out the window.

'I haven't seen any birds yet,' she complains. 'Isn't this place meant to be, like, bird central?'

There's a rustling outside our front door. I sit up. 'Do you think it's a bird?' I try not to sound scared.

The bird knocks on the door, then yells, 'Guys! Open the door! It's so fucking hot out here!'

Estelle looks at me. 'Are we expecting someone?'

I have no idea who our visitor is but, appreciating how sweltering it is outside, I go to the door and open it.

A man is standing there, looking thoroughly aggravated.

'Fuck, Katarina.' He sounds annoyed. 'I've been trying to find you for ages.'

I examine his face carefully, and realise we know each other. It's one of the other interns from the hospital. I think I might've spoken to him once in the first week and then I never crossed paths with him again. Pete someone or other. I recall someone telling me that he's super uptight and gunning to do cardiothoracic surgery, and repress a groan. Great. We're stuck in a tiny town in baking heat with a junior version of the Joker.

'Thank God I found you,' he says. 'Do you have any cigarette paper? I really need to roll a spliff. I'm fucking desperate.' Then, seeing Estelle's less-than-impressed expression as she realises who he is, he adds defensively, 'I've brought my own weed, and three bottles of wine.'

My mouth is open.

'It's a bit warm,' he says apologetically, 'but at least it's something.'

'Is this a test?' Estelle's staring at him suspiciously. 'Like, we aren't falling for it.'

He looks as if he's about to protest, but we're distracted by the creaking of hinges as someone else pushes open the door and enters the house.

The first intruder seems relieved. 'Thank God you found the bottle shop. Can you please tell Kitty and Estelle that I'm not a psycho and find me some tobacco paper?'

'It's all right, guys,' Max says, walking through the door with a carton of beer. 'He's clean.'

I don't know whether to be more surprised by the appearance of Max, who's meant to be back in Sydney about to start his surgical term, or by his apparent friendship with our uninvited guest.

'By clean he means really dirty,' the uninvited guest explains.

Max throws himself onto the couch and grins. 'Ladies, it's time you met the Godfather.'

Max and the Godfather met for the first time at the airport gate, we learn. They were the only two on the afternoon flight to Wingabby who weren't wearing Akubras, so they correctly assumed they were both junior doctors on the way to their rural secondment. The Godfather, formerly known to us as uptight heart surgeon wannabe Pete, was drinking from a hip flask of whisky. On identifying Max, he immediately offered him a sip.

Max, who was about to start his surgical term, had managed a swap at the last moment with a girl who had anxiety issues and claimed special consideration. Figuring he was going to be sent to Wingabby at some point anyway, Max had decided he'd rather go with his mates, but instead of just telling us the good news like a normal person, he'd decided to surprise us with a dramatic entrance.

By the end of the ninety-minute flight, Max quite liked uptight heart surgeon wannabe Pete. As well as sharing his flask of Jack Daniel's, Pete revealed that to earn extra money on the side of junior doctoring he dealt marijuana; he'd already lined up some connections in Wingabby. Max rightly acknowledged him as the Godfather, and the name has stuck.

'We thought you were obsessed with being a cardiac surgeon,' Estelle says as we gaze at him in amazement. 'But you're actually a pot dealer!'

'I also dabble in a bit of blow now and again,' the Godfather says. He's puffing away happily on the spliff he's creatively fashioned out of a page of Estelle's emergency medicine pocket book.

'You kept that quiet!' Estelle, not normally impressed by any doctors, looks floored.

'I find it best to keep my private life private,' he says sensibly, leaning back on a mouldy cushion. 'And I was interested in cardiac surgery for a while, but I've changed my mind since.'

'Sensible,' I say, thinking back to my own experience on surgery and shuddering.

'The G wants to do anaesthetics now,' Max says cheerfully, opening his third beer. 'The access to restricted prescription drugs appeals to him.'

We all nod our understanding. I remember Tom the anaesthetics registrar from our house party and his little bag of cocaine and tell the Godfather he'll be in good company.

Sometimes you meet someone and know straight away they'll become your friend. Call it serendipity, or fate, or bad luck that we're all stuck in Wingabby together, but the Godfather slots into place as the final member of our doctor quartet like the winning token in a game of Connect Four.

Despite, or maybe because of, his less-than-legal extracurricular sources of income, I like the Godfather. He tells us he was a lawyer before becoming a doctor and we're all suitably impressed. He's good-looking and deceptively quiet, which we soon learn has afforded him much success with the hospital nursing staff.

'There's gotta be some nurses out here,' he says hopefully. 'Every hospital has at least two decent-looking nurses.'

'You might want to pace yourself,' Estelle advises. 'We're here for over eight weeks, so that's an average of two a month, if you stretch things out.'

The Godfather and Max have been placed in the old fibro shack next door to ours, and are similarly dismayed.

'These places aren't exactly hot-nurse magnets,' the Godfather says, looking demoralised as he gazes at the brown decor. 'We want a love shack, not an actual shack.'

'It looks like it's been painted with shit,' Estelle says, not bothering with niceties.

Max laughs gleefully. 'The princes of Poo Palace!'

'Or fifty shades of shit.' Estelle grins despite herself.

The Godfather passes me his spliff, and I relent and take a long drag. I pass it to Estelle, who passes it to Max, and soon we're giggling like schoolchildren on the brown couch, staring at the brown walls which match the brown ceiling and brown floor.

Estelle turns on the ancient brown radio, which only seems to pick up one station.

'Classic hits on a steamy Wingabby weekend!' the broad Australian accent tells us enthusiastically as the music starts to play. 'Hope you've all got your fans on!'

As the haze of marijuana smoke floats above us, the radio blasts out classic hit after classic hit. Max is arguing with the Godfather about the best surgical program to apply for, Estelle has taken a valium and her eyes are as hazy as the room, and I sink into the brown couch, watching the words of the classic hits of Wingabby walk through the air in front of me.

Dr Katarina Holliday—this is YOUR life.

seventeen

THE DAYS, WE SOON REALISE, ARE LONG AND HOT OUT IN rural New South Wales. We wake up in the heat, go to work in the heat, walk home in the heat, then go to the pub to try to drink ourselves away from the heat. I'm too scared to swim in the river in case I encounter a snake; I don't trust that anyone in the local hospital is competent enough to save me in the case of a fatal bite.

Wingabby Base Hospital has the dubious honour of being named worst hospital in the country a few years running. (I'm not exactly sure where the data comes from for this study, but I believe it.) For some reason the electricity is faulty, and I don't believe for a second the hospital's claims it can't be fixed. This means that the heating is left on even on thirty-plus-degree days, because it can't be switched off. The hospital might as well have a big sign out the front saying, WELCOME TO DANTE'S INFERNO.

'All the doctors from Sydney do is complain,' says Maureen, a thin blonde with a taste in fashion surprisingly similar to

Nicole's, when we meet for our rural induction at the end of the week. 'The last group were absolutely impossible.'

Despite the obvious shortcomings of Sydney doctors, Maureen has enough kindness in her heart to cease the berating and instead offer everyone a homegrown orange. 'Wingabby has the best oranges in New South Wales,' she tells us proudly.

We dutifully eat our oranges, which to my surprise taste incredible.

'Medical admin don't give us homegrown oranges in Sydney,' Estelle whispers to me. 'Quite nice of her, really.'

I'm so used to steel scalpels and synthetic antibiotics and plastic cannulas I'd forgotten there's magic in the world not performed in an operating theatre or created in a pathology lab.

My phone pings. It's a message from the Godfather, who's sitting on the other side of the room.

Wonder what else Maureen grows on her farm, with a winky emoji.

I show it to Estelle.

'It'd be hydroponic for sure,' she says. 'Everything's so natural and clean out here, man.'

'And we have our country races coming up this weekend,' Maureen says, looking excited. 'It's the biggest event of the year!'

Estelle smiles. 'Who knows, mate,' she whispers, nudging me, 'might find me a farmer!'

As we file out of the room and into the sweltering heat of the ward, I say, 'It hasn't been all bad out here so far. I mean, imagine if we'd never met the Godfather!'

'The guy is a genius,' Estelle agrees as we struggle up the stairs. 'Yesterday he corrected the consultant nephrologist because he'd got the patient's creatinine clearance wrong. Like, he figured it out in two seconds. Without the calculator.'

The Godfather, it turns out, is a regular Stephen Hawking, which is handy in a place like this, where the computers crash regularly, and also because I often need his help. Wingabby is my medical term, unfortunately for me. Being more interested in surgery means I find the long ward rounds and physician-like discussions more tedious and confusing than ever. There's no operating theatre with Dr Prince to pop into to break up the day a bit, just neverending discussions about Mr Larson in bed 9's worsening renal failure.

I arrive on the ward and ring Dr Woo, my consultant, to tell him our sickest patient, Mrs Richards in bed 4, has a high fever and her blood pressure is dropping. The consultants are all fly-in fly-out from a variety of other, bigger hospitals, and when it's time for the fly-out part of their contract their plane waits for no man, meaning they wait for no patient or junior doctor. Dr Woo is already at the airport, even though it's only midday.

'Call the registrar,' he tells me. I can hear flights being announced in the background. 'I'll be back on Thursday.'

I've only met the registrar briefly. She's so busy we usually only have time for a cursory discussion about the patient list first thing in the morning then we go our separate ways. We have so many patients it's nearly impossible to keep track.

I call her anyway. 'I think Mrs Richards is septic.'

'Who?'

'Urosepsis, seventy-two, has a glass eye,' I remind her.

'Does she have an advanced care directive?'

'I don't think so,' I reply.

'She's not for resuscitation though, is she?'

'I don't think that's right,' I say. 'I heard her saying to the nurse the other day that she wants to be resuscitated if she has a heart attack.'

'Has she said that to you directly?' She sounds irritated.

'Well, no,' I admit, 'but she's delirious now, probably because of the urosepsis, so she wouldn't be able to tell me even if she wanted to.'

A sigh of relief pours down the phone. 'Okay, palliate her.'

'What?'

'That's what Dr Woo told me last week,' my registrar says. 'She's got an NFR, she's suffering, it's time. Call the palliative care nurse.'

'But she's got a treatable infection,' I point out. 'We charted the right antibiotic this morning, the nurse just hasn't given it yet.'

'What? Okay, stop the antibiotic. Chart the palliative care meds.'

I want to argue but I'm met with a dial tone. I go and take a look at Mrs Richards, who is curled up in the foetal position and letting out an occasional tortured groan.

'I've called the palliative care team,' the nurse informs me.

'Really?' I'm surprised at how efficient she is. Normally nurses force junior doctors to do everything, even tasks they can easily do themselves.

'Dr Woo called the ward.'

I'm impressed that Dr Woo has somehow managed to get in one last palliation before take-off. But I can't shake the uneasy feeling that something not quite right is happening.

The Godfather confirms my instincts. I'm charting the palliative care crisis medications and actively stopping Mrs Richards's lifesaving antibiotics when he appears beside me.

'Do you feel like they palliate a lot of patients in this hospital?' I ask, worried that I'm just being paranoid.

'Of course,' he says, hovering over the medication chart. He takes a pen from his pocket to increase the morphine dose I've just written up. 'They need the beds.'

'No!' I drop my own pen. 'They can't do that! We can't kill off old patients when they get a little bit sick just to free up bed space!'

He raises his eyebrows. 'How many times have you been to the morgue this week?' He hands me the penny and it drops, like a ton of lead into a bath.

'My God!' I am shaking my head. 'Mate.'

'Look, they're all old and suffering anyway,' he says reasonably. 'Maybe it's for the best. In the city we keep people alive for so long it's cruel, if you ask me.'

Right on cue, my pager goes off. It's the nurse manager. Another of our patients has died, and I have to go to the morgue to certify the death and do the paperwork.

I finish charting the medications that will free up Mrs Richards's bed and think about what the Godfather said. He's right; I seem to be going to the morgue to certify deaths surprisingly often.

The whole act of certifying a death is a little weird. I mean, everyone knows when a person is dead. But for the sake of making sure that nobody (or bodies) slip through the cracks, I guess it isn't a bad policy to have a doctor make sure.

This little exercise involves me popping into the fridge, where, using a key I've been given by hospital security, I unlock the drawer and pull out the body. This can be dangerous: if I pull on it too enthusiastically, there's a risk the drawer will tip down and the body will roll out on top of me. This happened to another junior doctor the year before, the security guard has warned me.

Once the body is exposed, you have to listen to the heart, the lungs, look at the eyes and try to elicit pain. Nothing happens, of course, since the person is dead. I feel like a total weirdo as I go through the motions. The most awkward part of the whole procedure is feeling the chest for a pacemaker. This is important, because if a pacemaker remains in the body when it's being cremated, it'll explode. Still, there's something totally off about feeling a cold corpse's chest.

I arrive at the morgue, to find one of the nurses looking flustered.

'Katarina, we've had three triage sixes arrive. The emergency department would normally deal with it but they're too busy. Can you sort it out, please?'

I stare blankly at her. Triage 6?

'You know,' she says, rolling her eyes at my ignorance, 'DOA.'

DOA?

'Dead on arrival,' the morgue attendant explains helpfully as he walks past.

This leads to my introduction to what I like to refer to as 'the death van'. The death van is a non-descript white van driven by anonymous contractors no one seems to know anything about, who drive around New South Wales fetching dead bodies that need their deaths certified by a doctor.

The van rolls up outside the hospital; the contractors tell the staff they need a doctor to certify a triage 6—or dead on arrival—then they wheel the body back into the van and disappear mysteriously, as if they were never there.

I stare at the van doors, almost morbidly fascinated, wondering what is about to declare itself. The death van driver then helpfully explains. 'And sorry, Doc, but one of them's a decomp.'

I'm getting sick of all these abbreviations. 'Sorry?'

'Decomposing. You know . . . smell's not great.'

Holding my breath, I watch with voyeuristic horror as they wheel out the 'decomp' and unzip the blue body bag. I stare at the withered, blackened corpse in front of me. 'Looks pretty dead to me,' I say, holding my nose. 'Do you reckon I need to do everything? Like do I really need to check his pupils and stuff?'

I wonder whether I should go through the proper motions and listen to the corpse's chest to ascertain there are no breath sounds or heartbeat, but I start to feel a little queasy at the thought of my stethoscope touching a dead body, which has been decomposing for the last month. I settle for putting on some gloves and palpating the chest for any movement, which is horrible enough.

'Yep, dead . . . definitely dead,' I say firmly, signing off on the clipboard.

'Okay, there are two more to go, Doc.'

'All right, wheel them out,' I say, trying to breathe normally now the 'decomp' is safely back in his zipped bag on the van shelf.

I look down at the face of an elderly lady and feel a twinge of sadness. She's been found by a neighbour, dead on her lounge.

This is how it all ends. With me, an ineffectual junior doctor, standing outside the hospital morgue while I check her off as 'dead'.

Death is an abstract concept, even for doctors. It's not until I find myself standing there, staring down at the dead face of a woman I've never met and who no one will ever meet again, that I stop to think for a moment—this is life, playing out in front of me. The end of a life. The enormity of the concept hits me, hard, and then it's gone.

'Some doctors yell out their name,' the death van driver says helpfully.

'EVELYN!' I yell at the corpse, wondering why I'm trying to elicit a response from somebody who's clearly not going to respond.

'I think her friends called her Evvy,' the death van driver offers.

I look at him. 'EV—' Halfway through yelling out her nickname I realise how ridiculous this is. Evelyn isn't going to suddenly wake up and say hello just because I use her nickname. Evelyn—nickname Evvy—is dead as a doornail and it doesn't matter how many anecdotal forms of address I use, Evvy isn't coming back.

I listen to Evvy's chest—no breathing sounds. I listen for her heart—no heartbeat. I shine a light in her pupils—fixed and dilated. 'Ah, yep, dead too,' I say, awkwardly, signing the form.

The contractors who drive the death van pack up their grisly cargo and vanish off into the steaming Wingabby summer afternoon. Out of habit, I quickly cross myself. I sort of hope even as a person of science that the dead have a safe passage somewhere into their next journey. I wish for a moment we were like the ancient Greeks, where every dead person had a gold coin placed on their forehead, to give to the boatman to take them across the river and away from Hades, but there are no gold coins and no boatman waiting. Just the death van, a steel slab, and a half-unzipped body bag.

I remember, out of nowhere, one of Mum's more fatalistic quotes, a biblical reference that she liked to toss around when I bemoaned the misery of studying and life generally.

Remember man that thou art dust, and to dust thou shalt return.

'There was this one time when the doc certified the wrong body.' The morgue attendant is back, hovering next to me.

I jump up, out of my thoughts. 'What?'

He laughs, coffee-stained teeth flashing at me. 'Yeah, it was a doc like you, from the city. He certified a death and signed the back of the form then, after the van was long gone, he checked the name and realised it was an old Italian bloke, when the death he'd certified was a sheila in her early forties.'

'What?' I feel horrified. 'But couldn't he just ring the . . . you know . . . van drivers?'

'Well, that's the thing,' the morgue attendant grins ghoulishly. 'No one really knows who they are. They're just contractors, you see.'

Fantastic. 'So what happened?'

'Ah, it turned out all right. He called the police and cross-checked with them and found the body but, you know, it was a scare.'

'Hmm.' I feel disconcerted, to say the least. I imagine the death van drivers running some kind of organ-pilfering ring, which hapless junior doctors become accidentally party to. There's a good horror movie in that for sure.

This proximity to death has me standing on the edge of a full-blown existential crisis, I realise, as I wait outside the morgue for my friends to walk home, in my mind halfway through the screenplay for *Death Van: Part 3*. I feel an intense longing for the shallow days of binge drinking, arguing with Winnie about putting out the bins, and my pathetically huge crush on my surgical boss.

Max arrives first, looking pleased with himself. The only other gay man in the hospital, a nurse called Robert, has invited Max to the Wingabby races this weekend.

'I've heard the country races are pretty fun,' I tell him, having listened to the nurses on my ward gossiping about them. 'Maureen looked super excited when she told us about the races at orientation. I think it's like the biggest event of the year.'

Max looks pleased. 'It'll be a good story, don't you reckon? That time I went to the country races when I was a junior doctor in a town of seven thousand people.'

Like me, Max sees the value of a good story. Even the biggest catastrophe can be turned around a few months later over some wines and a good laugh. Not that one ever wishes for a catastrophe, I remind myself, thinking about my colleague and his lost body, shuddering. I've had enough to do with the death van for one lifetime.

eighteen

ON SATURDAY I SIT ON THE COUCH IN POO PALACE considering Max's chosen outfit for rural race day. 'The light blue is better than the pink,' I decide. 'And I like your R.M. Williams.'

Estelle is still asleep, even though it's after midday. She 'treated herself' to a heavy dose of wine and sedation last night and will be in bed till at least 4 pm.

'Are you sure you don't want to come?' Max says.

I shake my head. 'I need to email the German guy and keep going with this research,' I tell him. 'Prince sent me this hectic email before I left and it's not like I have a raging social life here in Wingabby.'

'Fair enough,' Max says. 'The Godfather's at the pub already with one of the nurses so I'll catch up with him later. See you.'

'Bye,' I say as he heads out the door.

I open my laptop and immediately feel exhausted. Novel immunotherapy for tackling recurrent glioblastoma multiforme, while undeniably worthwhile, sounds about as exciting as watching paint dry.

These are the sacrifices junior doctors have to make, I remind myself. To have a competitive CV, I need to actually have something written on it. I also realise I don't have Dr Dietrich's email address.

I wonder for a crazy moment if I should text Nicole, but banish that thought before it can implant, and realise the only person I can really ask is Dr Prince.

I pick up my phone, and stare at it. Hmm.

I haven't seen Dr Prince since the awkward M&M meeting. I think about him quite a bit, but in fairness there isn't much else to think about on thirty-eight-degree nights surrounded by brown walls.

I reassure myself that Dr Prince has no idea of his starring role in my after-dark fantasies and that there is nothing wrong with texting him to ask for Dr Dietrich's email address.

I write a draft text which I then waste close to an hour editing. My head starts to hurt. If I can't even write a text, I have no idea how I'll manage to write an entire research paper.

Miraculously, Estelle emerges from her bedroom, looking sleepy but pleased. 'I just had the sleep of death!' she announces. 'I've finally found exactly the right temazepam-to-wine ratio!' She looks over to where I'm hunched, staring at my phone on the couch. 'What's wrong with you? Have you been called in to the hospital?'

'I have to text Dr Prince for his friend's email address,' I explain. 'You know, the German guy he's asked me to do research for.'

Estelle, aware of my feelings for Dr Prince, looks at me sympathetically. 'Have you been working on a draft?'

I nod, ashamed.

She grabs my phone and, before I can protest, types quickly. She throws it back to me.

Hi, would you mind sending me Dr Dietrich's email address so I can let him know where I'm at with the research? Having a really fun time out here in Wingabby! Thanks. Katarina.

'I don't know about the "having fun in Wingabby" bit,' I say nervously.

'Too late.' Estelle is merciless. 'I already sent it.'

I whimper. 'What if he doesn't reply?' I feel the churning fear of anyone who's ever sent a text message to someone they have a massive crush on. Even if the text is only work-related.

'Of course he'll reply,' Estelle says dismissively. 'It's about boring research that he asked you to do. Don't be ridiculous.'

My phone beeps, causing my heart to skip a beat.

'It's probably Max,' I say, trying not to get my hopes up.

'Nope, it says *Dr Prince*.' Estelle looks excited. 'I'm opening it.'

I don't know what she was expecting, but she looks disappointed.

Wolfgang.d@universityskane.se

'He didn't even acknowledge the fun line about being in the country.' She rolls her eyes. 'Do you reckon he ever goes to strip joints?'

'Doubt it,' I reply.

She sighs and sits next to me on the couch. 'Old surgeons just aren't what they used to be. Everyone is fucking PC now. It's so boring.'

As Estelle raves about the good old strip-joint days, when surgeons were into champagne and cocaine rather than surgery, I open a new email and copy in the address Dr Prince has sent me.

Hi Dr Dietrich,

I'm Dr Prince's surgical intern and he has sent me details of the paper I'm going to be writing. I'll send you updates as I go for advice and feedback. Dr Prince mentioned that the paper will be presented in Sweden. I'd be happy to help present if you think it's appropriate. Please let me know the deadlines etc. I'll be on secondment at a rural hospital for the next 9 weeks, so I'll have some time on my hands.

Best,
Katarina

Estelle suggests a wine, which I feel I deserve after going to all the effort of writing an email, and we leave Poo Palace for the bright lights of the backyard.

Estelle takes off her top and throws herself onto the grass, face first. Her breasts squash out to the sides and I bite back a laugh. She looks like a human pancake.

'I should have put a towel down,' she mumbles into the grass. 'It's really itchy.'

I take off my top as well and lie on my back, enjoying the liberation of being semi-nude outside in a place where no one can see us.

'When we first met five years ago, did you ever imagine we'd find ourselves here together?' Estelle asks. 'Like, lying on this itchy grass, in forty-degree heat, in the middle of fucking nowhere while working at the worst hospital in the world as junior doctors?'

'Nothing surprises me anymore,' I say, looking up at the bright blue sky, tracing the marshmallow clouds with my finger.

'Well, mate, there's no one else I'd rather be having this glorious experience with than you,' Estelle says formally, 'my colleague and friend, the esteemed Dr Kitty Holliday.'

I feel myself grinning at the ridiculous use of the word 'esteemed', when we're definitely the least-esteemed doctors I know—not to mention the fact that the esteemed are exposing themselves indecently and spending the afternoon getting drunk.

Two hours and two and a half bottles later, the esteemed stumble into the house of brown, and resettle on the couch. I look down at my phone, which I have happily neglected, and see that I have a reply from Dr Wolfgang Dietrich. In my happy wine haze I start to open it when I see I also have eleven missed calls from Max.

Estelle, meanwhile, finds her own phone and discovers a similar number of missed calls from the Godfather.

'I bet they've found a party,' she says, looking excited. 'I'm calling him back.'

The Godfather answers immediately. I hear him yelling into the phone but can't make anything out.

'Slow down!' Estelle interrupts him. 'What? You're where?'

More incoherent yelling.

'Okay, okay. Shit.'

'What's going on?' I ask.

She waves me silent. 'Okay, Kitty and I'll walk there as fast as we can. How far is the police station from our place?'

The police station?!

She hangs up and looks at me.

'Get your clothes on,' she says. 'We're going to the police station. Max has been arrested!'

nineteen

ESTELLE FILLS ME IN AS WE BEGIN THE WALK TO THE police station. We have a car, supplied by the hospital, but we're both too drunk to drive—which, I discover, is the crux of our immediate problem.

'Max was driving the nurse's car,' Estelle begins. 'You know—the guy he went to the races with? Anyway, he was on his way home, but then he crashed into an ambulance.'

I stop walking.

'I know.' Estelle's shaking her head. 'Of all the luck, right?'

The Godfather assured Estelle it was only a minor scrape, but the paramedic, being a responsible member of the local community, insisted on calling the police. They attended the scene, mobile breath-testing kit in hand.

'The nurse Max was with said he couldn't drive because he was too drunk, but Max thought he was fine.' Estelle grimaces. 'It's this hot weather—it really fucks with you.'

We're nearly at the police station when the Godfather calls Estelle again. 'Wait there, I'm coming outside,' he says.

We stop on the lawn. I admire the architecture. PROTECTING THE COMMUNITY SINCE 1911 a sign proclaims.

I see the Godfather exit the station and hurry towards us. I can't help but notice he looks a little . . . on edge.

'Are you high?' Estelle asks him incredulously. 'Your pupils look like dinner plates!'

'I didn't realise I'd have to pick Max up from the fucking police station!' he whispers fiercely, trying to wipe sweat off his brow. 'I'd just had some MDMA when he called me!'

'How did you get here?' I ask, fearing the answer.

'How do you think? The races are in the middle of nowhere—I had to drive!' he shout-whispers, looking over his shoulder.

'Oh, great,' I say. 'So, Max gets arrested for drink driving, then you arrive at the police station high as a kite after drug driving.'

Both Estelle and the Godfather turn on me. 'Shhhh!'

'Sorry, sorry,' I say. Moralising isn't exactly helpful in the present circumstances, I concede. 'Well, you'll have to leave your car here. We can't drive either—we've been drinking wine for hours.'

I swear all three of us roll our eyes at exactly the same time.

'You'd better come and say hi to Max.' The Godfather's face creases with pity. 'He's in the cell.'

'Maybe you should wait here,' I suggest, 'and just, you know, chill out.'

He looks relieved. We leave the Godfather hiding behind a large shrub and head into Wingabby local command.

I walk up to the reception counter.

'Hello, Officer . . .' I pause. 'We're here to see our friend, who's currently incarcerated.'

The policeman smiles cheerfully. 'Oh, the doc? Yeah, poor bastard. He was barely over the limit. It was just that ambulance driver. He really wanted to make a stink about it.'

He leads us down the hall and gets out his keys. When he opens the door to the cell, Max looks up fearfully, then promptly starts to cry.

'It's all right, mate,' the policeman says kindly. 'Your friends are here now.'

'It was the ambulance driver!' he tells us, wiping his nose on the sleeve of the blue Ralph Lauren shirt I'd admired only this morning. 'I swear, the ambulance wasn't even scratched!'

'Oh, we've heard,' Estelle assures him. 'The cop said you only blew just over. Why didn't you get a blood test? By the time they would have taken your blood you'd have probably been under.'

Max nods, more tears leaking from his eyes. 'I thought of that, but guess where the blood would have been taken?'

I groan. 'The hospital.'

'Oh, right.' Estelle nods her understanding. 'Well, that's not an option.'

I agree. I can't imagine anything worse than being dragged into the emergency department in front of my colleagues and then having to face their disapproval. It's a dilemma unique to doctors. I make a mental note to carry a card in my wallet that gives specific instructions in the event of an emergency that I only be taken to certain hospitals, where it's least likely that I'll know anyone working there.

'Do you reckon I should tell my mum?' Max looks up at me, his eyes wide with trepidation.

'I don't know, mate,' I say honestly.

Estelle gives him a hug. I pat his shoulder.

'I'd stopped drinking hours before,' he sniffles, his beautiful face stained with tears. 'I swear I thought I was right to drive. Then they made me go in the paddy wagon to the cells.'

This is too much. We all start to laugh so hard that soon I can't breathe. I try to picture Max, in his designer shirt with his perfect smile and big blue eyes and razor-sharp intellect, sitting in the back of a police truck in the middle of the Australian bush.

'What did you say to the police?' I ask him.

'I started crying straight away,' Max says, looking a bit embarrassed. 'But, like, you know . . . Then they told me I was under arrest and when I got here I tried to call you guys but no one answered.'

'We were drunk in the backyard,' Estelle explains sheepishly.

'So, I called the Godfather. I was so desperate I could barely talk, and he said he'd come straight away and get me but when he got here . . .'

'Yes, we know,' I say quickly.

'Lucky they didn't drug test him,' Max whispers, looking around anxiously. 'I mean, wouldn't look too good, would it?'

It's funny how quickly abnormal things become normal. My compass is constantly in full spin. North is south and east is north. I feel myself acclimatising too quickly to situations the younger me would have been horrified by.

'You doctors are crazy!' our friend the local policeman says happily a few minutes later as he liberates Max from his cell. 'Have you heard the news?'

'I'm on the news?!' Max turns pale. 'I think I'm going to vomit.'

'Not you, mate,' the officer says. 'I mean your friends in the big smoke.'

He informs us that back in the city two surgeons have been found operating after doing cocaine all weekend, and the media's jumped on it. The health minister has been on a rant about how disgusting we all are: we're meant to be doctors, he scolded, not drug lords. (No doubt doctors in hospitals all over Australia agree loudly and then go home and text their dealers to start using a less-obvious car.)

The police officer signs Max out of custody and gives him his list of criminal charges as a parting gift. 'We'll be in touch with the court date,' he says cheerily. 'Great to meet you guys!'

You have to hand it to country folk; they are pleasant to a fault.

We find the Godfather lying down behind the shrubbery, staring at the darkening sky.

'I feel amazing,' he says dreamily. 'Look at how big the world is.'

Estelle and I drag him to his feet, and the four of us walk home.

'Cheer up,' I say to Max as we stroll along the main street, the sun setting behind us and the dusk settling on the shops and old pubs that line the wide road. I throw my arm around him. 'Just think, in a while this will be such a great story.'

After all, even the biggest catastrophe can be turned around a few months later over some wines and a good laugh.

twenty

THE REST OF THE WEEKEND IS SPENT FORMULATING MAX'S legal defence. Once the Godfather sobers up, he steps into litigation mode. As well as picking Max up from the police station while high on MDMA, he is also generously taking on Max's case pro bono.

'I can't believe you used to be a lawyer.' Estelle is shaking her head. 'What kind of psycho are you? Law then medicine?'

'Maybe don't answer that,' I say quickly as the Godfather looks thoughtful and opens his mouth to launch into a lengthy description of the inner workings of his mad mind.

'The first thing you need to do is a remedial drivers' course,' the Godfather announces.

Max looks startled. 'What do you mean? Like an online quiz?'

The Godfather smiles.

Remedial Drivers, we learn, is a six-week weekend program created for traffic offenders. The Godfather reckons it's non-negotiable. It will send the message that Max is taking his crime seriously and genuinely wants to reform.

'You have to watch videos on dangerous driving, and then you listen to talks by occupational therapists about patients who've suffered brain injuries from drink-driving accidents,' he tells Max, who's looking more and more horrified. 'Then there's a big reflection session at the end. I think you have to write an essay about your feelings and stuff. And you get a certificate,' he adds, as a sweetener.

'At least it'll give you something to do on the weekend,' Estelle tells Max encouragingly. 'You might learn something.'

I'm amazed a town as small as Wingabby has such a service, but the Godfather explains that all country areas have them, due to the high volume of offences. Apparently, a significant proportion of the community is spending their Saturdays at the local church hall being lectured about road and traffic safety.

As the other three start arguing about what else to include in the remedial drivers' curriculum, I remember that I still haven't read the email from Dr Wolfgang Dietrich.

I open my laptop and locate the email. I discover that he sent me a second one while I was at the police station. I read both.

> Hello Katarina,
>
> How lucky you are being Jack's intern! He is a fun person. He was very good to me when I am in Sydney. Has he taken you to his art gallery?

I grin at his slightly off English and I wish I'd been to Jack's gallery.

He launches into a description of the research, which sounds hard and boring. The paper is on novel immunotherapy techniques for treating horrible brain tumours. He wants me to do a literature review and has a few links to add to those Dr Prince sent me.

> As Jack told you, if you do well and the paper is accepted you can have most of the poster with that, then you present it at our conference.
>
> You write me and we be in touch.
>
> Best regards,
> Wolfgang

Then another email, sent five hours later:

> Sorry, I forgot. The paper is due in nine weeks. I know not much time but Jack promises me you are a clever writer so it will be all right.
>
> Best regards,
> Wolfgang

Jack promises me you are a clever writer! I'm thrilled—and concerned.

'Do you reckon it's possible to do a really detailed lit review in nine weeks?' I ask the rest of the group, who are still arguing about remedial drivers.

'Yeah, easy,' the Godfather and Max say almost simultaneously.

Estelle looks sickened. 'God, why would you want to do that?'

'Is this Prince's research?' Max is interested. 'I've written a few surgical papers. I'll help you, Kitty.'

'Good idea—it'll keep you out of trouble.' The Godfather looks at Max sternly.

It's decided. In exchange for Max helping me do the research, I promise to pick him up every Saturday evening after remedial drivers and buy him a beer.

Later that day, Estelle and the Godfather go for a walk to the corner shop, and Max and I sit outside Poo Palace together, listening to the birds.

He looks over at me. 'Do you think I'm a bad person?' he asks out of the blue.

'What?' I'm genuinely surprised.

His face is creased with worry. 'Do you?'

'Of course not!'

'I just feel like such a fuck-up,' he says, sounding truly sad. 'Like, I'm living in the middle of nowhere, I work a million hours a week for barely any money, and then I go and do something as stupid as getting done for drink driving.'

I shake my head. 'Mate, everyone makes mistakes.'

I remember the morning I woke my housemates up, screaming from my nightmare, with Max's concerned face gazing down at me. Sometimes I see him on the ward at work, when he thinks no one is watching, sitting on the edge of some old patient's bed, having a laugh with them. Max wants to be a surgeon, but he possesses human qualities that I rarely see in the hospital. I secretly think that a low-range drink-driving charge, compared with the changes surgical training will inflict upon his soul, is the least kind of assault that could take place on his character. Max is only a very junior doctor like me, but I fear the years won't be good to him. He thinks the worst that can happen is that he misses out on his training place or annoys the wrong consultant. I silently worry that he will be chewed up and spat out by a system that doesn't care much for loveable larrikins.

'Give your mum a ring and tell her what happened,' I suggest. 'I think it'll make you feel better.'

To my surprise, he doesn't argue. He looks relieved.

When he reappears on the front porch ten minutes later, he's a new man.

'She told me the same thing happened to her when she was my age!' he crows. 'I knew I got it from her!'

It turns out that Max's conservative, successful, terrifying businesswoman mother has made her share of mistakes.

Well, haven't we all?

twenty-one

AFTER OUR WILD WINGABBY WEEKEND I THINK I WILL be glad to get back to the hospital. Then I'm called in to work the Monday night shift in emergency even though I've been at work since 7 am, and I start to wish I was still at the police station.

'You know what they call this area?' one of the consultant emergency doctors asks me as we sit in the emergency department, watching the list of patients waiting on the computer grow longer, then longer again.

I refrain from uttering one of the many less-than-positive answers that float through my mind. It's nearly midnight and I'm dog-tired. 'What do they call it?'

'The killing fields,' he says, staring wistfully into the distance, looking as if he's thinking of other, more appealing times and places. 'They call this hospital and its surrounds the killing fields.'

I believe him. Even if the patients aren't actively dying in front of us, it feels as though death is always stalking the corridors.

A twenty-three-year-old man-boy walks into the department an hour later after being kicked by his mother's horse.

'Fucking animal,' he says loudly as I examine his wrist. 'Fucking piece of shit, that horse. As soon as I'm out of here I'm going home to shoot it.'

I prod his scaphoid bone harder than necessary.

'*OWWW!* Fuck!' He glares at me. 'Take it easy!'

'Sorry.' I don't mean it.

I order the X-ray and offer him some pain relief. I look up his file on the computer and notice he was in hospital six months earlier for punching someone at the local pub. He'd broken several bones in his hand.

When he returns to ranting about shooting the horse, I can't take it anymore. To the amusement of the rest of the staff in the emergency department, when the patient leaves I call the police.

'Look, I'm not sure if you can do anything,' I say to the slightly bemused officer on the other end of the phone, 'but I don't think a person should be able to shoot a horse when the horse was, well, just being a horse.'

After assuring me that, no, people can't just randomly destroy horses, the officer promises to conduct a search of my patient's property for illegal firearms and check on the wellbeing of said horse.

'Maybe just don't say who it was who made the call,' I add quickly, remembering I have to walk home alone.

'You city doctors are mad,' says a gruff old paramedic who stood behind me listening as I made the phone call. 'You're mad as cut snakes.'

Eight hours and fifteen complicated patients later, I walk home to find Max sitting on the front porch of Poo Palace.

After relating how I prevented cruelty to animals from inside the emergency department, I ask him what he got up to last night.

'Remedial drivers' orientation, mate,' Max informs me, grinning a bit.

'How was it?'

'There's about a hundred people there and only ten of us can read,' he explains. 'So I was voted group leader and I helped everyone with filling in their workbooks. Everyone else in my group is over fifty.'

I'm overjoyed. This will keep us going for days.

'That's not even the best bit!' Max tells me. 'You wouldn't have seen the local news—there was a shoot-out!'

To his horror, a local news crew showed up at the end of remedial drivers' orientation with the intention of filming proceedings to show what a successful intervention the local community has organised. By a stroke of pure serendipity, at exactly the same time, two of Australia's most wanted, on the run in the local area, were spotted nearby. The police immediately cordoned off the whole town, surrounded the convicts, and the media rushed off to cover the subsequent shoot-out.

'Thank God for the escaped felons!' Max says.

With the sun beating down on us, me still in the filthy scrubs I've been wearing for nearly two days, we look at each other and start laughing so hard I feel as if my stomach is going to explode. How far away we are from our inner-city life of bars and Mardi Gras and Bondi now!

I suddenly have a terrible thought. 'If the police were busy with the escaped felons, then who was stopping that boy from shooting his mother's horse?'

Max looks horrified, then he shakes his head. 'No way, Kitty,' he says firmly. 'That's not how the universe works. The horse will have sensed what was coming and staged its own escape. I know it.'

I don't want to believe anything else, so I decide to keep the faith. I imagine the horse running across a field, its mane flapping in the wind.

I feel relieved that, against all odds, we are still capable of hope.

twenty-two

THE WATER IS VERY BLUE. IT'S SARDINIA, THE MALDIVES, Sydney on a perfect day. I'm fascinated by how blue it is. I lean over the edge of the yacht and run my fingers through it. After the heat of Wingabby, it's glorious. I let it wash up my arm, enjoying the sensation. I lie back, looking down at my legs, which now have a golden tan.

I decide I should try to enhance the tan so I untie my bikini top. I lie topless in the sunshine as the water laps the side of the boat.

I close my eyes, relaxing into the moment.

Then I feel a hand tapping along the skin above my bikini bottoms. I open one eye. *Hello there.*

He's wearing a white shirt and is tanned and perfect and so masculine. My fears that he's a bit old and overweight prove unfounded. I have never been this attracted to a man ever, in my entire life. He leans down and kisses me, hard, on the mouth, and I feel myself getting very wet.

His tongue traces my lip, and I reach down and push off my bikini bottoms. He unbuttons his shirt and shrugs it off, and

I am underneath him as he kisses me. His hand wanders down between my legs and he starts to rub me there, and I'm so wet it feels as if his fingers are moving along molten silk. I'm so turned on I can barely breathe.

I reach down and feel him. He's hard, and I spread my legs as wide as I can. He teases me, hovering above me until I beg him.

'Please . . .'

He smiles. I can't believe I ever thought he was awkward. There is nothing awkward about him now. He pulls my legs around him and thrusts inside me, and I let myself enjoy the feeling, savouring it in my legs and stomach and the throbbing between my thighs as I start coming around his cock and the orgasm is so intense that I feel myself . . .

BEEP! BEEP! BEEP!

For a second, I don't know where I am. I lie on my back, still feeling the after effects of the orgasm I've obviously just given myself—in my sleep, disappointingly.

I allow myself five seconds of enjoyable reminiscing about the dream and then force myself to wake up properly. This is unpleasant for a few reasons, the first being that I'm actually on night shift and the beeping that has woken me is my pager. I've been asleep in the tiny doctors' room, underneath a cotton sheet, having a filthy sex dream about one of my bosses. I really need to get a life, I think, feeling depressed.

I sit up and look down at the pager. Code blue. Paediatric ward. I feel a twinge of relief. I'm not covering that ward, so technically I don't have to respond, but a code blue is a life-threatening situation so I should attend, just for support. Plus, Estelle is covering the paediatric ward and I don't want her stuck in some horrific situation alone. I rub my eyes, roll off the mattress and hurry down to level two.

I burst through the door of room 214, expecting to see the intensive care doctor in the middle of a resus. I look around. There's no one here. Not even a patient.

Someone clears their throat behind me.

I turn and see a nurse hovering. 'Where's the code?' I ask.

'Been airlifted out,' he says, looking weirdly uncomfortable.

'That's fast.' I'm surprised. I only just got the page.

'The pager system went down,' he explains. 'It actually happened about half an hour ago.'

He tells me the patient was a three-year-old boy who was having trouble breathing and needed intubation.

'Where's Estelle?' I ask. 'Has she gone with the kid in the air ambulance?'

The nurse tilts his head slightly and gives me a meaningful glance.

'What?'

He points over my shoulder and I look around to see that he's indicated the door to the patient bathroom.

'In there,' he mouths.

I walk over and push open the door.

Estelle is sitting on the floor with her arms wrapped around her knees, staring at the wall. She's staring so intently I have a quick look at the wall to see if I'm missing anything. I glance down and notice her shirt's soiled. On closer inspection I realise there's some blood, and what looks like vomit. Her hands are shaking. It's very quiet.

'Are you all right, mate?' I ask, trying to sound casual.

'No one came,' she mumbles.

I don't think she really knows that I'm there. I put my hand on her shoulder, and she starts so violently I stumble backwards.

'Get away from me!' she screams, lashing at me with her hand. 'Just go away!'

My mouth drops open. I hardly recognise her in this state; it's like she's a completely different person.

Disturbed, I back out of the bathroom as she resumes staring at the wall.

The nurse and I exchange looks. I have no idea what's going on with my friend, but I know it isn't good. My stomach churns anxiously.

'When you say the paging system was down,' I ask the nurse quietly, 'do you mean over the whole hospital?'

He nods.

'Even the code blue team?' Surely not, I think. The way the system works, the intensive care code blue team receive the page before anyone else. Their paging system is the one thing in a hospital that always works—even a hospital as underresourced as Wingabby.

'Even them,' he says grimly. 'They didn't arrive until one of the other nurses ran to get them. They were dealing with a sick guy on level six, so it took her ages to find them.'

'What other doctors were here?' I demand. 'Who was here with Estelle?'

I glance over at her, huddled in the corner of the bathroom. She's an intern, like me. We're not trained to manage life-threatening emergencies by ourselves, let alone an emergency involving a child. Holy Innocents has no paediatrics ward, so we barely know how to deal with measles.

I almost hope he doesn't answer, because I have a sinking feeling I know what he's going to say.

'It was just Estelle,' he says, looking increasingly uncomfortable. 'Well, her and me.'

'So, you're like a paediatric nurse, right? You've seen a resus? You kind of know what to do?'

He shakes his head. 'I'm just an agency nurse.' He sounds apologetic. 'Someone called in sick, and they were desperate. Normally I'm on the orthopaedic ward.'

What a fucking shit show, I think.

Estelle stirs, and I walk back into the bathroom. Very gently, I put my hand on her shoulder. She doesn't react this time.

'It was just me,' she says, tears spilling down her cheeks.

Behind me, the nurse says, 'I rang the flight doctor, because we just didn't know where the team was. Estelle had to intubate the little boy by herself . . . They gave us instructions over the phone.'

I feel my eyes widen. 'You intubated a three-year-old? But we don't know how to do that!'

Sticking a tube down the airway of an adult is no mean feat; it's something we've only ever practised on plastic models. To intubate a dying child by yourself . . . It takes specialist paediatric anaesthetists years of training to master it, and still they sometimes fail. And here was Estelle, at two o'clock in the morning, forced to do it on her own, in a hospital in the middle of nowhere. I shudder.

I don't ask if the child's still alive. Suddenly, I don't even want to know. All I want to do is teleport the three of us out of this horrible little room to somewhere familiar and safe. I want to be sitting at the pub down the road from 19 North Avenue, at our regular table, gossiping about boys. *Get us out of this godforsaken place!* I scream inside my head. No one hears me. No one comes to our rescue. The airlift we so desperately need is flying over a crystal blue sea, delivering supplies of champagne and cocaine to Bond girls sitting on yachts.

'She got the tube down, though,' the nurse says, crouching beside Estelle. 'She did really well.'

I'm deeply impressed.

'You did everything you could and more, man,' I say, sitting on the floor beside her. 'You were stuck in an impossible situation no one in our position should ever be put in, and you did a fucking good job, all right?'

Estelle remains motionless on the floor, hugging her knees. 'His whole body was blue,' she says, finally looking up at me. Her eyes are so blank they scare me a little bit. 'Like, he was blue. As blue as your scrubs.'

I cringe.

'I've never seen anything like that.' Estelle sounds almost reflective. 'It was like a picture from a textbook, you know?'

Fantastic. What a great on-the-job learning experience.

'It's weird,' Estelle continues. 'All that keeps going through my head is that guy, the one who told us that story in our last year of uni.'

She's delirious, I think.

'You know.' She sounds frustrated. 'That emergency doctor. Tim . . . No, Toby.' She frowns. 'He told us that story about the kid who'd tried to cut off his own hand.'

How could I forget. Toby Henderson.

'I asked him how he coped.' She laughs, but there's no humour in it. 'Remember what he said?'

'You just don't,' I hear my voice saying.

'I didn't believe him.' Estelle's voice is rising. 'I didn't fucking believe him!'

The paediatric room has cartoon characters painted on the wall to make it seem like a cheerful place. But as I look closely I can see that the paint is cracking, and the smiles on Mickey and Minnie's faces are fading. There's an abandoned Lego set on the table.

I have the sensation that I'm looking down on the scene from above. We are Lego figurines. The floor is grey, splashed with red, and Estelle is a white Lego woman, sitting in the corner of the Lego room. I'm blue, and the nurse is black. A big hand picks up the figures and moves them. I hear the voice of a child playing doctors and nurses. 'Then the doctor moves here and saves the patient!' But the game is no fun anymore. The doctor is crying. The patient is dying. The grey Lego floor is dirty with blood. Our puppet master doesn't like the way the game is going. The doctor isn't doing what doctors are supposed to do. The child has a tantrum, knocking over the Lego hospital and leaving the figurines scattered on the floor. Discarded, until someone decides to pick them up again. We are little dancing doctor bears made of Lego. Tug our strings, and we move on command.

Toby Henderson was right. How do you cope? You just don't.

There's an unusual feeling welling up in my stomach, burning a path to my chest before flaring in my brain. I don't recognise it at first, but when it roars into my consciousness there's no mistaking what it is.

It's anger.

I look at Estelle, still slumped on the floor, muttering to herself. Estelle is one of the smartest, most beautiful, most fearless people I have ever known. To see her in this position enrages me.

My fury is pierced by the shriek of my pager. We all jump. Estelle's face is raw with panic.

Mechanically, I reach for the pager and read the message.

Room 312, chest pain. Urgent.

There's another shriek. Estelle's pager is going off now. She struggles to her feet.

'You should just go home,' I tell her. 'Just get your stuff, tell them you're sick, and go home.'

Estelle's eyes plead with me; she is fighting an internal battle I know only too well.

'I can't,' she says, the battle already lost.

The hand picks up the little Lego doctors and puts them back into position. A child giggles. The string is tugged. Up! And they begin to move.

Dance, little doctors! Dance!

twenty-three

EVEN THE LONGEST OF NIGHTS ENDS WHEN THE SUN RISES. I stand on the top level of the hospital, watching as light starts to flood the town beneath me. The world looks so calm outside, it's disconcerting. That people have been sleeping peacefully in their beds feels impossible.

The morning doctors start to arrive, and I meet Estelle out the front of the emergency department. She looks haggard. I put an arm around her shoulders.

'Let's get the fuck away from this place,' I say with feeling.

Estelle manages a small grin. 'You know, even Poo Palace doesn't seem that bad at the moment.'

We walk home in silence, lost in our own worlds. We're just about to turn into our street when I feel a sense of recklessness come over me.

'Let's go for an adventure,' I tell Estelle.

She doesn't look too enthused, but I force her along anyway.

'Come on, run!' I say, and start to sprint towards the road that heads out into farmland.

Estelle shrugs, but she runs with me.

It feels good to stretch my legs. I take huge strides, flying through the air in the quiet of the morning. We run and run and run, until we're surrounded by grass and trees, with the hospital and the memory of the night fading in the light of the morning.

When we finally stop, we both bend over, our chests heaving. My face is covered in sweat. Estelle's cheeks are flushed a bright pink, and she is gasping for breath.

'I need to lie down,' she says, panting.

I crawl under the fence running beside the road, and she follows me. We're surrounded by rows of orange trees laden with fruit. Some of the oranges are small and hard, but others are big and ripe, ready to be picked.

We throw ourselves down among the trees.

'I don't know why life feels so hard all the time,' Estelle says, shielding her face from the sun with her hand as she stares up into the oranges, 'when really it's pretty simple.'

I know what she means. I close my eyes, and let the gentle breeze soothe my frazzled mind.

I hear Estelle's breathing become regular sighs. Totally exhausted from the night, she has fallen asleep.

I don't wake her up.

I relax into the soft grass, for some reason remembering the odd conversation I'd had with the Smiling Assassin just before I left for Wingabby. She'd recited a passage from one of my favourite books.

Lines from *Through the Looking-Glass* float across the blue sky above me now, threading around the fluffy white clouds.

In a Wonderland they lie,
Dreaming as the days go by,
Dreaming as the summers die.

Ever drifting down the stream—
Lingering in the golden gleam—
Life, what is it but a dream?

It feels like we have stepped into Wonderland. This comforts me. Even in pain, I think, I can still find beauty.

In the orchard of orange trees, my nightmares are no more.

twenty-four

AFTER THAT NIGHT, ALL WE CAN THINK ABOUT IS GETTING back to Sydney. Max crosses off the days on a calendar. 'Thirty-four to go,' he says grimly one afternoon, 'which means five more remedial drivers' lessons.' It's also crawling towards winter, which is a relief. The ward, despite still being hellish, is at least a more tolerable temperature.

The Godfather has slept with nearly every single nurse in the hospital and is feeling the pressure. 'I don't think people really like me out here,' he says nervously over a beer in our living room. 'The nurses are all banding together against me.'

'Well, you didn't have to sleep with all of them,' Estelle points out. 'You didn't have to take such a mass destruction approach.'

'Or mass seduction,' I pipe up, smiling.

I spend every waking minute that I'm not at the hospital reading about glioblastoma and trying frantically to finish the literature review for Wolfgang Dietrich. It's becoming incredibly tedious. Wolfgang tears to shreds every draft I send him but offers only vague suggestions for improvement. I'm starting to wonder whether I should bother persevering; his feedback has been largely negative, and I doubt I have a chance of the paper being accepted into the conference line-up. I'm halfway through a draft email suggesting that I withdraw from the project, when Wolfgang beats me to the punch.

> Great news, Katarina! The abstract has been accepted! We have prevailed!

The word 'we' is a little galling, considering I've done all the work—but, as Max points out, that's the beauty of being a senior consultant surgeon.

'Everyone does the work for you and you take most of the credit,' he tells me. 'Don't worry, Kitty, only another twenty-five years before we get there ourselves.'

I send admin an email confirming I'm going to use my study leave to fly to Sweden to present the paper, and they respond more positively than usual, knowing it will reflect well on the hospital to be seen as a centre of research excellence that offers its juniors such wonderful opportunities.

I ring Mum to tell her the good news. She is over the moon. 'My daughter, the future surgeon, off to present at an international conference!' she says. 'I've told you that story about when you were born, haven't I? About your fingers being long? Surgeon's fingers!'

'Yes,' I say, refraining from adding, *Like a billion fucking times. Why do you think I'm doing this?*

I'm so focused on surviving Wingabby and finishing the research on time I can barely think about the fact that I'll return to Sydney only to get on another plane to fly straight to Europe. I want to be excited but only feel anxious.

The good thing about being so busy is it makes the time go much more quickly. The days are long, but the weeks are becoming shorter, and shorter again. Before I know it, Max's calendar has only six days and one remedial drivers' lesson remaining.

And there's another bright spot on the horizon. Despite my fear that it will only lead to heartbreak, when I see on Facebook that Fabien is leaving South America and heading to Europe, I send him a message to tell him about my own trip.

Maybe we can meet at a coffee shop, he messages back as I'm wading through the Johanssen paper on glioblastoma operative outcomes.

Or we could just get really drunk at a bar, I write back.

I didn't think doctors got drunk.

I allow myself a small smirk.

We decide we will meet. The conference only goes for a day and I assume I won't want to be spending a huge amount of time in Sweden with surgeons I've never met, so I allow myself to do something that makes me truly happy. I book myself a flight to Amsterdam, and Fabien books his. We send each other screenshots of our respective e-tickets and I nearly cry with joy.

Maybe I'm just a simple creature after all. Away from the operating theatre and glioblastomas and dying children, what fills my heart is booking a flight across Europe to see the ski bum I met three years ago.

'Being a doctor doesn't make a person happy,' Estelle says bluntly when I tell her this. 'It just makes you confused.'

'Agreed,' Max chimes in. 'You leave the operating theatre at midnight and feel great because you've just done a heart transplant or something equally hectic. But then you get home and there's no one there, or worse a partner you've been cheating on every other second because you're such a fucking mess, and all your mates are at work or asleep, then you realise you're actually really lonely and depressed, and all you have to look forward to is waking up and going back to the hospital.'

'That's why you've got Stilnox,' the Godfather points out. 'To avoid all that unnecessary reflection.'

We spend our final night in Wingabby getting drunk at Poo Palace. Estelle says she has a surprise for us and produces a huge bag of oranges and a juicer.

'I went back to the orchard Kitty and I found,' she says, looking pleased with herself, 'and I picked as many oranges as I could.'

I recall the rows of trees. Estelle, stricken from her terrible night shift, had found comfort among the trees and returned to pick the oranges to make vodka oranges for her friends. Life continues, glass by glass. Who says that alcohol doesn't bring people together?

Max loves the juicer, and orange after orange goes through. Vodka after vodka is thrown back. We toast the best orange juice in the world, Max's remedial drivers' certificate, the Godfather's nurse success rate, Estelle's survival of her night shifts (just), and me finishing my research paper. We toast each other well into the night.

'We survived,' Max says before we retire to our beds. 'It was touch and go for a while there, but we survived.'

I raise my last vodka and orange. Cheers to survival.

Doctors worry constantly about patients surviving. We fear death and suffering and blame. Our own survival seems unimportant by comparison. The doctor saves the child, or doesn't. Who saves the doctor?

These questions are hard to answer, and my brain is tired. On my last night in Wingabby, I dream of a horse eating an orange. The horse is alive and the orange is ripe. I wake up to the sun rising and hear Estelle in the shower, getting ready to take one of the only two taxis in Wingabby to the airport.

We have orange juice for breakfast. Survival tastes sweet.

twenty-five

WINNIE IS SHAKING HER HEAD IN DISBELIEF. 'MAX, YOU are *so bad*!'

Max looks sheepish. 'Did I tell you I came top of the remedial drivers' course, though?' he says.

We're back at number 19, having coffee with Winnie in the kitchen before work. We'd kept in touch with her from Wingabby, and while Max had kept quiet about his misadventures I'd happily spilled the beans.

When Max produces his remedial drivers' certificate, Winnie loses the plot and laughs so hard I worry she'll aspirate.

'It's good to have you both home,' she says when she has regained the power of speech.

'Yeah, but Kitty's flying to Sweden the day after tomorrow,' Max reminds her.

'I know,' Winnie says, looking jealous. 'I wish I was going to Sweden, instead of being stuck here arguing with the neighbours about who owns which bin.'

Max and I leave the house together and walk to the front entrance of the hospital, where we stop for a second, prolonging the inevitable.

'I almost envy that guy, you know,' Max says wistfully, looking at the homeless man who's asleep at the bus stop, wrapped in a quilt. 'He looks so peaceful.'

After Wingabby, which was largely populated by white farmers, I am much more aware of the diversity of the city. The area around the hospital is a good example. While it's in a very well-to-do beachside paradise, it also has its seedy sections, populated by homeless people and backpackers hanging out in old pubs with saltwater-stained windows. I admit to myself that I have missed the place a tiny bit.

The feeling passes almost immediately. The junior doctors who were away last term are hauled into reorientation by medical admin to remind us that while things may have been different in the country, we're back in the centre of teaching hospital excellence and must behave as such.

Nicole, wearing yellow and looking like a voluptuous buttercup, starts with a friendly welcome which quickly turns into a disciplinary ear-bashing.

I get a text from the Godfather.

You know what this is about right?

I reply in the negative.

Some nurse accessed the file of the football player who had a drug overdose and the media got on to it. So now we're copping it.

Fifteen seconds into the friendly welcome, Nicole has already used the word 'terminated' three times. As if we are pests that need exterminating, we're informed that if we do anything to compromise the confidentiality of any of our more famous clients (apparently when you're famous you're a client, not a patient), we will be terminated immediately.

'We've introduced a new system that you should all be aware of,' the buttercup chirps.

While we were away, the hospital has entered the twenty-first century and put us all under surveillance, she explains. The hospital computers now have an electronic tracking system that alerts the administration directly if an unauthorised doctor accesses a patient file. So, if a famous patient is in the hospital and you decide to sneak a look at their CT scan, an alert will be sent to the executive, who can then terminate you.

'It's for your own protection,' Nicole tells us cheerfully, neglecting to point out the obvious: that protection and termination can be used interchangeably.

As the lecture continues, I find out that there are plenty of grounds on which the executive can terminate me. If I don't wash my hands enough, if I don't use the right code on my discharge summaries . . . the list goes on and on.

After the talk ends, Nicole corners me. 'So you're off to Sweden tomorrow!' she exclaims. 'Are you seeing Wolfgang?'

I remember mentioning the research to her briefly, but I'm surprised she knows about my trip. She must realise this from my expression, because she rushes to explain. 'Jack told me,' she says, smiling. 'He said you're presenting the poster.'

I'm momentarily pleased that Dr Prince remembers who I am, as I've not heard from him in months. Then I feel irritated that he has discussed my research with Nicole but has never communicated with me. Then I tell myself to stop being so pathetic.

'Ah, yeah,' I say noncommittally, 'but I'm only spending a few days there. I'm meeting a friend in Amsterdam afterwards.'

I think of Fabien, and the light, fairy-floss feeling of happiness floats around me.

'A special friend?' Nicole probes. 'Is he a doctor?'

I refrain from pointing out that doctors can find happiness with people who aren't doctors themselves, probably more so, and shake my head. 'No, he's just a friend,' I lie. 'We used to ski together.'

'I can't believe he treated me like that, you know,' she complains, and I'm confused for a moment, before I realise she must be referring to the mysterious Dr Wolfgang Dietrich.

'Men,' I say vaguely, reluctant to get caught up in the saga.

I'm almost relieved when the Joker calls me on my mobile. No doubt he knows that I'm leaving the country tomorrow and wants to make the most of the one day we have together.

'I don't care that you've been away,' is his opening line. 'It doesn't make up for the fact that half the bloods haven't been ordered.'

'That's the job of the doctor who was on last night,' I point out, 'when I wasn't actually here.'

'Don't make excuses,' he snaps.

I hold my phone in front of me and mouth, 'FUCK OFF!' as forcefully as I can.

His voice, unfortunately, continues to spew out of the microphone. 'Come to theatres now,' he instructs. 'I wanted you there five minutes ago.'

I walk as slowly as possible to the operating theatre, wondering why it is that I can be terminated for failing to wash my hands thoroughly, while the Joker and the Smiling Assassin can be as heinous as they like and suffer no consequences.

I arrive at theatre six to see a man covered in blood fleeing the area. I step back as he charges towards me.

'Are you all right?' I ask. Normally people covered in blood are lying unconscious on the theatre trolley, not running out of the place.

The man is spluttering with indignation. 'He threw a tub of betadine at me!'

'What?'

'I'm one of the porters,' he explains, 'and that surgeon just threw a tub of betadine at me because he said I wasn't holding my hands up high enough.'

'So that's not blood?' I gesture at his shirt.

'No! It's fucking betadine!'

He storms out of theatres, raging about physical abuse in the workplace and threatening to lodge an official complaint. I raise my eyebrows as I start to scrub in. It appears the Joker has now progressed to physical harassment. Things have obviously escalated in my absence.

I hear stories like this a fair bit. Max has told me that he once saw an orthopaedic surgeon throw an IV pole at one of the residents because he didn't have his scrubs tucked in.

'How did he get away with that?' I asked Max.

He shrugged. 'Who knows? The more senior you are, the harder it is for them to touch you, I reckon.'

Personally, I don't think being a senior surgeon should excuse someone for being a total maniac, but that's how medicine works. I also don't understand how being an arsehole will increase your surgical dexterity, but maybe I just haven't had enough experience yet.

I finish scrubbing in and reluctantly enter the operating theatre, where I put on the sterile gloves and gown.

The Joker tells me to get a move on.

'I don't understand why Prince asked you to do this research.' He sounds more disdainful than usual as he starts to shave the head of the unconscious person on the table. 'You've been doing surgery for months and you're still hopeless.'

'Maybe he thinks I've got potential,' I can't resist saying.

'Potential to do what? Kill someone?' He laughs loudly.

The Smiling Assassin, who has joined us and is silently standing behind me watching what I do, joins in, laughing much too enthusiastically.

Maybe one day I'll tell them what I think of them, I muse. Maybe the day I quit. Maybe that will be today.

Yeah, right, a little voice in my head scoffs. Who's going to pay your rent and credit card debt then, Doctor?

The Joker starts quizzing me on brain anatomy, which I answer more proficiently than usual after my weeks spent reading about recurrent glioblastoma multiforme.

After an hour of me making him angry by not making as many mistakes as usual, he accuses me of ruining the sterile field and tells me to scrub out and stand in the corner to watch instead. The Smiling Assassin eagerly takes my place.

I relocate to the corner of theatre six and stare at the clock, willing it to move faster. Mercifully, my phone starts to ring. Even better, it's the hospital switchboard.

'It's switch,' I announce joyfully, waving my phone around as if I've just got engaged. 'I'll duck out and answer it.'

The Joker and the Smiling Assassin are trapped elbow deep in brain tissue, which means I'm able to exit without delay. Once outside I consider not answering, but then remember the Shark wants to do a round so, with a sigh, I put the phone to my ear.

'Hello?'

All I can hear is static, and a weird loud whooshing sound. I walk quickly out of theatres to the meeting room. I don't want the Shark to think I'm ignoring him.

But even away from the lead-lined rooms I still can't hear anything.

'HELLO!' I shout into the phone. 'DO YOU WANT TO DO A ROUND?'

I hear some clunking, as if the phone is going down a ladder.

'Sorry about the wind,' a voice says, now fairly clearly, into my ear. 'I'm out on the harbour.'

'Oh . . .' I stutter, realising I'm not talking to the Shark.

'It's Jack. Jack Prince.'

Even though I'm standing alone in the dictation room next to the operating theatre and he's many nautical miles away, I feel my cheeks start to burn. I nearly laugh. Of course he's out on the harbour, while I'm at work, struggling through a day that feels like it will never end.

'Hi, Dr Prince!' I manage. 'Sorry, I thought it was one of the other consultants wanting to do a round.'

'Don't worry,' he says, sounding relaxed. 'I never round on Wednesday afternoons. It's my sailing time.'

I nod, then realise he can't see me. What can I even say to that?

'Lucky you,' comes out accidentally. 'I've just been in theatre with your esteemed colleague.'

I must sound more sarcastic than I intended because he laughs. 'That bad?'

'Yeah,' I say, forgetting myself, 'he's a total jerk.'

The wind whistles in my ear. I wonder, for a second, what the yacht looks like. I forget that I'm leaning against the wall outside the operating theatre in my oversized scrubs and imagine what it would be like out on the harbour. Wind. Water. All that wonderful freedom. Sailing must open the soul in a way not even the sharpest scalpel can.

I forget that Dr Prince is my boss and start to tell him about my day. 'You know, he's just so mean all the time,' I explain. 'Like, I've been away for ten weeks and he can't even ask how my trip was. It's always just how I'm never good enough.'

'I can't stand the guy,' Dr Prince says, then there's a silence as if he realises he's gone too far.

'Me neither,' I agree with feeling, and even though all I can hear is the wind it whistles with agreement.

'I actually didn't ring to talk about him.' He sounds brisk all of a sudden, once again my senior consultant. 'I know you're off tomorrow, so I wanted to say good luck with the paper and ask you to tell Wolfgang I said, *Tjena*.'

'*Tjena*?'

'It's colloquial Swedish for hello,' he explains. 'Now he's been on sabbatical there for nearly a year from Germany he needs to practise his Swedish.'

I can't believe that in less than twenty-four hours I'll be on a plane to the south of Sweden where I'll say *tjena* to Dr Wolfgang Dietrich.

'Well, thanks,' I say. 'Thanks for offering me the research, too.'

'That's my pleasure.' There's a moment where neither of us say anything, and more wind whooshes through my ear. We both start to talk at the same time. He stops.

'Okay, I guess I'll let you get back to it.' I feel embarrassed and I don't know why.

'Have a safe flight.'

He ends the call.

I let my body flop against the wall and release a breath I didn't know I was holding. What is going on here, exactly? Do consultants normally call their interns from their yachts on the harbour?

Maybe they do. Maybe he's just being supportive. He's a busy, important man. The only time he probably gets to make calls is when he's out sailing.

My thoughts are interrupted by my phone ringing again. This time it is the Shark. I bury my questions with no answers, remind myself they're questions I shouldn't even be asking and, pulling off my scrub cap, walk up to the ward.

None of this will matter tomorrow. This time tomorrow I'll be on a plane to the other side of the planet, and the Joker and Jack Prince and his yacht on Sydney Harbour will be far, far away.

twenty-six

IT'S EARLY AFTERNOON WHEN THE PLANE LANDS IN Copenhagen. Despite taking a concoction of sedatives kindly prescribed by Max, I'm wide awake and desperate to escape my economy window-seat prison.

One day soon, I think as I nearly cop an elbow in the head from the woman sitting next to me, I'll have to fly business class. Which means I'll be commencing work as a female escort, considering my job as a doctor isn't providing me with the funds to do so.

'Welcome to Denmark,' the flight attendant offers in perfect English as we slow to a stop on the tarmac. 'It's nineteen degrees with light winds.'

I rub my eyes and remind myself that this trip is my chance for a mental recharge, as well as a career development opportunity. I wonder if Dr Prince somehow knew that I needed something to help repair my badly dented surgical confidence. Change, as they say, is as good as a holiday. New places, new people, new perspectives.

I disembark, and make it through customs and to the train station underneath the airport with surprising efficiency. I start to feel as if I have stepped into the twilight zone. Everyone is very calm and polite. In my experience, airports are normally stressful and rushed. Not this one.

'Excuse me, is this the platform for the train to Lund?' I ask a tall blond (everyone here is tall and blond) standing in front of me. An ancient university town in the south of Sweden, Lund is only half an hour by train from Copenhagen, Wolfgang has told me.

'It is,' the blond man says. 'So you are travelling in Sweden?'

'I'm attending a conference there,' I explain. 'So it's work, really.'

He smiles. 'Still, you must see the cathedral. And the bridge. Lund is very beautiful, and so is the journey.'

He's not wrong, I soon discover.

As the train pulls out of the station and rockets along the bridge linking Denmark and Sweden, I stare out the window. At first all I can see is water. Then, gradually, shapes start to form, emerging from the ocean like sea monsters. I squint, trying to work out what they are. I'm amazed to discover they're windmills. It's as if the Vikings woke up one morning and decided to hurl the windmills like javelins into the water, where they landed perfectly in a line, silhouetted against the horizon of the world.

I could have stayed on that train for hours. It's almost a disappointment when the words, 'Next stop: Lund', echo through the carriage.

More mundane sights greet me as the train slows. Factories, fields, houses.

When the train shudders to a halt and the doors open, I'm greeted by torrential rain. It's the start of June and meant to be the European summer but Sweden hasn't got the memo and it's freezing. The lift is broken, so I drag my suitcase up what feels like three hundred stairs. After asking a woman in the ticket office for directions to my hotel—there is no need to take a taxi, she assures me; it is only a five-minute walk away—I step out of the station into a cobblestone square lined by rows and rows of pushbikes.

Despite the seemingly straightforward directions, and even with the attempted use of Google Maps, I manage to get lost trying to find the hotel. By the time I reach the Grand Hotel I'm feeling anything but grand. My clothes and hair are so wet I feel like I've been on some kind of military exercise. The staff kindly ignore my bedraggled state and check me in with admirable Scandinavian efficiency. I finally make it to my room, and collapse onto the bed.

Then, reminding myself that I should text my parents to let them know I've arrived safely, I lift my head off the bed to rummage in my bag for my phone. I hear the rumble of thunder, and a flash of lightning illuminates the scene outside my window. There's a church standing in the rain, light shining from its stained-glass windows. The walls sparkle, even in the storm. I step back in time and see the stonemasons carving each brick, one by one, to build that fantastic cathedral. 'Wow!' I whisper involuntarily.

I had planned to review my research before the meeting I have scheduled with Wolfgang Dietrich at the hospital tomorrow morning, but it stays untouched in my suitcase. Instead, I lie on the bed and stare at the magnificent edifice in front of me. Only a divine hand could have created such exquisite beauty. There must be a God, I think drowsily, as my eyes start to close, to have inspired humans to build a place like that.

twenty-seven

I WAKE THE FOLLOWING MORNING WITH NO MEMORY OF having fallen asleep. When I reach for my phone I find fifteen missed calls from my parents and seven messages from Max.

How was the flight?

Are you there yet?

Are the Scandinavian men hot?

Are you alive?

Your parents called me.

Your parents are going to call the police.

ARE YOU ALIVE?

I spend ten minutes being yelled at by my mother for not having called sooner, text Max to assure him that I am still in the land of the living, then hastily shower and dress and, grabbing my folder of papers, run down to the hotel lobby.

The girl behind the desk promises me that the hospital is easy to find. To my relief the rain has stopped, so I take her word for it and make my way through the streets of Lund.

The town is beautiful, like something from a fairy tale. I'm so taken with the old architecture and the narrow streets that when the hospital comes into view I'm momentarily disappointed. Hospitals, even in fairy tales, look pretty much like any other hospital. And, I discover, have a similarly confusing layout.

Standing in the foyer, I re-read Wolfgang's email: *Meet me at 8 am on level 5. It's the surgical floor.*

I look around. The hospital is huge. There are blocks of lifts to different wings and floors all over the place. Hmm.

I approach the information desk and say, 'I have a meeting with Dr Wolfgang Dietrich on level five. Can you direct me, please?'

She turns and speaks quickly in Swedish to a man beside her.

'Come with me,' the man says. He leads me around the corner and up a flight of stairs to another set of lifts. He swipes his card and presses the button for the fifth floor. 'You'll need a code to get through the door when you get up there, but I don't have it,' he says apologetically. 'Maybe if you bang on the door someone will hear you.'

'Wait . . .' I don't think this sounds like a particularly good plan, but the lift doors are already closing.

They open again on level five, and I find myself facing two huge closed doors. There's no one in sight.

I sigh. I try knocking, which achieves nothing. Then I see an intercom. I press the button a few times, again with no result. I'm just about to get in the lift and go back to information when the doors miraculously open and an attractive older man in white scrubs steps towards me.

'Thank God!' I exclaim. 'Thank God you appeared! Can you let me in, please?'

He looks at me. 'Ah, do you work here?'

I look down at my faded jeans and grey hoodie and realise I don't quite fit the surgical mould. I curse Wolfgang Dietrich and his suggestion of a 'casual meet-up' and realise I should have dressed more formally.

'I'm here to meet Dr Dietrich,' I say, my confidence faltering. 'I'm Dr Katarina Holliday—from Australia.'

Understanding dawns on his face. 'You're Katarina! Katarina from Sydney!'

'Yes!' I nearly hug him.

'Yes, yes. You know Jack!' The man reaches forward and shakes my hand enthusiastically. 'I'm Tomas Johanssen. Very good to meet you.'

'Johanssen, like the 2014 paper on glioblastoma?'

He laughs. 'That's nothing too important, believe me.'

I admire how humble the Swedes are.

He leads me into a room where there are more men in white scrubs having an animated discussion over cups of black coffee. Everyone stops talking to stare at me.

'Wolfgang, I have found Katarina from Sydney!' Tomas says. 'Jack has sent her to us!'

A man with sandy blond hair steps forward, smiling.

'Hi,' I say, then remember. 'Sorry—*tjena*!'

His smile turns into a laugh. My irritation melts away and I immediately warm to him. He turns to the rest of the white scrub brigade, who are also chuckling.

'Jack has taught her well! *Tjena!*'

We shake hands. His eyes are bright blue, and the smile reaches them. Wolfgang Dietrich looks as if he doesn't take life all that seriously, though I know he must, given the kind of work he does.

'Katarina from Sydney! You made it!'

'Well, eventually,' I tell him as he motions for me to sit down. 'Your directions were hopeless!' I start to pull out my research folder, but all he wants to talk about is Jack Prince.

'Has Jack told you we used to go to the museum all the time?'

'Um, well . . .'

'It was great.' His expression is animated; it's clear he has fond memories of his time in Sydney. 'We used to go there to look at his latest acquisitions, and then out for drinks, then sometimes we operate. And his house! Have you seen his house?'

I'm not sure how to tell Dr Wolfgang and Co that in Australia interns don't socialise with their consultants and that our main interactions take place on ward rounds or in the operating theatre. Fortunately, he doesn't seem to need an answer, as he's lost in his reminiscing.

'And his yacht! Tomas!' Wolfgang looks over at Tomas. 'Remember his yacht?'

Tomas, it turns out, has also met Dr Prince, and is as impressed as Wolfgang.

'Surgeons make no money here,' Tomas tells me as I am poured my third cup of black coffee. 'Not like Jack.'

Another man in white scrubs joins in. 'After I met Jack, I really wanted to move to Sydney to have a life like his, but my wife wouldn't let me.'

'Yes, Henrik wasn't allowed to become an Australian,' Wolfgang explains to me, looking amused. 'Here in Sweden we are very controlled by our women.' Suddenly Wolfgang changes tack. 'So,' he says, 'let us talk about the conference tomorrow.'

He leads me into his office to show me the template for the poster and explain how the presentation will work.

'It's not so hard,' he assures me. 'You just stand next to it and for two minutes answer some questions. We will be there if it gets too difficult.' He looks at his watch. 'We have to go and operate,' he tells me. 'You can join us if you like.'

To be totally honest, the last thing I feel like is standing in an operating theatre for ten hours, but it would be rude to turn him down, so I half-heartedly agree and follow him out the door.

Within minutes I am standing at a sink, scrubbing in next to Wolfgang as he peppers me with questions about Dr Prince and life back in Australia. I can't believe I've gone from a scrub sink in the southern hemisphere to one in the northern hemisphere and wonder for a second why we couldn't have done something slightly more relaxing, like go for a drink, instead.

Doctors, I think with a sigh. It doesn't matter which part of the world they're in, they still can't help themselves.

A nurse comes over to let us know the patient is asleep. She gives me a funny look.

'*Tjena!*' I say brightly, since it's the only Swedish word I know.

'*Hej Hej*,' she replies coldly, before exchanging a few quick words with Wolfgang in Swedish.

Wolfgang clears his throat. 'Kitty, this is Astrid, my girlfriend.'

Astrid gives me a frosty smile. She is extremely slim, with honey-brown hair and piercing blue eyes. Her features are so symmetrical it seems impossible. She is undeniably beautiful, in a perfect Scandinavian ice queen kind of way. No wonder he wanted to sleep with Nicole, I think. She might not look like a Scandinavian supermodel, but she exudes sexuality.

Astrid says something else in Swedish, then turns and enters the operating theatre.

Wolfgang looks at me. 'You're coming?'

'Ah, yes . . . yes!' The jetlag is kicking in and I just hope like hell there's a stool I can sit on.

The Europeans, I soon discover, are even more psychotic than the surgeons back in Sydney. After seven hours—including a lunchbreak during which they leave the patient asleep on the table, and then the discovery that there's a slight complication, so the operation will now probably take another seven hours—I've had enough.

'Um, guys, I'm going to head back to the hotel.'

They're so focused they don't even raise their heads, but Tomas acknowledges my words with a nod. Wolfgang, without taking his eyes off the brain, bids me farewell.

'We meet outside the hospital at eight in the morning,' he says. 'We will all go to the conference together. You have your notes?'

'Yes, of course.'

I flee the operating theatre and almost run back to the hotel bar.

There I pull my laptop out of my bag to review the points I'm going to make. I have rewritten the paper so many times and made so many summaries, I don't feel overly nervous. Wolfgang doesn't seem too worried either, which is reassuring.

The barman catches my eye. 'Would you like another drink, perhaps some food?'

I throw caution to the wind and order another red wine, and a huge bowl of meat and dumplings.

'This is good Swedish food,' he tells me as I start to devour the enormous plate in front of me. 'You'll sleep well after this.'

I'm yawning even before I finish the meal. I think of Estelle and her experiments with wine and sedatives, and resolve to tell her the magic trifecta: temazepam, pinot and Swedish dumplings.

twenty-eight

'YOU HAVE DONE VERY WELL,' WOLFGANG WHISPERS TO me the next morning as I stand beside my poster, explaining the best new immunotherapy techniques for treating recurrent glioblastoma multiforme. 'I'm impressed.' The poster presentation is much more congenial than I'd feared. I'd had horrifying visions of me standing on a big stage as surgeons rapid-fire interrogated me. Instead, I just parked myself next to my poster between two other posters, and people have been milling around, asking questions and being surprisingly pleasant.

Tomas appears with three cups of black coffee, grinning. 'Well done, Kitty!' he says. 'You have answered all the questions so confidently.'

To be fair, I haven't been asked that many questions about the poster. Everyone seems far more interested in the fact I'm from Australia. Most of the questions are about sharks and Bondi Beach.

The Swedish approach to medical training is vastly different from the Australian one, I'm finding. Even though they're just as keen to spend hours in theatre, probably even more so, they seem less prone to asking mean questions and teaching by humiliation. When I describe life on the ward with the Joker and the Smiling Assassin, Tomas shakes his blond head in exquisite Scandinavian confusion.

'But, Kitty, you are so clever,' he says. 'You will be such a wonderful surgeon. I don't understand why you are not more encouraged.'

'Maybe your friend the Joker is not having enough sex,' Wolfgang suggests.

I smile, well aware that Wolfgang was having plenty of sex during his time in Australia.

'Who is having enough sex?' Tomas says, looking amused. 'I know I'm not.'

'Oh, me neither,' I agree.

We all grin.

I am overwhelmed with warm feelings I find difficult to recognise, particularly while standing inside a hospital. I am really starting to appreciate the Scandinavian approach to surgical life.

'Kitty's hospital teaching system is more based on the American one,' Wolfgang is saying to Tomas and another Swedish surgeon who has come over to say nice things about my poster. 'Don't you remember that conference we went to in Boston?'

'It was unbelievable!' Tomas recalls. 'They invited us into theatre to watch, and I've never forgotten the junior doctor in there! He was like a robot!'

Wolfgang adds, 'The surgeon was just firing off question after question—I didn't even know the answers to some of them—and this intern was just answering and answering and answering . . .'

'And then, when he finally got one wrong, the surgeon started shouting about how stupid he was.' Tomas shakes his head. 'If we did that here, we'd be fired!'

'Might make our junior doctors more scared of us, though,' Wolfgang says with a grin.

I feel as if I have fallen through a crack in the universe and stepped into a parallel world. The operating theatres look the same and the scrubs are the same but in other respects it's totally, wonderfully different. I can't believe there are surgeons other than Dr Prince who think the idea of bullying their juniors is needlessly cruel.

I have had to travel to a hospital on the other side of the planet to rediscover my love of doctoring, but miraculously it has happened. Standing in the conference room on level four of Lund University Hospital, I feel happy with myself for the first time in a long while.

'I think this will look good on my CV,' I tell Wolfgang, feeling cheerful. 'I reckon it's pretty impressive.'

'Very impressive,' he says kindly, even though he's published a million papers and regularly performs lifesaving operations. 'We will tell Jack how great you've been.'

Wolfgang insists we have a photo taken of the three of us and tells me to email it to Dr Prince. He stands over my shoulder, reading my message.

Hi, Dr Prince,

I made it to Lund. I've had a great time. Here's a photo of me, Wolfgang and Tomas with the poster; the conference was a big hit.

Thanks again for organising it all for me. See you back at work.

Kitty

'Say we said *tjena*!' Wolfgang instructs me.

I add: *Wolfgang and Tomas say* tjena, then attach the photo. I'm wearing white scrubs to match the Scandinavians. We look like evangelical Christians rather than doctors, I think.

Wolfgang studies the photo. 'We look like we are from a mental institution,' he says mournfully. 'The blue Australian scrubs are much better.'

I laugh so hard he looks suspicious.

'You were thinking the same! I know it!'

'Not at all!' My half-hearted attempts at denial are drowned out by uncontrollable laughter.

When we have recovered our poise, Wolfgang turns to me. 'We have planned a dinner for you tonight. Tomas spent all last night cooking. You must come.'

'Sounds great,' I say.

twenty-nine

MY ALREADY EXCELLENT MOOD IS ONLY IMPROVED BY A message from Fabien as I am deciding what to wear to dinner with the surgeons: *32 hours*. He's right, in thirty-two hours we will be seeing each other in Amsterdam.

I can't wait. After months of telling myself we aren't right for each other, the fact that I am tingling with anticipation seems to suggest otherwise. I can't believe what a fantastic time I'm having. The research went well, the Europeans seem to like me, and soon I'll be having wild sex with an age-appropriate hot man whom I've never been able to forget. Sweden, I decide, has been very good to me.

Two hours later, I'm trying to resist as Tomas pours me another schnapps.

'Tomas, you don't know what I'm like when I'm drunk,' I protest. 'You have no idea what you're unleashing.'

'Don't be silly,' Tomas retorts as he hands me a shot glass. 'You're an Australian!'

I concede defeat, and down the drink. As they say, when in Sweden . . .

I see Wolfgang watching me. He looks amused. Astrid glowers next to him, although she seems less fierce than she did yesterday. This, I'm sure, is down to the fact that I'm quite tipsy and have been regaling the gathering with accounts of my regular Friday night activities, which always involve me making a huge fool of myself and waking up not remembering what I've done the night before, usually sharing my bed with a pizza box. Astrid is no doubt comforted by the fact that I'm a disgraceful Australian mess and clearly no threat to her.

'You know, sometimes I dream of Sydney,' Wolfgang tells me as dinner wraps up and we put on our coats. 'I dream of the ocean, the sun . . .' He sighs, then smiles. 'Tomas and I are coming to Sydney in a few months. We must see you there.'

'I'll have you over for dinner!' I promise, forgetting in my schnapps-addled state that I barely know how to switch on the kettle let alone cook a passable meal. 'It'll be great!'

'If it would not be too dull for you,' he teases. 'Now I know you are used to such adventurous Friday nights. You must find Sweden very boring.'

'I like Lund,' I tell him. 'Even though I've only been here for two days, it has really cheered me up.'

'Were you not cheerful?' I laugh the question away, but he looks me in the eye. 'Being a doctor is not always so fun,' he says simply. 'I would prefer to be James Bond, for example.'

I'm surprised into genuine laughter. 'No way! You've stolen my idea! I want to be a Bond girl!'

Tomas walks us out, and we all exchange awkward hugs on the street. I watch as Wolfgang and Astrid stroll away, arm in arm. Then Wolfgang turns back. The streetlights illuminate his face, and he smiles at me. It's not a longing smile, or a flirty smile. It's the smile of a man who understands. There isn't any attraction between me and Wolfgang Dietrich, it's not quite like that. It's as if we're kindred spirits.

'See you in Sydney,' he calls. 'You've promised us dinner.'

I see it, just for a second, the glint in his eye. Wolfgang Dietrich is staring at me through his own looking-glass, behind him the crashing Australian ocean and a long mane of shining brown hair tumbling over a woman's breasts. When I dream of Lund's cathedral, he will dream of Sydney Harbour. It brings a new, much more personal meaning to the term 'the grass is always greener'. Or maybe it's just the simple fact that even as doctors we aren't immune to the basic human desire of always wanting what we can't have.

thirty

I ARRIVE IN AMSTERDAM AND CHECK IN TO THE HOTEL only to receive a message from Fabien telling me he's missed his flight. He's trying to find another one, but it's not looking good. My buoyant mood instantly evaporates.

When he calls me a few minutes later, I'm tempted to hurl my phone out the window into the canal. I press answer, and stare into the camera.

When I see the worried look in his brown eyes, I feel my anger dissipating. I almost feel bad for him.

'I'm so sorry, Kit,' he says as his face goes fuzzy with the bad reception. 'Don't be angry—the bus broke down on the way to the airport.'

'So now what?' I say, trying to get my disappointment under control. 'I only came here to see you and instead I'm all alone in this stupidly big hotel room.'

'I'm sorry,' he repeats. He looks stressed. 'I think there's another flight tomorrow morning, so I should be able to get there by tomorrow night.'

My frustration is rising to the surface again. 'I just don't understand how I've managed to get from Australia to Sweden, present a research paper, and fly to Amsterdam on time, and you can't even get one lousy flight!'

He's saved by the lousy connection.

'It's okay, Kit,' I hear coming through brokenly. 'Lightning strikes, remember?'

The connection dies just as I am considering smashing the screen with my fist. This is typical of Fabien, I tell myself. He's just so charmingly *agenda-less.* Everyone else I know lives by the ticking of a clock. Fabien, though, never wears a watch and seems to just go where the wind takes him, which is why we have no future—and is also why I like him so much.

The heart wants what it wants, Winnie says in my ear, even though she's back home at number 19 and I'm alone in a hotel room in the Netherlands.

Rather than drowning in self-pity, I decide to skype my housemates.

'You're *alive*!' Max shrieks into the camera, slurring his words. I realise, too late, that it's 1 am at home. In the background, I see the usual suspects.

'Did you meet Fabien?' Winnie's face bobs onto the screen. Her voice is higher-pitched than usual and she's holding a giant wineglass.

'He missed his flight,' I say, wishing suddenly that I was back in Sydney getting drunk with my mad friends.

'What?!' I hear Estelle exclaim indignantly. 'What a fucking dick!'

'He wouldn't have meant to,' Winnie defends him. 'If you met the guy you'd understand. He never means badly, he's just a bit . . .'

'Hopeless?' I say.

'So, what are you going to do, mate?' Max asks. 'Are you going to fuck him off?'

'I might wait one more night,' I say. 'He thinks he can get the next flight and I've got the hotel for three nights.'

'Just go and smoke some hash and meet another guy,' Max advises, ever the pragmatist.

'Look, Kitty . . .' Winnie is back. 'If Fabien can't make it tomorrow, just forget about it. Like, I love the guy but he needs to be more organised. You can't put up with this shit. If he doesn't come just fly somewhere else. Where does your flight home leave from?'

'Copenhagen.'

'Well, just fly back to Copenhagen.'

'I agree!' I hear Estelle shouting from behind her. 'Kitty Holliday waits for no man!'

I leave them to their night out—or night in—and decide to go to bed. I feel drained of energy now. The whole whirlwind trip has exhausted me.

I sigh and switch off the light. Outside, the red-light district is just kicking off. Welcome to Amsterdam.

I fly back to Copenhagen at five the following evening. My three-day European love fest had turned into a twenty-four-hour sob fest. The last I heard from Fabien, he was still trying to get a seat on a plane. I take Winnie's advice and cut my losses.

This, I tell myself, is why following your heart never works. It only leads to one place, and that's heartbreak town. Much easier to have an unrequited crush on a fifty-year-old surgeon.

I knock back five glasses of wine on the two-hour flight and am only prevented from requesting a sixth because the plane starts to descend. The one good thing about being back in Copenhagen so soon is that I'm a pro at the train and make it to Lund like a local. I've had the foresight to rebook into the Grand Hotel, and they welcome me back as if I never left—probably because it's barely been twenty-four hours since I did leave. I decline to explain my sudden reappearance and tear-stained face, and they kindly refrain from asking.

I don't really know why I've returned to Lund when I could have flown anywhere in Europe. There's something about the place that draws me back.

I'm about to recommence the serious business of drowning my sorrows with the help of the minibar when my phone rings. Glancing at the screen, I see Fabien is trying to skype me.

I press *end* and hope it hurts.

He rings again.

I press *end* again.

He rings again.

I press *end* again.

He sends me a message. *Pick up.*

I answer the next call, and glare into the camera. Unbelievably, he is smiling.

'Kit! Where are you?'

'What?'

'I'm here! How come you're not in the room? The hotel people said you went out and gave them the key.'

I start to feel a bit sick.

'You said you didn't think you'd make it,' I say, trying not to admit to myself that it looks suspiciously like he's standing in the hotel room I've just left behind in Amsterdam.

He laughs. 'That's because I wanted to surprise you. But look—I'm here!' He must notice my expression of horror because he starts to look worried. 'You're surprised, right?'

'Very,' I confirm.

'We booked the hotel for three nights. I thought you would have just stayed here, and then I was going to make up for missing the plane by surprising you with this.'

I resist the urge to put my head on my knees and start sobbing as he pulls out a bottle of expensive French champagne and a teddy bear in a little pilot's uniform holding a sign saying, *Sorry I'm late. Flight delayed.*

'Where are you, anyway? Did you move to another room?'

'You could say that,' I tell him.

Understanding dawns on his face. 'You've gone, haven't you?'

'Well, what was I supposed to do?' I shout. 'How was I supposed to know you were planning a fucking surprise? Why can't you just communicate like a normal person?'

He starts laughing, half in irritation and half in disbelief. 'This is just like that time in Zermatt when you thought I'd left you at the top of the run and you skied off in a huff. By the time I found you in the bar at the bottom of the slopes, you were drunk with a group of German guys on a bucks' weekend.'

'I thought you'd left me stranded!'

'I had to go to the bathroom!'

We yell at each other for a few more minutes, until I give in and start to laugh.

'I guess I could try to find a flight to Sweden,' he suggests, grinning. 'Then we could fight in person.'

Fabien and I spend our romantic night together on Skype getting drunk on the contents of our respective minibars. He looks up flights to Sweden, but they're all over a thousand dollars one way.

'I'll do it,' he offers, opening his fifth beer. 'I reckon Dad would lend me some money.'

'Nah, don't worry,' I say. 'I think I might have overreacted a bit.'

He smiles sheepishly. 'I shouldn't have tried for a surprise.'

'I'm not much good at surprises,' I admit. 'Being a doctor has really killed my spontaneous side.'

We stay on Skype until the early hours of the morning. I can't believe it, but it's the best date I've ever had.

'Maybe we do better being in different countries,' he says, his head resting on the hotel pillow, looking into the camera. 'This has been a really good night together.'

'I'm leaving in two days,' I say sadly. 'I don't think we'll get to see each other.'

'I think I'm going to come home at the end of the year anyway,' he says. 'Life on the road is getting a bit old, you know?'

I laugh in disbelief. 'Sure.'

He grins at me. 'Maybe I'll surprise you.'

'You know how much I love your surprises.'

I don't believe him for a second. He's been saying this for the last two years, so I've learned to ignore it. I know he thinks he means it, but then another adventure will beckon and the pull of home will be lessened by a new mountain, or a new beach—or, I think regretfully, a new girl.

'Lightning strikes, remember?' he says.

I nod. 'I remember.'

It's bittersweet, our European night together. I want to feel happy, but I can't, then I try to feel sad, but that doesn't quite work either.

How do I really feel about Fabien? I ask myself after we've said goodbye. Love? What is that, anyway? Feelings and longings and desires . . . where do they even come from? Organs and blood vessels make up my body, but love and desire exist somewhere else, don't they? Somewhere away from an operating theatre, inside the light of a candle that burns every day and night, and never dies. I hear Mum's voice again. That bloody quote, following me around.

Remember man that thou art dust, and to dust thou shalt return.

Is there any point in love if it'll turn to ash anyway? Why waste all this time and energy on feelings that will only end up scattered as particles among the ether? At least surgery is tangible. Love is just air and words, and painful disappointment.

Being in Lund has renewed my sense of purpose as a doctor, and that fills me with deep satisfaction. But larger questions about life swirl below the surface. Surgeons cut open skin and touch the organs that give us our life's blood, our personalities, our souls. The intimate places that my future scalpel slices into are still shockingly unknown to me. Maybe I am afraid of feeling too much. How can I possibly be a good surgeon if I can't learn to suppress my emotions? My head begins to ache, and I can't think about it anymore. Doing neurosurgical training, I thought the brain was confusing—but I realise now that it's got nothing on the heart.

thirty-one

WINNIE AND MAX MEET ME AT SYDNEY AIRPORT. I'M SO surprised to see them waiting for me at the gate I nearly fall over.

'How did you get here?' I ask, knowing Max's licence is suspended for at least six months and Winnie doesn't like driving.

Winnie looks affronted. 'We did a few practice runs. I was good!' She turns to Max, who is keeping very quiet. 'Wasn't I?'

'Really good,' Max says encouragingly, then mouths from behind her shoulder, 'I nearly died.'

We drive back to number 19, trying not to wince too obviously every time Winnie turns a corner.

'We're meeting at the pub,' Max informs me. 'Everyone wants to hear about your trip.'

'I was only gone a week,' I say. 'Nothing that great happened!'

'So what?' Max retorts. 'While you've been overseas having fun we've been at work, which has been shit as usual.'

Reality slaps me in the face like a brick. I suddenly forget about my jetlag and am desperate for a beer.

Max and I head straight for the pub on the corner. Con is in his usual form.

'You know I get fined if I smoke outside?' he says as I approach the bar. 'What is this fucking city?' He flings his hands in the air. 'It's like living in a fucking police state. I tell you, I'm going to go back to Kythira and leave all this shit behind.'

Con hails from Paradise Lost, aka the small Greek island of Kythira. He always shows me photos. It's all turquoise water and bleached white stone houses. His favourite line is 'This wouldn't happen in Kythira'.

'I just got back from Europe,' I tell him, 'but I didn't make it to Kythira, sadly.'

The Godfather and Estelle appear on either side of me. 'Thank God you're back,' Estelle says with relief. 'Wining and whining wasn't the same without you.'

I laugh. 'I was gone for, like, a week!'

'Felt like six years,' the Godfather says. He shakes hands with Con then orders a round.

'A trip to Europe and a great addition to your CV,' Estelle says enviously as we carry the beers to our usual table.

Everyone is worried about trying to make their CVs look more impressive so we have a better chance at getting onto a good training program.

'My CV is terrible,' Max says gloomily.

The Godfather sighs. 'Same.'

'Did you hear about Matt Whittaker?' Estelle asks. 'He topped the neurosurg exam, got the highest mark in the whole of Australia and New Zealand, and he still didn't get a spot on the training program.'

'What's he doing now?' Max asks, looking horrified.

Estelle shrugs. 'Still working as an unaccredited. This will be his fifth year.'

'I can't believe that I thought being a doctor would mean job security,' I say. 'If I'd known there was no such thing, I could have been a fucking actress and actually had some fun.'

'I'm getting this paper published,' Max tells us, though he seems strangely morose about it.

'That's a big deal, isn't it?' I ask him. Most junior doctors love bragging about publications in prestigious journals. These days, it's becoming near impossible to specialise without a PhD.

Max lifts one shoulder. 'I guess.' He sighs. 'I just don't know anymore. I mean, it's so much work and I don't even know if I'll get onto the program anyway. And the exam is six grand. I can't even pay the rent—how am I going to come up with six thousand dollars?'

The general public is under the impression that doctors make exorbitant amounts of money. That might have been true back in the day, but not for our generation. Even if I pass the surgical primary exam, there's no guarantee I'll get onto the training program. Realising this, the government and the surgical colleges have created a system of 'unaccredited registrars'. This means you can do the job, but you're not on the program and there's no guarantee you'll ever make it. In fact, a lot of people we know are in this unfortunate predicament: they're working as surgical registrars but don't have the ticket to allow them to progress to being a consultant. This means years of being on call, working night shift, being shipped out to the middle of nowhere on a fairly paltry government wage, all without any kind of security for the future.

After our year as interns, my friends and I will spend another year in the hospital as residents, but then we'll all be under pressure to decide which path we want to take: physician, surgeon, GP—whatever we decide, it will involve expensive exams and arduous training requirements, often far from Sydney.

No wonder I don't have a personal life to speak of, I think to myself. I don't even know where I'll be in a year, let alone three. It's a bit hard to start planning a future when I can't even take a lease beyond six months and all my money is going towards exams I don't even know if I'll pass, all to apply for a training program I have no guarantee of being allowed onto.

'At least you're not relieving on neurosurgery like Kitty,' Estelle points out. 'I can't believe you've still got another few weeks with those people.'

'Lucky I had the week away,' I point out. 'Even small reprieves are a blessing.'

Rather regrettably, before starting my internship I requested as many surgical terms as possible. Knowing that I had an interest in neurosurgery, admin kindly assigned me to that department for my relief month, which is a period when interns cover for doctors who are going on leave. I was thrilled to pieces by this initially, but all this means to me now is an extra month with the Joker and the Smiling Assassin when I could have just helped fill in on respiratory or something equally painless.

My next term after relief is emergency, which will be hard and tiring, and I wish even more that I'd used this month to take it easy. Hindsight is always such a powerful kick in the teeth.

'At least I'll get to see Dr Prince,' I say, trying to find the silver lining.

Max looks sorry for me. 'Nah, he's away, mate. I heard them talking about it in theatre the other day. There's some big conference in New York or something.'

'Great, so it'll just be me and the Joker and the Smiling Assassin then.'

Everyone looks at me sympathetically.

Estelle stands up, yawning. 'I'm buggered,' she says. 'I'm going to head off.' She gives me a quick hug. 'Glad to see you back, mate.'

The rest of us stand up too. Max and I walk home, and find Winnie smoking a cigarette out the front of number 19.

'I know I said smoking is disgusting,' she says, 'but my boss is being a bastard and I really need to relax.'

'Good to know even non-doctors have a shit go as well,' Max tells her, taking the cigarette from her and having a long drag.

Winnie rolls her eyes. 'I'm calling in sick tomorrow,' she informs us. 'You guys should try it sometime.'

thirty-two

THE NEXT MORNING, I TAKE WINNIE'S ADVICE AND, FOR the first time in my life, I call in sick.

'Everyone needs a mental health day,' Winnie says sensibly, having just called her own office to inform her boss that her chronic gastroenteritis has struck again. 'I don't know why you guys don't do it more often.'

Winnie's gastro and my viral upper respiratory tract infection (caught on the plane, I tell the Joker in a text) miraculously resolve after we spend an hour sitting on the couch together.

'Do you want to go somewhere for lunch?' Winnie asks.

'Let's go to the beach,' I say. 'It'll be too cold to swim but we can paddle.'

We call a taxi and head to one of the beaches not far from number 19.

There, Winnie and I stretch out on the sand and sigh simultaneously. It's one of those perfect crisp winter days. There's no wind, and the sun feels surprisingly warm.

'God, this is so much better than work,' Winnie says.

'Beats being yelled at in theatre,' I agree.

'I don't get why doctors are so nasty to each other.' Winnie shades her face with her hand. 'It really makes me wonder, you know . . .' She pauses.

'What?' I ask.

'About my mum,' she says. 'I remember the team of doctors that used to see her. They came around every day, and I used to think how professional and great they all were.'

'They probably were,' I reassure her. 'I think I've just hit a bit of bad luck with my seniors this year.'

Winnie looks over at me. 'But think about all our other mates. Max spends all his time trying to fit in more research to get onto surgery even though he's already written so many papers, and Estelle had that shit experience when you were out in the country.'

'Well . . .'

'And the Godfather! He's so smart, but all he wants to do is get himself so wasted that he can't think anymore!'

'Well, it's a stressful job,' I say weakly.

'And your nightmares, Kit. It's not normal, you know.'

I don't know what to say. I feel defensive and embarrassed, and confused too. It dawns on me how it must look to Winnie from the outside. It's easy for those of us who are living through it to lose perspective.

'I know how it must seem,' I say, 'but don't start questioning the way the doctors in England looked after your mum. I'm sure they gave her the very best care.'

I don't want Winnie to think that the medics caring for her mother at the end of her life were jaded cynical burnt-out alcoholics who had stopped caring about their patients. I can't blame her for thinking they might be, living with us, but I want to tell her that the patients are the single most important reason why I chose to become a doctor in the first place. I want to tell her I still think about Mr Wilde, I dream about the deaths I certify, I admire doctors like Dr Prince who care about their patients—but I don't know how to. I feel like a fraud.

Winnie is watching the waves in pensive silence, and I presume she is remembering her mother. Pancreatic cancer is one of the worst cancers to get, with a terrible prognosis and a quick decline. They would hardly have had time to get used to the idea that she was sick before she was gone.

Winnie turns to me abruptly. 'I never told you, did I, what happened at the hospital?'

I shake my head.

'There was one doctor, this young guy called George,' she says. She leans back again to stare up at the sky. 'He was so nice and attractive—you know, like the doctor you think you'll meet from stupid TV shows.'

'Yeah, I know.'

'And when Mum died, I was the only one with her. Dad and my brother had gone out for the afternoon, just to get away, and I said I'd sit with her.'

I nod. Winnie is lost in the memory.

'Anyway, Mum started breathing sort of weirdly. The nurse came in and looked at her and said she was close to the end. I started crying and she went out to get me some water. She must have run into George, because he came in.' Winnie shook her head. 'And when Mum died—like, five minutes later—I just couldn't stand up, I couldn't do anything.'

I reach out and touch her shoulder, but she doesn't seem to notice.

'So I sat on the edge of her bed and I just cried and cried. And that doctor, George, he must have had so much other stuff to do, and patients to see, and whatever.' Winnie's voice wobbles slightly. 'But he just sat with me on the bed for, God, it must have been close to an hour. He didn't say anything, he just sat with me.'

'What a decent guy.' I feel a sense of gratitude for Dr George, whichever hospital and whatever job he's working in now.

Winnie looks over at me, as if suddenly remembering I'm next to her. 'Yeah, he was. He was so kind to me. I've never forgotten it.' She runs her hand over the sand. 'Anyway, a few days later, when everything had calmed down a bit, I went back to the hospital to find him to say thanks, but he wasn't there.'

'Where was he?'

'He hadn't shown up for work so his girlfriend went to look for him.' Winnie makes an odd sound, like a repressed sob. 'He'd overdosed on some kind of drug he'd taken from the ward.'

I push my fingers into the warm sand, feeling the grains slip between them.

'He killed himself,' Winnie says, staring out into the endless blue of the ocean. 'He must have been thirty? Thirty-two? And I thought, what on earth could have been so bad that he went and did something like that? My mum had just died, and my world had collapsed, but I still wasn't anywhere close to wanting to . . . you know.' Her voice trails off.

'Maybe he had some other stuff going on,' I suggest. 'Maybe he had family problems, or debts—you never really know.'

'Maybe . . .' She doesn't sound convinced.

'Look, none of us are going to kill ourselves, all right?' I jump up. 'I know we drink too much and love whingeing about work, but I for one intend to remain in the land of the living. How am I going to have an affair with Dr Prince if I'm dead?'

This breaks the tension, and Winnie laughs. 'Yeah, I know. I just remember that lovely doctor sometimes, and now, seeing the pressure you guys are under . . . I just get worried sometimes.'

'Come on, let's go for a swim!' I urge, pulling her upright and dragging her towards the water. 'It'll do us good.'

'It's too cold!' But I ignore her protests, and soon we're both screaming with laughter as we fall into the freezing water and start thrashing around like beached dolphins before running back to the warmth of our towels.

'Fabien reckons he's going to come home,' I say, as feeling gradually returns to my extremities. 'I don't believe him, obviously.'

Winnie laughs. 'I love that guy,' she says fondly. 'I've never met anyone quite like him.'

'You know what he's like, though,' I point out. 'He's got too much wanderlust.'

'Speaking of . . .' Winnie says, rolling over in the sand. 'I know we drink too much, but alcohol is good for throat infections, right?'

'Oh, absolutely,' I say.

'Let's go to a bar,' Winnie says, grinning, 'and have some prosecco.'

I don't need to be asked twice. We pull our clothes on over our swimming costumes and head to a bar around the corner, where we spend the rest of the afternoon sitting in the sun, drinking prosecco and eating chips.

'Kitty,' Winnie tells me seriously as we clink glasses, 'this is the best sick day I've ever had. You're such a good doctor. I'm cured!'

In that moment, I am completely overwhelmed with appreciation for my wonderful life.

thirty-three

I GO TO BED AS SOON AS WE GET HOME, CERTAIN I WILL have a perfect sleep after my relaxing day. I'm lost in peaceful oblivion when my phone starts to ring.

Shocked, I sit up and start fumbling around, trying to find my phone. My sense of inner peace is washed away by waves of dread as I try to remember where I've left my scrubs.

When I finally locate the phone it has stopped ringing. I check the caller ID, expecting it to be the hospital number. I see that in fact it was Estelle—and it's not the first call I've missed; she's been calling me since eight o'clock and it's now a little after ten. I was sleeping so deeply I didn't hear a thing. I roll my eyes. She's probably out drinking and wants me to join her.

Beep beep.

I open the text, already preparing my excuses.

Meet me at the hospital. Now. I'll be in the utility room next door to the men's theatre change rooms.

I stare at the words, confused. Why the hell does she want

me to meet her at work at this hour? And in what's essentially a cupboard? Is she fucking serious?

My phone beeps again.

I'll be there in five minutes. I'll wait all night if I have to. Please, Kitty.

I rub my eyes. What the hell is going on? I dial her number, but her phone rings out.

I'm on the verge of rolling over and going back to sleep, convinced it's all a big joke, when I hear Winnie's voice in my mind. *What on earth could have been so bad that he went and did something like that?*

Estelle is not trying to be cryptic, I realise, and she's not joking. She needs me. *Now.*

As a medical student I sat a lot of exams. As a junior doctor I will sit more, and to get onto specialist training more again. Doctors are examined until eternity, but this may be the most important test I ever face. I must not fail.

I scramble out of bed, pull on some clothes, grab my keys and slip out of number 19, shutting the door quietly behind me.

I hurry up North Avenue towards the hospital, which looms over the street menacingly in the dark. Whatever Estelle is going to tell me, I know it has to be bad. There's no way we would be rendezvousing in a utility cupboard at this time on a Thursday night unless the situation had reached a crisis point.

I walk into the hospital, trying not to look too conspicuous. I rehearse in my head what I'll say if I run into anyone I know. ('Can you believe it? I left my wallet at work. I got so stressed out I had to come in now and look for it.')

The hospital is deserted, the hustle and bustle of the daytime replaced with the eeriness of the dim lights of the after-hours shift. I go up the stairs and swipe myself through the door that leads to the operating theatres. As I get closer to the utility room, I see that the door is slightly ajar—Estelle has beaten me here.

I take a breath and steel myself for the worst.

When I push open the door I see Estelle sitting on the floor with a mop between her legs. She looks up and our eyes lock. For a moment I can't say anything.

Her eyes are so puffy they're like slits. Her beautiful thick hair is dishevelled and she is wearing a ripped scrub top. It looks as if she left the house after dressing herself in the dark.

'It's happened, mate,' she says. 'The worst has happened.'

I wait.

'I've killed someone.'

I stare at her. I don't understand what she means.

'All interns kill people,' I say. 'It happens all the time. It's just part of being a doctor. It's not our fault.' Estelle knows this as well as I do, and inside I know that we're not meeting in a utility room late at night because a ninety-nine-year-old with pneumonia has died on Estelle's night shift.

I sit down next to her, moving a mop and a bag of adult nappies out of the way.

'Do you remember that little boy I had to intubate when we were out in the middle of fucking nowhere?' she asks, her voice hoarse.

'I thought that turned out okay!' I say, feeling the panic rise.

Estelle shakes her head. 'Apparently it went to the coroner.'

I hadn't realised the patient died.

'But that doesn't mean you killed him,' I protest loudly. 'Every unexpected medical death goes to the coroner.'

We hear a clanging sound from the wall behind us, where some hapless registrar is undoubtedly getting ready to go into theatre.

'Shhh!' Estelle hisses.

'Sorry,' I whisper. 'But why has this come up now?'

Estelle puts her head in her hands. 'They're doing an inquest. I've been called to give evidence.'

'Fuck!' I exclaim.

The clanging next door stops.

'Shhhhh!'

I put my hand over my mouth.

'I got home pretty late,' she explains in a whisper, 'and there was a letter in the mailbox.'

I cringe. I can barely handle an electricity bill, let alone a career-ruining summons to appear in court.

'I freaked out. I decided to wait until I knew less people would be around, then I came back here to see if I could access the Wingabby system from our computers. You know, to see what I'd documented at the time. But I couldn't access it.' Her fingers are tapping the ground nervously. 'I tried to call you, but you weren't answering. So I texted you and then came and hid in here.'

I'm still trying to take it all in. 'So what did the letter say?' I ask finally. 'Do you have to go to court? Can't you just—I don't know—submit a written statement?'

'No,' she says, sounding tired. 'I don't think they're looking to blame me, necessarily, but I have to go to court. Everyone will know what happened . . . It'll be in the paper for sure. You know how the media loves slamming doctors. It'll probably wreck my job prospects—no one wants to hire someone who's been linked to such a major fuck-up this early on in their career.'

'What was the cause of death?' I say, almost too afraid to ask.

She looks totally defeated. 'They're not one hundred per cent sure yet—they still need to wait a few weeks for the forensic analysis. But apparently when they opened him up the ETT tube was in his oesophagus, going into his stomach.'

I swallow.

'I intubated a child's fucking oesophagus,' Estelle whispers, wiping away tears. 'I stuck a tube that was meant to go into an airway into the food pipe instead. It's no good, mate. I definitely killed him. He wouldn't have been getting any oxygen. I shoved the tube down the wrong hole, and now he's dead.'

I can't think of a single thing to say.

'I killed him,' she repeats.

'But it was just a mistake!' I whisper furiously. 'You had no support, you were stuck there alone, you did the best you could! Mistakes like that happen all the fucking time!'

'Yeah, and kids don't always die,' Estelle replies flatly.

We sit there in the dark in complete silence.

I feel sick.

'Inquests are standard practice,' I say finally, trying to reassure her. 'They have to do them—heaps of surgeons have shit go wrong and go to inquests and then everyone forgets about it. Remember that cardiac surgeon ages ago? When that kid died? I'll show you the articles.'

'It's different when you're a boss,' she points out. 'They're protected because they make the private hospital so much money.

No one gives two shits about putting us in situations they know we can't handle then throwing us under the bus.'

'That's not true!' I protest, knowing even as I say it that she's right.

We've lapsed into silence again when another clang comes from behind the wall, a little louder than the previous sounds. It seems to be uncomfortably close to where we're sitting, and Estelle and I shift uneasily. The last thing we need is for anyone to overhear us discussing this train wreck.

'I shouldn't be telling you this here,' Estelle whispers. 'I don't even know why I suggested we meet in this cupboard. I just felt so overwhelmed and I couldn't breathe and it was the only place I could think of to hide.'

'Well, I know number nineteen is a bit shabby, but maybe next time you should just come over,' I tease gently.

Estelle half smiles. 'I better go,' she says, the horror of her situation crossing her face like a fleeting shadow.

We both stand up. I push the door open and we step into the corridor. As we walk quietly towards the stairs, I feel suddenly like we are ghosts. Shadows of ideas and happiness, echoes in time, floating through an old dimly lit hospital corridor with all the other memories of people suffering.

It isn't until we get to the front of the hospital that I realise with dismay that I have left my keys in the utility cupboard.

'You go,' I tell Estelle, annoyed with myself. 'I'll see you tomorrow.'

I return to the operating theatres, jog back down the hallway to the cupboard and push the door open. Using my phone light, I manage to locate my keys almost immediately. Relieved, I pick them up and turn to leave when I'm startled by the sound of a high-pitched giggle floating through the wall.

I stop.

It sounds like a woman, I think, confused. But I'm sure the cupboard adjoins the men's change room.

Could it be the cleaner?

I hear a shuffling sound, then the giggle again. It's definitely female. And it sounds almost familiar.

I know I should leave, but curiosity gets the better of me. It sounds like one of the surgeons is getting a little bit of extra action with a theatre nurse.

I hear a moan, and then a man's voice says, 'That's it, you little slut. That's it, take that dick.'

Jesus. This is getting heavy. Okay, I understand that people might get into that kind of role play in the privacy of their own homes, but to do it in the operating theatre change room is too much. And I find the word 'slut' offensive.

'Suck it, bitch.'

All of a sudden I want to vomit. I know who the voice belongs to. He's only been making my life hell for the last eight months. It's the Joker.

I stand there, paralysed. In my moment of indecision, which feels like an eternity, I hear the Joker panting and groaning his way through what sounds like the world's most disgusting blow job. When it finally ends, I have my fingers in my ears. I can't imagine what poor nurse would think it's a good idea to go down on a man as revolting as that.

There's some murmuring, and then the squeal of hinges as a door is opened. Thank God, they're leaving.

I give them a few minutes' head start then push open the door of the closet. I need to go home. I need to get out of this parallel universe of mops and dead babies and inquests and blow jobs and go the fuck back to bed.

As I step into the corridor, the door of the men's change room swings open.

'Katarina! What the fuck are you doing here? Aren't you meant to be sick?'

I gape at her. I can't believe it. It's the Smiling Assassin.

thirty-four

WE BOTH STAND VERY STILL.

I stare in horror at the Smiling Assassin, who isn't smiling now. Her eyes have such a frightening glint in them, I fear for a moment that she's going to hit me.

'Ah . . .' At first I can't speak. For the second time this evening, I'm rendered speechless. Then the words rush out in a flood, unfiltered. 'You gave him a blow job? But he's disgusting! He treats everyone like shit—he *is* a shit! I mean, seriously? A blow job in the men's change rooms? What the actual fuck? Are you—'

'You think I enjoy it?' she hisses, cutting me off. 'You actually think I enjoy doing that?' Her eyes burn like coals. 'It's all right for you,' she spits at me. 'You don't even care. You'll never make it as a surgeon. You don't have what it takes. You have to want it more than anything, and you have to *give it everything*. Don't you get it? DON'T YOU FUCKING GET IT?!'

No, I think, staring at her. I definitely don't get it.

'But you've just sucked off the most horrible man I've ever met!' I say incredulously. 'Are you out of your fucking mind?'

'I want to keep my job!' she nearly screams at me. 'Do you know how hard it is for a woman to get a surgical position at this hospital? I don't have any choice! I have worked so hard to become a surgeon. I have sacrificed years of my life. And if I have to give one creep a few blow jobs to keep this job, then I'll fucking do it. Don't you understand, you naive little girl? Don't you know what he'll do to me if I say no? This is how the hospital works! OPEN YOUR FUCKING EYES!'

Her words echo around the deserted hallway. I just stand there, dumbstruck. Every word is like a sharp slap in the face.

She's out of breath, and I can see her eyes glistening with tears. Sadness, or anger—probably both.

'If you tell anyone about this, I'll ruin you,' she says.

Then she turns and walks quickly away.

PART III

death

'Sex is also the revenge on death. Don't forget death. Don't ever forget it.'

Philip Roth, *The Dying Animal*

thirty-five

WHEN I WAS A CHILD I WAS A BIT OF A WORRIER. MUM liked to say I was the only five-year-old with a frown line because I worried so much. My parents thought about taking me to a child psychologist but, in the end, Dad started to meditate with me before I went to sleep.

Every night Dad and I went and stood under the worry tree, which was in fact of the lemon variety. Together we hung my worries out one by one on the branches and watched them flutter in the breeze. I was able to go to sleep, knowing that my worries were somewhere else, and that the next day I could take any new worries I thought of to the tree.

Now, as I sit on my bed after walking home from the disaster inside the utility room and outside the change rooms, I think to myself that the lemon tree from my childhood isn't nearly big enough. I need an enormous oak.

I don't sleep a wink. Estelle texts me first thing in the morning to let me know that she's taking three days off. She asks if I can write her a script for valium. I text her back asking if she's okay, but she doesn't reply. I mentally remind myself to nick a script from the ward.

I get dressed for work with an ever-increasing sense of dread and leave the house deliberately early, avoiding Max and Winnie.

I reach the surgical ward to find the Smiling Assassin is already there, also unusually early.

I nod in her direction. 'Hey.' I can't look her in the eye.

'Hey.' Her tone is clipped. We round in complete silence, apart from her occasional instruction.

When we reach the fourth patient, I comment that his blood pressure has been a little on the low side. She nods.

'I have to go to theatre,' she says suddenly, looking me in the eye for the first time. 'You can finish the round without me.'

'Ah . . .' I think of some of the really sick patients that we haven't seen yet, like Mr Trajevski in bed 9, who has had a huge tumour removed and has only just come out of intensive care.

Then I remember what her face looked like after our unexpected encounter last night and nod. 'No worries,' I say. 'I'll let you know if there are any issues.'

By the time I've seen the rest of my list, I pity the Smiling Assassin so much it makes me feel incredibly depressed. It was a lot easier to hate her, I realise as I order a CT scan for Mr Trajevski. I like giving blow jobs to men I'm wildly attracted to, but I firmly believe the act should be enjoyable for both parties. To fellate someone as revolting as the Joker surely isn't worth it, not even for a good reference. *Especially not* for a good reference, I correct myself.

I walk down to the cafeteria for a break, feeling incredibly tired. I can't wait until the year ends. Maybe I can request a transfer to a new hospital, or something.

'Hey!' I look up from my coffee to see Max walking towards me.

'Hey.'

I don't know whether to tell Max what happened last night with Estelle and then the Smiling Assassin. I have a feeling these are things that shouldn't be shared lightly. Luckily, Max is starting nights, which means we won't see much of each other. Usually when he works weird hours he spends half the time at his mum's place; his room there is darker, which makes it easier to sleep in during daylight hours.

'You left early this morning,' he says, plonking down next to me. 'That desperate to get to work after your sick day, huh?'

'Something like that,' I agree.

'I didn't get home until pretty late last night.' Max takes the lid off his coffee and scoops up the foam with his finger. 'I was helping Dr Glass in theatre. I reckon he'll give me a good reference.'

'That's good.' I try to sound enthusiastic.

Max doesn't seem to notice. In fact, he seems distracted himself. Probably the stress of surgical applications.

'Estelle wants to meet up with me and the Godfather after work,' he says after a pause. 'Said she has something to tell us. You know she's taken a few days off work?'

I'm momentarily relieved. A problem shared is a problem halved, or quartered.

'Estelle's in the shit,' I tell him. 'I'd better let her tell you in person.'

Max looks at me but doesn't push. 'Is that why you're a bit flat?'

'Yeah, I guess.' I don't elaborate. 'You don't seem that thrilled to be here either,' I point out.

'I really don't want to start nights,' he says with a frown. 'I wish I was still on respiratory.'

Max's night shifts cover the medical ward, which is probably the worst job in the entire hospital—aside from mine, I realise.

'At least I'm going to Europe in a month or so,' he says, forcing a smile. 'Thank God we get annual leave. I mean, they wouldn't give it to us if they didn't have to, but at least that's something.'

I wish I was going to Europe with Max, I think with a sigh.

We sit in silence, staring into our coffees. My pager goes off. It's the Joker. *Come to theatre.*

I leave Max to his misery and walk towards the operating theatre.

The oak tree, overwhelmed with leaves of worry, has transformed into a forest.

thirty-six

I COUNT DOWN THE MINUTES TO THE END, SECOND BY second. The remaining days on neurosurgery are nothing short of torture. I'm dreading starting my term in emergency after Estelle's less-than-positive descriptions of her time in there ('Totally fucked up'), but anything has to be better than this.

The atmosphere in operating theatre six is so tense it feels like the scalpels can cut air as well as skin. The Joker, having no idea of my recent insights into his relationship with his registrar, is his usual intolerable self.

The Smiling Assassin and I have gone from active dislike to active avoidance. She starts showing up late to the ward rounds and finishes early, by default leaving me in charge of all the post-operative patients, which isn't ideal. The Shark notices I am a single-doctor show and corners me after the trauma meeting on my last day of neurosurgery.

'Doesn't your registrar round with you anymore?' he asks as I press the button to take the lift. 'The nurses tell me you're running the neurosurgical ward these days.'

'It's fine.' I try to smile reassuringly. 'She's usually there. It's just because they're so busy in theatre now with all the traumas coming in, you know . . . I can always call her.'

'Mmm.' He doesn't sound convinced.

'I'm liking the responsibility,' I lie, wondering why I'm protecting the Smiling Assassin and briefly considering what will happen if I tell him the truth.

'You're doing well,' he says, to my surprise. 'You should think about doing surgery.'

Despite the fact I have spent the last God-knows-how-many years imagining myself as a surgeon, for some reason the remark seems totally ridiculous, and I can't help laughing.

The Shark looks offended. 'It wasn't meant as a joke,' he says tersely.

I pull myself together. 'I don't know if it's for me anymore,' I say honestly as I get into the lift, 'but thanks.'

I walk onto the ward for my solo round, still grinning. It isn't that funny, but the irony amuses me. What is it the French say? *L'humour est la politesse du désespoir.* Humour is the politeness of despair. Regardless, I enjoy the politeness; laughter has been somewhat lacking in recent times.

'Dr Prince is back from New York,' a nurse informs me. 'He wants to do a round.'

Despite everything that has transpired, I feel butterflies flapping around in my stomach as I walk into the nurses' station. He's staring at the patient board. I clear my throat.

He turns around, and the butterflies start whirring their wings more frantically. I can't believe, after everything I now know about surgery and surgeons, that he still has this ridiculous effect on me.

His eyes are grey today, I notice, as he pulls off his scrub cap absentmindedly. 'I'm sure I have another patient I've forgotten,' he tells me. 'I must still be on New York time.'

'Sounds pretty fun to me.'

We both grin.

'Oops, sorry!' I remember. 'I'm meant to say *tjena*!'

He looks thrilled. 'How was Lund?'

'It was great,' I tell him, sitting on the edge of the desk next to him. 'Wolfgang and Tomas were fantastic.'

'You know they're coming out here in two months or so. They'll be in Sydney for a few days before we go to this conference in Fiji.'

'I know,' I tell him. 'I've invited them over for dinner.'

He looks surprised. 'That's very kind of you.'

'Tomas had me over for dinner,' I explain. 'I can't cook as well as he can, but I promised them I'd give it a go.'

He nods and doesn't say anything. I take in his face, the grey-blue eyes and the half-smile, the wrinkles etched into his temples, not quite covered by short brown hair. I want to tell him everything—about what I overheard in the theatre change rooms, about Wolfgang and Nicole, about Estelle. I want to get to know him, properly, away from the operating theatre and the neurosurgical ward. But I can't think how to begin. So I ask him which patient he wants to visit first, and the round begins.

We walk to bed 3, and he talks to Mrs Jackson about how she's feeling. I check the obs chart. Stable.

He turns to me, closing the curtain behind him. 'Did you cross the bridge?'

'Sorry?' I'm still recording Mrs Jackson's respiratory rate.

'The bridge between Denmark and Sweden,' he says. 'Wolfgang has told me it's beautiful.'

I look up from the chart. 'God, it is amazing, you know,' I say with feeling, remembering the windmills emerging from the ocean. 'I've never seen anything quite like it.'

'Good enough to write about?'

I smile. 'Definitely good enough to write about.'

He looks around. 'Do I really only have the two patients?' he asks. 'There's no one else to see?'

'You're pretty quiet,' I explain. 'I guess because you've been away and everything.'

I wish suddenly that he had every single patient in the hospital, and that the round could go on for days.

He pushes his scrub cap back onto his head, signalling it's time to return to the operating theatre.

'I believe this might be our last round together,' he says lightly.

'I know,' I reply. 'And to think we're spending it here in Sydney when we could be in Lund!'

'Maybe another time,' he says, catching my eye as we stand there in our scrubs at the end of the ward. 'I'm sure stranger things have happened.'

You've got no idea, I think.

I watch him walk away, a blue blur returning to the fluorescent lights and open brains, and take a big breath.

'You know—' a nurse moves to stand beside me '—I've never

known Jack to round so much. On some terms you never see him. He's really made an effort this term.'

'He has?'

'Admin must have had a word with him,' she says knowingly. 'He's been in their bad books for years.'

I walk home from my last day of neurosurgery feeling cheerful. The feeling lasts all the way until number 19, when I enter the house and hear Estelle say, 'Yeah, so, I'm totally screwed.'

I find her in the living room, talking to Max and Winnie.

'The eternal optimist strikes again,' I can't resist saying as I throw myself down next to her.

'Estelle really is screwed, though,' Max points out. 'Even more than me, and I've got a criminal record.'

Estelle glares at him. 'Thanks, friend.'

I shoot Max a look. 'I thought you were going to stay at your mum's.'

'I was,' he explains, 'but she started on at me about paying her rent and how I eat too much of her food. I just needed some time out.'

Whenever Max gets stressed, he vanishes to his mother's place. He likes the home-cooked meals and the cleanliness. He usually stays until she starts hassling him about paying rent, which is when he reappears at number 19.

'You do eat too much food,' Winnie pipes up. 'Where's that chicken I made the other day, for example?'

Max looks irritated. 'God, don't you start,' he snaps. 'Just give me a fucking break, okay?'

'I think we all just need to calm down,' I say, surprised at how high tensions are running as Winnie and Max glower at each other. 'It's been a stressful week.'

'And what would you know?' Max demands, standing up and turning his glare on me. 'I'm going to get some sleep before I start this fucking run of nights.'

Estelle raises her eyebrows as he storms into his bedroom. We hear the door slam.

'Max is really on edge,' Estelle says. 'What's wrong with him anyway?'

'I think it's the shift work,' I say. 'He really hates working nights.'

Winnie looks over at me. 'Estelle's been telling me what happened,' she says, sounding worried.

'I figured maybe Winnie could give me some advice, since she's a lawyer.'

'I work in tax,' Winnie reminds her.

'Hey, did you end up finding your keys that night?' Estelle asks me out of nowhere.

'Did you lose your keys *again*?' Winnie is amused.

'Yes, I lost them again,' I snap, 'but I found them, okay?' I'm surprised to hear the edge in my own voice. I hadn't meant to sound so angry. 'It was a few weeks back.'

Winnie looks affronted. 'All right, no need to be so aggro.'

'I'm not!'

Winnie stares at me. 'Kitty,' she says gently, 'what's wrong?'

We've known each other for two decades; I don't know why I ever thought I could hide anything from her. 'I have to tell you something,' I hear myself saying.

Winnie raises her eyebrows.

'So the night I thought I lost my keys . . .'

I tell them everything. By the time I finish, with the Smiling Assassin warning me not to tell anyone what I saw or she'll ruin me, Estelle is shaking her head so hard I think it's going to fall off, and Winnie is looking appalled.

'But of course you have to tell someone!' Winnie exclaims.

There's a silence.

'Well, it's not that simple . . .' I say hesitantly.

'It sounds totally fucked, though,' Winnie interrupts indignantly. 'Like, it's a total abuse of power, not to mention unhygienic. Who blows someone in a place they're meant to get changed in before doing an operation?'

'Yes, okay. But what are you proposing? That I go to admin and say I heard my registrar blowing the junior consultant while I was hiding in a utility room late one night?'

Estelle, quick to understand the likely outcome of a very junior doctor going over the heads of her superiors and also adopting the usual medic approach of being a huge fence-sitter, takes my side. 'I agree. I don't think you have much choice other than to stay quiet. As far as I'm concerned it doesn't leave this room. We shouldn't even tell Max or the Godfather.'

Winnie looks even more horrified. 'But someone's abusing someone and getting away with it! Of course you have to report it! Kitty, you know you can't just turn a blind eye to this stuff.'

'I know!' I get where Winnie's coming from, but at the same time I can't see an easy way out. 'I don't like it either, but . . . well, it's tricky.'

Winnie is shaking her head. 'You guys are always talking about the shit you have to deal with as junior doctors, but then you're too scared to say anything that might lead to change.'

I sigh. 'Maybe I could talk to admin,' I say half-heartedly. 'I guess I could at least make them aware of it.'

Estelle isn't convinced. 'Winnie, you don't get it,' she says straight out. 'You don't know what it's like to actually work inside a system like that. Weird sexual shit aside, we're all copping heaps of abuse in different forms every day. The best thing you can do is stay quiet and try to survive.'

'Yeah, but at what cost?' Winnie sounds incredulous. I know she's thinking about her mum and Dr George.

At what cost? It's a good question. One I can't answer, or don't want to.

Estelle, tired of the argument, announces she's going home.

When she's gone, Winnie gives me a long look. 'I can't believe you, Kitty. You know what he's doing, and you're just going to say nothing? What has happened to you?'

'You didn't see her face when she realised I'd heard,' I try to explain. I feel miserable.

'No wonder she's been so mean to you.' Winnie runs her hands through her hair. 'No wonder! I'd be being fucking mean too if I thought I had to give my boss a head job in the toilets at work to get a fucking promotion. She must be so fucking on edge and stressed out. She wasn't in her right mind when she threatened you. You have to report this, Kitty!'

'You don't understand, Winnie,' I say, feeling the anger rising—at who I'm not quite sure. At Winnie, because I know deep down that she's right; at the system for allowing such a situation to occur; at the Joker for being such a pig; at the Smiling Assassin for wanting to be a surgeon so much she is prepared to do whatever it takes—even this.

'You don't work as a doctor,' I continue. 'You think we just go in there and heal people—that we wake up every day just not being able to wait to get into that hospital to commence the fucking healing. There's not actually that much healing, don't you get it? There's so much pressure coming from every angle. And tomorrow I've got a ten-hour shift in emergency, with drunk people and sick people and the unrelenting pressure to SEE MORE PATIENTS. I'm barely keeping my head above water, and to deal with this on top of it is bringing me to breaking point!'

'Bringing *you* to breaking point? What about *her*?!'

'If I tell anyone and she denies it I'll be in so much shit!' I hear my voice getting louder as I attempt to justify why I sound like such a selfish wimp. 'And even if she doesn't deny it, there'll be people who don't believe me or who'll just blame me for causing trouble. I'm so junior that nothing I say really matters. You think you get what it's like being a doctor because you live with me and Max, but you don't get any of it! YOU JUST DON'T GET IT!' I am shouting now.

Winnie is looking at me with an expression on her face I've never seen before.

'I'm sorry,' I say weakly, feeling my heart beating uncomfortably in my chest. 'That wasn't fair. I'm sorry.'

For a few moments neither of us speaks. Then Winnie says, 'I don't know who you are anymore, Kitty. I just don't know who the fuck you are.'

Her words hang in the air. The lump in my throat and chest is the size of Everest.

She stands up and lunges at me.

Absurdly, I fear she is about to hit me and I jerk away, but instead she grabs my hand and drags me to my feet, then pulls me over to the mirror on the wall.

'Look in the mirror, Kitty!' she orders. I can tell she is trying very hard to make me understand, even through the waves of anger and disappointment. 'Look in the mirror and tell me what you see!'

I look. I see my long dark brown hair, pulled back in a messy bun because I didn't have time to brush it. I see my green eyes and my slightly too big nose, and my frame, thinner than normal because I exist on a diet of wine and coffee and overpriced salads from the cafeteria. I look afraid.

Beside me I see Winnie: short blonde hair, big blue eyes, an angry expression.

'I . . .' I don't know what to say. 'I don't . . .'

'What are you so afraid of, Kitty?' Winnie's voice is steady now. 'What the fuck are you so afraid of? You never used to be like this. Remember my first job in a law firm, when I was too scared to quit even though I was being bullied? And I said to you, *I can't leave, I can't. I'll never get another job; I just have to stay and be miserable.* Do you remember what you told me?'

I do remember, but I am too ashamed to say.

'You told me never to make decisions based on fear,' she reminds me, her words as piercing as a laser beam. 'And what are you doing now? Tell me.'

I can't speak. I just keep staring at the reflection of that girl with her messy hair and her green eyes, and I ask myself the same question: *What are you doing now?*

'You're making decisions and choices that are driven by fear!' Winnie shouts, finally losing control. 'And not just about this—about every fucking thing! I was in Switzerland when you met Fabien. I saw how happy you were! I see your face when he's called or messaged you! And yet you can't even bring yourself to mention his fucking name. Why? Why can't you let yourself be happy?'

'I . . .' I can't speak. I just keep staring at my reflection.

Who is that girl?

'Is it because he's not a doctor? Because he's not as smart as you, the amazing Dr Katarina Holliday? What's so great about being a fucking doctor anyway? All it does is make you fucking miserable!'

'It's not that,' I say. 'It's . . .'

'What is it?' Winnie asks, sounding almost desperate. 'Tell me, because at this moment I don't understand. When we were younger all we used to talk about was the pursuit of love and truth and comedy and whatever else would make us happy. Love and truth and fucking laughs, Kitty, and you and me and our happy lives! Where's the love and where's the truth? There aren't any laughs at the moment, I can tell you that.'

Truth and love and laughs—lost to me now. I'm in a dark place and I have no idea how to find my way back.

'I hate this!' Winnie says suddenly, stepping away from the mirror. She gestures angrily, and her wineglass slips out of her hand, a perfect arc until it hits the ground. It smashes on the floorboards, and instinctively I step back, like a dog with an injured paw, trying to avoid the glass, but a shard pierces my foot. I reach down without even thinking and pull the piece of glass straight out. It hurts, but part of me enjoys the pain. The blood drips everywhere, down my toes and onto the wooden floorboards.

Winnie, snapping out of her anger, looks horrified.

'God, Kit, I'm sorry. I don't know what came over me.'

'No, no, it's all right.' I am numb, staring at the blood falling on the wood. 'I'll fix it.'

I limp into the bathroom, but instead of washing the blood away I just sit on the edge of the bath. I watch it drip onto the floor, the red shocking on the white ceramic, pooling on the bathroom tiles.

Out damned spot.

I lift my head up and gaze at my reflection in the bathroom mirror. I hear Winnie, imploring me: *Look in the mirror, Kitty. Look in the mirror and tell me what you see.*

I see Alice falling down the rabbit hole.
Going under a white sea of Propofol.
Lost in blood and knives
And other people's lives.

My intern is a poet.

I sit there, staring at myself in the mirror, the blood on my foot coagulating.

I wish I was skiing with Fabien, I think. I wish I was standing next to him on a ski slope, a bit tipsy after a peach schnapps or two, as he says, 'Let's just see where we end up, sexy bum!'

Let's just see where we end up.

I bite my lip, tasting blood. Is this it? Is this where I've ended up?

In a daze, I wipe up the blood with some tissues, and limp up the stairs to my bedroom. I lie down and close my eyes, ignoring the light of the hospital streaming through the cracks in my shutters, and wait for the nightmares to come.

thirty-seven

I OPEN MY EYES THE NEXT MORNING AND IMMEDIATELY close them again. Never, I think to myself, lying there with my eyes shut, have I been so close to full-blown melancholic depression. I feel like I'm in a very deep and dark ocean, swimming against the tide. The feeling is so strong that my limbs are heavy, and just the thought of dragging myself out of bed and into my new scrubs, with *Holy Innocents Hospital Emergency Doctor* inscribed on the pocket, fills me with lead.

Emergency. Casualty. A&E. The way people on TV carry on, you'd think A&E stood for Adventure and Excitement, not Accident and Emergency.

I spent time in emergency as a medical student, so I already have an idea of what's waiting for me. The emergency department is another world. There are no windows and the fluorescent lights are bright 24/7, because it's a place that literally never sleeps. Whether it's 1 pm or 1 am, it feels the same. It's like a chaotic morgue, where the patients are alive (mostly).

Theoretically, my emergency term, sandwiched as it is between my relief and next surgical term, means a break from the likes of the Joker and the Smiling Assassin, but it isn't really the kind of reprieve I long for. I want a villa on the Amalfi Coast, not a resuscitation bay.

The only good thing, I remind myself, picking up my phone to see the time—8 am—is that I'm starting on night shifts. This isn't a good thing per se, and it won't feel anything close to good tonight, but it does mean that right now I have an excuse to down a glass of wine and a valium, and drift off into pharmaceutically induced oblivion. A benefit is that it will enable me to avoid an encounter with Winnie, who might come home from work wanting to talk about our argument. Nothing will penetrate this combination, I think almost gleefully as I walk downstairs to fill my own prescription.

I wash the tablet down with wine, then go back to bed. A sense of enormous relief comes over me as I let myself go under the wonderful ocean of dense, dark sleep for ten straight hours.

As I walk into the hospital to start my first night shift in the ED, I wonder whether the odd feeling in my stomach is excitement or dread, or a combination of both. Then I step over a drunk twenty-something-year-old girl by the hospital entrance whose stream of vomit nearly hits my shoe, and I just feel tired.

I lean down. 'Are you all right?' I ask her, trying not to gag at the smell.

'Urghhhh,' she moans, her head lolling to the side.

Her friend, not quite as smashed but swaying next to her, looks at me. 'Are you a nurse?' she slurs.

Ignoring the question, I ask the girl who's vomited, 'Have you taken any drugs tonight? Or just booze?'

'Just booze,' she mutters. 'Can't you give me something to stop me being sick? Aren't nurses meant to help people?'

'There's a girl vomiting outside,' I inform the triage nurse as I swipe myself in. 'She's conscious but she's pretty drunk.'

The triage nurse rolls her eyes.

'Booze, apparently,' I say, pointing to the front door.

'Tell the paramedics inside,' the triage nurse says flippantly.

I sigh.

'Drunk girl outside the front door vomiting everywhere,' I tell the ambulance guys hovering by the main desk. 'I'd get her in here, but I think it needs man power.'

At least the paramedics don't argue. Nurses are a different story.

The relationship between doctors and nurses is a tricky one. There's this misconception that everyone should feel sorry for nurses, and the doctors are always the bad guys. We are, members of the general public tell me, overpaid, arrogant and difficult to deal with. Nurses, conversely, are underpaid and overworked, and always seem to make the patients feel so much better. I hear people say all the time in social settings that their medical team 'did nothing for them' (aside from saving their life), but the nurses, 'well, they were lovely'. There are even bumper stickers that say: BEHIND EVERY DOCTOR IS A SKILLED, INTELLIGENT NURSE SAVING THEIR ARSE. Of course, these are treacherous waters I'm entering—saying anything less than positive about nurses is sort of like saying anything less than positive about Nelson Mandela.

On that note, I walk into the department to meet the consultant on the floor that evening for a quick orientation, and within the first five seconds she's warning me that the nurses in the emergency department are extremely territorial. 'The best thing to do,' she advises, 'is to just let them boss you around for a while. I'm not sure why they're like that, but if you resist they can make your life very hard.' Then she laughs a bit nervously—this consultant emergency physician of over twenty years' experience—leans in and says, 'But for God's sake, don't tell anyone I said that.'

It takes about two days working in a public hospital as a junior doctor to realise that nurses love nothing more than bitching about how useless we are, how much more experience they have, how they always know better than us, but in the end it all comes down to one sticking point.

When a nurse doesn't know what to do . . . they call a doctor.

When a nurse needs a medication charted . . . they call a doctor.

When the patient's blood pressure drops even slightly . . . they call a doctor.

When the nurse makes a mistake and starts panicking . . . they call a doctor.

When someone makes a mistake and it ends up in court, the person who takes the stand will inevitably be . . . the doctor.

On an evening shift on the ward, a nurse of ten or more years' experience still looks after the maximum of four or five patients. A doctor in their first week of training is looking after three wards—maybe a hundred and ten patients.

Emergency nurses, I realise about two hours into my first night shift, are particularly problematic. They have more skills than ward nurses, which gives them more confidence. The nice ones are a dream to work with. The not-so-nice ones add another layer of anxiety. In the eyes of emergency nurses, all new junior doctors are put on trial. Apparently, they give you a month and then, if they decide they don't like you, they refuse to help you. With anything. The Godfather slept with the wrong nurse early into his emergency term and he paid for it until his last shift.

'Katarina, your cannula field isn't clean enough,' Mandy, the head nurse in emergency, snaps as she picks up the cannulation equipment I've arranged in order to stick a drip in a seriously dehydrated patient. 'I'm throwing it out. Get yourself another one and I'm going to watch and see that you're doing it properly.'

'Maybe you can put the cannula in, Mandy,' I suggest. 'I've got five patients at the moment and one is about to go into theatre.'

'I'm not up to date with my accreditation,' she says smugly, 'so you have to do it.'

Nurses love not being up to date with their accreditation, which is an excuse not to work. Doctors don't need to be accredited or taught new skills. We're just expected to learn on the job.

'It's all right, Kitty.' James, one of the other doctors, appears next to me. 'I'll do it for you.'

He rolls his eyes as Mandy storms off in a huff, annoyed that I have managed to avoid her on-the-spot cannulation assessment.

'Thanks, mate,' I say, feeling grateful I am on with decent doctors tonight. 'Appreciate it.'

It's nearly midnight, and James and I still have a good nine hours ahead of us. Maybe tonight there won't be many patients, I think hopefully.

I walk around the corner to have a look in the waiting room.

Every chair is full. Some of the people waiting try to catch my eye. Their expressions are angry, as if saying, 'We know you're a doctor—why haven't I been seen yet?' I feel my stomach clench.

When Max did his emergency term, he told me, he started altering his opening line when he saw patients. 'If they look well and the triage says they've come in for something like, I don't know, elbow pain they've had for a year, I used to open with: "Good evening, I'm the doctor seeing you tonight. What is your emergency?"'

I like that. 'What is your emergency?' I practise, trying not to sound as passive aggressive as I am feeling.

I walk back to the main department, where the doctors on the shift before mine are finishing up, leaving me, James and Matt, the senior, on overnight.

'How's it been?' I ask one of the doctors who's about to leave.

He shakes his head ruefully. 'Have you seen the waiting room?'

I nod. Have I ever.

'Yeah, it's been fucking shit,' he tells me, suppressing a yawn. 'Sorry to leave you with it.'

'It's all right,' I say. 'It's not your fault.'

'A patient told me tonight if I missed his vein when I cannulated him that he'd kill me,' the doctor tells me. 'I said, "Is that a threat on my life, sir?" And then I missed his vein anyway.'

We both laugh, even though it isn't that funny. If someone makes a threat like that on a flight, they'll be arrested. But threatening a doctor inside an emergency department while they're trying to help you is apparently nothing to worry about. People probably think it's a good thing; it might make us work faster.

Our hospital is, apparently, the best-performing emergency department in the state. It's debatable what this actually means. To the hospital board, it means that we're the best at meeting the government's arbitrarily created key performance indicators. Some genius, in all their wisdom, has created a timeframe called 'the four-hour rule'. If a patient isn't seen, reviewed, assessed, investigated, diagnosed and then treated or admitted to the ward in less than four hours, we're informed by the 'emergency department navigator' that 'we have breached'. The emergency department navigator is a nurse whose sole role is to harass the doctors on the floor when they fail to meet the timeframe. To ensure maximum humiliation, they call your name over a loudspeaker so the entire department knows you're going too slowly.

'Katarina, to the navigator's desk, please.'

They don't give two shits that you're seeing three or four patients at any given time, that most or all of them have something complex wrong with them, that you've called about a million specialists to come and review them but they're all stuck on the ward or in theatre. All that matters to the navigator is that every patient is either cured or at least shipped into an overcrowded ward within two hundred and forty minutes.

'Kitty, can you pick up the ear pain in the waiting room?' Matt asks me as I stare at the computer, trying to figure out which will be the least taxing patient. 'He's been here a while . . .'

He clicks my name off before I can respond, as if I actually have a choice, and I trundle into the waiting room to meet Jason, a thirty-seven-year-old male with a sudden onset left ear problem.

'Jason?'

Two men stand up, one looking pained. Jason, I discover, has brought along a friend, who happens to be a private ENT surgeon.

'I've already assessed him,' the surgeon tells me as I faff around asking Jason if he has any allergies. 'He's got sensorineural deafness. He needs to be admitted under ENT and given IV steroids, now.'

'Do you have admitting rights at this hospital?' I ask him hopefully, praying that he does and that I can fast-track an admission and avoid any awkward confrontations.

'No,' he says, looking annoyed, 'but it doesn't make any difference. That's what he needs.'

I examine the patient and quickly establish that Mr Private ENT Surgeon is indeed correct: Jason does have sensorineural hearing loss and does require urgent IV steroid therapy, stat.

'I think he needs to be admitted under ENT,' Mr Private Surgeon advises me for the third time.

I agree with him. I run it by Matt, who tries to bluster around the issue for a while, because no one likes being told what to do by other doctors on their own turf, but the outcome is inevitable.

'You're going to have to call ENT,' he tells me gloomily.

Reflexively, I check the time. It's 1.20 am. I swallow. If a patient has to be admitted or there's a problem that can't be solved by the emergency doctors, it means waking someone up and asking what to do. And even though senior specialists or their registrars are listed as on call overnight in case one of the emergency doctors needs some urgent advice, what 'on call' really means is: *I'm asleep. In bed. If you call me and wake me up, I'LL BE VERY FUCKING ANGRY.*

My stomach, irritatingly, clenches slightly at the thought of making the call. But no one in the best-performing emergency department in the state knows the correct dose of dexamethasone to administer for this kind of problem, so I really have no choice.

I call through switch. 'Can I have the ENT registrar, please?'

'Sure, love,' says Susan, who's on switch tonight. Then, 'Oh, it's Dr So and So.'

'Is he mean?' I ask with trepidation.

Susan sighs. 'Good luck, love,' she says. 'Putting you through now.'

'Wait!' I shout into the phone, panicking wildly, but it's too late; the phone is ringing. I'm committed.

The ringing stops abruptly, and I hear mumbling, like someone trying to wake up, then, 'Yes? What do you want?'

'Ah, hello. I'm so sorry to call you at this hour. I'm one of the junior doctors in emergency, and I have this patient . . .'

'What?'

'Ah, do you have a moment to discuss a patient?'

'It's one o'clock in the fucking morning!' the voice on the other end of the phone exclaims, sounding seriously annoyed. 'Why are you calling me at one in the fucking morning?'

Maybe Susan has put me through to the consultant, not the registrar. Maybe there's been a mistake and this person isn't even on call. Maybe this is a complete misdial, and this person isn't even a doctor but a complete random whom I've woken up in the early hours of the morning.

'Sorry, are you the ENT registrar on call?' I ask.

'Yes,' the voice says flatly.

'Oh, right.' I'm relieved. 'Look, I know it's a bad time to call, I'm really sorry, but it's kind of a touchy situation. This thirty-seven-year-old guy has come in with sudden onset hearing loss in his left . . .'

'You're calling me at one in the morning about hearing loss?' the voice interrupts me, dripping with disgust. 'What kind of idiot are you?'

'It's sensorineural deafness!'

'Give him some fucking steroids!'

'How much?'

'You're a fucking idiot! Don't call me again and don't admit him under us! He's not coming in under ENT!'

'If you could tell me the dose . . .' I plead, but it's to no avail; I'm now speaking to a dial tone.

I put the phone down. The waiting room's full and I still don't know what dose of steroid to give my patient.

I quickly wipe away the tears that have sprung to my eyes. This is no time for crying.

Matt walks over. 'How'd you go with ENT?' he asks.

I clear my throat. 'He wasn't very interested,' I confess. 'He said we couldn't admit to the ward under ENT. What should I do?' I'm wondering how I'm going to tell Mr Private Surgeon that his friend isn't going to be admitted under ENT.

'Well, admit under ENT, obviously,' Matt says cheerfully, patting me on the back. 'That's why they gave ED direct admitting rights.'

I try not to think about the ENT registrar's reaction when he arrives on the ward tomorrow morning to find I've admitted the patient he refused to discuss. I decide to make my signature extremely hard to read in the chart so he won't know what my name is. The reason why doctors have such messy handwriting suddenly becomes crystal clear.

'What dose of steroid should I start him on?' I ask.

Matt doesn't know.

'His surgeon mate would probably know,' I say.

'Maybe just ask him,' Matt says finally.

I walk down to the bed where my patient and his surgeon are waiting to see what will happen next.

'I've spoken with ENT,' I say, forcing a smile, 'and we're going to admit you.'

Mr Private Surgeon looks satisfied.

'So we'll just, ah, start you on the IV steroids now,' I add, my confidence faltering. I hold the medication chart and a pen. 'Just out of interest,' I say awkwardly, 'what dose of dex do you think you'd start on?'

'Oh, fifty milligrams,' the surgeon says, seeing straight through me, 'but it depends on what you want, of course.'

'Just what I was thinking!' I exclaim enthusiastically. 'Very good. Ah, good.'

I quickly chart the fifty milligrams of dexamethasone and tell the nurse in charge to get Jason to the ward as quickly as possible.

I look at the time: 2.30 am. Nothing stops the clock, I remind myself. As bad as things can get, nothing can stop the clock. In seven hours, I'll be crawling into bed.

I walk into the waiting room and call the next patient.

'Just come with me, I'm one of the doctors on tonight,' I say, forcing a smile.

The patient gets up, swaying. She glares at me. 'Well, it's about time, you motherfucker!' she declares loudly before falling over.

I'm so tired I don't even blink. 'I'd probably prefer it if you called me Katarina,' I say, grabbing her under one arm and hauling her off the floor.

Nothing stops the clock.

thirty-eight

THE WEEKS IN THE EMERGENCY DEPARTMENT, WHILE stressful, move quickly. It might be the odd shifts or the fast pace, but it starts to feel as if I'm going to sleep, waking up, going into the emergency department, then going home. During my runs of night shifts I lose contact with my friends aside from the odd text and spend daylight hours in a chemically induced coma before waking up in the dark to go to work.

I emerge from my stupor only briefly to a text from Wolfgang Dietrich informing me that he and Tomas have booked their flights to come to a conference in Australia and they are looking forward to the dinner I promised them. I feel forgotten emotions of excitement and happiness, and file this information away, telling myself that when the run of night shifts ends I will patch things up properly with Winnie and also tell her the good news that we will be hosting a dinner party. For now, though, it's back to the grind.

As I drag myself through the front doors of the emergency department at eleven for a night shift and see, yet again, the packed waiting room, I realise that most patients have zero idea of what constitutes an emergency.

Emergency means life-threatening anaphylaxis. Emergency means high-speed motor vehicle accident and abdominal trauma. Emergency means suicide attempt and huge drug overdose with acute liver failure. It doesn't mean a mild tummy ache that could be cured with Panadol, or a mosquito bite.

It occurs to me that there are a lot of very sad and unloved people in society for whom coming into the emergency department means that, at least for a little while, someone will care for them. I develop this theory as I sit in one of the assessment rooms five hours later, as the clock ticks over to 4 am, listening to the woman in front of me cry about her hip, which has been hurting for seven years.

Something breaks inside me.

'Look, Sandra,' I say, interrupting her long story, 'what's really going on?'

Most of the time they just want someone to talk to. Sandra came into the emergency department consciously seeking medical care but subconsciously seeking something else, something that I can't give her and something that no hospital can provide.

There are so many lonely people in this world. Their loneliness shrouds them, so they become invisible. They're in the corner of your eye, hovering in the periphery. Yet we always miss them—sometimes even when they're sitting right in front of us. For every attention-seeking time-waster who floats through the doors of the emergency department, there's another patient, invisible, who slips in between them. I'm always meeting these people at 4 am, I think sadly, hearing these stories when we all should be peacefully asleep in bed.

'I think my husband is cheating on me,' Sandra says, and starts to cry. 'And I'm scared I've got herpes.'

I take a look. Sandra is right. She has such a severe case of herpes she ends up being admitted under gynaecology for pain management. I write her up for regular morphine, feeling guilty.

People say you see life when you experience certain things. When you travel around the world, or get married, or have a baby. But the most I've learned about life has been while working in the emergency department in the early hours of a Tuesday morning. We're always told in magazines and online and in movies that life is this endless notion of possibility. We dream of the adventure, but we live a different sort of reality. The kind of reality that walks into a hospital at four in the morning. At 4 am in the emergency department, people feel like they don't need to pretend anymore.

I sit at the desk, writing up Sandra's notes, and wonder what they think of doctors, to give up these intensely personal things so easily. The stethoscope and the scrubs must give me an invisibility cloak of my own. People come in because they're seeking someone or something to make them feel better. A doctor in a hospital seems like a good answer.

But where do doctors go when they wake in the early hours and want reassurance and someone to talk to? It isn't inside a hospital. I suppose we think we know better than that. Or at least know that the answers we want won't be found in here.

All we'll find are people just like us, who know no more or less than all the things we already know.

Ay, I think as I close Sandra's chart and click off on the next patient, there's the rub.

thirty-nine

'HAVE YOU SPOKEN TO YOUR OLD REGISTRAR?'

I look up from my glass of prosecco, poured from a bottle that Winnie has gone and bought for me from the bottle shop up the road—kindly refraining from mentioning that it's only 9 am—and sigh. 'Mate, I'm really tired,' I say, trying to avoid the question. 'Can we talk about this when I finish this week of nights?'

'I bought you the prosecco so you'd talk to me!' she says belligerently. It's been weeks since our argument and we're yet to have a proper conversation about it. I've used the excuse of my weird hours and general fatigue to avoid any deep and meaningful discussions with Winnie, and we've kept it to pleasant exchanges.

'I thought you were just being nice.' I smile at her.

She shakes her head.

'You would have been a great surgeon,' I tell her. 'You really know how to cut to the chase.'

'I really think you should speak to her,' Winnie says, ignoring my remark. 'You don't know what could be happening to her now. He might be raping her for all we know.'

'She is a grown woman,' I point out, tired of where the conversation is going. 'She is above the age of consent.' Even as I say this, I know that, in my heart of hearts, I agree with Winnie. I just don't know what to do about it. 'You haven't said anything to Max, have you?' I ask.

Winnie shakes her head. 'God, he's been as distant as you lately. The night shifts really aren't great, are they? He's back at his mum's this week. Good thing he's going to Europe soon—the guy needs a happy infusion . . . Ah, fuck it,' she says suddenly. 'I'm going to have a prosecco too. I'm working from home today.'

'Gastro again?' I can't resist teasing.

She smiles. 'They're renovating the office,' she informs me, 'so we're not allowed to go in.'

As she pours herself a glass my phone pings with an incoming email. I glance down.

'It's from Wolfgang Dietrich!' I say to Winnie. 'The German guy living in Sweden. He and his mate Tomas are coming to Australia soon.'

I open the message and read it aloud.

Dear Kitty,

As per my text to you, we are arriving in Australia at the start of September. We are much looking forward to some Sydney sunshine, is very cold here in Lund and we have been working too hard and getting very fat. Tomas and I gratefully accept your dinner invitation . . . if it still stands? Just checking.

Best regards,
Wolfgang

Suddenly, there's a bright spot in the mess that is my life.

Winnie is grinning, the Smiling Assassin forgotten. 'We've got to do it! I love dinner parties. If we clean the house a bit, it'll be great!' Then she frowns. 'We don't have a dining table,' she points out. 'Do you reckon we could do a Japanese theme and eat on the floor?'

'I'll just buy a table,' I say. I can't really imagine Wolfgang appreciating eating on the floor. Surgeons are, after all, notoriously clean. 'It's an investment.'

We spend the morning exchanging emails with Wolfgang Dietrich. Dinner is planned for three and a half weeks away.

Will you invite Jack? Wolfgang asks. *He loves dinner parties. We can talk about art.*

Winnie looks at me. 'Maybe you should invite him. It's because of Dr Prince you even met these guys.'

'Wouldn't that be weird?' I feel a bit sick at the thought of asking Dr Prince over to number 19 for dinner, even with the excuse of his European friends.

She shrugs. 'I don't think so. It'd be weirder if you didn't invite him, I reckon. He'll most likely say no, but at least then you can say you did the right thing.'

I bite my lip. 'Should I . . . call him?' I immediately reject this idea as soon as I suggest it. I don't possess that kind of courage.

'Maybe text,' Winnie suggests. 'Just say, *Hey, Dr Prince, I've invited Wolfgang and Tomas to my house for dinner when they're in Sydney. You're very welcome to join us or swing by for a drink.* You know—just be cool about it.'

'I guess I did mention that I was having them over for dinner,' I agree. 'Like, this isn't a big surprise or anything.'

'You're work colleagues,' Winnie says confidently, with the air of someone who doesn't work inside a hospital. 'This makes sense.'

'Well, yes and no . . .' I don't know any other doctors as junior as me who casually invite consultant surgeons over to their crumbling old sharehouses for dinner.

'Come on, Kitty.' Winnie looks excited. 'Since when are you scared of anything? Like are you a man or a mouse?'

'I'm a mouse,' I admit freely, 'and I'm a lot more scared of things since being a doctor initiated the destruction of my personality and self-esteem.'

'That's exactly why you need to invite Dr Prince for dinner!' Winnie sounds more and more enthused by the idea. 'Get a bit of the old Kitty Holliday back—the one who used to take on double black ski runs without thinking twice!'

'This is Sydney, not Zermatt,' I remind her.

'God, Kitty! Stop thinking so much. Just send a fucking text!'

'Fine,' I say. Maybe the old me is lurking underneath the night shifts and the operating theatre and the doctor's scrubs. Maybe the old Kitty never really left; she was just waiting for the right moment to reappear.

Hi, Dr Prince,

I type, schussing down the proverbial black diamond run in my mind.

Wolfgang and Tomas are coming over to my house for dinner Sat night, in just over three weeks. You're very welcome to join us or come by for a drink, if you're free. Would be great if you could make it. Katarina.

I press send and throw the phone at Winnie. 'I did it,' I announce. 'I invited him.'

Winnie's eyes widen. 'You didn't,' she breathes. 'You didn't actually.'

'What? You're the one who told me to!'

We both start laughing uncontrollably.

'Oh my God, what if he doesn't reply?' I moan, staring at my phone which has taken on the appearance of a ticking time bomb.

Winnie busies herself with formulating the menu, and valiantly tries to distract me.

My phone sits on the table, taunting me with its silence.

'Do you think Italian?' she says. 'I make a really good lasagne.'

'Mmm.' I reach forward and put my phone under a cushion.

'Maybe turn it off,' Winnie suggests.

'But then I'll just have to turn it on again,' I point out.

'I reckon still turn it off.' She reaches forward, about to press the off button when the phone pings. Winnie starts. 'God,' she says, 'my heart is racing.'

We glance at each other.

'It's probably Mum,' I say, trying to ignore the butterflies boxing in my stomach.

'I can't look!' Winnie is staring at the phone. 'You look!'

I turn the phone over to see a miracle.

Dr Prince.

'Is it him?' Winnie's eyes are wide.

I nod. 'He's probably going to say no.' I press open.

The phone takes an eternity.

Hi Katarina, That sounds great. Let me know when and where. Looking forward. Jack.

I look at Winnie. She looks at me.

'Fuck, mate,' she says, shaking her head in complete disbelief. 'We really need to buy a dining table now.'

forty

I'M MERCIFULLY ROSTERED ON TO DAY SHIFTS FOR THE next month in the emergency department, but that still means 8 am to 6 pm, making it difficult to achieve any decent efforts at life admin—which has never been a strong point even when I'm not working a billion hours a week. I flee the emergency department as soon as possible, after explaining to Mr J why I can't feed his opioid addiction by giving him the four boxes of Endone he's requesting for his headache, suggesting that he should be linked in with the chronic pain service instead. He tells me to fuck off, which I agree to do enthusiastically, just so long as he offers me the same courtesy and lets me finish my shift in peace.

I'm a woman, I tell myself as I run home, change out of my scrubs, and stare at the to-do list on my phone. How hard can it be? I have less than twenty-fours in which to become a domestic goddess. Despite having had three and a half weeks to prepare for the dinner, my Nigella ways have been stymied by my long shifts in the emergency department, and Winnie has suffered a stress-related bout of tonsillitis. We have left all preparation until the night before.

I am about to run down the stairs to head to the shops when I hear Winnie climbing up to my attic room.

'I've made the list for the entrees,' she is saying, waving a piece of paper at me. 'I just need to confirm the numbers.' She stops talking and stares at my bedroom the evening prior to the most important night of my entire life, and winces. 'Mate, this is no good,' she says. 'This is no good.'

'I doubt we'll be coming up to my bedroom,' I say defensively. 'Can't I just shut the door?'

'What if they want a tour?' she says. 'You can't let them see this. You look like a hoarder. Anyway, back to the numbers: Max is working, so he can't come, but do you know if Dr Prince is bringing his wife?'

'That's a good question,' I respond. I've been wondering the same thing.

'I mean, I guess you didn't specify when you texted him whether or not she was invited,' Winnie points out. 'So he might bring her. And that means we have a problem: we don't have enough chairs.'

'Should I text him to say if he's bringing his wife he has to, you know . . .' I pause, realising how ridiculous this sounds.

'BYO chair?'

Winnie and I collapse into tears of laughter. Here at 19 North Avenue, we'll supply the booze and good times, but you have to bring your own chair.

'Look, he knows it's just Wolfgang and Tomas and us,' I reason. 'He might realise we're all, you know, going it solo, and do the same.'

Winnie shrugs. 'Well, either way it doesn't really matter. I think we should prepare ourselves for the possibility of Mrs Prince and just roll with it regardless.'

With that small hurdle workshopped, we return to the tasks at hand.

My room takes ages to clean. It will be a tight race to get to the shops before closing at this rate. The food is our next challenge. Winnie has wasted her entire day at work poring over every cookbook. She is capable of culinary genius, she assures me, but due to time pressures the only sensible thing to do is go and buy everything preprepared from a gourmet food hall and let the VIP guests think that we've made it ourselves.

'You doing anything fun tonight, Doc?' my patient asks me the next afternoon as I explain that his fractured scaphoid bone means he needs a cast on his wrist if he's to avoid avascular necrosis (bone death, in layman's terms). 'You look like a girl who knows how to have fun.'

The patient is a young flight attendant who fell over in the middle of a gay orgy while high on MDMA last night. Not only did he sustain a fracture, but I also had to remove a buttplug that had been jammed in a little too high (miraculously I was able to tease it out with forceps and he didn't need an operation), so I allow the overfamiliarity.

'Not quite as fun as what you got up to last night,' I say, grinning and taking him into the plaster room. 'But now that you ask . . .' I explain my plans for the evening.

'God, so you're just having all these sexy old surgeons over for dinner,' he says, looking thrilled. 'What are you cooking?'

'I'm not,' I admit freely. 'We've bought everything from a food hall and I'm pretending we made it.'

His cackles set me off, and we sit in the plaster room giggling as I apply sheet after sheet of plaster of Paris. Vincent is actually pretty helpful, and gives me plenty of advice on serving prawns and transitioning between courses.

'It'll be great, gorgeous,' he says supportively as I farewell him at the doors of the emergency department. 'They won't be able to believe how well you've catered. I can't believe you're having five courses! Don't let them know the menu in advance, just keep bringing out course after course, and surprising them.'

It's not till I'm on my way to Coles to purchase some napkins at the end of my shift that I start to feel nervous. I've been so excited that I haven't really paused to consider the enormity of the situation. My boss, to whom I am sexually attracted, is coming over to my place for dinner along with two of the best surgeons in the world.

I wonder what the hell I'm doing. I can barely check the mail. We have an ironing board I bought at the beginning of the year with great intentions, yet I've never opened it. I can't host a dinner party for the best surgeons in the world! What the fuck was I thinking? I start wishing like mad I had just suggested we go out to a restaurant, like a normal person.

I stand in aisle four, staring at all the napkin options in front of me. Fuck, it's just the party aisle at Coles and yet there are so many damn napkins. Do I want the white napkins, the blue, the red, the novelty patterns? What does a napkin really say about a person? Will Dr Prince judge me if I lay out the wrong napkins? Should I be using linen napkins, like the ones Mum puts out at Christmas? And the glasses . . . I cringe. Our glassware is all from Big W. Dr Prince's crystal ware is probably worth more than my entire year's salary.

I run home and dump five packets of napkins on the new dining table.

Winnie rushes out from the kitchen, where she is making canapés. 'Well, we're well sorted for napkins,' she says briskly. 'Probably didn't need this many, though!'

I check the time: 6.45 pm. The clock is ticking, and I'm starting to feel as if I'm a contestant on the final round of *MasterChef*.

'I'll handle the serving,' Winnie says, like a true friend. 'You just keep the conversation rolling.'

I admire how clean number 19 looks. The table is set, the prawns are in a bowl, the canapés are made, and the champagne is chilling on ice. No one would ever guess that we don't usually live like this.

'We'd better get ready!' Winnie says. 'Don't worry, Kitty. Everything looks great. It'll be great. *We'll* be great.'

After trialling a variety of outfits I've settled on something innocent yet racy, pure yet naughty, decent yet indecent. It's a high-necked sleeveless white lace dress that's cut dangerously low at the back. But it's a cotton blend, so it has a casual summery look to it without being too skimpy.

I never normally bother too much with make-up but tonight's a special occasion. I even put on eye shadow. I actually use a blow dryer and brush on my hair, like a normal woman.

Winnie and I stand in the kitchen, allowing ourselves a glass of champagne to relax prior to the guests arriving.

'We can do this,' I say, breathing out.

Winnie looks less sure. 'Should we have one of Max's valiums?' she suggests.

'Good thinking!'

But before I can act on the idea we hear a knock at the door.

'It must be them!' Winnie half whispers, half shrieks, throwing back her champagne in one gulp. 'It's them! Go to the door.'

It's a perfect night for a dinner party. It's an early spring evening and the sun is just beginning to creep down, casting a glow over the house. Everything looks warm and welcoming, and the evening takes a magical turn. My shift in emergency is a distant memory. Real life is suspended. That can start again tomorrow, I decide. Everything can wait until tomorrow. The crack in the universe opens, and I let myself fall through it. *Into the rose-garden*, I hear Mum say. *Let yourself walk into the rose-garden*.

So glamorously holding my glass of champagne like the hostess with the mostess that I have miraculously become, I walk to the door to greet my guests.

forty-one

'YOU GIRLS SHOULD DEFINITELY COME AND SEE MY LATEST acquisition,' Dr Prince—Jack—is saying. Now that he's in my home, I have to keep reminding myself to call him Jack. *Jack*, I practise in my head as I refill his wineglass, trying not to stare at him too creepily.

I can't remember what bottle we're up to, but all the food has been served, and everyone seems to be enjoying themselves. There was just one slightly awkward moment when Winnie and I were carrying the plates to the kitchen. Winnie turned to me and whispered, 'God, Dr Prince—I mean Jack—can't stop staring at you! He's seriously into you, Kitty.' And before I had a chance to respond we heard a noise and turned around to see the man himself offering to help us wash up.

Any resolutions to drink sensibly and remain sensible have completely gone out the window. Everyone is cracking into the wine as if they are the last bottles on earth. In addition, Tomas has brought two bottles of Scandinavian aquavit, a horrifically strong liquor which apparently has serious effects on one's ability to think or act clearly.

'Let's open it,' Dr Prince—Jack—suggests.

I wonder if this is such a good idea. I've been doing so well. I might be drunk, but I'm in control of most of my faculties. I haven't taken off any clothes or said anything sexually inappropriate (that I remember), nor have I vomited. I'm doing a fine job. The aquavit might change that, however.

Of course, everyone else thinks it's a top idea and suddenly Winnie is producing plastic shot glasses we bought for our house party a few months ago.

We spend the next hour shooting strong Scandinavian schnapps and yelling 'Skol!' at regular intervals.

'You know there's something about this house,' Jack is saying to Winnie.

She looks across at me and raises her eyebrows.

I swear I feel number 19 smirk, if houses can even do that.

'Really, Jack,' she says, her English accent, a hangover from her time in the UK, more pronounced than ever after a few wines, 'whatever could you mean?'

'These old terraces behind the hospital,' he says, catching my eye, 'they were all owned originally by the church.'

Now this possibly explains a few things.

'So, this place would have definitely at some point housed a few of the sisters, back in the early days of the old hospital.'

'Well, Kitty here is such a good Catholic girl,' Wolfgang chimes in, grinning at me.

It all makes sense. After decades of enforced purity, number 19 is as repressed as I am! I'm as controlled by the hospital as the house was by the convent!

'Let's skol to this naughty little house,' Wolfgang says, raising his glass. Everyone obliges with enthusiasm. *SKOL!*

I've stood next to these men in the operating theatre. I've watched them remain almost scarily calm under the most extraordinary amount of pressure. Men like this are so rare, I think. And they're not thanked enough for the incredible, indescribable things that they do every single day. And here they are, throwing back schnapps with two young women who've assembled a table from Fantastic Furniture. I've experienced a lot of surreal moments in my life, but as I down another aquavit I think that this really might take the cake.

'I have to head home,' Jack says, putting down his glass. 'I'm on call for the emergency list tomorrow afternoon, then it'll be straight on the plane for the conference. Don't forget we're all going sailing next week!'

After a bottle of wine, he invited us all out on his yacht when he, Wolfgang and Tomas get back from their conference in Fiji.

I offer to walk him out, trying not to trip over my high heels.

We talk about sailing as we walk through the front garden and out to the street.

'So, what do you even wear sailing?' I keep asking, drunkenly fixating on the fact I own no suitable clothes.

As we stand beside his car, the hospital looms over us. I hardly notice. For once, the hospital is the furthest thing from my mind.

'Should you really be driving home?' I ask him. 'I mean, we've had quite a bit to drink.'

'I'll take the back streets,' he assures me, which for some reason I think is a completely reasonable solution.

'Okay,' I say.

We stand there under the streetlight, looking at each other.

'Thanks for tonight,' he says. 'It was really something.'

'Oh, thanks for coming,' I reply brightly. I'm not quite sure what's happening between us. I convinced myself halfway through the dinner that my fantasies about me and Dr Jack Prince are ridiculous. He's too important, too old, too married, too wealthy, and way too out of my league. I'm lucky just to be kind of friends with him. That's enough, I tell myself. It is definitely enough.

The silence lingers and neither of us moves to break it.

Then all of a sudden, friends isn't enough.

I reach forward and rest my hand on his cheek, just for a moment. Just to check that he's there, that I'm there, that we're real.

'Katarina . . .' he says.

I wait, hardly breathing.

'I feel such a strong attraction for you. It has made it very difficult at work. This effect you have on me when we're near each other, on the rounds, in theatre . . . I felt like I didn't know how to behave at times, I couldn't understand where these feelings were coming from, I didn't want to be . . .' He pauses. 'I can't help it,' he tells me simply. 'I lose myself around you.'

I lose myself around you.

Usually, we're protected from each other. There are invisible boundaries everywhere: in the operating theatre, on the wards, in the hierarchy of the medical profession. As doctors, we always tell our patients to resist their urges. Stub out that cigarette, don't eat the slice of mudcake, cork the bottle of wine. Resist temptation.

Until now.

I can't remember who leans in first, perhaps because we both lean in at the same time.

When his lips meet mine something deep inside me comes to life, something that's been carefully suppressed for a long time. I push my tongue inside his mouth and he wraps his arms around my waist, his hands running over my body: surgeon's hands. Our lips together are perfect. I vanish completely into the kiss. He tastes like wine and ash and all things good and bad, and I never want it to end. It's the kind of kiss that dreams are made of.

When we break apart the magic is still hovering in the air between us. I want to lie next to him, and to see what he feels like after we make love. I want him to touch me gently, with all of the power he exudes in the operating theatre and a tiny bit of the pain. I want him to play with my hair against a pillow and I want to show him how much pleasure we can make together.

Much like a futile last-ditch intervention for someone who is about to die, it's all too much, and not enough. It never has been, and it never will be.

I stand there under the streetlight, the shadow of that damn hospital above us, and I let him step away from me. Don't go, I want to scream. I am filled with a wild, irrational desire to shove my hand inside my chest and pull out my heart, with the blood running down my fingers. Don't leave me, don't leave this, don't let this moment become just a memory! The crack in the universe is closing, and I am helpless to stop it. The words of T.S. Eliot return to me.

Footfalls echo in the memory

Down the passage we did not take

'Safe drive home,' I offer lamely.

So quiet. So controlled. The door is closed and we are back in the operating theatre once more.

Towards the door we never opened,

Into the rose-garden.

He drives away, one of the world's top surgeons, after a few bottles of booze, some strong aquavit, and the world's most potent kiss.

As I walk back into the house, nearly tripping over my front step, I can't fight the funny feeling that the nuns, even though they're shaking their heads, have deep down, just a little bit, enjoyed the show.

forty-two

THE NEXT EVENING, I'M LYING ON MY BED STARING AT the ceiling, feeling the inevitable sense of anticlimax that always follows after something incredibly exciting has happened. Where to from here? Jack and I texted a bit this morning, but it was all pretty G-rated. The fact he's texting me at all is unusual, though, so maybe . . .

Maybe what, Dr Holliday? I ask myself sternly. An affair? Destruction of both our personal lives? Which would no doubt lead to the worst outcome of all: nothing. The loss of our friendship, if you could even call it that, and then never seeing each other again.

I sigh. Self-control only ever seems like a good idea sober and in hindsight. It's hard to live in the moment and wisely at the same time.

I have just resolved to put the whole thing from my mind when I hear my phone ringing. I pick it up from the bedside table and look at the caller ID. Wolfgang. I'm surprised he's calling. They should all be in Fiji by now, about to start their conference in paradise.

'*Tjena!*' I say into the phone.

'How have you recovered from the feast?' he asks me.

I laugh. 'Almost,' I say. 'That aquavit is—'

'Kitty,' Wolfgang interrupts, 'I have to tell you something.'

He sounds serious, and I wonder what's coming next. A lecture maybe, about my appalling behaviour. How much does he know about what happened between me and Dr Prince? I didn't *tell* him, did I? With a sinking feeling, I realise I might well have, in my drunken state.

'It's about Jack,' he continues.

Uh-oh. I knew it . . .

'What about him?' I say.

'He had some chest pain this afternoon, just after we landed. It got very bad.'

Suddenly my bedroom becomes very small, the air very thin.

'It's okay,' he says quickly, clearly sensing my distress. 'He had a heart attack, but he is still alive. He's in intensive care at Holy Innocents. They flew him there because it's the closest cardiothoracic trauma centre.'

The seconds tick away. The sound of nothing bounces around my head.

'He had a heart attack?' I repeat stupidly. Oh my God, I'm thinking. I've given the guy a heart attack.

Waves of nausea start to roll over me. Dr Prince came for dinner, kissed me, and then had a fucking heart attack? That wasn't meant to happen! That is not how the story is supposed to end!

'Is he all right?' I ask finally.

'He is okay. He had surgery—a CABG. He is being transferred to the ward in a few days.'

Coronary artery bypass graft: open-heart surgery. 'I see,' I say. I feel my lips moving but I can't really hear the words I speak. My head starts to pound. I put my finger on my temple, trying to calm myself.

'Listen, I don't know who is meant to know,' Wolfgang says, sounding worried. 'I was just saying to Tomas that we had to tell you, but maybe don't message him yet or tell anybody.'

'Okay.'

He's right. The last thing a surgeon wants is for people to know that they're sick. People would already be talking, but it's good to minimise damages. Surgery's cut-throat enough; you don't want it getting around that you're physically incapacitated and can't operate. Plus, his wife will be by the bedside, which makes me feel very awkward. God.

We finish the call, and I walk over to my window and gaze out at the lights of the hospital.

I see Dr Prince standing beside me under the fluorescent lights of operating theatre six.

I see him standing beneath a streetlight, leaning towards me . . .

Then I see him lying in a hospital bed, completely, unexpectedly, human, all the power and control he normally wields handed to somebody else.

Dr Jack Prince has become the most unacceptable thing of all to any doctor—he's become a patient.

forty-three

TWENTY MINUTES LATER I'M SINKING LOW-CARB BEERS with Estelle at the pub on the corner. Usually it's fun to watch the poor suckers who have to work that night walking past us, giving us evil looks as they drag themselves towards the hospital, although I don't know how much pleasure I'll derive from anything tonight.

It's good to finally catch up with Estelle, though. What with me working crazy hours in emergency and her now being on her surgical term, we've hardly seen each other in the past few weeks, just when we need each other most.

'How are you feeling about everything?' I ask.

Estelle looks at me, and laughs. 'Which part of my disastrous life are you referring to specifically?'

I shrug. 'You know, the inquest. Or anything. Our shared reliance on alcohol?'

I don't want to sound too serious, but I am worried about Estelle. I've been texting her daily to see how she's coping and I know she's struggling.

'Well, the inquest is in two months,' she says, staring into her wineglass. 'I spoke to the lawyer, and he said I'll just have to wait it out. He seems to think I probably won't lose my registration, but it'll be stressful. I'll have to appear in court to answer the coroner's questions.'

'I'll come with you,' I say.

Estelle smiles sadly. 'Thanks, mate. But I don't think I want anyone there. I don't even really want to talk about it, to be honest. It's not like I'm trying to be brave, it's just with the hours on surgery and this hanging over my head, if I don't compartmentalise the fuck out of everything I think I'll go under, know what I mean?'

Doctors, I am realising, have to be extremely good at compartmentalisation. I'm not that great at it. My brain is like a big airy house with no doors between the rooms. Other doctors, I think, picturing the Smiling Assassin, seem to have brains with millions of little locked panic rooms, and staircases and dungeons and attics. Although, recent events considered, it's probably time for me to get good at compartmentalisation quick smart.

'Yeah, I understand that,' I say.

'Anyway, tell me what the fuck is going on with you. What happened with the dinner party?'

I take a deep breath. 'Dr Prince had a heart attack today and is in intensive care. He nearly died twenty-four hours after kissing me.'

Estelle is so startled she starts to laugh uncontrollably. 'I know it's not funny,' she keeps repeating, gasping for air. 'Don't think I'm laughing at him being sick, I'm not, I'm not. But, Kitty, you actually have the kiss of death!' She is still in hysterics.

'Yes, thanks for that.' I can't help grinning a bit. It's so good to see Estelle laughing. 'But I mean—a heart attack? I just can't believe it. I mean, can you fucking believe it?'

Estelle, still giggling, assures me that no, she can't fucking believe it.

'You've given your boss a heart attack,' she says, abruptly turning serious. 'I've killed a patient, and you've nearly killed your boss.' She reaches for the bottle of wine. 'It's not really how I saw our first year as doctors panning out,' she continues. 'I mean, I always knew it was going to be bad, but I can honestly say that I didn't predict this.' She fills her glass, then drains it. 'Do you have any benzos at your place?' she asks me, looking desperate.

I'm tempted—Max is on night shift and we all know where his secret stash is—but we do have to go to work the next day. 'All out, mate,' I say, feeling bad for both of us, Estelle especially.

She's putting up a good front, aided by the fact she's so beautiful it's hard to see that underneath there's something wrong. But we've been through a lot together, and if anyone can sense that things are awry, I can. I make a vow to myself that no matter how hectic our schedules, we will do a weekly in-person check-in. I will not just text, I decide. Her wellbeing is too important. I will force her to come over or meet her for a coffee or go to her place.

'Another bottle of the same, thanks,' I say to the waitress as she comes by.

'I'll get you some water too,' she says, giving us a look.

'Don't need water.' Estelle looks affronted as she enunciates her words carefully in an effort to appear sober.

'You do realise you've got a problem with alcohol,' a voice says behind me.

I turn around to see the Godfather, still in his scrubs, clearly having just finished work. I feel drunkenly relieved. I can deal with the Godfather.

'You're going to pour me one, right?' he says, instantly sitting down and stretching out his legs. 'I've earned it.'

'There's another bottle coming,' I say, catching the eye of the waitress, who's staring at the Godfather.

'I think the waitress wants to have sex with you, mate,' Estelle whispers, trying to be subtle but failing. It works, in any case, as she heads off to replenish our dwindling supply.

'Give her my number,' the Godfather says. 'She's cute.'

The Godfather's had the shift from hell, he tells us. 'Everyone tonight is just really high on ice,' he says. 'Man, we had to shackle at least three people to the bed. It was pretty fucked up.'

Ice is scary, even for the Godfather, who has been exposed to so many recreational drugs that he's like a walking illegal pharmacy.

'Speaking of,' he adds casually, 'do you guys want some charlie?'

Estelle's face brightens. 'Ye—'

'No!' I say firmly. 'Come on, guys! It's Sunday.'

Estelle gives me a filthy look. 'I'm Dr Katarina Holliday and I'm such a good doctor,' she mutters in a high-pitched imitation of my voice.

'Right, sorry, sorry,' the Godfather says, looking sheepish. 'Yeah, so, anyway, just as I was leaving, right—' he takes a huge sip of my wine '—apparently some registrar came in.'

'As a patient?' Estelle says.

'Yeah,' he replies. 'She'd taken like fifty valium and half a bottle of gin. Apparently she wanted to, you know . . .' He pauses. 'You know, she wanted to kill herself.'

We all look at each other.

'Who was it?' Estelle asks finally.

The Godfather shakes his head. 'Don't know. She was brought in just as I was leaving, and when the boss realised what was going on he immediately cleared everyone away. I only know she works at Holy Innocents because one of the nurses started crying. I think she's one of the cardiology registrars, someone was saying.'

I feel an odd twinge of relief. Not one of the surgeons then.

The waitress arrives with the extra glass and bottle, smiling at the Godfather.

'Thanks, darling,' he says, flashing her a grin.

'Finish the story?' Estelle urges, shooting him a disgusted glance.

'Well, that's pretty much it.' He gives the waitress's backside a considered stare as she walks away. 'Or she might have been someone who used to work here or something, but people definitely looked like they knew her.'

Dr George, the man who cared for Winnie's mother, taps on the glass behind my mind's eye. I try to block him out, but I can't help feeling vaguely unsettled.

Admin sends us weekly emails telling us how great everything is in the hospital and how resilient we all are. We spend our days at work, our nights dreaming about work, sharing our beds with imaginary corpses, and our years trying to force ourselves through training programs to finally get somewhere. It's like trying to run up an escalator that's going down. You just keep on going until eventually you can't run anymore and have to step off. Or you jump off.

Or you have a heart attack at fifty.

forty-four

AT SEVEN O'CLOCK THE NEXT MORNING I WALK INTO THE emergency department to start my shift, trying to pep myself up for another ten hours of action. Using the power of positive thinking, I've nearly convinced myself that cannulating drug overdoses in the resus bay can be exciting, when I throw myself forehead first into another human being.

'God, I'm so sorry!' I exclaim, clumsily stepping back from the person I've headbutted in my haste to enter the workplace. 'I wasn't looking where I was going.'

'Honestly, Katarina,' my victim says, grinning. 'You can never just say hello like a normal person, can you?'

I stop and take a long look at the man I've just accidentally assaulted. My self-control, which I'm determined to improve, dissolves like sugar in boiling water. The drama of the recent weeks somehow fades away. I stare at the vision in front of me, and my pulse rate shoots up to about a hundred and fifty.

'Oh my God!' I exclaim. 'Lucas!'

He starts laughing, and my heart beats even faster. The soundtrack of my life immediately starts playing the *Grey's Anatomy* theme. I'm standing in an emergency department in scrubs stained with old blood and other unmentionable bodily fluids about to struggle through a painfully long shift, but I feel as if I've been instantly transported to Seattle Grace.

Dr Lucas Lang is without a doubt the sexiest, most charismatic, most charming man I've ever met. If Dr Prince is my Dr McDreamy, Lucas is Dr McSteamy. He's a cardiothoracic surgeon, and I was under him (not in the fun way, sadly) when I was a medical student. It's probably no surprise that I finished cardiothoracics thinking that I definitely wanted to be a heart surgeon. This was misguided—I soon realised that my true ambition was to sleep with the man wielding the scalpel. He'd let me come into the theatre to watch him operate a few times, and after every single encounter I left feeling I had been on a journey of sexual discovery without actually having sex.

Fast-forward to the present day and amazingly, I realise as I admire the very fine specimen standing in front of me, I still feel the same. Lucas Lang inspires feelings of raw sexual hunger in me, made even more tantalisingly painful because I know they'll never be sated.

We walk into the emergency department together, chatting.

'How come you're not doing cardiothoracics?' he asks.

'I haven't been given a term,' I reply.

'You were a great student,' he says, smiling. 'You should think about it.'

'That's very kind of you to say,' I tell him, 'but you don't have to.'

He looks surprised. 'I mean it.'

His eyes are a bright honey-brown, and I find myself growing rather lost in them.

'Hey, look,' he says, as I'm wondering how to respond, 'the department is having a dinner this Friday night, for the registrars who are finishing up and for anyone else who might be interested in applying for cardiothoracics. Maybe you should come.'

I almost shout, 'No!', remembering how my last dinner with surgeons ended, but catch myself just in time.

'Have you thought about what you want to do?'

I sigh. 'No, not really . . . The only thing I really want to do is spend six months lying on a beach somewhere in the Mediterranean.'

He laughs. 'You haven't changed.'

As I look at him, at his warm eyes and tall frame and slightly flirtatious smile, I remember the old Kitty from years before, when life was a lot easier. Maybe a night out with Lucas Lang and the other heart guys will take my mind off things. Cardiothoracic surgeons have a reputation for being massive egomaniacs. Because they operate on the organ that pumps our life's blood through our bodies, they tend to consider themselves superior to all other doctors, so there's always plenty of testosterone, as well as oxygen, floating around. Lucas is the surgical opposite of Dr Prince. Surely this is safe.

'So you'll come to the dinner, right?' he says.

'Okay.'

He looks pleased. 'Great, I'll email you the details.'

It will be good for my career, I tell myself as I avoid the glares of the people sitting in the waiting room. Cardiothoracics isn't such a bad idea, really. Plus, as hot as Lucas is, he's resting safely on a pedestal way above my position under the stairs, so it will be a nice safe environment for me to expand my surgical networks.

I go along to the dinner on Friday night not really knowing what to expect. It will probably be pretty dull, I warn myself as I walk into the restaurant. Heart surgeons love crapping on about how many lives they've saved, and bitching about how other heart surgeons or, even worse, lowly cardiologists are trying to steal their work. Not to worry, it is Friday after all. I also should be celebrating, I remind myself. My emergency term has finally ended, and I have the entire weekend off. It's a rare luxury, and I vow to enjoy my freedom before Monday and the return to the operating theatre for another surgical term.

The other real highlight is seeing Lucas Lang in a social setting away from work and, fortuitously, we are sitting opposite each other. I realise almost immediately that cardiothoracic surgery isn't the career path for me and enthusiastically refill my wineglass as the people around me rave on about Bentalls procedures. The only slightly interesting tidbit of information I hear is in a hushed conversation between Lucas and the guy next to him. I hear him say 'settlement' and 'she'll take the kids' and 'I should just push through it'. I wonder if he's going through a separation. Okay, big ears, I reprimand myself. That is quite enough.

Lucas is exceptionally professional and loves talking about aortic valve replacements. By the end of the dinner I'm starting to realise he genuinely wants to foster my interest in cardiothoracics.

'Look,' I say honestly when he asks me for my thoughts as we all stand around outside the restaurant saying our goodbyes, 'I don't know if I want to give up the next ten years of my life training to be a heart surgeon.'

Some of the registrars are planning to kick on, I notice, but all the consultants seem to be heading home. Lucas is still standing next to me.

'Ah, are you going for drinks?' I ask him, not really knowing what else to say now the subject of cardiothoracics has been totally exhausted.

He looks at me. 'Are you?'

I suddenly decide maybe I should go for a quick drink. It is Friday, after all.

'Yeah, of course,' I say, ignoring my cringing subconscious self. 'As if I'd turn down a Friday night drink!'

We follow the group up the road and I begin to realise that Lucas's personality is multi-faceted. Now we're away from the table, he's less keen on talking about heart operations and more keen to probe me about my personal life.

'There is this one guy,' I say, not wanting to go into too much detail, but the wine is loosening my tongue, 'although, well, I don't think we're that compatible.'

Even as I say the words, I see an image of Fabien in my mind and know I'm lying to myself. I quickly try to repress the feelings but all at once I realise that Lucas looks a lot like Fabien. Same height, same honey-brown eyes, same big white smile.

No wonder I think Lucas is so hot. What on earth am I trying to re-create here? Is this some desperate grab at memories and happiness?

'Anyway . . .' I clear my throat. 'Let's talk about something else.'

'How long have we known each other, Katarina?' Lucas asks as we walk around the corner, slowing down ever so slightly so the distance between the two of us and the rest of the group starts to increase.

'Years!' I reply. 'Remember when I was your student and used to come and watch you in theatre?'

He laughs. 'And you always used to tell stories about some guy you were seeing and what a disaster it was.'

I laugh too. 'God, I really need to learn how to keep my mouth shut!'

'I like that about you.'

The group is now so far in front of us that I can barely see them. We're also dangerously close to the corner of North Avenue.

Every single intelligent part of my brain is screaming at me. My subconscious is screeching so loudly I can barely hear myself think. *This is a terrible idea. Stop this now. Jack Prince is still lying in hospital. Another doctor recently tried to kill herself. You're just drunk. Lucas Lang is extremely bad news. He's too hot and too married* (maybe separating, a rogue voice whispers) *and too sexy. He just looks like Fabien, this is all this means. Honestly—when will you learn? Behave yourself! Behave!*

'Gosh, we're right near my house!' I hear my voice saying.

We both stop walking.

'Well, we've kind of lost the rest of the group,' he points out.

'Fancy a nightcap?' As soon as the words leave my mouth I try to reel them back in. 'Sorry,' I say. 'I know—not really appropriate . . .'

He smiles at me. 'I think it's completely appropriate.'

We walk up the road and through my overgrown front yard.

'So, you're a keen gardener then?' he asks wryly, stopping to observe the weeds which are almost thigh height.

'My housemate Winnie calls it the ecosystem of life,' I tell him. 'There are lizards and stuff living there. We can't just knock down their house!'

He looks at me and we both start laughing again.

Still laughing, I open the door and we enter number 19, leaving the outside world conveniently far behind us.

I listen for my subconscious, expecting resistance, but there's none. Excellent!

forty-five

THE HOUSE IS IN A TERRIBLE STATE. MY BEDROOM IS SO messy not an inch of floor can be seen, with at least two pizza boxes sitting somewhere inside my bedclothes, so there's no way I'll be inviting him up.

He insists upon the tour anyway, and though I try to block him from looking into my room he's so tall that my attempts are hopeless.

'Oh my God! You're the messiest person I've ever seen!'

'I told you we can't go in there!'

I also realise that my offer of a nightcap is a little optimistic as all we have in the house is a seedy old bottle of red, and all our wineglasses are dirty. I serve the wine anyway, in two matching Christmas mugs.

'I love what you're doing with the mugs,' he says, grinning at his Santa mug and my Christmas tree. 'It's so kitsch.'

'Well, I like to make a statement.' I try not to shudder too obviously as I sip wine reminiscent of arsenic from my own mug. 'You know how it is.'

Lucas Lang is pretty cool. He's taking it all in his stride. In fact, I feel surprisingly comfortable hanging out with Dr Lucas Lang (top cardiothoracic surgeon) on my couch in my hovel of a living room.

'Do you live with anyone?' he asks.

I try not to laugh. Max, as I discovered when Lucas went to the bathroom—I can only imagine what kind of state that's in—is at this moment lying in bed covered in chips, drunk as a skunk. I'd woken him up with a firm prod of the shoulder.

'Yurghhhh,' Max slurred, half opening his eyes. 'Whaddyawant, Kitty?'

'I thought you were staying at your mum's!' I hissed.

'She started hassling me to pay her board again.' He tried to sit up, looking irritated.

'Don't come out of your room!' I whispered urgently.

He tried without success to focus on my face. 'Why not?'

'Dr Lang's here,' I whispered.

'The cardiothoracics guy?'

'Yes!'

'The one you always used to crap on about?'

'Yes!'

'Well done, mate.'

'Where's Winnie?' I asked.

He looked confused.

'You know—the other person who lives here!'

'She's gone to stay with one of her English mates who's out here from London,' Max said after a long pause, before lying back down among the chips.

'Good. So just stay in here!'

He was sound asleep again by the time I shut the door.

'Um,' I say in answer to Lucas's question. 'Sort of . . .'

He raises his eyebrows. 'Are they home?'

'Well, yes and no,' I fumble.

There's a loud snore from the direction of the front bedroom.

'So that's a . . . yes?' Lucas guesses.

'You're too clever for me, Dr Lang,' I say, smiling.

'Does your housemate work at the hospital too?'

'Oh, definitely not,' I lie.

Unfortunately, he turns to the shelf next to the couch and lifts an empty bottle of champagne from it. Stuck to the bottle are two name badges.

Dr Katarina Holliday is typed on one, *Dr Max Henry* on the other. Both have the Holy Innocents logo on them.

Dr Lucas Lang raises his eyebrows, again.

'Look, he's super drunk.' I'm trying not to laugh. 'He won't even know you're here.'

This all may be a bit too close to home, or hospital, and he might decide it isn't worth the risk and leave. I wouldn't blame him. Instead he takes a sip of horrible red wine from his Christmas mug and starts to laugh.

We talk for ages. We talk, and talk, and talk. We talk so much we become long-lost mates who've finally reconnected. Maybe Lucas wants new friends; I guess even surgeons need mates.

There's an unfortunate moment when he asks me about my surgical term.

'Who was your boss again? Jack Prince?'

I nod into my mug, feeling it's safer not to elaborate.

'What's he like?'

I shrug. This is typical of surgeons. They love having a gossip about their counterparts. They know juniors always hear the juicy bits, which is why it's a good idea to get us drunk and let us spill the beans. In this case, the juice is so concentrated I feel like he might choke on it.

He tries to catch my eye, which I avoid.

'I don't really know him that well,' I offer.

To my relief, Lucas nods. 'I don't think anyone really knows him,' he says thoughtfully. 'You know, I grafted him a few weeks ago.'

I swallow a huge gulp of wine so quickly I spill some down the front of my dress. Thank God it's black. 'You grafted him?'

'Yeah,' he says. 'Urgent bypass. I saved the guy's fucking life, and when he finally came out of it a few days later he told me I'd not done a bad job.'

I smile despite myself. Typical.

Lucas Lang shakes his head, not realising that the night before he had his hands on Jack Prince's heart, the neurosurgeon had been in this very room.

'Not done a bad job,' he mutters, looking half amused, half irritated.

I know the world of medicine is a small one, but this is getting a bit ridiculous.

I notice that his hand has moved, so it's resting on my upper thigh, and I realise that as much as I want us to be friends I'm fighting against the inevitable.

I start rabbiting on at a mile a minute, plucking random subjects out of the air, until Lucas puts his hand over my mouth. 'Kitty,' he says, smiling, 'can you stop talking for one fucking second?'

My eyes widen, and he drops his hand. I can still feel the touch of his skin on my lips. 'Did you just have your hand . . . on my mouth?' I ask incredulously.

We stare at each other.

'I think I did.'

If there was ever a time to say the one thing I've been wanting to say to this guy for the last six years, that time is now. 'I think we should have sex,' I tell him. 'We don't have to do it right now, or even this year. But some time, in some place, I think you and I should have sex.'

There's a pause. He shakes his head, laughing slightly in disbelief.

'I agree,' he says. 'I've actually wanted to have sex with you for about six years.'

'Oh my God, me too!' I exclaim enthusiastically, as if we've just discovered we both love the same TV shows.

You really like British crime drama? My God, SO DO I!

I examine him closely. I admire his chest underneath his shirt. Fuck—he's so hot. I mentally shake myself—wait until I tell Estelle about this! Lucas Lang, after all these years, finally at my fingertips!

Speaking of fingers, I look down to where his hand rests on my thigh and feel a bit short of breath when I see how huge his hands are. His fingers are massive. My mouth goes dry. Wow. He probably has the most perfect penis.

Maybe being a junior doctor is a bit like *Grey's Anatomy* after all, I think, as I take in the truly fantastic sight of Dr Lucas

Lang, top cardiothoracic surgeon, moving his hand further up my leg.

'You look lost in thought.' He smiles at me.

I decide immediately that I'm sick of thinking, I'm sick of worrying, I'm sick of the bloody hospital and all its associated stress and anxiety, and instead of doing the sensible thing and changing the topic to mitral valve regurgitation or, even better, quickly escorting him out, I let my vagina take over and I leap across the couch.

'God, you are sexy,' he breathes, roughly shoving his fingers through my hair. 'Do you even know how sexy you are?'

Now this is more like it! I straddle him and he grabs my arse, squeezing it as we kiss. I feel myself getting wet.

'God, you're so hot.' He pulls me closer to him. 'You're just so fucking hot.'

He starts kissing my neck, and I feel my nipples hardening. I push myself onto him, wondering whether I'll have the self-control to stop. Instead, I pull my dress over my head so I'm wearing only black stockings, high heels and a black bra.

He's a man possessed, and as his tongue runs over my breasts I realise that I've forgotten about anything particularly serious or work-related and that all I want to do is fuck, hard, on my couch.

I undo my bra clasp and he groans, staring at my breasts. 'God, those tits,' he says, smiling slightly. 'I always knew you'd have the most perfect tits.'

He leans in, running his tongue over my nipples, and I close my eyes, trying to fight the urge to take off my stockings as well.

'Are you wearing undies?' he asks, feeling my naked arse through my stockings.

I sigh. 'No,' I say, to his obvious delight, 'but it was just because I had a really obvious visible undie line! This wasn't deliberate!'

Also because I didn't have a clean pair, I admit silently.

He laughs, a deep masculine sound that makes me wetter than I've ever been in my entire life.

He pulls me closer to him, and I can feel how hard he is through his pants. He slides his long fingers beneath the waistband of my stockings, and slips them inside me. I close my eyes, moving against him.

I have a vision of me at work, running from the operating theatre to the ward. I hear myself being yelled at on the phone by some overworked registrar, I see the Joker being nasty to me in theatre, I see Dr Prince and me kissing underneath a streetlight as if the world is ending. I see me six years ago, flirting with Lucas Lang and thinking he's totally out of my league. I see everything and nothing and realise that for all the things I think I know, I actually don't know *anything at all.*

Life's a wild unpredictable beast that nobody can control, not even doctors, and it's such a relief just to let go. Consequences belong in another time, far from this moment.

Lucas pushes his tongue inside my mouth, and I let him bite my lip, hard. I know immediately that he wants the kind of sex that I want. I want to open my legs for the man and get down on my knees in front of him.

'You are such a bad girl,' he whispers into my ear, shifting his finger down to where I want it to stay. 'You really are a very naughty girl.'

He's right. I am a bad girl. Two senior consultants in almost as many weeks. At least we aren't in the operating theatre change room, I think, acknowledging the irony.

He starts to unbutton his pants and I realise that in another fifteen seconds Dr Lucas Lang's cock is going to be deep inside me. I'm tantalisingly close to the best feeling, my body exploding . . . I want him so fucking badly. Sex is, after all, the world's best distraction. From work, from life, from reality. Sex is the furthest thing from death, isn't it? Doctors know that better than anyone. We try our hardest to avoid death but remain preoccupied by it, and we're preoccupied by sex but force ourselves to avoid it, especially with the wrong people.

Until we don't. Then temptation isn't even temptation, it's full-blown reality. Jack Prince lies in the shadow of death only a few hundred metres away, while I am sitting on top of Lucas Lang, every nerve alive.

He pushes my stockings down. It's been so long since I've had any kind of sexual encounter I feel my legs turning to liquid.

'Come on, babe,' he groans, shifting me further onto him and parting my legs even more. 'I can feel how wet you are.'

I'm obsessed with sex, but preoccupied by death. It stands there in the corner of the room, a woman wearing lacy lingerie but holding a scythe.

Suddenly I can't breathe. I want Lucas so badly, but the scythe is raised and the man beneath me becomes Jack. I feel as if I am on the verge of a panic attack, and I don't even really understand why. I stand up abruptly, pulling myself away from Lucas and clearing my throat.

'Ah . . .' I say, wondering what is happening to me. 'Fuck, I want to have sex with you so bad.'

Lucas leans back on the couch and sighs. 'This isn't happening.'

'Like, it nearly is, but . . .'

'You just killed me,' he says ruefully. 'My old student has just killed me.'

He doesn't realise what he's saying, but the figure in the corner slinks away, scythe lowered. Lucas is all sex, and life, beating hearts and throbbing desires. No death here tonight.

'I think we should call it here,' I say, letting out a breath. 'I just don't know if this is the right, ah, time, you know.'

He doesn't argue but pulls me back towards him. We kiss. He is warm and strong, and I already feel regret starting to course through my veins.

I tap his chest with my finger. 'You'd better go, Dr Lang.'

'Very sensible, Dr Holliday,' he says, fixing his clothes.

I nearly laugh. Yes, me, the absolute epitome of sensible.

I walk him to the front of the house, topless, in my stockings and high heels. We kiss at the door, and he pushes me against the wall. This goes on for a while.

'I really would love to have sex with you,' he says, pulling me towards him. 'You drive me fucking crazy. You always have.'

'Some other time.'

'Some other place.'

We look at each other. We'll meet again, I think to myself. The looking-glass shimmers at me. Serendipity, fate, words we use to explain things that can't really be explained. Like Latin medical terms. Or miracles.

Maybe nothing's ever really over. Maybe we all just ride the carousel, and when it stops we think that it has stopped forever, but then the music starts again and we find ourselves flying past things that we thought we'd already left safely behind.

He kisses me slowly.

'So, you want to be a writer,' he says to my surprise.

I don't ask how he knows. I probably told him when I was at peak intoxication at dinner, based on previous behaviours.

'Yeah, I do.'

He runs his long fingers down my face. 'Of course you're a writer,' he says. 'What do you write about?'

I look into his brown eyes, admiring the way they catch the light. 'Moments like this,' I tell him truthfully.

He laughs and opens the door. 'Can't wait to read it.'

I smile. 'Well, you'll definitely be a chapter.'

He smiles back. 'You know what you are, Dr Holliday?' he asks.

I raise my eyebrows in query.

'You're a panacea.'

Dr Lucas Lang, the flawed hero from a book I'm yet to pen, vanishes into the night.

I close my eyes. When I open them, I'm still standing there with my hand against the door. For once, I haven't even been dreaming.

Before I go to sleep I look up the word *panacea*. It is, I learn, a solution or remedy for all difficulties or diseases. A heal-all, nostrum, magic bullet, elixir.

Panaceas are an impossible fantasy in medicine, but that night I'm his, and maybe he's mine. Miracles, different from the ones he performs every day, sometimes actually happen.

forty-six

I WAKE UP ON MONDAY MORNING AND REMEMBER THAT I'VE finished my emergency term and am back to neurosurgery. I feel instantly relieved then immediately nauseated. Again, I berate myself mentally for begging for two neurosurgical terms at the beginning of the year. Although, I comfort myself, I could hardly have known how bad it would be. And I won't even have Dr Prince around to protect me.

I walk into the hospital at the ungodly hour of 6.30 am to attend the weekly radiology meeting and cheer myself with the glorious memory of Lucas Lang sucking on my nipples. This distracts me so thoroughly that at first I don't notice as I walk into the meeting that it's unusually crowded.

I look around. 'Why are there so many people here?' I whisper to Max, who looks as exhausted as I feel. Max has finished nights, which is a relief, but he's now on vascular surgery and is, in his words, already completely fucking over it. And it's only been ten minutes.

'It's a special meeting today apparently, they're only doing cardiac angiography,' he whispers, 'so the cardiothoracic department's here.' He nudges me. 'Maybe Dr Lang's here, mate.'

'How come you're here?' I whisper, changing the subject. 'I thought you were meant to be in theatre.'

'My old consultant told me I needed to go to more meetings for my CV,' he says. 'My team told me about the radiology meeting. They have it every week. I wanted the free breakfast and a break from the fucking ward, and I can say that I'm so keen I attend extra education sessions.'

I look around me, the realisation dawning that half the men in the room were at the cardiothoracic dinner on Friday evening. A few are giving me curious glances, and I realise I need to abort mission. Immediately.

'I'm not that interested in hearts,' I whisper to Max, quickly gathering my things. 'I might just, ah, head back upstairs.'

'Don't even think about it,' the Joker says, appearing before me like an evil spirit accidentally invoked at a séance. 'We're staying. One of the patients they're presenting the angio of is also having neurosurgery under us so we need to be here. Your anatomy is hopeless. I'll be quizzing you after the meeting to see what you've learned.'

Sandwiched between the Joker and Max, I sit back down.

'Why are you wearing your jacket over your head?' the Joker asks. 'Have you converted to Islam?'

I ignore the political incorrectness and cough. 'I've got a cold,' I say. 'I need to keep my head warm.'

The room goes quiet as Lucas Lang stands up to start commenting on the angiogram.

My face burning, I stare straight ahead, trying not to draw attention to myself, as he points to the left main coronary artery and describes the threatening stenosis present.

'Stop being so obvious!' Max whispers. 'You look like you're about to have a heart attack.'

I glare at him. 'I need to get out of here,' I whisper back.

'Ah, perhaps one of the juniors can offer an opinion on the angio,' Lucas suggests, smiling at me. 'It seems like they're very interested in talking about it.'

The burn is worsening. By now I must resemble a lobster. Thank God the lights are dimmed.

'Dr Holliday?'

I try not to look too pained. 'Hi, Dr Lang,' I say. 'Ah, yeah.'

'What do you think?' His smile widens.

Next to me, Max snorts.

The cheek! I can't believe the nerve of the man! He knows very well what I think, and it has nothing to do with the angiogram in front of me. For a second, I imagine saying, 'I think the angio is nowhere near as interesting as Friday night, when I was straddling you topless and you had a huge erection and your hands were inside my pants!'

Instead, I flush redder and mumble something incoherent.

'Speak up!' the Joker barks.

'I think it's at least eighty per cent stenosed,' I shout, glaring at Dr Lucas Lang, hating him at the same time as wanting to drag him from the room and rip his trousers off. 'I guess surgery would be the preferred option.' (As if I have any real idea what that involves.)

'Not bad,' he says, raising his eyebrows.

Despite everything, I grin.

'He's so hot,' Max whispers, nudging me. 'Wonder if he'd give me a go?'

'Oh my God, mate!' I hiss. 'He's not fucking gay, all right?'

'Maybe he's bi,' Max whispers again, 'You never know . . .'

I kick him under the chair.

'Fortunately for the patient the stenosis was bad enough that the cardiologists did end up asking the humble surgeons for our assistance. He had three grafts yesterday, and is doing well.'

Everyone looks appropriately morose and gleeful simultaneously.

Lucas smiles, rather smugly. 'Anything else to add, Katarina?' He's staring at me again. The smile broadens.

I glare back. 'Um, the right coronary seems a bit diseased too,' I squeeze out painfully.

The Joker snorts. 'A medical student could have picked that—I'm surprised you missed it earlier.'

'I'm sorry I don't have a brain as gigantic as yours and am unable to interpret cardiac angiography before I've examined them,' I snap. 'I know you can probably tell a patient's pathology before they even actually get sick.'

There's a silence, and I immediately, desperately try to grab the words from the air and stuff them back into my mouth. Max squeaks, trying to hold back a laugh, but in the end he doesn't need to. Dr Lucas Lang guffaws into the microphone and that sets off the rest of the room.

'You shouldn't be so mean to your boss,' Lucas says, still laughing. 'He's under a lot of stress, you know, Kitty.'

The Joker, fuming at my victory, and also looking confused by Dr Lucas Lang's use of my nickname, gives me such a scathing look I feel my stomach curdle a bit. He'll get the last laugh, as we both know, back in the operating theatre where there are no Lucas Langs to rescue me.

When the meeting has ended, Lucas saunters over to me. My legs go a little weak at his proximity. The man emanates sexual charisma. Regret at not having sex with him hits me like a freight train.

Max, ignoring my obvious eye signals, stays glued to my side. The Joker thankfully has been distracted by another consultant and has vanished, no doubt to argue about operative success rates.

'Dr Holliday,' Lucas says.

'Dr Lang,' I reply.

Max clears his throat.

'This is my housemate, Max,' I say grudgingly.

Lucas lunges forward, grabs Max's hand and gives it the most enthusiastic shake I've ever seen.

'Um, hello,' Max says weakly. 'I, uh, I guess I'd better go check on the ward.' He is looking dazed as he turns and walks away.

Lucas looks into my eyes and smiles. 'God, you make me laugh,' he says, flashing his perfect teeth at me.

'I just love being put on the spot by senior surgeons who've seen my breasts,' I say in a low voice, smiling back at him. I might not be very good at interpreting cardiac angiograms, but he isn't the only one who specialises in the flirt under pressure.

He laughs under his breath. 'Katarina,' he murmurs, 'naughty.'

Another surgeon comes over, giving me a glance. 'How'd your CAGs go on that old bloke last week, Lucas?'

'Yeah, fine,' Lucas says dismissively.

I break in. 'I read an article that said more people are choosing stenting by cardiologists nowadays because they don't want their chests cracked open, even if open-heart surgery may end up better for their vessels.'

He ignores the jibe and says, 'That's a special interest area of mine, actually—can you send me the link?'

'I would, but I don't have your number . . .'

'That's easily resolved,' he says. 'I'll give it to you.'

I type the digits into my phone as he recites them. Where is this little exchange heading? I wonder.

As I walk back onto the ward, I take an indulgent trip down memory lane.

God, you're so hot . . . I always knew you'd have the most perfect tits.

I can't help grinning as I follow the Joker to the bedside. He is looking at me suspiciously, clearly perturbed by my unusually cheerful demeanour, when his phone starts to ring.

He glances at the caller ID. 'It's your boyfriend,' he says sarcastically, putting the phone to his ear. 'Hi, Lucas.' The Joker listens then rolls his eyes. 'Yeah, she's here with me.' He turns to me. 'What's your number?' he asks impatiently.

I tell him, and he repeats it.

'Don't poach my intern,' he says into the phone, like he's trying to make a joke but failing. He presses end and looks at me, his mouth a hard, mean line. 'Why does Lucas Lang want your number?'

'I'm sending him a research article,' I explain, wondering what the hell is happening. Have I finally cracked the

Grey's Anatomy life of medicine? Is this what I have been waiting for?

My phone starts to ring. I pretend it isn't, and busy myself with fixing the end of my stethoscope, which isn't broken.

'Answer it,' the Joker says, curiosity getting the better of him.

'Hello?'

'Kitty,' says Lucas's voice on the other end of the line. 'I just want to check I gave you the right number.'

I don't know what to say, and choose not to ask the obvious question: how many phone numbers does the guy actually have?

I confirm that, yes, he has given me the right phone number.

'Good,' he says, and hangs up, leaving me to continue the ward round with a seething Joker.

'He must have two phones,' Max says as I relate this tale in the cafeteria. 'It's the only explanation—I mean, he's married, right?'

'I think he's going through a divorce . . . but who knows.'

'Gee, the secret life of surgeons,' Max muses. 'I always knew they were filthy bastards.'

I don't ask Max how he knows this, but I don't doubt he's right.

'So now I have Lucas's phone number,' I say, 'what am I going to do with it?'

'Maybe send him a nude,' Max suggests.

We both go quiet, considering.

'Boobs, would you reckon?' I ask. 'Or an arse shot?'

'Tricky to capture the arse,' Max says thoughtfully, being a connoisseur of the nude selfie. 'Would vag be too much? I mean, that'd be an easier angle.'

'I can't send Lucas Lang a photo of my vagina!' I exclaim, going red. 'What if someone saw it?'

We both start giggling. I feel like I'm starring in an episode of *The Real Doctors of Holy Innocents Hospital.* Sitting in the cafeteria with my mate as we debate sending photos of my genitalia to one of the married surgeons at work. Another hard day spent saving lives.

'Give me your phone,' Max demands.

'No way!'

He grabs it out of my hands and goes straight to the fake calculator app where I keep a collection of artistic erotic photographs in case of emergencies.

'God, this one is great!' He zooms in on my breasts in a white lace Italian bra I bought on a trip to Europe.

'I know, right? I got that at Milan airport—like, it was at the *airport*. Europe's the best.'

Before I can stop him, Max is opening a new message and typing. When he's done, he holds my phone up in front of me, teasing. 'I'm going to send this.'

He has written, *You like? Have a great weekend, sexy*, underneath my not-unimpressive (if I do say so myself) Italian lace-clad breasts.

'Give it back!' I shriek, making a desperate grab for my phone while also trying not to draw anyone's attention to the fact that we aren't having a heated argument about the best antibiotic protocol for post-op cholecystectomy patients.

Max is laughing so hard he's crying. 'Of course I won't send it. I just wanted to see your reaction.'

He hands me my phone and I press delete, only my hand is shaking so much from the close call that my finger slips . . .

I let out such a loud scream, the people at the table next to us look over, concerned.

'Fuck, I think I've sent it! I've sent it to him! Delete it! Call Vodafone! Get it sent back! Is that, like, a thing?'

Max is bright purple by now and he's having trouble breathing. 'It's too late, Kit,' he says. 'It's gone.'

'Oh my God! No! This can't be happening!'

'It's not such a big deal,' Max reminds me. 'He's seen your tits in real life anyway.'

'This is different!' My stomach is churning with anxiety. 'What the fuck am I going to do?'

'Wait!' Max says, looking down at my phone, which is sitting on the table between us. 'He's replying!'

'WHAT?!'

'Look! I can see the three dots that mean he's typing.' Max sounds excited. 'Do you reckon he's sending you a photo of his cock?'

I nearly scream again but as we look at each other I feel the laughter bubbling up. I try to suppress it but fail.

'He might be in his rooms, between patients,' Max says. 'He's probably masturbating!'

'Shut up!' I hiss, trying to look angry but unable to stop laughing.

We both stare intently down at the phone, waiting for the dots to reveal the sentiment behind them.

There's a ding.

'It's here!' Max says. He grabs the phone.

'Give it back!' I screech.

Max rolls his eyes. 'Kind of boring really.'

We both look down at the message.

Babe . . . you're killing me. That is sooo fine!

'Wow, he's calling you babe these days?'

I shrug. 'Maybe that's what a tit shot does to men, mate. You should try it.'

Max looks at me. I look at him. We both look down at my phone and start laughing again, so hard I feel the muscles of my abdomen cramping.

I'm a very bad example of a junior doctor, and so is Max, I remind him as we take the lift to our respective destinations, still giggling.

'This hospital isn't the centre of excellence,' Max says to me seriously. 'It's the centre of sexcellence.'

I walk into the ward, still laughing to myself.

Sex, death and nude selfies. Not a bad book title, if you think about it.

forty-seven

I WALK TOWARDS OPERATING THEATRE SIX, DREADING what's to come. I've been so gloriously momentarily distracted by my eventful morning that I almost forgot the array of awful situations facing me: the Joker and the Smiling Assassin; Dr Prince; my future.

I'm starting to wonder where my future lies in medicine. The hospital has become a place I'd rather avoid. I've learned this year that working as a doctor in a big hospital means that the most important person in the equation is your boss, the patient comes somewhere in the middle, and the least important person is you.

What are my options, realistically? I ask myself. I have to complete my intern year, otherwise I won't be eligible for my full medical registration. I could take some time off next year, maybe, in residency, but then I'd struggle to get onto a training program—and if I still really want to be a surgeon, I can't afford to take time off to go travelling or write my book.

Will I ever write my book? I ask myself, feeling my soul cracking a little bit more. When I was young, I loved writing detective stories. I invented a character called Detective Hamburger who could crack even the most challenging of cases. I suddenly wish Detective Hamburger was real and that he could solve the questions I have about my life and future.

Someone should have warned me, I think to myself, that once you stand on the platform that says *Medical School* and board the train, there are no further stops. You can't get off the train again, not even for a bit of a scenic stopover. Destination: eternity.

I just need a holiday, I think a bit desperately. If I could just go away for a few months and sit with my thoughts, and process them, I might have a better sense of what to do. It doesn't escape me that my year as an intern has provided me with a lot of material, maybe even enough for a novel. Everyone loves a bit of medical literary sauce, right? I should start writing things down more, I remind myself. Sometimes, when something particularly mental happens, I make a note in my phone, but really I need to start a full-blown diary. Maybe tonight, when I get home. If I don't drink too much.

I push open the door to theatre six, bracing myself for the worst. To my surprise, the Joker's there but the Smiling Assassin isn't. Maybe, I think hopefully, she's found a better job with another surgeon somewhere else.

There's a different woman in her place.

'Where's the usual registrar?' I ask.

No one replies. I notice one of the nurse's eyes tracking towards me, looking nervous.

The Joker totally ignores me. 'Hand me the right equipment next time,' he scolds the scrub nurse.

I wonder what's going on. I've never not seen the Smiling Assassin in the operating theatre. Maybe she's at the police station, I think optimistically, reporting the Joker for sex crimes against vulnerable junior female doctors!

'Well, are you just going to stand there or are you actually going to do something useful?' the Joker fires in my direction, looking angrier than usual.

I dutifully walk outside to the sink to start the tedious process of scrubbing in. The Smiling Assassin's probably on sick leave, I think; the kind of stress she was under would give anyone an ulcer.

It's nearly 7 pm when the list ends. I walk straight from the operating theatre to the pub. I tell myself it's okay to be drinking alone, as it's been an extremely trying few weeks.

'Kitty?'

Of all people, Nicole from admin is walking towards me. I wonder if I should pretend that I'm meeting someone. Boozing alone after work in my scrubs probably isn't a great look. Fuck it, I decide. I don't care anymore.

'Are you by yourself? I've just come in to use the ATM. I'm having dinner over the road with some friends. Come and join us if you like.'

'Nah, I'm all right. I just felt like a drink before I went home. Long week, you know?' And it's only Monday, I think . . .

Nicole sits down next to me, looking concerned. 'Is this about the doctor?'

I'm not sure what she means. Does she know about Dr Prince? Lucas Lang? Is she testing me? Could she know something?

'Which one?' I ask, feeling slightly on edge.

'The overdose . . .' She sounds awkward.

'Right . . . Yeah, I had heard.'

Nicole looks uncomfortable. 'I'm really sorry. It must be hard for you.'

'What? Why would it be hard for me?'

'Kitty . . .' She stops. 'Don't you know?'

'Know what?'

Nicole's eyes fill with concern. 'It was your registrar. I thought somebody would have told you.'

For a moment, I just gape at her. And then it hits me. Sitting at the bar, with Nicole from admin being weirdly kind, I start to cry. My whole body is shaking and I can't seem to stop it.

Nicole gets me to my feet and walks me home.

'God, you live close to the hospital,' she remarks as we turn into the front yard. 'Must get a bit much sometimes.'

She sits me on the couch. I'm so confused and overwhelmed, I don't know how to make sense of my thoughts. I just ramble, with no idea what I'm saying. 'I should have told someone,' I keep repeating. 'I should have told somebody. Winnie was right. I should have told someone.'

'Told them what?' Nicole presses.

'She was being taken advantage of by one of the senior surgeons,' I say, even now worried I'm going into too much detail. I wipe away the tears that keep forming. 'She said not to tell anyone, and I didn't. But I should have, shouldn't I?' I repress a sob. 'Is she all right?' I ask, trying to get myself under control. 'Will she be all right?'

Nicole looks anxious. 'I think so. They had to intubate her, though. I think it was pretty serious.'

I picture the Smiling Assassin lying in a hospital bed, a tube shoved down her trachea and the harsh noises of the mechanical ventilator breathing for her. I imagine her waking up to the horrible realisation she has a piece of plastic down her throat, and her coughing and spasming, trying to rip it out. It's the natural instinct of any patient to do that. As a doctor watching that, you feel strangely removed. It wouldn't happen to us, because we are the people who operate the machine and give the drugs and have the control and power.

I try to imagine what she was feeling before she took the valium with the intention of ending her life. I see her eyes as we stand locked in a silent battle outside the operating theatre change rooms and recall the words she spat at me. *If you tell anyone about this, I'll ruin you.*

We are all just teetering on a precipice. Estelle and I have talked about the feeling of standing on a thin wire—well, it turns out the Smiling Assassin—'Rachel' I remind myself, using her name for the first time—was standing there right next to us, invisible. It doesn't matter how competent she seemed in theatre or how forceful she could be on the ward. Throw into the mix the disastrous situation with the Joker and the stress of surgical training, and she's slipping off the wire, tumbling down into the abyss.

I know why she did what she did, because I've been tempted myself. I've never reached the point of jumping, but I've definitely lifted one foot off the wire occasionally. I have; Estelle has; Max probably has too.

'Can I go and visit her?' I say, feeling a sudden urge to see for myself that she is still alive, still breathing, her heart still beating and her neurons still firing.

'I'm sorry, but her family has said no visitors.' Nicole looks apologetic.

I nod, breathing slowly.

'God, Kitty, it must be difficult being on neurosurgery again what with this *and* Dr Prince.'

I look up at her.

'You know about Dr Prince, right? Apparently, his heart attack was really serious. If they hadn't got him into surgery when they did, he would have died.'

Of course I knew about Dr Prince, but the words 'he would have died' pierced through my soul.

The wire creaks, and all at once I am falling. In my mind's eye, Estelle catches me, and I grip onto her hands for dear life, my legs flailing in the wind. Maybe it's the booze, or the sheer amount of overwhelmingly bad news, but I completely lose it.

Struggling to speak through my sobs, I tell her everything, starting with the Joker and the Smiling Assassin and including my feelings for Dr Prince. To her credit, she doesn't even seem fazed when I tell her that Dr Wolfgang Dietrich, her German flame, came over for dinner.

'Did he ask about me?' she wants to know.

'I think we discussed it briefly,' I lie.

'Have you been in touch?'

'A bit.'

She shrugs. 'It sounds like you've had a lot going on.'

When I get to the bit where I kissed Dr Prince, her eyes widen but she doesn't say anything.

'I'm such an idiot,' I say pathetically when I've finished. I wipe my nose on my scrub shirt. 'It's all my fault.'

'Of course you didn't cause his heart attack. God, Kitty, you're a doctor—you know better than that.'

Nicole is actually being pretty reasonable. I feel bad for having had misgivings about her. She waits until Winnie gets home before she leaves. She promises me she won't tell anyone what I've told her, but if I want to make a complaint about the Joker, she says, she'll help me write it.

'Thanks, Nicole,' I say as I walk her out. 'You've been really nice.'

'It's okay,' she says, giving me a hug at the door. 'I see how hard it is for you guys. As doctors, you're not given much support. People expect you to be so perfect all the time.'

As soon as the front door closes, the door to Winnie's bedroom opens and she emerges. 'What was that about?' she asks. 'Why were you crying? Is that the woman from admin with the sexy clothes?'

I'm reluctant to tell Winnie what has happened, remembering uncomfortably how adamant she'd been that I should report it. If only I'd listened.

'You were right,' I say, giving in and sliding down the wall to sit in the hallway. I stare at a crack in the plaster and suppress a sigh. Me and the house, my beloved old house, we are both falling apart.

Winnie looks at me. 'Right about what?'

'The Smiling Assassin tried to kill herself,' I tell her flatly, seeing no other way to put it.

Winnie opens her mouth but doesn't say anything.

'I know you told me I should tell someone. You were right.'

'Oh, Kit,' Winnie says, her face crumpling with sympathy. 'I didn't want to be right.'

'Yeah, but you were.'

'How is she?'

I shrug. 'She's in intensive care. Overdose.'

'Shit.' Winnie grimaces. 'At least she's still alive.'

'You can say it,' I tell her. 'I fucked up.'

Winnie sits down next to me in the hallway, looking thoughtful. 'No, you didn't,' she says, too kindly. 'I don't think anyone truly understands, me included, exactly what it's like to be in that position.'

'But you did.' I can't shake the guilt. Since when had I lost my empathy? When I started medical school, if someone have told me I'd be too afraid to report a potential sexual assault, or sexual coercion at the very least, I would have laughed in their face. Look at me now. The brave and powerful Dr Katarina Holliday.

'It's all just so extreme,' Winnie points out. 'Jack professes his love for you and nearly dies; she professes her hate for you and tries to kill herself; you're constantly dreaming about dead bodies and having to look at dead people. Like, it's fucking weird, man. When you take away all this medical bullshit and pretence, that's exactly what all this is. It's fucking WEIRD.'

To hear the words is a strange relief. It simplifies everything. Doctors are once-normal people who get stuck in totally fucking weird situations—and it makes us all crazy.

forty-eight

I LOOK AT MY WATCH, MESMERISED BY THE SECOND HAND as it ticks onto 2 am. I rub my eyes. Just for something different, I'm sitting on the surgical ward, listening to my pager go off. I'm exhausted. All day and night my thoughts have been crowded with images of the Smiling Assassin's face. It's like she's on the ward with me.

Please call the private hospital on 7806.

I read the message on my pager and wonder why the private hospital is calling me at two in the morning when I'm the intern covering the surgical wards at the public hospital. The private hospital is a painful ten-minute trudge up the road. It's not that far, I guess, but the two hospitals exist as separate planets. The private is an otherworldly paradise, the garden of medical Eden, where the patients can choose a wine that matches their hospital dinner, and the doctors are paid huge amounts of money.

I dial the number, curiosity almost breaking through my exhaustion.

'Hi, it's Katarina Holliday,' I say into the phone.

The nurse on the other end is breathless with relief. 'Are you the surgical intern? At the public?'

'Yeah.'

'We have a cannula that fell out,' she says—the words every intern dreads. 'No one can put it back in and the night doctor has gone home sick.'

I picture the long walk to the private and immediately try to deflect responsibility. 'Are you sure it's me you call? I don't even know if I'm allowed over there,' I say, stalling.

'You're the surgical intern?'

'Yes,' I admit, sensing defeat.

'Our protocol is if our doctor isn't here and the intensive care registrar is busy, we call you.'

When a nurse invokes a protocol, there's little point in arguing.

'Is the intensive care registrar busy?' I ask, already knowing the answer.

'Yes,' the nurse replies flatly. 'So as soon as possible would be good.'

Sighing, I stand up and start the trek through the dimly lit ward down the stairs and out the front doors to climb up the hill to the private hospital. Surely there are better things to be doing at two o'clock on a Thursday morning. For example, I could be having sex with a nice man, who I would have met because I had a normal life where I wasn't at work all the time. Or I could be at a bar with some friends meeting said man. Or, even better, I could be asleep in my own bed.

Entering the private hospital, I locate the nurse who called me and she directs me to room 834. I gather up the cannula equipment and head down the corridor. Just as I'm about to turn into room 834, I notice the door to the room opposite is open and the light is on. Peering in, I see the patient is standing up, wrestling with his IV pole.

I'm about to step into the room and offer him some assistance when he looks up and our eyes meet.

For a moment the world spins, and I drop my equipment on the floor.

I don't know how to react, so I tear my eyes away from Dr Jack Prince, patient, hastily gather up the equipment I dropped, and charge into room 834.

'Hi, I'm the doctor from the public hospital just here to put a drip in!' I exclaim, my face flushed and my heart pounding. I start to put in the cannula, my hands shaking.

'Have you done this before?' the patient asks me, looking suspicious. I swallow a laugh. How can I tell him the truth? That I've put in thousands of cannulas and the reason why my hand's trembling is because the man in the room opposite is my former boss who nearly died the day after we kissed, *Casablanca*-style, under a streetlamp outside my house?

'A few.' The cannula goes in smoothly, almost to my distress. Now I'll have no excuse to stay. I hover at the door, stalling. 'Do you need anything else?' I ask desperately.

'Yes,' the patient snaps, irritated. 'I need to go to sleep.'

I step into the corridor. I can just leave, I tell myself. That isn't unreasonable. Maybe Dr Prince doesn't want visitors, especially me. Plus, it is two o'clock in the morning. Perhaps I could just give him a wave, call out, 'Hope you get better soon', and make a quick exit.

Then I notice that his door's closed. Well, that makes things easier. I can just leave and he'll never see me walking away.

I'm still hovering outside the door, feeling foolish, when the nurse appears.

'Thanks for doing that,' she says.

'No problem,' I say, trying to conceal my interest in Dr Prince's room. Nurses are the gatekeepers to patients, particularly patients who work as surgeons in the hospital. There's no way she would allow me to see him.

'Ah, I just better jot something in the patient's chart,' I lie, gesturing to the room I've exited.

The nurse shrugs and continues up the corridor.

When she's gone, I step over to Dr Prince's door and take a deep breath. I tap on the door lightly and give it a little push. It swings open and I poke my head into the room.

Dr Prince is still standing up, preoccupied with his IV pole. When he sees me, he looks surprised, but not horrified. He doesn't look angry, just a bit . . . startled.

I don't blame him. I'm feeling pretty startled myself.

'Um, hi,' I say quickly. 'Ah, I saw you before and I just wanted to, ah, see if you need any medication charted before I go—like sleeping tablets or painkillers or . . . something.'

I'm pleased with this sentence. Now he can politely decline, I can leave, and we can both go back to struggling through the rest of the night, and the rest of our separate lives.

'Or, you know, champagne,' I say, laughing. I immediately regret it. What's wrong with me? What kind of a joke is that? The last time he and I drank champagne together he ended up here. God, I'm such an idiot.

'No, I think I'm all right,' he says.

It's strange to see him wearing a blue patient gown, like, well, a real patient.

He *is* a real patient, I remind myself. Being a doctor doesn't preclude you from being a patient. Moron.

He doesn't look so different from when I saw him last—just a bit tired.

I'm about to make my excuses and leave when he says, 'Do you want to sit down?'

'Um . . .' I don't know what to say. 'Ah, okay.'

He shuffles around the small room and sits down on the bed.

'Do you mind if I sit on your bed too?' I ask timidly.

He motions me over. I sit down next to him. I've fantasised about the two of us in bed together after dark, but this isn't exactly the scenario I had in mind.

'Sorry, I didn't say hi before. I felt kind of awkward and I didn't want to . . . bother you.'

'That's okay,' he says. 'I wasn't sure whether I'd see you again.'

I turn my head to face him. 'I've been really worried about you,' I say.

He looks surprised, and touched.

'How are you?' I ask.

He laughs. 'How do you think? Kitty, I'm so fucking over this.'

I see the expression in his eyes and I know what it means because I've seen it before, many times. I've seen it when jabbing people's veins to put in cannulas or take bloods. I've seen it in the emergency department palpating someone's abdomen. I've seen it in the anaesthetic bay before a person is sedated. I've seen it in Estelle that night in the ward in Wingabby when the baby died, and I've seen it in myself when I look in the mirror.

It's the bone-aching weariness that I've only ever seen inside a hospital, and in the eyes of two groups of people: patients and doctors. He's flipped a coin and, impossibly, it's landed on both sides.

'I bet.'

Our eyes meet.

'You look tanned,' he says. 'Have you been away?'

'It's fake,' I confess.

He grins. I blush.

'I might go away, though,' I tell him. 'I'm thinking France. Maybe next year, when I have some money.'

'Have you been before?'

I nod. 'I love the south especially. The food, the people, the wine . . .' For a moment I'm lost in memories.

'I should have spent more time in Europe,' Dr Prince says almost wistfully.

Being stuck in a hospital bed allows plenty of time for brutal reflection. The impossible question reverberates around my head: what is it that we recall when we are dying? Would it be the last operation we couldn't complete, the tumour we didn't get to excise? Or would it be a beach we never walked along in the south of France, the wine we didn't drink, the love we didn't make?

The people we didn't make love with?

Perspective: the most bitter pill of all to swallow.

The thing between us—whatever you want to call it—hovers in the air. Our eyes, which are just eyes and have no special significance, meet, and I swear just for a second neurosurgical research means nothing and the door blows open and I stare directly into the man's soul.

'My wife really likes the south of France,' he says suddenly, looking down at the bedsheet.

I nod.

He looks up and, oddly, the door stays open, the shutters up. He doesn't have to say anything, but I get it. It's why I like him so much, I realise. There are always rumours in hospitals; people having sex with other people, affairs, bad behaviour, sleaze, lust. But sitting there on his hospital bed, as we both silently acknowledge the painful truth that we have simply just missed each other in time, I realise that what draws me to Dr Jack Prince is his decency. And our wonderful connection, forged against all odds, remains intact inside a place neither of us will ever visit. He goes back to his wife, and I go back to my life.

But we will meet in the rose garden, that metaphorical place where what never happened is as true as what did. And our story will forever be imprinted on the pages of the life of Kitty Holliday, the writer.

The thought, as foolish as it may be, comforts me. I wonder if he realises the impact he has had on me, quite apart from our mutual attraction. Any senior consultant who shows an interest in the wellbeing of their struggling juniors and is kind to them can make an enormous difference. Perhaps if someone had cared about the Smiling Assassin, things would have turned out differently for her.

My pager goes off. I ignore it and stay there, next to him on that bed. We talk about sickness, about my plans for the future, about the hospital and about the other doctors. He starts to look exhausted, so I move to get up. As I do, to my surprise he pulls me towards him. He holds me tightly, as if he never wants to let go, and I place my lips on his cheek and let them linger on the warmth of his skin. We lie there, gripping each other, for several minutes.

'I'd hug you tighter, but I'm in pain,' he says as we break apart, and we both laugh softly.

I get up and leave the room, shutting the door behind me. I walk the long road back to the public hospital and into the doctors' room. There I gaze out the window overlooking the houses below, where people are sleeping peacefully in their beds, only their dreams as distractions. I see the roof of my own house, two short blocks away. I see another me, dreaming through my sleep, and I let myself ask the unaskable question, the one that most doctors bury because they've already given or lost too much by the time they're desperate enough to ask it. Was it a mistake, choosing to be a doctor? In another life, could I have done something different, something better, something that made me better? I thought when I finally finished medical school that everything would fall into place. *Let the healing commence, Dr Holliday.*

Is this what you really want? I ask myself. Is this the person you really want to be?

I finally understand who is on the other side of the looking-glass. I'd always thought there must be some glorious other self or alternate universe. Now I understand that's not it at all. There's no one particularly special on the other side of the mirror. It's just plain old human Kitty. Forget the prestige and the intellect and the grand future plans and the absolute power of the surgeon. Forget all of that. On the flipside of the mirror I am no one, but I am everyone. I love my mum and dad, and I cry in sad movies. I worry about losing weight and I feel the sting of unreciprocated love. On the public side, the side my patients see, the side I present to my colleagues, the esteemed Dr Katarina Holliday, I wonder now if it's all just a bit of an act. On one side of the looking-glass there's rather unextraordinary me, on the other side a consummate performer. Maybe it's the same for all doctors. Maybe we are all just actors, pretending to be doctors, inside a theatre with a curtain that never falls.

I stand there with my chin on my clenched fist and watch the darkness of the night for a long time.

forty-nine

FOR THE NEXT WEEK I DO NOTHING BUT GO TO WORK, then go home. I also start exercising and I even cut down on the wine. After everything that has happened, I need to clear my head.

As I'm arriving home one evening, I run into Max, exiting the front yard with a toiletries bag in hand.

He looks as miserable as I've been feeling. It's strange to recall that the last time I saw him we were laughing our pants off in the cafeteria over #accidentalboobgate. Vascular surgery is a far cry from his summer respiratory term, and he's stressed.

'Hey,' I say. 'Long time no see.'

'Hey,' he says. 'Work's been fucking bad the last two weeks. Sorry I haven't been around—I couldn't handle the thought of cooking so I'm back at Mum's.'

'Don't worry,' I reassure him. 'I've had a lot of shit going on too. It sucks.'

He opens his mouth as if to speak, then pauses.

'What's up?' I prompt him.

'Did you hear about . . . ?' He stops.

'Yeah,' I say. 'It's pretty terrible.'

He has a funny look on his face.

'Are you sure you're—?' I start.

He interrupts me. 'Apparently they've sent her to the psych ward. I heard that yesterday.'

'Fuck.'

We lapse into silence.

Psychiatry is all about electricity. Little pathways in the mind that are burnt-out or need rewiring. Inside the psych unit is where we rewire them. More dopamine here, less dopamine there. A current through this part, but not that part. Fix those little electrical pathways, the ones that allow people to smile. Maybe they'll smile again, maybe they won't.

The place where the Smiling Assassin lies now. Probably not smiling.

What is it, I wonder, that causes us to tip over the edge? All it takes is one trauma, one bad trip, one too many stresses, an illness, a death, or—and this is what's scariest—nothing at all to send someone tumbling into the void.

I think about Fabien, skiing down that fantastic mountain. That's the very opposite of the abyss—the wonderful peaks of the Swiss Alps, a paradise where things like shock therapy and shackles are far, far away. Fabien always told me that he doesn't care where he is or what he does, so long as he is happy.

What is happiness, anyway? It's just some electricity and some dopamine, I think viciously. You can get that shit in a pill and an electrode. All it really takes is a prescription and a broken spirit.

I hear my voice speaking, lifting me out of the rabbit hole I've found myself falling into.

'Listen, Max, if there's something you want to talk about . . .'

He gives me a sharp look. 'Like what?'

'I don't know, anything. You seem a bit flat.'

'So do you,' he points out. 'Is there anything you want to tell me?'

I'm so close to opening my mouth I can see the words floating into the air. *Yes*, I shout, *yes! I heard the Smiling Assassin giving the Joker a blow job in the theatre change rooms even though she didn't want to, and now she's tried to kill herself and I feel like if I'd told someone I could have stopped her. I'm a pathetic coward and I don't know how to fix it.*

'Not really,' I say, hating myself. 'You know, just work getting me down.'

He nods. 'Me too.'

We sigh simultaneously.

'Don't forget I'm going on annual leave next week,' he reminds me, looking happier for an instant.

'That's right—Europe!'

He grins. 'I can't wait. I'm gone for a month.'

'Make sure you get regular STI checks!'

'Maybe you can take me to the airport,' Max says, his grin broadening as he walks towards the gate.

'If you're lucky!'

He waves as he disappears up North Avenue. I wish I was going to Europe with him. I want to be sitting in a little bar with Max in Greece, drinking cocktails and talking about the hospital as if it was just a vague, distant memory.

Reality, I think to myself as I unlock the door, is seriously overrated.

fifty

ONE WEEK LATER I'M CALLED INTO THE OPERATING theatre to assist with the last case of the list, a head trauma. I'd been hoping to leave work at a respectable hour to go and meet Max before his flight, but the Joker is trying to ruin my day again. He knows that calling someone in late means they'll be stuck in theatre well into the evening. 'Just ask for overtime,' he says, knowing very well that I can't.

The good news is that Dr Prince has been discharged and is deemed fit to operate again after one month. I haven't seen him since our 2 am rendezvous on his bed at the private hospital, but I think that's a good way to end things. It's important to know when it's time to leave the party.

'You're late,' is the first thing the Joker says to me as I walk to the sink to start scrubbing in.

'You called me pretty late.' I refuse to look at him.

He makes me sick. I turn on the tap with my elbow, ignoring the fact he is standing next to me.

'You're not going to get very far in surgery with that kind of attitude,' he says, starting the tedious process of washing his hands.

'I don't think I want to get very far in surgery anymore, thanks.'

I must have finally reached the end of my tether to be so overtly rude. I'd normally be too intimidated. I know I should tread carefully, but I'm feeling reckless. A lot has happened over the course of the year, and it's hardened me.

He looks at me, but I continue to avoid eye contact. Picking up the nailbrush, I focus all my attention on getting the grime out from under my thumbnail.

'You'd never make it anyway,' he says. 'You don't have the right temperament.'

I don't have the right temperament?

I turn off the tap with such force it makes a clanging sound; I actually think I might have broken it. I don't care. I turn to face him, red swarming everywhere. I reach over and turn off his tap too so there's no noise and it's just the two of us.

'Hey! What the fuck are you doing? You're going to need to rescrub!' He leans forward to turn the tap back on.

I reach out and block his arm with my hand. 'Listen to me,' I say quietly, and I'm so angry I can feel my pulse rate shooting up. 'I know what you did. I know you were making her give you blow jobs after hours, you disgusting pig.'

All I can see is the red; it's everywhere. In front of my eyes, in my ears, roaring through my body.

'I heard you, you idiot,' I hiss. 'I heard everything. I know why she took all that valium. It's because of *you*. She was too scared to tell you to fuck off, and because you were abusing her all that time she's now lying in the fucking psych ward. You evil man. You fucking horrible man.'

He moves his mouth slightly, sort of like a smile. 'Prove it,' he says calmly.

'I'll get her to back me up,' I say. 'She's got nothing to lose now. You'll pay for this. I'll be a credible witness and you're going to get deregistered—or at the very least sacked!'

He moves his mouth again, and I see he really is smiling. I feel a bit uneasy. He's clearly totally unhinged.

'You're very self-righteous for someone who isn't exactly a saint,' he says.

I look at him.

'There's a certain favourite consultant of yours who just got out of hospital and who wouldn't be too pleased to know that his little intern has been telling everyone that they're having an affair.'

I feel bile rise up in my throat. I turn back to the sink and take a breath.

'I don't know what you're talking about,' I whisper, feeling my face getting hot.

He laughs. 'I'm sure the hospital executive would be very interested to hear that one of its most senior members of staff has been carrying on with his intern. Who knows how long you've been at it for? Did you think he'd help you get onto the training program?'

'Who told you this?'

'You're not the only one who has friends in the admin office,' he says. 'Maybe they're better friends with me than they are with you. You're an intern. I'm a surgeon. Who do you think they're going to believe?'

Nicole. My stomach twists. I was right about her all along. She caught me in a weak moment and I, as per usual, wasn't able to keep my big mouth shut. She was probably so jealous to hear that I'd been hanging out with Wolfgang that she decided to screw me over.

'So I'd think twice before I go and make any big statements,' the Joker says casually, as he turns the tap back on to finish scrubbing in. 'It's not only your career that you'd be ruining, but his too—and so soon after he nearly died. But, you know, we can't have this sort of thing going on, so I'd be doing the right thing for any other innocent interns he might want to take advantage of. Really, when you think about it, I have no choice but to tell the executive everything.' He tilts his head. 'I always wondered why he liked you so much and gave you so much support,' he muses. 'I mean, it made no sense to be that nice to someone who's so hopeless at surgery.'

I take a step back from the tap.

'Except now,' he continues, 'of course, it does make sense.'

I stare at him, wondering how long I'd have to serve in prison if I ripped the tap off the sink and charged at him with it. I imagine beating him across the head until he is lying, whimpering, in a pool of his own blood, at which point I would finish him off with a swift hard kick to the testicles.

'So just think about it,' he says, smiling at me. 'Are you going to finish scrubbing in now?'

I shake my head. 'I don't feel very well,' I say coldly. 'I'm afraid I'll have to sit this one out.' I leave the operating theatre, go down the stairs and sit in the deserted change rooms.

My medical career lies in tatters. Even if I technically can't be sacked for kissing Dr Prince, the Joker could probably spin it to make it look as if we've been having a full-blown affair since the start of my internship. That would effectively destroy Jack's career and also look very bad for me. They'd probably start to question what other sexual favours I've been performing to get through my neurosurgical term.

However I look at the situation, it's a complete catastrophe. I wonder if I could just deny everything. Of course I'll have to do that anyway, but the seed of doubt will be planted and my job at the hospital will be toast either way.

I wonder if I should go and talk to the Smiling Assassin. But as soon as the thought enters my mind, I reject it. She's probably loaded up on so many different psych meds she's completely out of it. And even if she wasn't, I'd be the last person she'd want to see. I don't want to make things any worse for her and I don't have anything really constructive to say. Clearly she hasn't said anything to anyone about the Joker, as he is still very much employed, and I don't want to force her into exposing her private life, which she obviously wants to keep hidden.

I wonder if I could take some sick leave. Or move to another hospital. That's probably my best option, I think as I pull off my scrub shirt. There's no point in getting all upset and carrying on; I need to be pragmatic and think logically.

I've seen better days, I think as I zip up my bag and head out of the theatre change rooms to go home. I've definitely seen better days.

fifty-one

ON THE WEEKEND, FOR THE FIRST TIME IN A MONTH, I make the long drive home to see my parents. It isn't the bravest of moves, but I just don't know where else to turn.

My parents left Sydney many years earlier and live down the coast on a small farm. It's very peaceful there. When I look out at the green hills and the blue sky my mind is always calmed.

I tell my parents everything. I expect them to be shocked, but they're not. I guess after twenty-nine years there's nothing I can do that would surprise them.

'Look, in the end,' Mum says, 'even though you're an intern and they're surgeons, you're all just people. Jack Prince is just a person. And the Joker is just another dickhead in the workplace, like a dickhead in any workplace.'

The difference, of course, is the added complication of trying to heal people who are sick and dying, but all that really does is tack on another layer of stress. She's right. The principles are the same as in any workplace.

'I'd just keep your head down for a while and see what happens,' Dad says, taking his usual slightly conservative approach, which is ironic considering he has such a wayward daughter.

'It's like a Greek tragedy,' Mum muses. 'You've got all the elements.'

We both smile despite ourselves.

'Actually, darling, I bought you something,' Mum says, standing up. 'A book.'

Of course it is. Most gifts exchanged in our family are books. 'Is it a good read?' I ask.

'No, it's a book for you to write in,' she explains. 'I saw it at the post office and I thought you could use it to write down your thoughts. You're always saying you want to write a novel.'

Mum and I share a weakness for pink sparkly things, and when she hands me the little pink hardcover notebook I love it immediately, despite it being so kitsch.

Follow your dreams! the cover urges in sparkly silver lettering.

Mum rolls her eyes, still smiling. 'Yes, I know it's a bit chintzy but, you know, it's a nice colour. It's only a small thing, but I thought you might like it.'

'I do like it!' I say, giving her a quick hug. 'I'll use it every day to write down all my feelings and how depressed I am.'

Mum, Dad and I laugh. It feels good. It makes me realise that Mum's right; what's done is done and I'll just have to deal with it. It's very easy to get caught up in the hospital hierarchy and the dramas, but the point is that what I'm dealing with isn't actually that different to the shit most people have to deal with in their workplaces. I suppose there's this expectation that as doctors we should all be a bit better behaved.

Even Greek tragedies have to end somehow, I muse as I fly along the highway back to Sydney on Sunday evening. (Always badly, I admit.) What I really need now is the ancient deus ex machina used to transport actors on and off the stage. The winged bird in the machine flies down and airlifts the protagonist away from their plight regardless of what wrongs they've committed. It's a convenient way to wrap things up.

I never thought I'd say this, not having been a great fan of Greek tragedies at school, but if only real life were as simple.

fifty-two

THE NEXT NIGHT I'M SITTING ON THE SURGICAL WARD on the after-hours shift, dreaming of the south of France. Going home to see my parents seems to have unlocked something in me. Mercifully, it's a quiet night for once, so I take out the little book Mum bought me at the post office and start making some notes.

Chapter One, I write carefully with one of the hospital pens I've stolen from a nurse. Maybe I'll begin with my first day as an intern, the failed cannulation?

Failed cannulation blood bath, I scrawl, chewing on the end of the pen. Or maybe a prologue? Toby Henderson perhaps, and his line about doctors not coping . . .

Kitty Holliday the writer is interrupted by her pager going off.

Almost immediately, the nurse appears behind me.

'I just paged you!' she says, sounding annoyed. 'Why didn't you call me back? You need to go and see Mrs Davies in bed eleven.'

'Do I?' I say, feeling belligerent. 'Why?'

'You know how we thought she was aspirating this morning?'

I grunt in response.

'Well, ah, you know—she's kind of been near the end . . .'

'Is she dead?' I ask bluntly.

The nurse begins to stammer. 'Well, I—think so. I mean . . .'

'What do you mean you think so? Is she dead or not?'

'I don't know. I want you to come and have a look. That's your job!'

I sigh. 'Is she breathing?'

'No, she hasn't taken a breath for at least five minutes.'

I bite my tongue. I know what the nurse is doing. She knows as well as I do the patient is dead but she doesn't want the responsibility of calling it. I wonder what on earth she thinks is going to happen—that Mrs Davies will wake up after she's told me she's dead and then she'll be blamed for—what? Calling a false death?

No, I think bitterly. In the ridiculous and unlikely event of Mrs Davies rising like Lazarus down in the morgue—despite the fact she never will, except in a horror movie—the nurse wants me to cop the blame.

I walk over to Mrs Davies's bedside, where the nurses are speaking in hushed tones. I look down. Mrs Davies is indeed dead. I sigh. 'I think she's dead.'

The nurses look affronted, as if I should have put it more delicately. But I don't believe in euphemisms when it comes to death. Saying 'she's passed' or 'she's left us' doesn't change anything. Passed on what exactly? An auction? Left us for where—another house?

I go through the motions, then hurry out of the room. In my haste, I nearly walk straight into the cleaner, standing with her mop outside the door.

'Maybe don't go in there yet,' I suggest. 'She's just . . . died.'

The cleaner, an old Croatian lady I've seen on the ward before, doesn't look surprised. 'We must always be ready for death,' she croaks unexpectedly in her thick accent.

'Uh, yeah,' I say, trying to walk past her.

'He comes like a thief in the night.'

I stop. 'Sorry?'

'Thessalonians,' she says, looking me straight in the eye. 'Death comes like a thief in the night and we must always be ready.'

I'm lost for a response so walk away, feeling enormously unsettled. A thief isn't welcome in my home, let alone Mrs Davies's hospital room, but he's come anyway and stolen her last breaths with little regard for anyone but himself.

'Creepy Croatian cleaner,' I mutter, feeling spooked. Who gets around in dark hospital wards saying that death comes like a thief in the night? Outside the rooms of dead patients, for God's sake? Like, time and place, lady! Too soon!

'Can you call her husband?' the nurse asks, approaching from behind and making me jump.

'Yeah, I can,' I say, trying to ignore the hammering in my chest. 'But shouldn't the consultant looking after them do that?'

I call the consultant, hoping that he'll do the awkward job of calling the family, but he asks me if I can do it.

'Maybe just text me the husband's mobile number,' he says, 'and I'll call him later.'

'So, do you want me to tell Mr Davies you'll be giving him a ring?'

'No, no!' he says, sounding flustered. 'Just don't mention me! I'll think on it.'

I stare into the receiver. Seriously? I manage not to say, 'Thanks for nothing, fucko', and hang up.

'The husband, Keith, he always rings the ward around this time to check on her,' the nurse says, hovering behind me, sounding anxious. 'He lives pretty far away but he comes in every morning and stays till the afternoon, then calls at night to check how she is. You'd better call him straight away.'

She finds me the number for Keith Davies, and as the phone rings I flip through his wife's chart. It looks like she's been sick for a while. I feel a twinge of relief. He's probably expecting it, to a certain extent.

'Hello?'

'Ah, hello. Is this Mr Davies?'

Suddenly his voice changes. 'Yes,' he says, and I hear the trepidation in his tone.

I swallow. 'My name's Katarina Holliday, and I'm the after-hours doctor at Holy Innocents. I'm sorry to be calling so late. It's about your wife, Mary.'

'What is it?' His pitch rises. 'What is it? She's all right, isn't she? I knew I shouldn't have gone home! I was there earlier.'

I realise immediately that I've completely misunderstood the situation and that this isn't an expected death at all. I'm about to say words that Keith Davies will never forget. My voice will be indelibly imprinted upon his subconscious. He won't remember my name, but this phone call, this moment, this unwanted exchange between the two of us, will stay with him. What I am about to say will alter his life forever.

I start to feel mild panic rising in my chest. What the fuck do I say next? That she's dead? Isn't that too blunt? There's no going back, so I push forward.

'I'm so sorry to tell you this,' I start, and I mean it, 'but about half an hour ago the nursing staff noticed Mary's re—' I stop. 'Respirations' is a medical word. Too clinical. Too sterile. This is a human being I'm talking about. The love of his life, by the sound of it. The mother of the man's children, for God's sake. 'They noticed that, ah, Mary's breaths had started to slow down.'

'Oh, God,' he says, and his voice begins to break. 'But I can drive down now? I'll get there before she—'

'I'm really sorry,' I say again, cruelly forging ahead. 'They asked me to come up and see her, and I'm so sorry to tell you that around fifteen minutes ago Mary died.'

I didn't think phone receivers could bleed, but in that moment I realise I'm wrong. Never have I felt someone else's pain so acutely without being able to see them. His breathing is ragged, and his words are punctuated by sobs that go straight to my heart.

'No, no, no, no, no,' he repeats. 'No. Please, no.' He's in agony. The man is in complete, soul-destroying, bone-crushing agony. I'm horrified to feel my throat closing over and tears welling up in my eyes.

'I'm really sorry I had to tell you this,' I say, my voice hoarse.

'Me too,' he says, and we both manage a bit of a laugh before he collapses into loud sobs again. 'Where does she go now? Should I drive in?'

'No, no,' I say awkwardly. 'The body—I mean *Mary*—will be taken to the mortuary and you'll be able to see her in the morning.'

'The mortuary?' He sounds panicked. 'What happens there? Is she on a bed?'

'Well, um . . .' I wonder how to tell him that Mary's body will be put on a steel slab which is then pushed into a freezer.

Slab. Trolley. This was no good. No one wants to be told that the love of their life will be lying on a slab.

'It's sort of like a big chest of drawers,' I say finally.

'Mary's going into a drawer?'

'Well, no, not a drawer,' I reassure him quickly. 'It's, ah, more like a bed, but it's, ah . . .' I really don't want to say fridge. 'Ah, it's in a sort of cooling facility,' I settle on.

By this point Mr Davies is sobbing again.

'Keith, is someone there with you?' I ask.

He isn't coherent, having completely surrendered to his emotions, and another voice comes onto the phone. Keith and Mary's daughter is as upset as her father but she keeps it together, at least for the phone call. She thanks me, and I tell her, against all my medical instincts, to go and get a bottle of whisky.

'We're on the reds,' she says, and the Australian vernacular makes me smile.

'I'll say a prayer for your mum,' I say, and there's a pause. It's weird, in the middle of all this science, hospitals, slabs, medicine—in the end, it's the most comforting thing I can think of to do and say.

'Thank you. That means a lot.'

'She went peacefully,' I say truthfully. 'She really just sort of slipped away, the nurses said.'

I know that even if it had been a traumatic last few minutes I would have lied to her. I would have told her that Mary was prepared, that she was ready to go, that it was like she was drifting into the most peaceful sleep. I would have used platitudes like 'she had made peace with it all' and 'it was her time'. I would have said all those things, even if none of them were true. Sometimes, I realise as I hang up the phone, being a good doctor is just a case of being a good liar.

That's not a bad line. I find my new diary. *Follow your dreams!* it shrieks at me as I open the cover.

Sometimes, I write, *being a good doctor is just a case of being a good liar.*

fifty-three

'SOMETHING WEIRD IS GOING ON,' ESTELLE SAYS TO ME the next morning as I slide into a seat at our usual table in the cafeteria.

I'm tired from my late shift last night so I just yawn in response.

Estelle looks over at me. 'I mean it, Kitty! I just got out of the lift and one of the surgical registrars got in and it looked like he'd been crying. Then, when I was coming to meet you, I walked past one of the residents and she was, like, sobbing.'

'Job interview stress,' I say dismissively, stifling another, bigger yawn. 'It is that time of year.'

'Yeah, maybe.' She looks unconvinced. 'Maybe it's something to do with your old registrar—she did try and kill herself.'

'I don't think so,' I say. 'I saw the Shark on the round this morning, and apparently she's close to being discharged. She's doing much better, he said. They're having a meeting next week.'

The Smiling Assassin, according to the Shark, is 'much improved'. He also said—in not so many words—that her surgical career's probably over, in the city at least.

'There are always jobs in the country,' he told me uncomfortably. 'We need surgeons out there.'

'Life's probably a bit more chilled out in Broken Hill,' I said, trying to see the positives, and failing. Fabulous. Years of surgical training, sexual and emotional abuse by your superior, a suicide attempt, all for the glorious future of night shifts in Broken Hill, or equivalent.

'Kitty! Estelle!' The Godfather is striding towards us, looking flustered and upset.

Estelle looks at him. 'Have you been crying?' she asks incredulously. To me she says, 'See? I told you something weird was going on.'

'Is this about your job interview?' I ask him.

The Godfather gapes at me. Something about the way he looks at me makes me pause. The old saying 'somebody just walked over my grave' springs to mind.

We're interrupted by my phone ringing. It's the Shark, no doubt about something I've forgotten to do for one of the patients.

'Kit . . .' The Godfather is still staring at me intensely. 'I should tell you—'

'I have to take this,' I say. 'It's my boss.'

I answer my phone. Estelle is staring at the Godfather, he's staring at me, and I'm trying to hold my phone while eating my lunch at the same time.

'Is this about Mr Moretti's bowels?' I ask. 'He's passing wind today and feels like he needs to go, so I think his ileus is getting better. Do you want me to—?'

'Kitty,' the Shark says.

I stop talking immediately. I don't think he's ever used my nickname. Never. Not even in theatre when he laughed at one of my jokes.

'Where are you?'

I raise my eyebrows. Now this is definitely getting weird.

'I'm, ah . . .' I don't want to admit I'm in the cafeteria.

'Are you with people?'

'Yeah, I'm with my friends in the caf,' I say, now so confused I'm honest by accident. 'It's just a quick coffee,' I add defensively.

He sounds relieved. 'That's good. Kitty . . . Katarina . . . I need to tell you something. I would prefer to do it in person but I'm not at the hospital at the moment. I wanted to call you directly, though.'

I wait.

'It's about your registrar,' he says. 'Rachel.'

I look at the Godfather's red eyes and remember what Estelle just said, and I feel my heart sink into my shoes.

'She's dead.'

I hear the words but I'm not listening. The Godfather puts his hand on my arm and I see my phone clattering onto the table, nearly knocking over Estelle's coffee.

Dead. My mind rolls the word over. Asleep. More than asleep. Quiet. Silent.

Dead.

Just like Mrs Davies. Estelle is trying to talk to me but her words are a blur. I'm back on the ward last night, answering my pager. It's like someone hits rewind and I swear I look up and the Croatian cleaner is coming towards me, slowly dragging her mop and bucket.

Death comes like a thief in the night and we must always be ready.

But I'm not ready, I think, panicking. I'm not ready for any of this! I feel like I am Mr Davies. He wasn't ready either! How did Rachel die? Where's her body now? Did it hurt? Was she in pain? Did someone have to call her family? The whys, the hows, the questions swarm through my brain. Questions that no one, not even the smartest palliative care physician in the world, will be able to answer.

'Kitty?' The Godfather is staring at me anxiously. 'Kitty, are you okay?'

We always assume we understand death, I think, watching the world buzz around me in the hospital cafeteria. God knows we see enough of it. Now I know the truth. For all my medical experience, I have just as little comprehension of what death means as Mr Davies the night he sobbed down the phone when I called to tell him his wife had died.

Remember man that thou art dust, and to dust thou shalt return.

There are few true equalisers in the world, but death is one of them. Grief—the universal adaptor, almost cruel in its convenience—can fit any human plug.

fifty-four

RACHEL COPELAND WAS BORN ON 7 JULY 1985 AND DIED on 28 November 2016. She was thirty-one years old. When she was a child she liked playing tennis and told her mother she wanted to be an actress but gave it up for the pursuit of medicine. Children always dream of being actresses or writers but, like my mum always said, actresses and writers starve and doctors don't. Maybe Rachel's mum told her the same thing, I don't know. After medical school, she was set on becoming a surgeon. The only place she wanted to be was inside an operating theatre. She exchanged the ambition for one stage with another.

When she was my registrar I hated her. She reduced me to tears, belittled me, and made my work days a living hell. Other people told me that when they knew her, not so very long before I was her intern and the Joker her boss, she was funny and nice and loved doing karaoke. She missed her ex-boyfriend, who lived in another state, but she'd had to break up with him to come to Sydney to take the job of her dreams. She had a pet dog called Wolverine, and a collection of fridge magnets she'd bought on her travels through her early twenties. I found it hard to reconcile the woman I had known with the picture they painted. It made me realise that I hadn't really known her at all.

Her friends told me about her enormous intellect and determination, that these qualities could have got her anywhere. In the end, I guess they did. The morning she died she convinced the nursing staff to let her out on leave after her morning session with the psychiatrist, and she fled the psych unit on foot. She ran to the nearest major intersection and threw herself in front of a bus. They say she died on the footpath about two minutes later, and that she didn't utter a single word.

The hospital sends us a three-sentence email with a link to a counselling service and we keep going to work as if nothing has happened. They hold a small memorial service in the chapel which is interrupted by the constant beeping of pagers and awkward speeches by doctors who knew her and who have the same look in their eyes I'd seen in Dr Prince's the night I sat in his hospital room.

At home that night, I look at the memorial booklet with a picture of her on the front. The photo was taken in France, the caption says, in a town called Èze. I can see the Mediterranean in the background. As well as her many other skills, Dr Rachel Copeland spoke fluent French, having lived there for a year after she finished high school. I remember the morning on the surgical ward, and the funny expression on her face when she'd talked about the south of France. I wish to God that I had asked her about it then. I wish I'd known she could speak fluent French because of a conversation we'd had at work as colleagues, not because of a photograph on the cover of her funeral booklet.

I stare at the frozen image, at her smile and her hair. In the photo it's windblown and bleached white by the sun, not the neatly coiffed style I'd envied with perfect honey highlights. I stare at her smattering of freckles, dotted carelessly along her cheeks. An artist accidentally flicked his brush and sunlight scattered across the canvas of holiday skin, like gold poured into the crack of a finely wrought ceramic, the impossible contradiction of perfect imperfection.

I google Èze and discover it is a fortified medieval town that has been home to some of the world's most famous artists, writers and actors over the centuries. I try to imagine Rachel there, sitting in the sun, drinking wine and being happy. The images are distorted, mixed in with the look on her face when she saw me outside the change rooms, or on the ward rounds, when she told me that everything I did was always wrong. I wish I'd met her in Èze, and that I had known her as she was then.

The symbol of Èze is a phoenix perched on a bone, I learn, and the town's motto is *Isis Moriendo Renascor*—In death I am reborn.

All I can hope is that it's true. But who knows? Maybe at the end there is just the impact of a bus going sixty kilometres an hour, metal on flesh, and then nothing.

fifty-five

I'M NOT SURPRISED WHEN I RECEIVE THE EMAIL. I HAD a feeling that the Joker wouldn't just let things slide. I've no doubt that, after Rachel's death, a few questions are being asked—but, knowing the hospital, there'll be a quick internal investigation and the case will be closed. I've already heard the usual whisperings: 'She had issues', and, 'She was struggling', and, worst of all, 'Some people just can't hack surgery.' I've seen the Joker a few times since Rachel died and he's been his usual self. He doesn't seem to be particularly perturbed by what happened, and there's no sense that he realises her suicide was largely his fault. I know he must be worried that I'll tell the hospital what I saw, though, so I assume he's trying to destroy my credibility before I can destroy his.

Dear Katarina,

The hospital executive and myself have had a serious matter brought to our attention. We would like to request a meeting with you to discuss.

> We suggest Thursday at 4.15 pm in my office, which is on level 2 of the main hospital. Should you have any questions or wish to discuss anything prior, please call me.

It's signed by Dr Lawson, terrifyingly, the Director of Medical Services. I notice that the entire executive have been copied in.

'I think I'm about to get sacked,' I tell Winnie before I walk to work on Thursday morning. I'm feeling surprisingly relaxed about it. My main worry is still Dr Prince. I've decided long ago to fall on my sword rather than get him into trouble.

'I just had a really big crush on him, and I made up the kiss because I wished it would happen, but he was always so professional there was no way it ever would,' I practise saying to the mirror in the bathroom of number 19.

'Nicole had a relationship with a surgeon I am now good friends with,' I rehearse to Winnie, who's in the kitchen as I walk out of the bathroom, 'and I feel as if she became jealous of our friendship and has subsequently made up these vexatious lies.'

As for the Joker, well, I sought the counsel of the Godfather, who's become our go-to legal representative, and on his advice I documented every single time the Joker bullied me.

'I can't believe you used to be a lawyer,' I said to the Godfather in awe. I thought about that for a moment. 'Actually, maybe I can,' I corrected myself, remembering that lawyers are renowned for their copious cocaine use.

'Your mates can be full of surprises, Kitty,' he said seriously, putting his arm around me. 'I haven't even told you about the methamphetamine production line under my apartment building.'

I looked at him, eyes wide.

'Joking!' he said, grinning.

Was he joking? I wondered. Best not to go there . . .

I also wrote an account of my conversation with the Smiling Assassin about the Joker's coercion, but I'm not sure yet if I'll bring that up. Those are the big guns, the Godfather told me, only to be fired if things are truly dire.

'Okay,' I said, feeling a bit sick.

'Be confident,' he urged. 'You haven't done anything wrong. Yeah, you kissed your boss after a boozy dinner. Big fucking deal. This other guy, the Joker, he's behaved disgracefully.' He shook his head. 'Look, if it gets too much, say you'd like to call your lawyer, and I'll walk down from the ward and be there as your advocate.'

We both grinned, imagining me presenting my lawyer—another intern. At least it would be kind of funny.

The hours crawl towards 4.15 pm. I barely focus at work. I screw up cannulas on every single unfortunate patient who needs a drip on the ward because I'm so distracted.

I meet up with Estelle at 3.45 pm. I'm reluctant to tell her that the fateful night when I met her in the utility room has led to my demise, so instead I explain that Nicole has told the Joker I had an affair with Dr Prince and now I'm disgraced professionally and probably so is he.

'God, you didn't even have sex with him,' she says, rolling her eyes. 'At least then you could have said it was worth it. All you managed was a pash and a heart attack.'

'It's like the name of a band,' I can't help pointing out. 'Pash and Attack.'

'Or a dance move,' Estelle says and, despite ourselves, we both smile. 'You know,' she muses, 'I always did have this dream of opening a little ice-cream shop by the sea. I was going to call it Hot Licks. I think it would have been a huge success.'

I picture a nice little ice-cream place in an idyllic seaside location. I see Estelle and myself in matching aprons, with long sun-flecked hair and golden tans.

'Man, that would be so good,' I say wistfully, looking across at her.

'It's not too late,' Estelle says. 'By the end of this week we could both be out of a job, so why not?'

'I wonder if Dad would lend me some money to get Hot Licks started? I could sell it to him as an investment . . .'

'There's really nothing to worry about,' Estelle says positively. 'Just go in there, tell them the truth—what a fucking knob old mate is—then say thanks very much you're quitting anyway. This time next week, we'll be looking for a nice little shop to rent in Palm Beach or somewhere.'

Estelle and I have been through a lot together. If I'm going to throw it all in to open an ice-cream shop with anybody, I'm glad it's her.

'Hot Licks, mate,' are her last words to me before I leave the cafeteria to attend my own execution. 'It'll be way more fun than this.'

fifty-six

'*SEND NOT TO KNOW FOR WHOM THE BELL TOLLS, IT TOLLS for thee*,' I think gloomily as I make my way to level two. Well, I've been a doctor for a little less than a year, and it looks as if the journey is about to end.

I'd like to thank my friends, my family . . .

A billion years of hard studying only to find myself in this stupid situation, I think as I stand in front of the door to Dr Lawson's office.

I knock.

The door opens, and I see Dr Lawson, Nicole (to whom I give a dark look), Professor Trimby (who is the big boss overarching everything), and two empty chairs.

'Take a seat, Katarina,' Dr Lawson says—quite kindly, all things considered.

I sit.

'We're just waiting for a couple more people,' she explains, seeing me glance at the other chairs.

This is interesting. The Joker will be one of them, I suspect, but who's the other?

No one says anything. Professor Trimby offers me a glass of water, which I decline. Then I hear footsteps coming up the corridor. The door opens and in walks . . .

'Max?'

My housemate is standing in the doorway, looking extremely nervous.

I jump to my feet. 'Mate!' I exclaim, too loudly. 'I thought you weren't back from Europe for another ten days, at least!'

Max gives me a look that says, *Just shut up for a second.*

'Came home early,' he mutters, his eyes boring into mine.

No one else looks surprised to see him. I sit back down, completely speechless. What on earth is Max doing here? I suddenly remember the few times I'd seen him before he left for Europe, how stressed and anxious he looked, as if there was something he was on the verge of saying, but he was holding back.

Another tap at the door and the Joker appears, looking bored and irritated.

Dr Lawson clears her throat. 'Well, now we are all here, I suppose we can get started.'

I take a deep breath, and steel myself for the worst.

'I'd like to ask what the hell this is about?' the Joker demands, sounding incredibly angry.

I look at him in disbelief. What? Hadn't he been the one to call the meeting, to discuss my affair with Dr Prince? I try to catch Nicole's gaze, but she steadfastly refuses to make eye contact.

I start to feel extremely confused.

'I think Max should begin,' Dr Lawson says, giving the Joker a sharp look. 'Max, would you like to tell us what you saw on the night of June the twelfth, while you were in the male theatre change rooms?'

It suddenly dawns on me: Max was present that night as well. No wonder he's been behaving so oddly.

I stare at Max in shock as he starts to talk.

'I stayed back late to finish some research,' he says, 'and the person covering theatres after hours had called in sick. Because I'm keen to do surgery, I offered to replace her so the on-call doctor didn't have to come in.'

Everyone nods. I nod too. The Joker starts to look a bit uncomfortable.

'And the list finished at about ten-thirty that night,' he continues.

Yes, I think, that would have been right. That's when Estelle sent me the call-to-arms text, and I met her in the utility room.

'I went into the change room and then I needed to go to the bathroom. I didn't think I could wait till I got home . . .' He pauses, looking a bit sheepish.

'It's okay, Max, you don't have to justify needing to use the bathroom,' Dr Lawson says, sounding almost amused.

'Anyway, I was just about to flush the toilet,' Max says, embarrassed, 'when I heard some, ah . . . some unusual sounds.' He glances briefly at the Joker.

The Joker starts to speak, but Dr Lawson puts up her hand. 'Let him finish,' she orders.

'I heard someone calling someone else a . . . slut,' Max says awkwardly, 'and then what sounded like people taking their clothes off. I wanted to see what was going on, in case it was something bad, so I really quietly opened the toilet door and looked around the corner. They didn't see me, but I could see them.'

'What did you see, Max?' Dr Lawson leans in.

'I saw Dr . . .' Max tips his head towards the Joker, 'standing up with his pants off and one of the other doctors in the hospital . . . um . . .'

Everyone is silent.

'You know,' Max says uncomfortably, 'ah, performing oral . . . sex . . . on him.'

At this the Joker starts shouting and Dr Lawson starts shouting back, trying to calm him down. Max looks like he's about to be sick, and I just sit there, feeling completely numb. All this time, Max knew. If I'd said something or he'd said something, if we'd joined forces and done something sooner, together, maybe she would still be alive.

Through the numbness, I start to wonder exactly why I'm present at the meeting. No one has mentioned anything to do with me and Dr Prince. Max also wouldn't have known I had been there, as by the time I'd encountered Rachel she was out of the change room and Max's earshot.

'This is bullshit,' the Joker snarls. 'It's his word against mine. And just for argument's sake, say it did happen—and I'm not saying it did—but if two consenting adults should engage in such behaviour, well, doctors have done a lot worse behind closed doors.'

Even though I know it isn't true, I have to admit he has a point. I also know I can't back Max up, because if I say anything then the Joker will spill the beans about Dr Prince.

Dr Lawson looks at me. 'Katarina, you must be wondering why you're here.'

I nod. Well, sort of, yes.

I can feel the Joker's eyes burning into me. I feel less angry and more tired. I wish the Smiling Assassin (Rachel, I remind myself) was still alive so she could stand up and tell them what he had done to her. Unfortunately, she's dead, I'm alone, and he'll probably end up getting away with everything.

Dr Lawson clears her throat. 'Katarina, we have something that we'd like you to read.'

I have no idea what she's talking about. Crazily, I wonder for a split second if I've documented something incorrectly in the patient notes and that I'm getting in trouble.

'Have I done something wrong?' I ask.

Dr Lawson has a strange expression on her face. 'No,' she says, 'but I'm going to give you something and we are all going to leave the room while you read it.'

She pulls a piece of paper from a file. I notice that written on the front of the file are the words *Dr Rachel Copeland*.

Dr Lawson hands the paper to me. 'This was found in Dr Copeland's locker after she died,' she says. 'It's addressed to you, so we thought it was your right to read it.'

I feel the tears welling up in my eyes, and try to blink them away. It doesn't work, and I feel one, then two, then more tears begin to slide down my face. They drop onto the table. I worry, absurdly, that they will hit the paper and the ink will be smudged and then I won't be able to read the words.

Dr Lawson hands me a box of tissues. 'We'll give you some time,' she says. 'We'll be next door in the boardroom if you need us.'

One by one, everyone leaves the room.

Max catches my eye. 'Are you okay?' he asks quietly. 'Do you want me to stay?'

'I'll be all right,' I say, and he closes the door and it's just me and the piece of paper. I look down at the first words, *Dear Kitty*, and part of me wants to tear the letter into tiny pieces and throw them out the window. I imagine the white bits of paper falling through the air and down onto the grass under the hospital. I see them falling, like snowflakes, the words of a woman who has nothing else to say fluttering in pieces onto the earth, raining down onto the heads of the doctors underneath. The doctors won't notice. They'll be too busy rushing to their next ward round.

Dear Kitty,

Can I even call you that? I know it's what your friends call you, and some of the surgeons whom you seem to know, and like. When I was an intern I was too scared to speak to senior surgeons—you don't seem to be afraid. I never understood it. Maybe that's what it's like when you don't really want to be a surgeon; you have less fear and more words, and you can see life as an adventure rather than a set of chains. Once, when I was working late, I walked to the train station and saw you having drinks at the pub down the road with some friends. You were all laughing. You looked really happy, totally different from the way you were around me on the ward. Your friends were calling you Kitty, and I didn't even know that you had a nickname. I think it suits you. I've never really had a nickname. My ex-boyfriend called me Rachy and sometimes it annoyed me, but other times I liked it. I never spoke to you about my boyfriend. You probably think that I'm into surgeons and weird sex, and I don't blame you for thinking that after what you heard that night, but my boyfriend was normal and fun and sometimes we used to waste entire Saturdays watching episodes of The O.C. *Not even the latest series, but the really old ones. We'd pretend we were Marisa and Ryan. Sometimes we were Seth and Summer, but the further I got into surgical training the more I started to realise I'd always be Marisa.*

The tears are falling freely as I read the words. I see her face, pausing, thinking as she puts her thoughts to paper. I almost laugh at the *O.C.* comparison; I'd done the same thing with my first boyfriend, years before.

By the time I'd finished my residency all I wanted to be was a surgeon. I gave up so much for it. I moved away from my family, I left my boyfriend, I stopped seeing most of my friends, but I kept telling myself that it was worth it. There were times in the operating theatre when I felt like a superhero. Can you understand that? I think on some level you must. I saw your face, sometimes, while we were in there. You had that look of complete enthrallment. That's how it made me feel. Everything else became secondary.

She's right—I know exactly what she means. I'd said as much to myself: the operating theatre is a place where magic happens.

I don't know when it started to go wrong. It'd be easy to say it was when he became our boss and I started to turn into a nasty bitch, and then the sex stuff started and I didn't know how to say no—but it was before then. I would never have been honest about this before, but it's over for me now and I may as well tell the truth. It probably started in medical school, I'd say. I knew straight away that to do surgery you had to be strong and focused, and I saw what happened to students who let their emotions get the better of them and I told myself, over and over, that wasn't going to be me. They were weak, I was strong, and that was it. That's what I kept telling myself. I remember once, when I was in my final year, being quizzed on a ward round by some consultant and fucking up the name of the artery and him telling me how stupid I was. And I knew then that I wasn't good enough, that to get where I wanted I had to work harder, stay later, and be better. Only the strongest and smartest survive, and I didn't care if it meant I'd be staying back till one o'clock every morning or going in on the weekends—that was just what I had to do.

In my mind's eye, I remember Mr Waters. I see him vomiting up blood and the look of absolute terror in his eyes, reflected in my own. I remember how alone and isolated I felt. I see Estelle, sitting on the floor in Wingabby, tears running down her face. I see the Smiling Assassin, Rachel, sitting in front of me and picture her face after I'd heard the Joker calling her a slut. That is the trajectory. How does it happen? How do any of us let it happen? How do we go from wanting to save the world to this?

It starts the day you begin ignoring situations and your normal responses to them because you exist inside a system which tells you that you have to be tougher. You're dehumanising yourself and everyone around you to survive it, holding on to the mirage of finishing specialty training, of finally 'making it', whatever that even means. Then you meet yourself on the final day, the day you find that you're waking up, thinking today is the day you're going to throw yourself in front of a moving bus. We spend all our time trying to avoid death, but in the end for some of us death is the only way we can feel alive. Sex doesn't work. The only sex Rachel was having was the kind that wasn't even sex. It was just one step closer to the deafening silence.

When he started having a crack at me I was almost flattered at first. He's a qualified surgeon, he'd passed his exams and he has a public appointment—he has everything that I wanted, and I thought maybe because of that I wanted him. But I didn't want him, I'd only wanted what he had. When I realised that I wanted it to stop, by then it was too late. That night when I saw you, I saw myself through your eyes and I was so ashamed that I couldn't really face you anymore. I hated everything that I had become, but by then I didn't know what else I could do. I'd spent so many years of my life dedicated to getting this far that I didn't have anything else. I can barely have a conversation with my parents, let alone try for another career path. Surgery is everything, it is everything, and without it I have nothing. I am nothing.

He wouldn't leave me alone. If I didn't sleep with him, he told me, he'd give me a bad reference. And without a good reference from my direct supervisor, you and I both know I'd be screwed. I don't want to move to the middle of nowhere and be a shithouse surgeon because I couldn't make it here. In the end, if I had to give him a few blow jobs, so be it, I decided. I'd finish my term and move on and then I wouldn't have to think about it ever again. I mean, people have done worse things to get to where they want to be.

People have done worse things to get to where they want to be. The truth of the statement makes me wince. The conscious realisation that her experience was probably just the tip of a very large and very well-hidden iceberg shudders through my heart.

But then it got so bad I couldn't sleep, I couldn't eat, I started fucking up in theatre. It wasn't even just him; the other consultants were always calling me, the hours were horrendous, the hospital telling me off for being 'uncontactable' when I was just on the fucking toilet—I just can't see a way through.

People tell us we have options, but that's bullshit, Kitty. I can't quit surgery and I can't change my job and I'll never win against them. I'll never win. You must know that too. I don't even know why I'm writing you this letter; it's all pointless in the end anyway. I think I just wanted to explain why I behaved the way I did, and you were the only person who knew what was happening. And I wanted to say that I'm sorry. Maybe I wish you'd ignored my threat and had reported me to someone, but then I wouldn't have been able to handle everyone knowing, and whispering, and the nurses looking at me like I was this huge dirty slut who was trying to sleep her way through surgical training, even though it was only because I don't feel like I had any other choice.

I wish this mess hadn't happened, I wish it wasn't like this. I'm in this dark room with no windows and I can't even see a crack of light, Kitty, not even one crack. The darkness is everywhere and I'm so lost, I'm so lost and I'm so alone. I'm walking around in circles inside a prison cell of black and I just want it to stop. I wish I could make it better and go back and make different choices and do it a second time, but I think I've finished my race and I've screwed it all up.

Maybe this isn't the end, maybe it's just the start of something else. Maybe the light is waiting for me somewhere else, and I just need to get on with it and go there and leave this all behind.

I'm sorry, for what it's worth.

Rachel

A line from Tennyson, read to me by my mother long ago, floats through the aching fog in my brain. For some reason, it's all I can think of.

We die—does it matter when?
Sink me the ship, Master Gunner—sink her, split her in twain
Fall into the hands of God, not into the hands of Spain!

fifty-seven

BY THE TIME DR LAWSON AND THE OTHERS COME BACK into the room I've composed myself. I know what they're going to ask about: the event corroborated by Max and now, from the grave, by Dr Rachel Copeland. After warning me that if I told anyone she would ruin me, she'd then killed herself—but not before writing a letter naming me as a witness to her own ruin.

'When Rachel writes about "what you saw that night", what exactly is she referring to?' Dr Lawson asks me straight out, after I've reassured her that I am okay to continue with the meeting.

There's no point prevaricating now. 'I heard her in the change room with him,' I say tersely, gesturing at the Joker. 'And when she came out she looked like she'd been crying. Through the whole thing he was calling her a slut and other gross things.' I shudder.

'Exactly what Max heard,' Dr Lawson says.

Max and I both nod.

'But neither of you realised that the other was there.'

'No,' we both say at the same time.

The Joker immediately starts to bluster. 'She can't talk,' he says, glaring at me. 'She's been having an affair with Jack Prince.'

Dr Lawson looks at me with interest.

'That's a lie,' I say.

Dr Lawson catches my eye and I think I see the flicker of a smile hover on her lips before it is replaced with a grimace. 'Don't be ridiculous, David,' she says firmly. 'I know Dr Prince well. I'm close friends with his wife.'

I vaguely remember a story about Dr Lawson having an affair with her boss when she was his registrar and twenty years his junior, but no one talks about that anymore. They just say that she and her husband met at work and their attraction for each other must have overcome the age gap.

Guess I'm in good company, I think to myself wryly.

The discussion moves on to an internal investigation of the Joker. Realising our presence is no longer required, Max and I both rise and head towards the door.

'Actually, Katarina,' Dr Lawson calls after me, 'there's one more thing.'

I turn around.

'Dr Copeland left another note,' she says. 'The police have it now—it was in the pocket of her scrubs, which she left in her locker—but I wrote down the words.' She opens her file and leafs through it, pulling out a slip of paper. 'Her parents didn't know what this meant. Does it make any sense to you?' She reads: '*Isis Moriendo Renascor.*'

In my mind's eye, I see a phoenix perched on a bone, and a young woman smiling with a glass of wine in her hand in front of sea so blue it looks like something out of a film. A surgeon, but still an actress, bowing out with her final line.

'I've no idea,' I say, for the first time looking the Joker directly in the eye. 'I don't speak Latin.'

Then I walk out the door.

fifty-eight

'KITTY! WAIT!'

I ignore Nicole as we walk down the corridor towards the exit. I stupidly told her something in confidence and she betrayed me to the one person whom she knows I despise.

'Kitty!'

I turn around.

'Listen, I'm sorry,' she says. She sounds upset.

Sorry doesn't really cut it, but I pause anyway.

'You don't understand,' she pleads. 'After we had that conversation, and you were so upset, I finally rang Wolfgang—talking about him made me want to make things better between the two of us.'

I wait.

'And then he told me how well the two of you get along,' she says, straight out. 'That you're so smart and how he wishes when he was in Sydney doing work with Jack that you'd become friends then. And I just felt so jealous—of your friendship, of everything . . .' She trails off.

I don't know how to respond. I just stare at her.

'I was so angry,' she says honestly, 'that when I ran into you know who, and he was mouthing off about you and Rachel, I just blurted out that you were having an affair with the boss.'

I roll my eyes. 'It was one bloody kiss, hardly an affair. Exaggeration much?'

'It was stupid. I'm really sorry.'

I wonder how much of it is a genuine apology and how much is trying to save her own arse, but I'm too tired and too over it to care, so I tell her not to worry about it.

'Maybe we can have a drink after work some time?' she suggests.

I nod as we walk away, but I doubt it. There's one person whom I want to have a drink with, to whom I actually owe a whole lot of drinks, and that's Max.

'What I want to know,' I say as we sit down at the pub on the corner together over two glasses of the house white, 'is did you realise that I was there too?'

Max shakes his head. 'As soon as she walked out I couldn't hear anything else. I had no freaking idea you'd heard him as well! I would have told you ages ago if I'd known that . . . I can't believe you didn't tell me either!'

'I just can't believe we didn't tell each other any of this,' I repeat, shaking my head in disbelief. 'Like, we live together. We're best mates!'

'Well, I was going to tell you,' Max says, 'but then I was on night shift for months, and I was so fucking tired. I wasn't really coping, so I just moved in with Mum.' He pauses. 'And then, to be honest, all I wanted to do was go to Europe and forget about the whole mess. I mean I had some idea she'd taken the valium and stuff, but I was still too scared to say anything.'

It was while he was in Europe, he tells me, that he heard Rachel had killed herself, and he knew he had to speak up, no matter the consequences. Max had done what I wasn't brave enough to do: he emailed Dr Lawson and told her what he had seen.

'And there were a few pina coladas involved,' he adds. 'Dutch courage and all that.'

I nod empathetically. 'At least you said something! I was such a fucking coward, Max.'

'To be fair to you, mate,' Max says, 'Rachel didn't know I'd seen them, so she never threatened me like she did you. Plus I didn't have to work with them like you did.'

'So you don't think I'm pathetic for not reporting it straight away?' I ask him.

He shakes his head. 'Nah, I don't know what I would have done in your situation. Probably just wanted to move hospitals.'

We both laugh. God, it feels good to have a laugh.

'There's only one bit of it that's not quite true,' Max says, looking nervous and taking a large gulp of wine.

I look at him. 'What?' I say. 'Which bit?'

'Well,' he says, sheepishly, 'you know how I said that I'd stayed back late to help in the operating theatre?'

'Yeah,' I say, 'but that was true. You were helping Dr Glass.' I recall talking to Max in the cafeteria the day after I'd overheard Rachel and the Joker in the change rooms. *I didn't get home until pretty late last night*, he said. *I was helping Dr Glass in theatre. I reckon he'll give me a good reference.*

'Yeah, that *is* true,' Max says. 'But about Dr Glass . . .'

Dr Glass is head of one of the surgical departments and, like Dr Prince, a really big deal.

'So he asked me out for a drink,' Max says, grinning. 'And I was rushing to get changed after theatre because he and I were meeting afterwards.'

I start to laugh properly now, so hard I can't stop. 'I should have known! What happened?'

Max rolls his eyes. 'Well, what I was hoping was a rendezvous was actually just him introducing me to some senior surgical trainees he thought might be able to give me some more research—and you know how I am so over doing research. What a letdown!'

'Disappointing,' I say, grinning.

'What about Dr Lang the hot heart surgeon?' he asks. 'Have you sent him any more nudies?'

I hit him. 'I have *not* sent Dr Lang any more nudes. I think I only fancied him because he looks like an older surgeon version of Fabien anyway,' I confess.

Max reaches for my phone. 'I'm sure we can fix this.'

'Fuck off!' I yell.

'Jokes, mate!' Max yells back, a huge grin cracking his face. 'Watch out—you'll give yourself a heart attack and I'll have to operate on you!'

Max looks at me. I look at him. Then we laugh and laugh and laugh, and I feel better than I have in a very, very long time.

Con the Greek comes over carrying two glasses of wine.

'We didn't order more wine,' I say, trying to catch my breath as Max wipes tears from his eyes.

Con shakes his head. 'On the house.'

'What? But you're always saying the business is going broke!'

Con glares at me. 'It is.'

'So we'll pay,' Max exclaims, pulling out his wallet. He nudges me. 'I've got no money. Kitty, you pay.'

'Fuck off! I always pay!'

'No pay,' Con says firmly. 'This is the first time I've seen you two laughing together in a long fucking time. Doctors need more wine, and less work.'

'And more money,' Max says, gratefully accepting his glass.

'You don't need money in Kythira,' Con says happily, sitting on the stool next to us. 'In paradise, anything is possible.'

'We've just been in hell,' Max informs him.

They say the road to hell is paved with good intentions, but to paradise it's rocky and narrow and difficult.

I don't know where I'll end up; my penchant for kissing married men then nearly killing them probably means I've got my own special seat reserved in hell, but I feel like I've been trudging up the narrow road for years.

Maybe this time, I think, listening to Max and Con argue cheerfully about who's more broke, my paradise is here, and now.

Mum's voice reverberates through my mind again: year ten English, Milton's *Paradise Lost*.

Long is the way and hard, that out of Hell leads up to light.

fifty-nine

TWO WEEKS LATER, I SIT ANXIOUSLY ON THE WARD staring at my phone. The Joker has called in sick at the last minute, which isn't a surprise. Since the truth came out he's been calling in sick nearly once a week. According to the rumours he's either getting promoted or fired, so maybe he's making the most of his sick leave just in case. Regardless, the theatre list is cancelled so I retreat to the safety of the ward.

We're all waiting for the outcome of the inquest into the death of the child from Wingabby. The preliminary findings will be released in the afternoon, and Estelle texts me to say that she's expecting the worst.

I'll know by the end of the day. Stay tuned.

Finally, at around 4 pm, my phone beeps with a message from her.

Meet me in the utility room next to the men's theatre change rooms. NOW.

I stare at the words in disbelief. They could only mean one thing. Poor Estelle!

My phone starts to ring.

I answer it, preparing to say something sympathetic and supportive.

'JOKING!' Estelle shouts into the phone, sounding as if she's just won the lottery. 'Forget the utility room and get your arse down to the pub because we are celebrating, Dr Holliday! I've been cleared of any wrongdoing. I'm *innocent*!'

For once I feel no guilt about leaving work at the appropriate time.

I find Estelle at our usual table.

Con points at us. 'You have to pay today,' he shouts. 'I had to call in the plumber and you won't believe what he's quoted me. Fucking tradesmen.'

'So apparently the poor kid had congenital cardiomyopathy,' Estelle explains. 'Even if I had intubated the trachea, it still wouldn't have saved him. But it took ages to work out, because it's such a rare condition they had to get some pathologist in America to come and consult on it.'

We're both silent for a moment.

'Man, the inquest was stressful, though. I was shitting myself. It was horrible. The parents . . . Jesus.' She looks grim as she reaches for her beer. I reach for my own. Beer: thank God it exists. 'So, it's all over,' Estelle says, sighing. 'We don't have to start Hot Licks after all.'

I laugh. 'Man, it's almost a pity. Now we have to think seriously about the future.'

The Future. Just the thought of it makes me feel weird. After all of this, what's next for us? For me, for Estelle, for Max, for the Godfather, Dr Prince—where next? At least we have a next,

I realise soberly, thinking of the poor child from Wingabby—not to mention Rachel Copeland. Any kind of next is still better than cold hard dirt, a box, and my medical degree sitting silently behind a sheet of glass.

We're interrupted by a commotion at the bar. Max and the Godfather have arrived, and Max is trying to persuade Con to shout him another drink.

'We'll give you free medical care,' he promises.

Con laughs. 'The only time I see you is drunk, mate. As if I'm going to make you my fucking doctor!'

'Drunk doctors are the best kind,' the Godfather says, pulling out his credit card. 'It's okay, Max. I'll pay.'

Max doesn't even try to look remorseful. 'You know, I always forget my wallet,' he says, pleased with himself. 'Plus all my drink-driving charges have cost me a lot of money.'

'What?' I stare at him. 'What do you mean *charges*? I thought there was only one?'

The Godfather coughs. 'I'll get you a cocktail, Kitty,' he says quickly. 'Anything you want.'

I'm glaring at Max, the Godfather is paying for our drinks, Estelle is flirting with Con, and the paint is chipping off the wall next to us, the pub as old and seedy as ever.

People say that doctors save lives, but, being a doctor, I know the truth.

A routine operation can kill you, but friendship is forever.

Ashes, dust and beer.

sixty

ON MY LAST DAY OF WORK AS AN INTERN, THE LAST DAY I will be the most junior doctor in the hospital system or the world, I get a phone call from Winnie as I'm walking home.

'There's something for you at the door,' she says, sounding a bit confused. 'Um, are you going to be home soon?'

'It's not a bloody bomb, is it?' I ask, wondering if maybe the Joker has risen.

'No . . . but it's pretty explosive.'

I sigh. No doubt it's another parking fine. I make a mental note to have a go at Winnie as soon as I get in. Like, who calls someone up about a fine?

Walking down North Avenue, with the hospital looming behind me, I wonder how I will feel when I wake up tomorrow morning as a medical resident, now only the second-most junior doctor in the hospital. Probably much the same, I realise, allowing myself a small grin. Still, one rung higher is one rung higher. Medicine is nothing if not an exercise in delayed gratification.

As I near number 19, I notice there's someone sitting on the front doorstep. Oh, God—they've actually sent a debt collector?! I turn through the front gate and stop abruptly, unable to believe what my eyes are telling me.

He's as tall as I remember. His dark hair is the same, flopping over his eyebrow. He's tanned and looks like he's stepped off an island paradise—which he probably has, I remind myself. He's wearing a t-shirt with a picture of a cartoon dog on it, and he is holding a package. I stand gaping at him, speechless.

'Hi, Doc,' he says. 'We've got to stop running into each other like this.'

The violins which have started up in my head come to a screeching halt.

'Nice line,' I say. 'What do you think this is? A movie?' Then: 'Well, you took your bloody time! Good to see you're capable of actually making a flight!'

'Do you always have to start an argument?' he replies, looking irritated. 'I'm trying to be romantic.'

'Sorry, I'm a bit lacking in the romance department,' I snap. 'I've been working hard while you've been gallivanting around.'

He grins. 'Okay, angry pants.'

I try extremely hard not to smile.

'I got you a present,' he says, unwrapping the parcel he's holding. 'It's a leather purse—had it made by a tailor in Saigon in Vietnam. It has *Dr KH* inscribed on it, see . . . and I had it made with a blue zip, because I know blue is your favourite colour. Remember your blue ski pants? I carried it all over the world for you. Then I messaged Winnie and got your address so I could surprise you after work.' He gently lifts my stethoscope from around my neck. 'Wow,' he says, grinning, 'you *are* a real doctor.'

'Don't think you'll be working as a surf instructor while I slave my arse off in the emergency department,' I warn.

'I know.'

Then there's no more talking, and as we move towards each other I feel my mind completely empty, for once, of all lingering thoughts.

I am finally a real doctor, and Fabien has finally come home.

epilogue

One year later

I WALK ONTO THE PEBBLES FOR THE SEVENTH CONSECUTIVE morning and wave at the men building the bar on the beach at Èze. I flew into Nice eight days ago.

One morning I woke up and decided it was time to take six months off training to finally try to write my book. I found a tiny apartment on the French Riviera with an internet connection, and two weeks later I was gone. I packed only carry-on luggage, my laptop and the little pink book my mum bought me at the post office, its pages now filled with notes: it contains people, experiences, tears, pain, memories and love. My dreams, and my nightmares, encased in bright pink fake leather. The glittery cursive *d* has faded, and *Follow your dreams* looks more like *Follow your reams.* It's tattered and old now, and stained with red wine from when Estelle knocked over a glass as I was reading her and Max an excerpt.

'You have to write this book, Kitty,' she had said, looking at me intensely.

We were sitting on the floor of number 19, surrounded by wine bottles and words.

'You have to tell this story. Not just for us, or for yourself, because you want to be a writer, but for all those poor fucking medical students and junior doctors like us, for the patients and for the general public who think that doctors are superhuman machines. For people like Rachel, who didn't have mates or support like we do. Forget making a difference by being a surgeon or whatever—*this* is your difference, Kitty: *this* is what you were meant to do. You have to write it. If you don't, you'll regret it for the rest of your fucking life.'

'And cheers to that,' Max chimed in, laughing as we clinked our glasses together. 'Cheers to Kitty's book.'

I take them seriously. The hospital isn't going anywhere, and I have my whole life to work. I get off the train at freedom station; the looking-glass between Dr Katarina Holliday and Kitty Holliday the writer vanishes. I follow my reams.

'*Bonjour*,' says one of the builders.

I wave in response and am about to keep walking but decide I should practise my French. I'm in France, after all, and the morning is warm with the day stretching out in front of me into a glorious eternity. For the first time in a long while, I have nothing to do except whatever I like.

'*Il fait très chaud aujourd'hui!*' I say.

The men all turn to look at me. '*Parlez-vous français, Madame?*' one of them asks.

I laugh, holding my thumb and index finger an inch apart. '*Un peu.*'

He nods in understanding. 'You are English?'

I feign a look of horror. '*Non!* I'm Australian.'

'It is a long way. Are you here for holiday?'

I pause. 'Sort of,' I reply.

'What do you do?'

I look at him. The words *I'm a doctor* are on my lips, words I've waited so long to say. But I'm not in Èze to be a doctor. 'I'm a writer,' I tell him. I have a feeling Rachel would approve.

He smiles. 'Lots of writers come here. Nietzsche—he came to Èze. You must walk the Nietzsche trail; they say he walked it every day for inspiration.'

Nietzsche, the great philosopher, who wrote something along the lines of: *He who has a why to live can bear almost any how.*

Is this my why? This small French town that I have been led to by the echoes of a dead young woman, the place I have come to write down my story, her story, my friends' stories—is this my why? Maybe, I think, as the builder goes on to name other writers who have lived in the village, I am meant to be here.

I smile, say goodbye, and continue my walk along the beach.

My phone pings in my pocket. I pull it out. A message from Fabien.

Having fun?

I allow myself a small laugh. For once, he's stuck back at home working while I'm gallivanting around the world. I don't know what will happen with me and Fabien, but I've decided to listen to him and, like when we ski, just wait and see where we end up. To learn how to enjoy the moment feels liberating and unusual. It makes me smile. I turn my phone off. How times have changed.

I take my laptop from my shoulder bag and, with my little pink book beside me, I sit there on the pebbled shore, and start to type.

Thirty-three years ago, Toby Henderson was working in the emergency department of a hospital on the outskirts of the city . . .

author's note

IN 1978 THE SATIRICAL NOVEL *THE HOUSE OF GOD* WAS published, written by Samuel Shem, a psychiatrist who detailed the intern year of a group of young doctors at a fictional hospital. The novel describes the dehumanising, brutalising experiences of interns training at Harvard Medical School's Beth Israel Hospital in 1974. It was drawn from real life and, more than forty years later, is still part of medical folklore. It is now 2019, and this is a conversation that still hasn't ended.

In January 2017 an anonymous article was published on the physician blog Kevin MD called 'There is something rotten inside the medical profession'. It was shared thousands of times. It detailed the dire state of training for junior doctors, and a recent spate of suicides of young medics working in Australia. I had particular interest in the overwhelming response to this article as I was the doctor who wrote it.

I remember vividly sitting inside the emergency department as a friend told me that a colleague of ours had just killed herself. I remember the whispers and seeing people crying around the hospital. I also remember that, aside from among my close friends, I couldn't discuss it with anyone and I had to put on a brave face and finish my shift that night. It was the second suicide of a doctor I knew within twelve months. A few weeks later, another doctor killed himself. All of these people were under the age of thirty-five, and all based in Sydney.

I walked home and poured my anger onto the notes function of my iPhone, which ended up being published as the aforementioned article. The sense of disillusionment was overwhelming. There is something wrong when young people with a qualification as difficult as a medical degree, who have the skills and intellect to contribute to society in an enormously meaningful way, are pushed into a mental space where they think their only option is to take their own life. Every year in America four hundred physicians kill themselves. That's an entire medical school. I refuse to believe the apologists who infer there are other reasons for such drastic actions. There is a common denominator in all of these deaths: the job, and the system in which we train.

Being a doctor is all about control. Certainly, the expectations placed on doctors by themselves, their superiors, and the general public are enormous. Behind closed doors and with the knowledge you are going to be on call every night for one year (as is what happened to a surgical trainee I know well), between working sometimes sixteen-hour days, relatively paltry remuneration and extremely costly exams, is it any surprise that people then lose control? Be that with infidelities, abuse of drugs and alcohol, significant mental distress and, the worst case, suicide. I felt physically ill when the same surgical trainee told me on more than one occasion during this time period he had gone close to the roof of the hospital, with calm and clear intention to throw himself off.

The impact of superiors showing their juniors kindness and care cannot be overstated. I know this from first-hand experience. I was very fortunate to have some consultants who I trained under be extremely kind and supportive, and this, between having a close-knit group of friends I could be very honest with, made the difference between me finishing my training and going under, for want of a better term. It may come as a surprise to senior consultants or hospital administration how vividly their juniors recall a kind word, a signed overtime sheet, or just a sense that they have someone they can speak to who actually has the power to meaningfully assist them when they are feeling lost or isolated.

There is a kind of omerta that exists around the walls of a teaching hospital. Every now and again someone will break the silence and there will be shock and awe at the sudden window the general public is given into the mystical world of medical training, but the people who speak out know the cost at which their truth comes. The system promises change but the statistics surrounding junior doctor suicide and mental health remain dire. The flurry of responses to whistle blowers, if you want to call them that, dies down, and the cycle continues to perpetuate. This book I hope will contribute to breaking that cycle, and push towards meaningful and practical change. We are making steps, albeit small ones, to attempt to stamp out a culture of bullying, intimidation and unsafe working hours. Some hospital departments have had their training accreditations stripped from them until they improve the conditions their trainees work under, and I largely applaud this, despite the impact it undeniably has on doctors trying to finish their specialisation.

In the words of a good friend of mine, being a junior doctor is a tough gig. No one is denying the need to have highly skilled medics caring for the sick, nor that we need rigorous standards to adhere to. No doctor I know would argue with that, nor do we want to. You know on your first day of medical school you aren't signing up for an easy time, and we all accept the nature of the beast in that regard. However, there is a difference between a hard job, and a job that is made much harder by bullies, petty bureaucracies, colleges who refuse to open training positions, and an ingrained culture of abuse and brutality.

To quote the article I wrote after that long shift in the emergency department over two years ago: 'The only people dying inside a teaching hospital should be the sick patients for which doctors can find no answers.' I, like my friends and colleagues, have worked very hard to be part of an ancient profession whose oath is *Do No Harm*. Now is the time to stop harming ourselves, and each other.

Dr Sonia Henry
22 February 2019
Sydney, Australia

acknowledgements

THANKS TO:

My agent Sarah McKenzie. Without you none of this would have happened.

My publisher Jane Palfreyman, a legend, and an exceptional lunch companion.

My editors:

Haylee Nash (pre contract). And to Jo Butler for the introduction.

Ali Lavau and Christa Munns.

Greg Sioris, and the invaluable advice ever since the snorkel dropped.

The doctors who have offered particular kindness to me, encouraged creativity, or assisted with clinical details in the manuscript:

Dr Damien Boyd, Dr John Rooney, Dr Tom Pennington, Dr Jaci Hang, Dr Farnoush Noushi, Dr Sandy Beveridge, Dr Kirsty Hamilton and Dr Gareth Crouch.

Paul Blake for the ongoing advice.

Sally—for the title!

Dieter and Franz, for believing in me, and Cokes for the pen.

Peter, Sophie and Adrian Henry, for the love, and the literature.

Finally, my little house on the hill, and my brilliant friends, without whom I wouldn't have survived those years, nor been able to write this book.

J(esso) R, NF, LW, RH, RH, DR, DJ, JL and ND.

If only the neighbours could see us now.